W9-BTM-180

The Shadow Queen

ALSO BY REBECCA DEAN

The Golden Prince

Palace Circle

The Shadow Queen

A NOVEL OF

Wallis Simpson

Duchess of Windsor

R EBECCA D EAN

BROADWAY / NEW YORK

BROADWAY

This is a work of fiction. Names, characters, places, and incidents
either are the product of the author's imagination or are used fictitiously.
Any resemblance to actual persons, living or dead, events, or locales
is entirely coincidental.

Copyright © 2012 by Rebecca Dean

All rights reserved.
Published in the United States by Broadway Books, an imprint of the
Crown Publishing Group, a division of Random House, Inc., New York.
www.crownpublishing.com

BROADWAY BOOKS and the Broadway Books colophon are
trademarks of Random House, Inc.

Originally published in Great Britain by HarperCollins UK, London.

Library of Congress Cataloging-in-Publication Data
Dean, Rebecca, 1943–
The shadow queen : a novel of Wallis Simpson, Duchess of Windsor /
Rebecca Dean. — 1st ed.
     p.   cm.
1. Windsor, Wallis Warfield, Duchess of, 1896–1986—Fiction. 2. Windsor,
Edward, Duke of, 1894–1972—Fiction. I. Title. II. Title: Wallis Simpson,
Duchess of Windsor.
PR6066.E488S34   2012
823'.914—dc22   2011049963

ISBN 978-0-7679-3057-4
eISBN 978-0-307-98583-5

Printed in the United States of America

BOOK DESIGN BY BARBARA STURMAN
COVER DESIGN BY LAURA KLYNSTRA
COVER PHOTOGRAPHY BY POPPERFOTO/GETTY IMAGES

2 4 6 8 10 9 7 5 3 1

First American Edition

This book is dedicated with love to my granddaughters,

DAISY MAY GRUMBRIDGE

and

THEODORA PEMBERTON KEMP

The Shadow Queen

Chapter One

Although Blue Ridge Summit nestled high in Monterey County's mountains, on June 19, 1896, no cooling breezes relieved the stifling heat.

In a vacation cabin attached to the small town's Monterey Inn, Alice Warfield was struggling to give birth to her first child. She and her husband, Teackle, were from Baltimore and were on an extended vacation in Blue Ridge Summit because of its reputation as a health spa and because Teackle was a consumptive. The plan had been for their family physician, Dr. Neale, to travel out to Blue Ridge Summit in time for the birth. The baby, though, was uncaring of the plans made for it, and when Alice had gone into labor seven weeks prematurely, the doctor hurriedly dispatched from Baltimore was a newly graduated student of Dr. Neale's, Dr. Lewis Allen.

"We're nearly there, Mrs. Warfield!" the young man said exultantly, sweat beading his forehead. "Now when I say pant, pant as if your life depends on it."

Through a sea of unimaginable pain, Alice panted.

"And now push! PUSH!"

Alice pushed, and as above the bed the blades of a ceiling fan creaked and whirred, a red-faced squalling baby girl slithered into Dr. Allen's hands.

"It's a girl!" His voice was charged with emotion, his relief that there had been no complications vast.

An exhausted Alice eased herself up against sweat-soaked pillows. "Oh, let me see her, Dr. Allen! Is she all right? Has she all her fingers and toes?"

As the baby kicked and squirmed in his hands, Dr. Allen said in deep sincerity, "She's perfect in every way, Mrs. Warfield. In fact, she's fit for a king!"

"That is what the doctor said to your mama the instant you were born, Bessie Wallis, and as I said then to your now dear-departed daddy, Dr. Allen knew what he was talking about, for Warfields and Montagues—your mama is a Montague—are two of Maryland's oldest, most illustrious families *and* they have connections to British royalty, and not many people can claim that distinction in Baltimore!"

Because Bessie Wallis's dear-departed daddy had died young, he'd had no opportunity to earn a fortune of his own or to inherit one, and so, being penniless, Bessie Wallis and her mother had been invited to live with Grandma Warfield in her big tall house on East Preston Street.

Bessie Wallis loved living there and hearing Grandma Warfield talk about how special the Warfields and Montagues were. Something she didn't like was a sense of tension she didn't understand, but which she knew was caused by her dear-departed daddy's bachelor brother, Solomon, who also lived with Grandma Warfield. Uncle Sol wasn't a very tall man, but his imposing physique and erect bearing made him seem so. He had narrow eyes and a luxuriant well-clipped mustache, and he wore stiff high collars and wide formal ties that he fastened with stickpins.

Bessie Wallis was a little afraid of him—and knew her mother was, also.

Another cause of tension was the friction between her mother and grandmother. Grandma Warfield insisted on family prayers every morning, and her mother often referred to her as "a pious old bat." In return, her grandmother called her widowed mother "flighty." *Flighty* was another word Bessie Wallis didn't understand, but she knew it was something not very nice simply from the way her grandmother said it.

When Bessie Wallis was five, her happy life on East Preston Street came to an end in a way that left her confused and deeply troubled. She'd been in her favorite secret place, sitting beneath the giant chenille-covered table in the dining room. The cover reached nearly to the floor and made a wonderful darkened den. She was playing house in it with her two best dolls, Mrs. Vanderbilt and Mrs. Astor, when the dining room door opened and she heard her Uncle Sol say hoarsely, "All I want is for you to be nice to me, Alice. Surely it's not too much to ask? A little kiss now and then. You give other people kisses, don't you? So why not me?"

Bessie Wallis couldn't imagine her mother kissing anyone apart from her and she was just about to come out from under the table and say so, when she realized her mother was crying.

The sound froze her into absolute stillness. Even though her mother was a widow, she *never* cried. "Life is made to be enjoyed, Bessie Wallis," she would say merrily, dancing her around their bedroom, her azure blue eyes sparkling, her golden hair swept up to the top of her head with tortoiseshell combs. "Promise me you'll never grow up into a sourpuss like Grandma Warfield."

Her mother wasn't being merry now.

Bessie Wallis heard her say defiantly, through tears, "I've been widowed for four years and who I kiss is my own affair."

Bessie Wallis held her breath, certain that her uncle would now apologize for having made her mother cry. He didn't. Instead he said in a harsh, desperate voice, "You're lying, Alice! I *know* you're lying!"

All that Bessie Wallis could see was her uncle's booted feet and, a little distance away, her mother's tiny size three feet. Then, so suddenly it made Bessie Wallis gasp, her uncle closed the gap between himself and her mother and though she couldn't see him doing so, she knew he had seized hold of her by her arms.

"You sleep only two rooms away from me, Alice! It's a torment I can bear no longer! You have to be nice to me, Alice! You *have* to!"

Bessie Wallis dug her nails into the palms of her hands, not knowing what to do, certain that neither her mother nor her uncle would want to know that she was in the room listening to them.

"No, Sol!" Her mother's voice was hysterical as she struggled against him. "Please, no!"

There came the sound of material ripping.

Bessie Wallis pushed Mrs. Vanderbilt and Mrs. Astor to one side, knowing that no matter how cross her mother and her uncle were going to be with her, she had to run and beg her mother not to be so upset. After all, being nice and polite to her uncle wasn't such a hard thing to be. Her Grandma Warfield had told her that she, Bessie Wallis, always had to be nice and polite, that being so was a sign of good breeding.

She caught hold of the fringe of the table cover and pulled it to one side. As she did, her mother and Uncle Sol, still struggling, fell against an occasional table. A Chinese vase toppled to the floor, splintering into giant shards.

"Damnation!" Her uncle let go of her mother, staring in horror at the destruction of a family heirloom worth thousands of dollars.

With a gasp her mother whirled away from him, hurtling out of the room fast as light, the door yawning wide behind her.

Her uncle made a sound like a sob and brought his fist down hard on the mantelshelf.

He had his back to her, and Bessie Wallis let the table cover fall back down. Not for another twenty minutes, when her uncle also left the room, did she leave her hiding place.

Later that day her mother left East Preston Street and, taking Bessie Wallis with her, moved into a residential hotel. Although her mother never said so, Bessie Wallis knew why they had moved. It was because her pretty mother no longer wanted to live in the same house as Uncle Sol.

A year later, when she was six, they moved again, this time to go and live with her Aunt Bessie, her mother's sister. Her mother still took her to visit her grandmother, and she still sat on a little petit-point-covered stool at the side of her grandmother's rocking chair listening to stories such as the one about Robert de Warfield, who, a long time ago, had been a friend of King Edward III of England and of how Robert had been so chivalrous and faithful in serving him that the king had made him a Knight of the Garter, which was, her grandmother had said, the highest honor in the whole of the kingdom.

Another of her favorite stories was of Pagan de Warfield, who had accompanied William the Conqueror from France and fought beside him in the great Battle of Hastings. "And just as Robert was rewarded for his chivalry, so was Pagan," her grandmother had said with pride. "He was given a grant of land near Windsor Castle—the castle that kings and queens of England still live in—and it was named Warfield's Walk in his honor."

These stories of her long-departed antecedents made Bessie Wallis feel special and different from everybody else, and at school she worked hard to make sure that everyone knew she was special and different. She wore a green pleated skirt when everyone else wore a navy one, and at playtime, because her grandmother had also told her she was descended from the great Indian chief King Powhatan, she sometimes stuck a feather in the back of her braided hair.

The first day she had done so, John Jasper Bachman—who was the most popular boy in the class and who had once bloodied the noses of two older boys when he'd found them tormenting the school's pet rabbit—said, "Your feather looks swell, Bessie Wallis. How about you be an Indian princess when we play cowboys and Indians?"

His invitation was a great honor because the boys never allowed girls to join in with them when they ganged together at break time, and joining in with them was something Bessie Wallis had longed to do for ages and ages. After that, when the boys found out she didn't cry if she fell down and grazed her knees when playing football, and that she didn't complain about being tagged first in games of chase, it became understood she could join in their games any time she wanted to.

Bessie Wallis wanted to often, and she knew it was something that would never have happened if it hadn't been for John Jasper—and if John Jasper hadn't been someone all the other boys took notice of.

Another way that she found to be different was in being cleverer than everyone else. Her homework was always meticulously done. In class, her attention never strayed. She was a star pupil, always the center of attention, and that was how she intended things to remain.

· · ·

The day she was suddenly faced with a rival started out with her teacher, Miss O'Donnell, telling everyone she had an announcement to make. "A new girl will be joining our class later today." There was a touch of color in Miss O'Donnell's normally pale cheeks. "She is English and has only just arrived in America, and so we must try very hard to make her welcome."

"Please, Miss. What is her name, Miss?"

The question came from Violet Dix. The Dixes were one of the city's oldest families, but Violet never could get it into her head that it was vulgar to address Miss O'Donnell merely as "Miss."

"The new girl's name is Lady Pamela Denby."

Clamor broke out as everyone in the class wanted to know why the new girl had such a funny Christian name.

"'Lady' isn't a Christian name," Miss O'Donnell said when she had restored order. "It's a title. Lady Pamela's father is an English duke. Daughters of dukes are addressed as 'Lady.'"

John Jasper, whose desk was immediately in front of Bessie Wallis's, shot up his hand. "Is that what we have to call her, Miss O'Donnell?"

Miss O'Donnell shook her head. "No, John Jasper. In the classroom and in the playground, Lady Pamela will be known simply as Pamela. Now we will spend a little time on multiplication and division and then, after break, we will have history."

When Miss O'Donnell briefly left the classroom at break time, Violet Dix and her friend, Mabel Morgan, zeroed in on Bessie Wallis, eager to point out that the new girl came from a far more distinguished background than she did.

"A duke is someone who is royal, or nearly royal," Mabel, the class know-it-all said, happy at a chance to deflate Bessie Wallis's infuriating self-importance, "and that's a lot more than you are, Bessiewallis Warfield."

By the way Mabel said her name, Bessie Wallis knew Mabel

was running her Christian names together in a way she hated, and she itched to slap Mabel's gleefully smug face.

"And though you pretend to be nearly royal, you ain't," Violet Dix put in spitefully, abandoning the careful diction Miss O'Donnell insisted on and remaining a step or two behind Mabel so that Bessie Wallis wouldn't easily be able to hit her. "Worse than that, you and your ma ain't even got any money. My ma says the two of you live on rich relatives' charity and that you wouldn't even be at Miss O'Donnell's if it wasn't that your Uncle Sol pays the fees."

Bessie Wallis balled her fists and stepped forward in order to push Mabel out of the way so she could get to Violet. Violet screamed and was saved as Miss O'Donnell walked in on them to announce it was time for their history lesson.

Bessie Wallis seethed all the way through the first part of the lesson, but when Miss O'Donnell asked, "Who knows who tried to blow up the Houses of Parliament in London?" her hand went up immediately in order to answer.

Before she had time to do so, John Jasper beat her to it, leaping from his seat and yelling, "Guy Fawkes!"

Bessie Wallis was so mad at him and her nerves so strained, she seized hold of her pencil box and smacked him over the head with it.

Instead of being aggrieved, he hooted with laughter.

Miss O'Donnell didn't laugh. Instead, as a punishment, she made Bessie Wallis sit outside the classroom in the corridor. She was still there when Miss Smith, the school secretary, turned into it accompanied by a girl Bessie Wallis had never seen before.

"What are you doing outside the classroom, Bessie Wallis?" Miss Smith demanded, walking briskly toward her.

Well aware the girl must be Pamela Denby, and not wanting to be humiliated, Bessie Wallis said swiftly, "I was feeling faint,

Miss Smith. Miss O'Donnell thought there would be more air out here than in the classroom." The friendly amusement in Pamela's eyes—eyes that were a mesmerizing sea green—showed that she, at least, didn't believe a word of her explanation.

Bessie Wallis was overcome by a feeling she'd never experienced before: the feeling that, for the first time ever, she'd met her match.

"We're having a history lesson," she said at last, when she could trust her voice to be steady. "It's about Guy Fawkes and how he tried to blow up the Houses of Parliament."

Pamela shot her a wide complicit smile. "That's good. I'm English. I know all about kings and queens."

What neither of them could know, as the school secretary ushered them into the classroom, was that for as long as they lived, their lives would be inextricably entwined, and that though for the most part they would be best friends, they would also sometimes be enemies. Beyond her imagination was that both of them would enslave a king and that one of them would marry him.

Chapter Two

From the moment Bessie Wallis and Pamela walked into the classroom together, it was clear that Pamela was going to be Bessie Wallis's best friend and that no one else stood a chance.

The boys in the class were uncaring, but the girls were furious. "How come Bessiewallis always gets just whatever it is she wants?" Mabel had demanded at lunchtime as the rest of the disappointed clustered around her. "And where has Bessiewallis taken Pamela? Where have they gone?"

"They've gone to take a peek at the rabbit." Edith Miller sounded crushed. No one blamed her. Edith's daddy was a member of the state legislature and if anyone should have been showing Pamela the school's pet rabbit, it was Edith.

"I vote we never speak to Bessie Wallis ever again," Violet Dix said maliciously. "It isn't as if she should even be at Miss O'Donnell's. Not when she ain't even got a daddy to pay the fees."

There was a shuffling of feet, and then Edith put into words what most of them were feeling. "It isn't Bessie Wallis's fault her daddy is dead, and Bessie Wallis is fun. I don't want to stop speaking to her."

"An' if we stop speakin' to her," someone else interjected, "she'll make sure Pamela never speaks to us and then we'll never get invited to a duke's house for tea."

This was something none of them had thought of, and, even for Mabel, it settled the matter. Mad as they were at Bessie Wallis for cheating them all of the chance of becoming Pamela's best friend, none of them was going to run the risk of being ostracized by the only duke's daughter they were ever likely to meet. Also, as Edith had pointed out, Bessie Wallis, with her Indian feather in the back of her hair and her peppy way of talking—she'd once told Miss O'Donnell that arithmetic brought her out in hives—was good fun. Not speaking to her anymore would be just too boring for words.

If Miss O'Donnell's pupils were hopeful that a duke would have conjured up a castle in which to live, they were disappointed. Pamela's home was, however, in the very best part of Baltimore. An Italianate mansion set in vast grounds, if Rosemont wasn't a castle, it was certainly near to being a palace—a palace that Wallis was soon able to regard as her second home.

She was nine when she realized she and Pamela could well find themselves being separated. Miss O'Donnell's school only took children up to the age of ten, and when she left Miss O'Donnell's she was to go to Arundell, a Baltimore school with a prestigious reputation.

"Or she will be if Sol comes up with the fees," she'd once heard her mother say to Aunt Bessie.

It was a doubt that filled her with apprehension—but not nearly as much apprehension as when Pamela said, "Won't it be swell when we go to Bryn Mawr next year?" It was the summer of 1905 and they were on Rosemont's terrace playing jacks.

"Bryn Mawr?"

As Pamela scooped up four jacks, Bessie Wallis stared at her.

"Of course." Pamela missed catching the ball. "What other school is there to go to?"

Bessie Wallis picked up the ball, but she didn't continue with the game. There were three other schools in Baltimore—one of them being Arundell. And though Arundell was prestigious, it wasn't as prestigious as Bryn Mawr. No school in Baltimore was. Her nails dug deep into the ball. If there was doubt about Uncle Sol coming up with Arundell's fees, there wasn't even a chance of his coming up with Bryn Mawr's fees.

Her chest felt painfully tight. How would she and Pamela be able to continue as best friends if they began going to different schools? And what if Mabel and Violet—or anyone else in their class—went to Bryn Mawr? How would that make her look? She knew what the answer was. She would look poor.

"Well, we *are* poor, Bessie Wallis." Her mother was always cheerful and laughing, and even though she was now being frank about this very painful truth, she didn't sound glum or resentful. "Your Grandma Warfield didn't at all like me marrying your daddy, and the minute he did so, she cut him off without a penny. As for the Montagues—it's a long time since any of them have lived in the style they once took for granted." Laughter crept back into her voice. "I guess Montagues have just been too carefree to keep hold of their money, Bessie Wallis."

That her happy-go-lucky mother was every inch a Montague was something Bessie Wallis had long realized. She had also come to realize that she and her mother were funded almost entirely by Uncle Sol and that Uncle Sol increased or decreased their allowance in proportion to how nice—or how not nice— her mother was being toward him.

The knowledge gave her a nasty shivery feeling down her spine. How nice would her mother have to be to Uncle Sol before he agreed to pay Bryn Mawr's colossal fees? The answer made her feel a little sick, and she knew, right then and there, that she wasn't going to mention Bryn Mawr to her mother. No matter what the cost to her friendship with Pamela, she was going to settle for the school Uncle Sol had already half agreed she should go to. She was going to settle for Arundell.

"Arundell?" Pamela stared at her mystified. "But why?"

They were in their own private part of the playground, and as no one else could overhear and as they didn't have any secrets from each other, Bessie Wallis told her.

Pamela gave her the same knowing look she had given her when they'd first met and Bessie Wallis had lied about why she was sitting outside the classroom door.

"I don't think you're being very bright about your Uncle Sol, Bessie Wallis."

They were sitting on the warm ground and Pamela hugged her knees with her arms.

"I think he's in love with your mother." There was unnerving certainty in her voice. "I think that's why he increases his allowance to her when she's nice to him and cuts it short when she isn't."

The shivery feeling Bessie Wallis was beginning to get used to ran down her spine again. She wanted to tell Pamela she was wrong; that as Uncle Sol was her uncle, how could he possibly be in love with her mother? She thought about the scene she had witnessed between her mother and Uncle Sol just before she and her mother had left East Preston Street. She remembered Uncle Sol's angry desperate voice and the sound of her mother crying, and she knew one thing for sure. Even if Uncle Sol was in love with her mother, her mother most definitely wasn't in love with Uncle Sol.

The subject was so unpleasant she didn't want to discuss it anymore, not even with Pamela. She jumped to her feet. "Miss O'Donnell will be ringing her handbell in a minute."

"Let her." Though uncaring of Miss O'Donnell and her handbell, Pamela reluctantly rose to her feet. "At least that's one thing we won't have at Arundell." She tucked her hand in the crook of Bessie Wallis's arm. "High schools have whistles, not handbells."

"But you'll be at Bryn Mawr."

"No, I won't. If you aren't going to Bryn Mawr, then I'm not going. Don't tell Mabel or Violet, though. We don't want them changing from Bryn Mawr to Arundell." Amusement fizzed in her voice. "Wouldn't you love to see their faces when they get to Bryn Mawr and find that I'm not there!"

The thought was so delicious Bessie Wallis giggled along with her all the way back into their classroom.

Her happiness that she and Pamela would be going to Arundell together lasted for the rest of the afternoon and until she was back at West Chase Street in time for tea. She had been looking forward to telling her mother and Aunt Bessie that Pamela had chosen Arundell over Bryn Mawr—and why she had done so—but the minute she stepped into the house, she knew something was wrong, and the words died on her lips.

Her Aunt Bessie, like all Montagues, possessed a sunny disposition. Bessie Wallis had never known her aunt to be anything but equable and buoyantly good-humored.

She wasn't good-humored now. As she faced Bessie Wallis's mother across the dining room table, there were angry spots of color in her cheeks. "I'm sorry, Alice," she was saying as Bessie Wallis walked in on them—and not sounding sorry at all—"but a widow with a nine-year-old daughter has no call to be going out on an evening with unsuitable men. You're going to get yourself a reputation you won't ever be able to lose."

"What would you like me to do, Bessie?" There was color in her mother's cheeks, too, but in her mother's case the color only made her look even prettier. "Wear black and sit in a rocking chair all day like my mother-in-law?"

"I'd like you to think about Bessie Wallis." Her aunt looked toward her. "Go to your room, Bessie Wallis, dear. This isn't a conversation you should be listening to."

"No!" Alice sprang to her feet. "You stay just where you are, Bessie Wallis. Your aunt has brought you into this silly row, and so you just tell her that you don't mind at all if I go out and have a little fun."

In rising alarm Bessie Wallis looked from her mother to her aunt, and then back to her mother again. It was quite true that she didn't mind her mother going out and enjoying herself, but she didn't like it when her mother went out with gentlemen friends. Her doing so was the reason Grandma Warfield referred to her mother as being "flighty"—a word that thanks to Pamela, she now knew the meaning of.

To admit in front of Aunt Bessie that her mother's flightiness made her feel uncomfortable would be to let her mother down, but neither did she want to fib. Her cheeks flushed scarlet and, aware of her hideous dilemma, her aunt said with swift kindness, "Of course Bessie Wallis doesn't mind you going out and having a little fun, Alice. Nor do I. But while you are living under my roof, I draw the line at your having a succession of disreputable suitors cluttering up my front porch."

The row was on again with a vengeance, but at least Bessie Wallis was now no longer a part of it.

The last thing she heard as she escaped from the room was her mother snapping defiantly, "Then there's only one answer to that, Bessie!"

Sick with apprehension, Bessie Wallis ran up to the bedroom she shared with her mother, slammed the door behind her, and, sitting cross-legged on the bed, put her hands over her ears.

Minutes later her mother raced up the stairs and flung the door open. "We're leaving!" she announced, dragging a portmanteau from the bottom of their closet. "I don't have to be spoken to by my elder sister as if she's my mother!"

She began opening drawers, scooping up their contents and tossing them into the portmanteau.

"But where will we go, Mama? Where will we live? Are we going back to Preston Street? Are we going to live with Grandma Warfield again?"

"No, we are not!" Her mother slammed half a dozen pretty frocks into the portmanteau. "We're going to go to . . . we're going to go to . . ." She snatched up a pile of undergarments, and Bessie Wallis knew that her mother still hadn't thought of where they would go.

"We're going to go to the Preston Apartment House," her mother said suddenly, with a triumphant flourish. "It is where me and your dear-departed daddy once lived, and it will suit the two of us just fine, Bessie Wallis."

In her haste she had dropped a lace-trimmed chemise and a whalebone corset. Bessie Wallis picked them up, her anxiety deepening. "But won't it cost an awful lot of money to live in an apartment house? And we don't have an awful lot of money. We only have Uncle Sol's allowance."

Her mother scooped a silver-backed hairbrush and hand mirror from the dressing table and packed them on top of their underclothes.

"Uncle Sol is just going to have to increase our allowance, Bessie Wallis." Bessie Wallis's tummy turned a hideous somersault. It was so her mother wouldn't have to do such a thing that she hadn't asked if she could go to Bryn Mawr.

Her mother squashed down the lid of the portmanteau and

fastened the buckles on its leather straps. "Stop looking as if it's the end of the world," she said spiritedly, as if their leaving Chase Street were an adventure, "and let's be on our way."

In a sea of misery, Bessie Wallis followed her out of the room and down the stairs.

Aunt Bessie was waiting for them in the hall, her face anguished. "I wish you'd start acting like a grown woman and not a child, Alice," she said, stopping her in her tracks. "Where are you going to go? Mrs. Warfield won't give you a home again. She's too afraid Sol will ask you to marry him."

Alice gave an indignant toss of her head. "Then she's worrying over nothing, because he already has and I've already refused him." She switched the heavy portmanteau from one hand to the other. "And let me remind you that it's *your* fault Bessie Wallis and me are leavin'. It was *you* who gave the ultimatum—and don't you worry about how we're goin' to manage, because we're goin' to manage just fine!" And with that she opened the door and marched down the front steps, the portmanteau banging against her legs.

Her aunt gave Bessie Wallis a tight hug. "Be a good girl for your mama and make sure she brings you to see me often—and that she takes you to your Grandma Warfield's often as well."

"I will, Aunt Bessie. I promise." She was having to try very hard not to cry and knew that her aunt was fighting the same battle.

"Run along now after your mother, and remember that I love you and that whatever happens I'll always be here for you."

The words took the edge off Bessie Wallis's panic. If she was still going to see her aunt and her grandmother regularly, living at the Preston Apartment House might not be as bad as she'd feared.

Her aunt gave her a last good-bye kiss and lost the battle she had been fighting. Tears filled her eyes and streamed down her homely face. Bessie Wallis didn't mind. The tears meant her aunt loved her and, in a world that was becoming increasingly precarious, Aunt Bessie's love represented stability. Stability she was very much in need of.

"So what is it like, living in rented rooms?" Pamela asked, deeply interested.

"It's a lot different than living at Rosemont."

It was a typical blunt sassy Bessie Wallis answer, and Pamela grinned. "Come on, Wally. Because my father's too snobbish to allow me to visit an apartment house, I can't tell for myself, so spill the beans."

They were lying on the grass at the side of Rosemont's tennis court.

Bessie Wallis rolled over onto her back. Once it had become known that her address had changed from West Chase Street to the far less salubrious Preston Apartment House, all her classmates had been told by their parents that it was beneath them to visit her there. Some of them had even told her they were no longer able to invite her to their homes. That she was suffering this humiliation at the hands of families who didn't have an iota of her own family pedigree enraged her, but there wasn't a thing she could do about it. All she could be grateful for was that she hadn't been barred from visiting Rosemont.

"It's not half as bad as I thought it was going to be," she said now, in answer to Pamela's question. "Everyone else in the apartment block is very friendly. Most of them go to local restaurants to eat, and so Mama has thought up a way of earning pin money. She's going to throw dinner parties for them, which they will pay to attend. Mama will do the cooking, and I'll help her."

Pamela shot into a sitting position. "You're going to *cook*?"

"I may not actually cook, but I'll certainly bake. I can already make a pecan pie and a Lady Baltimore cake."

"What on earth is a Lady Baltimore cake?"

"It's a cake filled with raisins, figs, candied cherries, and chopped pecans and frosted with meringue."

Pamela's eyes nearly popped out of her head. "It sounds scrumptious. Could you show me how to make one?"

Bessie Wallis raised an eyebrow. "Have you ever been inside a kitchen, Pamela?"

"No, never."

The admission had them giggling so hard, their tummies hurt.

One thing Bessie Wallis didn't talk to Pamela about was her mother's partying. Without Aunt Bessie to keep a check on the number of evenings she spent with gentlemen friends, her mother's partying had increased dramatically.

"Now you just go to sleep and have pleasant dreams until I come back," she would say lovingly, tucking Bessie Wallis up in the big feather bed the two of them shared.

Her mother would always be wearing a very pretty dress. Sometimes it would be silk that shimmered in the lamplit room; sometimes taffeta would rustle. Always her mother's golden hair would be swept up high, and, instead of tortoise-shell combs, a glittering barrette would be holding her waves and curls in place.

When she kissed Bessie Wallis good night, there would be a touch of rouge on her lips, and when she left the room after snuffing out the lamp, the scent of violets would leave the room with her.

Then would come hours Bessie Wallis hated, for she never could do as she'd been asked and go to sleep and have nice dreams. Instead she would lie awake in the darkness, overcome by the fear that her mother might never come back; that she might disappear from her life just as the father she had never known had disappeared and just as the lifestyle she had once known at her grandmother's and then at Aunt Bessie's had disappeared; for if there was one thing Bessie Wallis knew for certain, it was that nothing could be guaranteed to last forever.

On her tenth birthday, something happened that had never happened before. Her Uncle Sol asked to have a private meeting with her at 34 East Preston Street.

Though she couldn't be certain, Bessie Wallis thought she knew the reason. West Chase Street, where they had lived with Aunt Bessie, was a distance from 34 East Preston Street, but the Preston Apartments were only a few blocks away, and Uncle Sol couldn't help but see her mother's gentlemen friends coming to call. His reaction had been to drastically reduce her allowance.

In order to overcome this blow, her mother had increased the number of dinner parties she gave for paying guests, and she and Bessie Wallis now spent backbreakingly long hours in the kitchen, slaving over the stove. If word of their doing so had gotten back to 34 East Preston Street, it would be the reason Uncle Sol wanted to meet with her—and he would be doing so to demand she cease letting his family name down by working like a servant in a kitchen.

"Sit down, Bessie Wallis," he said unsmilingly when she walked into his study. "I have some serious things to say to you." Having greeted her at the door, he retreated behind his large leather-topped desk. "I am a very wealthy man, Bessie Wallis," he said without preamble, stating what she, and everyone else in Baltimore, already knew. "And as I am unmarried and you are my only niece, I would like to do my best to see that as you grow and take your place in Baltimore society, you do so with all possible material advantages."

If it was possible to sit any straighter, Bessie Wallis did so. "I intend to adopt you, Bessie Wallis. It is, I think, what your father would wish. In looks you are very much a Warfield. You have the firm Warfield jaw, and your schoolwork shows you have the Warfield ability to work hard. Though you are perhaps too young to be aware of it, your mother's déclassé reputation has already damaged your social standing. As you grow into a young woman, that damage will affect you severely. It will, however, cease the instant it becomes known you are to be my heir."

Bessie Wallis gasped. Her mother had, she knew, always hoped that some Warfield money would one day be left to her, but even her mother hadn't dreamed that her uncle would leave her his entire fortune.

"And will I live here again, Uncle Sol?" Her head reeled at the thought of what that would mean. When she went to Arundell, instead of being one of the poorest pupils in the school, she would become one of the richest.

"Live here again?" Her uncle's steely blue eyes held hers. "Of course you will live here again. Your life is going to change dramatically—and in ways you are far too young to understand as yet."

She wondered how her mother would feel about living in close contact with Uncle Sol again, but considering the benefits that would now come with doing so, it was certain her mother would find a way of managing.

"Thank you, Uncle Sol." She was so transported by happiness she jumped to her feet, rounded his desk, and gave him a kiss on his cheek.

"Mama is going to be so happy when I tell her we're coming back here to live."

Her uncle's eyes narrowed. "Not so fast, Bessie Wallis. Your mother won't be coming back here to live. The Preston Apartments—and the life she lives there—were her choice, and it's a choice she's going to have to stick with. When you come back here, you'll be doing so alone."

Bessie Wallis's euphoric happiness drained as fast as an ebb tide.

Sol saw the expression on her face. "All that I'm offering comes with conditions," he said grimly. "Not only will you come back to live here without your mother, you will have no future contact with her. Not of any kind. Now what is it going to be, Bessie Wallis? A life of pinch and scrape with a woman who has lost her reputation, or a life as one of the richest heiresses in Baltimore?"

Chapter Three

"And so what choice did you make, Wally?" Pamela asked, riveted by Bessie Wallis's account of her meeting with her uncle.

"I told him I would never sever my relations with my mother. That there wasn't money enough in the world to make me do so."

Pamela let out her breath in a long, admiring sigh. "You're a heroine, Wally. *I* couldn't have done that." She shot Bessie Wallis her irrepressible grin. "But then my mother lives in England and I haven't seen her in over three years."

It was a Saturday and they were on their way to Guth's pastry shop for Kossuth cake and meringues.

"And even if my mother were around, she wouldn't be as much fun as yours is," Pamela added as they crossed St. Paul Street. "What did your uncle do when you told him you weren't going to leave your mother in order to be adopted by him?"

"He looked as if he'd been socked in the stomach by a baseball bat! He just couldn't believe what he was hearing. And when he did finally believe it, he got angry. He said it was a foolish decision I would live to regret."

"And what if you do?" Pamela's forehead creased in a frown. "What if he stops your mother's allowance?"

"He won't. He's an Episcopalian. It's his duty to provide for the widow and child of his dead brother, and though he doesn't always do it in a way my mother likes, he does always do it. My grandmother sees to that."

Bessie Wallis had been right in thinking that her uncle wouldn't renege on his promise to pay for her fees at Arundell. She went there in September 1906 and immediately knew that Arundell was going to be all she had hoped it would be. No one mocked her for having high and mighty airs about her family lineage, because she had outgrown the childishness of constantly referring to it. Pamela was still her best friend, but she made lots of other friends too.

She was even happy living at the Preston Apartment House, because thanks to her mother's irrepressible talent for turning adverse situations into something fun-filled, living there was enjoyable. All their fellow tenants at the Preston thought her mother a ray of sunshine, and there was never any shortage of takers whenever she announced she was going to give one of her pay-to-attend dinners.

"When people eat at someone else's table, they like the food to be elaborate," her mother said as she stirred a sauce she was preparing for the soft-shell crab that was to be one of the evening's side dishes. "They don't want to sit down to something they could have made themselves. You need to remember that, Bessie Wallis, when you're a married lady giving candlelit dinners for your husband's wealthy friends."

The thought of being married made Bessie Wallis giggle. She was far too young to have a sweetheart, but she'd confided to Pamela that when she was old enough she'd rather like her sweetheart to be her second-best friend, John Jasper Bachman.

"But you told me you once hit him over the head with your pencil box!" Pamela had said, hardly able to believe what she was hearing and keeping the fact that she was also sweet on John Jasper to herself.

"He deserved it." Bessie Wallis hadn't been remotely sorry for the incident. "But he has the thickest, curliest hair of any boy I've ever seen. I bet if you dug your fingers into it, it would be just like digging into a sheep's fleece."

When she had been at Arundell a week she asked Miss Carroll, the headmistress, if her name could be altered from Bessie Wallis to Wallis in the class register. When Miss Carroll knew the reason—that Bessie Wallis felt "Bessie" to be a cow's name—she said that as long as her mother didn't object, the alteration would be made.

Life was suddenly perfect. Just as she had been head of her class at Miss O'Donnell's, so she became head of her class at Arundell. It wasn't that she was brighter than the other girls— some of the girls at Arundell were very bright indeed—but none of them needed to prove that they were just as good as, if not better than, anyone else in the way she did. The insecurities she lived with—the knowledge that she owed her place at Arundell to her Uncle Sol's charity, just as she did the roof over her head and the clothes on her back—ran deep, and the result was a fierce competitiveness. She had to shine. She had to be best, and when she had set herself a goal, she had to achieve it.

Some things, though, couldn't be achieved by sheer determination and willpower, as she was painfully reminded whenever long school vacations came around.

When she was eleven and had been at Arundell for nearly a year, the arrangement for her summer vacation was that she would spend it at Pot Springs, a country estate belonging to her late father's youngest brother, her Uncle Emory. Pamela was going to be spending it in Europe with her father.

"I don't want to go, Wally. Truly I don't," she'd said with apparent sincerity. "I'd much rather be coming with you than going with Papa to Cannes and Biarritz."

Much as she would have liked to believe Pamela, Wallis found it hard to do so and couldn't help wondering if, unlike her, Pamela sometimes only told people what she thought they'd like to hear and kept her true opinions to herself.

Uncle Emory's home was a sprawling, verandahed, Southern-style mansion, and his passion was horses. Wallis was nervous of horses, having been brought up only with tame carriage horses, and she was determined that on this visit to Pot Springs she was going to conquer her nervousness and learn to ride really well.

"Henry will give you lessons," her Uncle Emory said indulgently when she told him what it was she wanted to do. "No one better. He's the best horseman for miles around."

Her cousin Henry was nine years older than she was, and she had never previously spent much time with him. That she would be doing so now didn't faze her, for her interest in the opposite sex was precociously well developed and the word *shyness* wasn't in her vocabulary. Henry was, of course, much older than anyone she had previously attempted a flirtation with, but that only made the thought of flirting with him even more exciting.

"How old are you, cuz?" he asked abruptly as they walked toward the stables together the morning after she'd spoken to her uncle.

Wallis hesitated, wondering if she could get away with saying she was twelve. Twelve sounded so much better than eleven. If Henry hadn't been family she most certainly would have done so—in fact, she knew that she would have said she was thirteen—but within family that sort of fib was hard to get away with.

"Eleven," she said carelessly, as if she didn't find being only eleven a handicap.

He gave a snort of laughter. "Merciful heavens, Wally. How d'you get to be eleven without having learned to ride well?"

Wallis stopped walking, forcing Henry, out of good manners, to stop walking as well. She eyeballed him as if she were one of his male friends. "I did it by choice," she said crisply, aware it was a fib she couldn't be found out in. "I live in Baltimore, or had you forgotten? And there are other things to do in Baltimore."

His mouth twitched at the corners. "And just what are those things, Wallis?" he asked, making no move to continue walking.

"Roller-skating. I can roller-skate better than anyone else you can possibly know."

He burst out laughing.

Wallis didn't mind. It wasn't unkind laughter, and, whereas when they had left the house for the stables he had done so in a bored, carrying-out-a-duty kind of way, his boredom had now vanished.

She had caught his attention, and the knowledge gave her a heady sense of power.

"Come on, then." He ran a hand through straw-colored hair. "I'll improve your riding, and the next time I'm in the city you can take me to the roller-skating rink and show me how ace you are on a pair of skates."

Reluctantly—for his eyes were gray-green with intriguing gold flecks—she broke eye contact with him and began walking again, knowing that the age barrier that had been here when they had started out from the house was there no longer. She'd made him like her and be interested in her, and it had all been done as easy as winking.

The summer of 1907 was long and hot, and not once did Henry make an inappropriate move toward her. There were, though, other thrilling intimacies. The heat of his hands around her waist as he steadied her when she dismounted. The pressure of his hand over hers as he corrected her hands on the reins. The way his arm would sometimes fall casually around her shoulders.

Sometimes she would catch an expression in his eyes when he looked toward her that sent a tingling sensation into parts of her body she'd been brought up to pretend didn't exist, and she knew without a shadow of doubt that if she were just a few years older, Cousin Henry would be behaving very inappropriately toward her.

She wondered how inappropriate behavior would feel. She could imagine the kissing part of it, for after all everyone knew what kissing was. You just pursed your lips and pressed them against someone else's pursed lips. She couldn't imagine what the other thing would be like. The thing that came after the kissing. All she knew was that it was a cardinal sin for a young lady to allow a man to go "too far"; but what "too far" meant she'd never been able to find out, for no one was telling.

"We'll just have to find out things for ourselves, Wally," Pamela had said breezily during one of their many discussions as to what actually went on when two people married, "and personally I can't wait to do so!"

By the time Wallis returned to Baltimore in September, she was glowing with the knowledge that she had aroused improper feelings in her handsome twenty-year-old cousin. The glow of burgeoning sexual confidence nearly compensated her for what had been the downside of her stay at Pot Springs: an even greater awareness of her poor-relation status.

Every relation she had lived with had the same kind of financial security as her Uncle Emory's family. A leisured lifestyle, such as the one lived at Pot Springs, was one her many Warfield and Montague cousins took for granted. Only she, out of all of them, couldn't do so. Without her Uncle Emory's kindness, her summer would have been spent in the heat of Baltimore, helping her mother cook dinner for their fellow tenants in an effort to make ends meet.

"Cannes was blissful," Pamela said as they walked in with the rest of their classmates toward the nearby gymnasium where their games lessons took place. "The British upper classes don't patronize it in the height of summer—it's too hot—but my mother visited with her new husband. He's an earl, which is a couple of degrees down in rank from a duke, and so Mama is now a countess, not a duchess. She doesn't seem to mind much, and I don't blame her. Tarquin is the most awful fun."

"Tarquin?"

They weren't supposed to talk as they walked the short distance from Arundell to the gymnasium, but Pamela never gave a fig for school rules and Wallis was now too mystified to care about any reprimand she might receive.

"Tarquin St. Maur. He's my new stepfather. He's quite young. Much younger than Mama. He said he didn't want me calling him Papa. He said it would make him feel as old as Moses. After Cannes Papa went to Nice to meet up with an old lady love, and I went to England with Mama and Tarquin."

"To London?"

The gymnasium was on the corner of Charles Street and Mount Vernon Avenue and was now only twenty yards or so away.

"No, silly. No one stays in London during August. Tarquin's pile is in Norfolk, quite near to Sandringham."

Wally had been a friend of Pamela's for long enough to know that in English slang, a *pile* was a stately home of mammoth proportions. And she knew what was meant by Sandringham. Sandringham was the country home of King Edward VII and Queen Alexandra.

Before she could even ask about King Edward, Pamela said, "The king wasn't at Sandringham. He was at Cowes, sailing. The Prince of Wales and his family were there, though. They live there all the time. Not actually in Sandringham House it-self, but on the Sandringham estate. Mama says Prince George and Princess May are pathetically provincial and she didn't re-ally want to spend time with them, but Tarquin was insistent. He went to naval college with Prince George, and between men that kind of thing matters."

"D'you mean to say that you met the prince and princess?" Wallis was so stunned she forgot to whisper, and in front of them several heads turned.

"Meeting royalty is no great shakes for me, Wallis. Didn't I ever tell you Queen Victoria was my mother's godmother?"

"No, you didn't!"

They were at the gymnasium now and Miss Noland, who took them for games and whom they both liked immensely, shook her head sternly in their direction.

"More later, Wally," Pamela said, and, because they were due to play basketball and she was on the team opposite Wallis, she sauntered off to join her teammates, leaving Wallis with a host of unasked questions.

By inclination Wallis was not particularly athletic, but her competitiveness ensured that she worked just as hard in the gym as in the classroom, and to her great satisfaction she was captain of her team. Within seconds of the game starting she was giving it all her concentration, and when she shot the ball into the net from outside the three-point line, she was so euphoric she almost forget about all the questions she wanted to ask Pamela about Prince George and Princess Mary.

"Well done, Wallis! Keep up the speed!" Miss Noland shouted from the side of the court. And then, seconds later, "That's a foul, Pamela! When will you understand that you can't impede another player if she is still moving?"

After the match, when they were again arranged in pairs for the short walk back to Arundell, she said urgently to Pamela, "The Prince and Princess of Wales. What were they like?"

"Stuffy. Neither of them even spoke a word to me. I was sent off to play with the children."

"The children?"

"Prince Henry, who is always called Harry, and Prince George, named after his father. Harry is seven and George is five. Needless to say, I didn't want to spend time with either of them. I wouldn't have done, either, if it hadn't been for their sister joining us. She's ten, and if she'd been any fun I would have broken my rule of never spending time with anyone younger than myself, but she wasn't. She's so shy and tongue-tied it's criminal."

Wallis was mesmerized. Pamela was speaking about a royal princess in the same offhand way she spoke about Mabel Morgan or Violet Dix.

"Then things got a whole lot better, because Bertie and David turned up. Bertie is twelve," Pamela continued as they turned off Charles Street, "and David is thirteen. Only he doesn't look it. He looks much younger."

Thinking of her own school vacation and the thrilling time she had spent with her cousin Henry, Wallis was vastly relieved that she did at least have the edge over Pamela where a flirtation with the opposite sex was concerned.

"And so did you ignore him?" she asked as they neared the school gates.

"Of course I didn't ignore him!" Pamela never wore her hair braided, and she lifted a long fall of golden waves back over her shoulder. "David is Prince Edward, and after his father he's next in line to the throne. By the time I'm a debutante he'll be just the right age for me, and so I made sure that we got on terrifically well and that he liked me a lot."

She grinned naughtily as they made their way into school. "Heirs to thrones always marry young, and I would make a terrific princess. As you are my best friend, Wally, I promise you that if David comes up to scratch, you will be chief bridesmaid at our Westminster Abbey wedding!"

Chapter Four

After that particular conversation, Wallis's interest in the British royal family increased. It was relatively easy to come across newspaper photographs of King Edward and Queen Alexandra—though the majority of photographs were of King Edward without his queen and had been taken at fashionable resorts such as Baden-Baden, or Cowes, or Biarritz. American news items about the Prince and Princess of Wales were much rarer, and in the only newspaper photograph of them with their children, Prince Edward looked quite nondescript apart from his naval cadet uniform and hair that looked to be an even paler gold than Pamela's.

She clipped it nevertheless. It was quite the rage at Arundell to collect pinup photographs of favorite sports stars or of any other personable young man they could fantasize and daydream about. So far the pride of Wallis's collection was a photograph of Henry. All the girls had oohed and aahed over Henry. Pamela, however, had stolen the show by flaunting a photograph taken in Cannes by her stepfather. It was of twenty-one-year-old Prince Sergei Romanov. And he had his arm around Pamela's shoulders.

Privately, Wallis would very much have liked to add a photograph of John Jasper to her growing collection, but there was little chance of doing so because John Jasper now attended a boys' school over on Lake Avenue and, much to her disappointment, the only time she now saw him was at the roller-skating rink.

Her mother's angry row with Aunt Bessie had long since been made up—though Wallis knew her aunt still disapproved of the way her mother persisted in spending time with gentlemen friends.

"The trouble with your mother," she said once to Wallis, when Christmas was over and Baltimore lay deep in snow, "is that she's a romantic. She doesn't have a commonsense idea in her head."

It was a remark Wallis remembered when her mother finally admitted she wasn't making money out of the dinners she was giving.

Nervously she showed Wallis a drawer crammed full of unpaid bills. "I don't know how people can think I owe them so much," she said, clutching a tear-sodden handkerchief. "Do you think some of those nice tradesmen are trying to cheat me?"

Wallis, who was no better at figures than Alice, didn't know. Aunt Bessie had known, though.

"Dear Lord Almighty, Alice!" she said when Wallis asked her to look at the bills. "No one is trying to cheat you. You've been cheating yourself! How could you ever hope to make a profit giving dinners as elaborate as you have been doing, for the money you've been charging?"

She fanned the bills out on their dining table.

"Diamondback terrapin? And lobsters? And prime rib and squab? You haven't been giving dinners, Alice. You've been giving banquets. I'm not surprised you were never short of guests!"

Alice's tears gave way to sobs. "I g-gave traditional S-southern-style d-dinner parties and that meant my m-menus included the b-best of everything."

"They certainly did—and now you're goin' to have to pay for being so foolish." Her voice softened and she reached out across the table and covered Alice's hands with hers. "You aren't a businesswoman, Alice. It's something you're just going to have to accept."

Alice's slender shoulders sagged. "But the bills, Bessie." Her voice cracked and broke. "I can't go to Sol with them. He can hardly bring himself to speak to me since someone told him about me and . . ."—she threw a quick glance in Wallis's direction—". . . since my friendship with you-know-who."

At the mention of "you-know-who," Bessie's mouth tightened, but there was only love and infinite patience in her voice as she said, "Sol doesn't have to know, Alice dear." She scooped the bills from the table and stuffed them into her handbag. "I'll see to these, but in future there are to be no more business ventures. And try to keep on the good side of Sol, Alice. He's all that stands between you and really severe financial difficulties."

Wallis had no idea who "you-know-who" was, but his existence troubled her greatly.

"But why?" Pamela asked when she told her about it.

"Because he's obviously in a different category than the others—and because my mother was so careful not to say his name in front of me."

Pamela shrugged. "That's just the way parents are. They don't realize that when you're nearly twelve you're not a child any longer. That's why I prefer Tarquin to my father. He doesn't treat me as though I'm still in leading reins."

Wallis couldn't imagine anyone treating Pamela as if she

were in leading reins, for she simply wouldn't have suffered them; she was far too precocious.

"Sergei Romanov kissed me on the lips," she had told Wallis, not long after coming back from Cannes. "It was a very peculiar experience because he didn't seem to know how to do it. He tried to push his tongue into my mouth, which was a very silly thing to do, don't you think? It wasn't at all pleasant, and I told him that if he wanted to kiss me again he had to do it properly, with his mouth shut."

Wallis had been round-eyed. No one in their class had been kissed by a boy—and Sergei Romanov wasn't a boy. He was a twenty-one-year-old adult—and a Russian prince into the bargain.

"And did he kiss you again?" she'd asked, wondering what it might be like to be kissed by John Jasper.

Pamela had given a careless shrug of a shoulder. "No," she'd said. "He looked panic-stricken and told me I must promise not to tell anyone what he'd done."

Still deep in thought as to who her mother's new beau could be, not able to be as dismissive about it as Pamela had been and for once not wanting Pamela's company, Wallis slung her roller skates over her shoulder and set off for the one place Pamela never went: the skating rink at Mount Vernon.

The first person she saw there was John Jasper. He was fooling around with a couple of friends, and she knew she couldn't just skate over and join them. That kind of camaraderie had ended the day they left Miss O'Donnell's for single-sex schools. Eleven-year-old girls didn't do that kind of thing. Girls hung together in groups. It was all right, though, for a boy to approach a girl, or a group of girls, on his own. That is, it was all right if he knew the girl or girls in question and if he approached them in a suitably polite manner.

Standing on the side of the skating rink as skaters noisily whizzed past her, Wally wondered how she could best attract John Jasper's attention. It was brought home to her, for the first time, that where boys were concerned a girl had to make herself stand out from the crowd. Pamela stood out from the crowd simply because she was a duke's daughter and had waist-length golden hair and mesmerizing sea green eyes.

She, Wally, had no such assets.

For one thing, she wasn't head-turningly beautiful in the way Pamela was. In fact, apart from having eyes that were an extraordinary violet blue, she wasn't beautiful at all. She wasn't even enchantingly pretty in the way her mother was. Though she was now counting the months off to her twelfth birthday, it was quite obvious to Wallis that she wasn't going to grow up looking like her mother. Her hair was far too dark for one thing, so dark an auburn that it was almost black. Because she liked to capitalize on her far-distant-in-the-past connection to King Powhatan and Pocahontas, she didn't mind being dark-haired. What she did mind was that she wasn't fine-boned. Her hands and feet were bigger than she liked—as was her nose—and she had a strong, almost boyish jawline. There was nothing softly rounded about her. Even her shoulders were bonily angular. It didn't matter too much now, but she was enough of a realist to know that it would in a few years' time, when she was a debutante and looking for a husband.

She had always tried to stand out from the crowd by dressing differently from her school friends, but now she determined that in future she would do so even more exaggeratedly. And she would capitalize on her boyish physique instead of being self-conscious about it. In one of her mother's dressing table drawers was a monocle that had once belonged to her father. She would begin wearing it. That would certainly make her stand out from the crowd, and she already knew that simpering never engaged any boy's attention and that it was far better to be confident and bold, as she had been with Henry.

With that decision made, all she had to do now was work out how she was going to disengage John Jasper from his friends. She looked at the way the other girls at the rink were skating. They were all doing so in twosomes or in a shrieking, chattering group, bumping into each other and regularly falling over. Confident in her own prowess, she buckled the straps on her skates a little tighter and set off to attract John Jasper's attention.

It didn't take long.

"Hi, Bessie Wallis," he said, leaving his friends behind and skating up beside her. "How are you doing?"

Wallis didn't break the rhythm of her skating. "No one calls me Bessie Wallis anymore," she said, shouting to be heard above the roar of fifty or so careering roller skates. "I'm called Wallis now."

He grinned, keeping pace easily with her as they expertly negotiated a curve of the rink. "Okay then, Wallis. How are you doing?"

"I'm doing just fine," she said, trying not to think of the painful scene that had just taken place between her mother and her aunt.

Fleetingly she took her eyes off the skaters in front of her in order to quickly glance across at him.

She liked what she saw just as much as she always had. His dark hair was still as thick and curly as a ram's fleece, and she still couldn't help wondering what it would be like to feel those tight curls springing beneath her fingers.

"How are you liking being at Bryn Mawr with Mabel and Violet?"

She noticed that he was roller-skating with his hands

laconically clasped behind his back. "I'm not at Bryn Mawr," she said, doing the same thing with her own hands and cross that he should be linking her with the two girls she had liked least at Miss O'Donnell's. "I'm at Arundell. With Pamela."

He chuckled, still roller-skating with perfect balance. "I ran into Lady Pamela at Guth's last year, just before the summer vacation. She said she was off to Europe to hobnob with royalty. She said if I wanted to tag along, her pa wouldn't mind."

Wallis lost her balance, crashing into him so hard it was a miracle they both didn't end up on the wooden floor.

Hanging on to her in order to keep her upright, he steered her to the side of the rink, where they were out of harm's way of the other skaters.

"What happened?" he asked, black-lashed brown eyes darkening in concern. "You were skating brilliantly."

Wally leaned against the rink's waist-high barrier, struggling to catch her breath. She could hardly tell John Jasper that Pamela hadn't breathed a word about meeting him in Guth's and of the invitation she had given him—and that Pamela's not doing so, when they were best friends and constantly confided every detail of their lives to each other, was a betrayal that stunned her. Especially so when Pamela knew she had been sweet on John Jasper for years.

"Thanks," she said in answer to his compliment, her mind whirling. "I just lost concentration for a moment."

"Come on." He took hold of her hand as if she still needed steadying. "Let's do another couple of circuits."

Her fingers interlocked with his in a way she found terribly exciting, but she couldn't give herself up to enjoyment of the experience because she was too busy thinking about Pamela. Why hadn't Pamela told her about running into John Jasper at Guth's? Even more to the point, why had she told John Jasper he was quite welcome to spend the summer vacation with her and her father? There was only one answer, and it wasn't one Wallis liked.

Pamela was just as sweet on John Jasper as Wallis was.

And though she and Pamela had always promised they would never have any secrets from each other, this was one secret Pamela had kept very firmly to herself. Just how she felt about it Wallis didn't quite know, but she found it disconcerting, for if she couldn't trust Pamela, who could she trust?

"John Jasper? At Guth's?" Pamela looked perplexed, and then her expression cleared. "Oh, way back last year? Yes, I did run into him. And he told you about my asking if he'd like to tag along with Papa and me to Europe?" She gave her distinctively throaty giggle. "Didn't you think that a hoot? What if he'd said he'd come? Can you imagine John Jasper Bachman at the Royal Hotel, Cannes, mixing with Russian royalty? Or, much, much worse, at York Cottage, Sandringham, in the presence of Prince George and Princess May?"

The images Pamela was conjuring up were so bizarre—and so unlikely—that Wallis found herself giggling along with her. Pamela had merely been teasing John Jasper and he should have had the sense to realize it, but then, as Pamela had once said to her, boys could be awfully dim.

A few weeks later, strange things began happening at the Preston Apartment House. Her mother ceased worrying about money and her new dresses were no longer ones she had made herself but instead bore the label of Baltimore's most prestigious fashion house. If that weren't bewildering enough, something even more bewildering followed.

"We're moving," Alice announced gaily. "Nineteen oh-eight is going to be a wonderful year for us, Wallis darling. There's going to be no more Preston Apartment House. We're going to move into a splendid little house on Biddle Street, and it will be our own house, Wallis. It won't be rented."

"Our own house?" The prospect was so magical, Wallis's legs felt weak. "But how can we afford our own house, Mama?"

Her mother laughed. "We can't, Wallis, but someone else can, and that someone is being extraordinarily generous."

Wallis gasped. Her own relationship with Uncle Sol had improved vastly over the last few years. Sometimes he would unexpectedly slip her a ten-dollar bill and had even begun kissing her on the forehead when saying good-bye to her. It had never occurred to her, though, that his relationship with her mother had also undergone a great change, and her relief that it had was enormous.

"A house of our own!" She hugged her mother ecstatically. "It's going to be wonderful, Mama! It's going to be perfect!"

Although the houses on Biddle Street were relatively small brownstone row houses, it *was* perfect. On the first floor there was a library, a parlor, a dining room, and a kitchen and pantry. On the second floor were two large bedrooms with a bathroom in between them, and on the third floor was another bedroom. Her mother took one of the second-floor bedrooms for her own use, designating the other bedroom on the second floor for use as a guest bedroom. Wallis's bedroom was the one on the third floor.

It was far better than living at the Preston Apartment House. Wallis thought it even better than living at East Preston Street, for though there was no grandeur at Biddle Street, it was all their very own. She even preferred it to West Chase Street, because at Biddle Street they were not living as guests—however well loved—in someone else's home.

"I'm happy," she said to Pamela. "Happy, happy, happy." It was a happiness that didn't last long.

Chapter Five

They had been in the Biddle Street house only weeks when her mother said to her, "I have a friend comin' over for dinner tonight, Wallis. A very special gentleman friend. His name is Mr. Rasin—and I'm very fond of him, Wallis."

Wallis stared at her, too shocked to think of a suitable response. She was still in a state of shock when, an hour later, she met up with Pamela at school.

Pamela was blasé about Mr. Rasin, but in talking about him Wallis's concern only deepened.

"Mama's never done this before," she said, trying to get Pamela to understand how she felt.

"What?" Pamela was chewing on a mouthful of taffy and spoke with difficulty. "Never become fond of anyone?"

"No. She's never invited an admirer home to dinner before."

Pamela continued to chew thoughtfully. Eating taffy at school was strictly forbidden, but like all the rest of Arundell's regulations it wasn't one she'd ever taken notice of. When her mouth was empty, she said, "Your mother had dinner guests when you were at the Preston Apartment House."

"That was different. They were paying to be there."

It was something Pamela had no answer for, and so she said, "But your mother won't be dining with him on her own. You'll be there. D'you want a piece of taffy? I've still got quite a bit left."

Wallis shook her head. She'd quite enough on her mind without being found by Miss Carroll with a lump of taffy in her mouth. Not only would Uncle Sol and her grandmother be appalled at the thought of her mother entertaining an admirer at Biddle Street, Aunt Bessie would be appalled as well. It wasn't the thought of her Aunt Bessie and her grandmother's disapproval that was filling her with fear, though. It was the thought of Uncle Sol's disapproval.

He had bought the dear little house on Biddle Street for them. What if he decided her mother was abusing his generosity and took the house away from them? The very thought gave her a sickening feeling of dread deep in the pit of her stomach. No matter how nice Mr. Rasin might turn out to be, she knew she wasn't going to like him. She couldn't afford to. He posed too much of a threat to the newfound security she had just begun to enjoy.

Mr. Rasin turned out to be nearly as old as her Uncle Sol, at least forty. And he wasn't as fastidiously well groomed as her uncle. He was a big man with a big stomach and a huge shock of bright red hair. His stomach looked as if it were trying to escape from his clothes, and his mustache was in need of a clip.

"How-de-do, Wallis," he said genially, a kindly smile splitting his face as he held his hand out to her. "I'm right glad to meet you."

Wallis stared at him in horror. Not only didn't he look to be a gentleman, he didn't sound like a gentleman either.

She became aware of her mother watching her with anxious eyes. "Where are your manners, Wallis?" she prompted. "Shake Mr. Rasin's hand."

Wallis did so.

Mr. Rasin beamed down at her and, withdrawing his other hand from behind his back, produced a prettily beribboned box of sugared almonds. "For you, Wallis," he said, giving them to her.

She accepted them, not wanting to, but not seeing what else she could do.

"There now, isn't that swell?" Alice said happily. "Aren't we just a nice little family?"

As far as Wallis was concerned, Mr. Rasin wasn't family, and she had no intention of treating him as if he were. To her vast relief, she found out her Aunt Bessie felt just the same.

"Of all the men to fall in love with, Alice," she said in exasperation and in front of Wallis, "John Freeman Rasin has to be not only the most unlikely, but the most unsuitable."

Alice narrowed azure blue eyes and put a hand on her hip. "And just why is Free so unsuitable, Bessie?"

"Because he's an 'out'—and with good reason, too."

To be "out" was a Baltimore expression meaning that someone wasn't, where Baltimore high society was concerned, "in." In high-society-conscious Baltimore, there wasn't a worse thing to be.

"Fiddle-dee-dee!" Wallis had never seen her easygoing mother so angry. She was even angrier than she had been when her quarrel with Aunt Bessie had resulted in their moving out of her house and moving into the Preston Apartment House. "John Freeman Rasin was educated at Loyola College, and his daddy has controlled state politics in Maryland for more than thirty years."

"Carroll Rasin may well be head of the Baltimore Democratic Party," Bessie shot back waspishly, "and he may well be wealthy, but he hasn't any pedigree. None of the Rasins have."

"Just because Free didn't come to America with the Pilgrim Fathers doesn't mean he isn't kind and good company and generous!" As always, Alice couldn't sustain her temper and was now on the verge of tears. "I've been a widow for eleven years, Bessie. I don't want to be a widow all my life."

Her elder sister regarded her with loving despair. "But Free isn't the kind of man women marry, Alice. He wouldn't still be a bachelor at forty if he were. Not only doesn't he hold any socially eminent position, he doesn't even work—or hasn't for as long as I have known him."

"Free doesn't need to work." Alice dabbed at her eyes with a handkerchief. "His daddy gives him all the money he needs."

"There you go!" Bessie threw up her hands and her eyes to heaven. "What kind of a husband would a man like that be? Lord Almighty, Alice dear. Open your eyes before it's too late."

For days after the scene between her mother and her aunt had taken place, Wallis was so quiet and withdrawn that even Pamela grew exasperated with her. Wallis didn't care. All she could think of was that word *husband*. What if her mother married Free Rasin? What would happen to her then? Her Uncle Sol would turn them out of the house on Biddle Street and, as Free Rasin didn't work, there was no telling what sort of a home they would then live in. As far as Baltimore high society was concerned, she and her mother would be social outcasts.

As she walked down Preston Street on her way to visit her grandmother, she was seized by fear of what the future held. How could she ever become a debutante if, because her mother had married Free Rasin, she was regarded as being an "out"? And if she didn't become a debutante, how would she ever meet eligible young men? The answer was, she wouldn't be able to.

As a highly suitable marriage was the only acceptable career for a well-brought-up girl, what kind of a future was she then going to be facing?

She was a block away from her grandmother's when she saw Mabel Morgan walking up the other side of the street. She wasn't alone, or with Violet Dix, but with a group of girls Wallis didn't know; girls who were, she assumed, Mabel's classmates at Bryn Mawr.

She averted her gaze, intending to ignore them.

Mabel didn't give her the opportunity.

"Hi, Bessiewallis!" she called out with nothing friendly in her tone. "How ya doin'? Is your Uncle Sol still ponying up for your school fees?"

The girls with Mabel looked across at her with prurient interest. Some of them began sniggering.

Wallis clamped her mouth tightly shut and clenched her fists. To engage in a shouting match across the street would be to lower herself to Mabel's level, and she wasn't going to do that; not when she was so near to number 34 and when word of a fracas might get back to her grandmother.

Seething with rage and frustration, she walked on, behaving as if Mabel and her friends didn't exist. It took all of her very considerable self-control, but as the sound of the sniggering faded into the distance she knew one thing for certain. One day she was going to be someone very, very special. Just how she would attain that goal she didn't know, but she knew that when that glorious day came, the snobs of Baltimore high society would bitterly regret the way they had so contemptuously treated her and her mother. As for the likes of Mabel Morgan and her friends—when she was *Someone* with a capital S, they could go down on their knees begging and she wouldn't even give them the time of day.

"Instead of spending the spring vacation at Pot Springs, how would you like to spend them with your Montague cousins in Virginia?" her mother asked her when, after spending time with her grandmother, she finally arrived home. "It will make a nice change, and you know Cousin Lelia just loves to have you stay at Wakefield."

"And I just love being there." It was true. Cousin Henry apart, she far preferred spending time with the Montague side of her family than with the Warfield side, for the Montagues were far more relaxed and easygoing.

Like Pot Springs, Wakefield Manor was a typical rambling Southern plantation house, with glistening white columns and long verandahs and balconies. It was set in the midst of vast grassy lawns studded with giant cedars and was somewhere the Montague clan tended to gather two or three times a year.

Her Aunt Lelia was her mother's first cousin and so, strictly speaking, not her aunt at all. *Cousin* and *aunt* were words used loosely among Montagues. Whether first or second cousins, or first cousin or second cousin once removed, they always referred to each other simply as "cousin," or, if there was a large age difference, as "aunt" and "uncle." When it came to her Montague cousins, Wallis had a lot of them.

Her favorite was her cousin Corinne, for twenty-one-year-old Corinne was glamour personified. She was a typical Montague in looks, being blond and blue-eyed, and she had only recently married a dashing Navy pilot, Henry Croskey Mustin. Flying was still such a novelty that a pilot of any kind was a figure of awe, and a naval pilot more so than most.

During her few weeks at Wakefield Manor, Wallis formed a firm ambition. When she was older, she wanted to be just like her cousin Corinne. She wanted to be thought enviably glamorous—and she wanted to be married to a Navy pilot as handsome, dashing, and fearless as Henry Croskey Mustin.

She begged a photograph of Henry from Corinne and added it to her pinup collection.

Pamela capped it by producing a photograph of Prince Edward that had been taken by her stepfather on his summer visit to Sandringham. Unlike earlier newspaper photographs of him, Prince Edward no longer looked quite so nondescript. He had obviously just finished a game of tennis because he was wearing white flannels and had a racket in one hand. With his other hand he was pushing a lock of pale gold hair away from his forehead, and he was smiling toward the camera with an engagingly quizzical expression in his eyes.

Arriving home from summer vacation wasn't as happy an experience for Wallis as it usually was, for it was quite obvious that, in her absence, Mr. Rasin had been spending a lot of time at 212 Biddle Street.

Some of his clothes now hung in the chifforobe in the guest bedroom. Worse, she came across a pair of his shoes in her mother's bedroom.

Nearly every night of the week, he was a guest for dinner. Large, moonfaced, and always amiable, he seemed to fill whatever room—dining room or parlor—he happened to be in.

"And he *always* brings me a gift," Wallis said gloomily to Aunt Bessie. "I don't want him to. I just don't want him to be there. I hardly ever have any time with my mother on my own any more. Sometimes he even stays the night."

Bessie, who had been knitting, dropped her needles into her lap so abruptly she lost half a dozen stitches. "Are you quite sure about that, Wallis?"

It was only when she looked into her aunt's appalled face that Wallis realized she shouldn't have told anyone—not even Bessie—about Mr. Rasin's sleeping arrangements.

"He sleeps in the guest bedroom," she said hurriedly, closing her mind to the thought of the shoes she had seen in her mother's bedroom, "I only mind it because he doesn't shave before coming down for breakfast."

It was information her aunt didn't look much comforted by.

When Wallis arrived home there was, for once, no sign of Mr. Rasin.

A smell of frying chicken drifted from the kitchen, and there was a plate of freshly baked oatcakes on the dining table.

"It's nice to be on our own, Mama," she said, giving her mother a loving hug. "Aunt Bessie is fine. She's thinking of taking a trip to Monterey County."

"That's swell." Alice gave her a kiss. "And you're right, Wallis. It is nice to be on our own together, but there are many times when you are not here, and then I get a little lonesome."

She sat down at the table.

Wallis, her antenna for disaster utterly failing her, sat down at the other side of the table and reached for an oatcake.

Alice hesitated, cleared her throat, and clasped her hands in her lap. "Because of the lonesome thing, I've something very important to tell you, sweetheart."

Wallis was so happy at having her mother once again to herself for a little while that she still didn't sense what was about to come.

"I'm going to marry Mr. Rasin, Wallis."

Wallis had just bitten into the oatcake.

She choked on it.

"Now, there's no reason for you be upset, Wallis darling." Alice reached across the table, taking Wallis's hands in hers.

Wallis snatched them back, pushing her chair away from the table, struggling to her feet.

"Of course there is!" Hot tears scalded her eyes. "I don't want you to marry him! I don't want you to marry anyone!"

Alice sprang to her feet, rounded the table, and tried to take Wallis in her arms. Wallis pushed her violently away.

"I don't want to share this little house with anyone else but you, Mama!" The tears poured down her face. "Uncle Sol didn't buy it for us so that someone else could come and live here! It has always been just the two of us, and if you marry Mr. Rasin it will never be just the two of us again! Not ever!"

"But Wallis darlin', in a family, three is better than two and Free is so kind and he's so lookin' forward to being your stepdaddy . . ."

Alice tried to put her arms around her once again.

Wallis struggled free. "No!" she shouted, backing away until the closed dining room door prevented her from backing any farther. "No, Mama! *No!*"

Alice was now crying almost as hard as Wallis was. "You're not being fair to me, Wallis." Tears dripped onto her hands. "You're too young to understand. You haven't even understood about the house. Your Uncle Sol didn't buy it for us. Free did."

It was a reality too much for Wallis. With a howl of anguish she spun around, wrenched the door open, and raced up the stairs to her third-floor bedroom. Once there, she turned the key in the lock, threw herself on the bed, and, ignoring Alice's pleas to be let into the room, pummeled her pillows in a fury of anguish until she collapsed on top of them, exhausted and still crying.

To her stunned surprise she received sympathy from no one. Pamela thought she was making a huge fuss about nothing. "So what if Mr. Rasin did buy the house on Biddle Street? You like it, don't you?" she'd said with her usual down-to-earth practicality on the day Wallis was twelve. "And if your mother has Mr. Rasin for company, you won't have to feel guilty about leaving her on her own when you're a debutante and out at parties and dances every night."

It was a line of thought shared by Aunt Bessie. "In five years' time you'll be seventeen and a young woman, Wallis," she'd said, speaking to her more sternly than Wallis could ever remember her doing. "Life will be much easier for you then if you don't have to worry about your mother being on her own."

"But I thought you didn't like Mr. Rasin!" Wallis simply couldn't understand the attitudes she was meeting with. "You told Mama he wasn't good enough for her!"

Bessie flinched, well aware that in the heat of the moment she'd said things in front of Wallis that she shouldn't have said. "Your mother could certainly have married someone far more socially eminent and more personable than Free, but it is Free she loves, Wallis. That your mother is marrying a man who is kindness itself is something to be very grateful for. And you should be proud of her for choosing to marry for love, rather than marrying for social advancement. Which, let me tell you, she could have done if she'd so wished."

Wallis knew her aunt was referring to her Uncle Sol. Even though the idea of her mother marrying her uncle was even more horrific than the idea of her marrying Free Rasin, it wasn't a comparison that helped her come to terms with the thought of having Free Rasin as a stepfather.

To her stunned incredulity, even her grandmother failed her as an ally.

"Your mother has been on the road to ruin for years," she'd said bluntly. "It's better she marry Carroll Rasin's son than continue living the way she has been doing. Free's a no-good layabout, but at least he's doing the honorable thing and putting a wedding ring on her finger. It's more than any of her other beaux were willing to do."

That her grandmother was raising no objections to the marriage was something she found almost impossible to believe until Pamela said sagely, "Well, of course she isn't going to do so, Wally. It means now she doesn't have to worry that your mother may one day say yes to your Uncle Sol. The last thing your grandmother wants is to be your mother's mother-in-law for a second time."

Once she knew she had no allies who would help her prevent the marriage, she used emotional blackmail.

"I'm not coming to the wedding, Mama. I'll run away rather than go to it."

Alice, who had never previously had a moment's trouble with Wallis, was in despair. "But darlin', of all the wedding guests, you are the most important. How can I get married without you there? It would break my heart."

Distraught at the thought of a wedding without her daughter present, Alice asked Bessie and her cousin Lelia if they would talk to Wallis and make her understand what a terrible thing her not being there would be.

"You see, honey," her Aunt Lelia said, an arm affectionately around Wallis's shoulders, "your mama loves Mr. Rasin, and her wedding to him should be a joyous occasion. If you aren't there, that won't be the case. You will make your mother very unhappy. So unhappy she may never get over it."

"If you come to the wedding," Bessie said, having run out of all other persuasions, "you will be the first to cut the cake. Being first, you'll probably find the good-luck token ring and silver thimble and bright new dime that are hidden in it."

Wallis wasn't remotely interested in the ring and the thimble and the dime.

As the day of the wedding approached, she was, however, realistic enough to know that however much she didn't want to be there, there wasn't really any other option. She couldn't very well run away, when she had nowhere to run to.

The wedding was to take place in the parlor at Biddle Street. Both Warfields and Montagues had accepted invitations to attend it. The dress her mother was to wear remained a closely guarded secret. The dress Alice had set aside for Wallis to wear was of embroidered batiste laced with blue ribbons.

It was the prettiest dress Wallis had ever seen, but it didn't win her over.

"I don't want to be there," she said mulishly to Pamela, "and I'm not going to behave as if I want to be there."

When the big day came, the sight of so many of her relations, all in their very best finery, almost weakened her resolve. Almost, but not quite.

Her mother wore a gown the same color as the ribbons threaded in Wallis's dress and, in her upswept hair, a white gardenia. Her grandmother wore black, as always, but instead of bombazine her gown was made of shiny silk. Her Uncle Sol wore a suit of pale cream linen, chamois gloves, and a thunderous frown. The bridegroom, despite his suit being carefully and expensively tailored, looked as if he were wearing something that belonged to someone else. He did, however, sport a red rose in his buttonhole—and he wore a very big, very happy smile.

Wallis didn't. Her emotions were in such tumult that she felt violently ill.

With a face set and mutinous, she stood a little behind her mother as her mother and Free Rasin began to take their vows. With every second that the service continued, her inner tumult increased. In the end she could stand it no longer. Uncaring that she was behaving badly, she began edging away. Though she could be seen doing so, no one disturbed the solemnity of the vow-taking in order to bring her back.

As her mother said, "I will," Wallis reached the door and left the room.

Across the hallway, the dining room door was open. A white napperied table was laid, all ready for the reception. In the center of it, in wonderful splendor, stood the many-tiered wedding cake.

Wallis walked into the dining room and stood opposite the cake.

From the parlor came the sound of Free Rasin's deep bass, "I will."

Something red exploded in Wallis's head. With emotion surging in a way she could no longer control, she made a fist with her hand and plunged her fist into the center of the cake.

Icing cracked and splintered. The decorative figures of bride and groom on top of the cake toppled and fell.

Instead of being appalled at what she had done, now that she had started, Wallis was determined to finish her work of destruction. She plunged her hand into the bottom tier of the cake again and again, pulling out great handfuls of raisins, currants, cherries, and candied peel and letting them fall on the table and on the floor.

There came the sound of clapping and then the sound of footsteps crossing the hall. Brought to her senses, she whirled around to find herself face to face with her stepfather.

For a long, never-to-be-forgotten moment, their eyes held. Behind him were a whole group of wedding guests, their mouths round in horror at the sight of the destroyed cake. She heard someone call for her mother and someone else call for her Aunt Bessie.

In a moment of blinding self-hatred, the enormity of what she had done and of how she had totally ruined what should have been one of the happiest moments of her mother's life flooded over her. Her mother would never again love her. Even Aunt Bessie would never again love her.

Free saw the emotions chasing through her eyes, and in one swift second he put an end to all her fears.

"Why, looky here!" he boomed jovially, stretching his arms wide as he stepped toward her. "Wallis has beaten us all in the race to find the good-luck tokens!" And he put his massive arms around her, lifting her off her feet and twirling her round and round, laughing so loud everyone else began laughing as well.

Chapter Six

"He made everything all right at a stroke," she said afterward to Pamela.

Pamela was impressed. People who could make difficult situations right at a stroke were worth the time of day, in her opinion.

"And so are the two of you friends now?" she asked, wishing she could have been there when Wallis had plunged her fist into the cake. "Do you call him Papa?"

"No." Wallis looked horrified. "I call him Mr. Rasin."

Pamela hooted with laughter. "You are a case, Wally. I know I don't call my stepfather Papa, but I do at least call him by his Christian name!"

Wallis shot her a wry grin. "Mr. Rasin's Christian name is Free. And somehow, Pamela, I just can't bring myself to make free with it."

They giggled at the awfulness of her quip, and then Pamela said, "How about we go to the Mount Vernon rink? You never know who's going to be there, and at least there'll be some boys to talk to."

There had been boys to talk to, but to Wallis's intense disappointment John Jasper hadn't been one of them.

Wallis had been correct in thinking Mr. Rasin's presence at Biddle Street would change her and her mother's way of life. It did, and though there were times when despite his constant kindness she resented his presence, for the most part the changes were all beneficial, the most beneficial being that her mother no longer had constant money worries.

Though Alice had told Bessie that Free's father gave him whatever money he needed, his income actually came from a trust fund. To Alice it was a seemingly bottomless well, and she spent joyously, transforming 212 Biddle Street with new carpets, new drapes, elegant furniture, and a magnificent piano.

For Wallis, the piano came with a drawback, for her mother insisted she learn to play it, and as she was tone deaf and had no musical sense whatsoever, her piano lessons were a form of prolonged torture.

Free left the running of Biddle Street and Wallis's upbringing entirely in Alice's hands, and he continued to give Wallis surprise presents. His very best present to her was a French bulldog puppy she christened Bully.

If there was any real drawback to Free—which was the name Wallis always used when speaking about him to Pamela or Aunt Bessie, even though she couldn't bring herself to call him it to his face—it was that he simply didn't have the knack, when he was at home, of living as a gentleman should live.

He was nearly always happily untidy, which was an agony to Wallis, who was fastidiously neat. Sometimes he breakfasted unshaven. Even worse, he liked to enjoy champagne with his breakfast, something Wallis knew would shock her Episcopalian grandmother to the depths of her being if she ever knew about it. Not having to worry about a lack of money, though, was ample compensation for Free's embarrassing habits at home.

"And though Biddle Street isn't a big house and though Free doesn't often leave it, he's never overly visible," she said to Pamela one day in 1911 when they were on their way to a school friend's fifteenth birthday party. "He spends most of the day in the library, reading newspapers and smoking cigarettes."

"And drinking?" Pamela asked.

Wallis grinned. "There is usually a bottle of bourbon by the side of his chair, but he never gets falling-down drunk. Not that I've ever seen anyway."

"How is your Uncle Sol? Has he ever got over your mother becoming Mrs. Rasin instead of becoming Mrs. Solomon Warfield?"

They began walking up the steps to the Mount Vernon mansion where the party was being held.

"If he is, he isn't letting anyone know." Wallis transferred the present she was carrying from one arm to the other. "Nowadays Uncle Sol is *very* nice to me—and he never mentions my mother's name. Not ever."

As at most of her school friends' parties, the guests were nearly all girls—something that bored Wallis and Pamela equally. Boys were a topic they never tired of discussing, but though Wallis spoke of her cousin Henry quite often to Pamela, she no longer brought John Jasper's name into their conversations. Although she still only saw him infrequently it was John Jasper, not Henry, who was the center of all her romantic fantasies, and for a reason she wasn't entirely sure about, she didn't want Pamela to know how important John Jasper was to her.

It was Pamela who sometimes brought up John Jasper's name. "Wouldn't it be fun for you," she said once, "if John Jasper

Bachman had your cousin Henry's looks and if he became a Navy pilot like your cousin Corinne's husband? Then he'd be your perfect beau."

Privately Wallis thought John Jasper just perfect as he was, but she wasn't going to admit it. "And if he were royal, like Prince Edward," she'd said, laughing the subject away. "But then, Prince Edward is going to be your beau, isn't he? Not mine."

Whereas it had once been hard to find photographs of Prince Edward in newspapers, now he was rarely out of them. A year earlier his grandfather King Edward VII had died and, with his father now king, Prince Edward was heir to the throne. If being royal had always imbued him with glamour, that glamour had intensified a hundredfold now that he was in line to be not only the next king of Great Britain and Ireland and all her dominions over the seas, but the next emperor of India as well.

The crowning of his father, as George V, had only recently taken place in the same week as Wallis's fifteenth birthday.

"It takes a year for preparations for a coronation to be made," Pamela had said to her when Wallis had been puzzled by the year time gap. "You would think in that year arrangements could have been made for me to be in London when it happened." There was disgust in her voice. "As a peer of the realm, my father is eligible for a seat in Westminster Abbey when a king is crowned. If he'd returned to London for the coronation—and taken me with him—think of how wonderful it would have been. But he simply couldn't be bothered."

"What about your mother?" Wallis found Pamela's family situation just as intriguing as Pamela found hers. "Tarquin is an earl, isn't he? Isn't an earl a peer of the realm?"

"He is." Pamela was so cross she could hardly get the words past her lips. "But he's married to a divorced woman and so wouldn't have been on the guest list. That doesn't mean my mother couldn't still have invited me to London."

"Why didn't she?"

Pamela's eyes had flashed fire. Wallis had never seen her quite so angry. "She didn't invite me, because she doesn't want to remind people she's old enough to have a fifteen-year-old daughter. She's going to have to remind people when I'm eighteen, because when I come out as a debutante, I sure as peas-are-green am not going to do so in Baltimore!"

Photographs of the coronation procession and of King George and his queen waving to the crowds from the balcony of Buckingham Palace, Prince Edward and their other children by their side, had been featured in every American newspaper, and nearly every girl at Arundell had clipped one of them.

Almost immediately after the coronation had come another sacred and spectacular royal ceremony, and this time Edward, not his father, had been center stage.

"As Prince of Wales, the ceremony at Caernarvon Castle was his formal investiture," Pamela had said when they were looking at a photograph in the *Baltimore Sun* and Wallis had questioned her about it. "I don't think much of his robes, do you? They look far too big for him. Let's hope he grows a bit taller. I don't want a husband who is shorter than I am!"

Wallis hadn't believed her, knowing that if Pamela's daydream ever came true she would accept Edward's proposal fast as light, not caring how small or slightly built he might be.

Daydreams about Prince Edward were daydreams they comfortably shared, though Wallis was well aware that Pamela's daydreams had a far greater chance of coming to fruition than had her own. When Pamela returned to London for her debutante coming-out year she would, thanks to her stepfather's friendship with the king, at least have the opportunity of meeting Prince Edward. Her own coming-out would take place in Baltimore, and though she was greatly looking forward to it, she wouldn't be being presented to King George and Queen Mary—as Pamela, along with all the other debutantes of her year, would be. It was something, whenever their debutante year was under discussion, that she had to try very hard not to be jealous about.

The years she was enjoying were the happiest she had ever known. Harsh words were never spoken at Biddle Street. On the rare occasions when she misbehaved, it was her mother who disciplined her—and Alice was far too loving to ever be cross with her for long.

At Arundell, too, she seldom found herself in trouble.

"That's because you're far too clever to be found out," Pamela said grumpily when, after it had been Wallis's idea that they and their classmates should spy on a Masonic ceremony they knew was taking place in a building close to Arundell, they had been discovered and hauled up in front of a furious Miss Carroll. All, that is, apart from Wallis, who had adroitly slipped away unobserved.

"You're just not fast enough on your feet," Wallis had said with a smirk, dodging away before Pamela could lay violent hands on her.

Other things, as well as home life at Biddle Street and school life at Arundell, were also going well for her. Every Sunday morning she went to church with her grandmother and her Uncle Sol, and afterward she had lunch with them on East Preston Street, where she enjoyed the sense of being part and parcel of a highly respectable family.

In the spring vacation of 1912 she went again to Pot Springs. It had been two years since she had last been there, and though she'd then been thirteen and eager for Henry to make a romantic move toward her, he hadn't done so. In Henry's eyes, her being thirteen had, apparently, been little different from her being eleven. He had still rated her far too young to be kissed. There was, however, a lot of difference between being thirteen and being fifteen.

On her first morning down to breakfast, she wore her glossy hair plaited into a long thick braid, a crisp white shirtwaist, a black currant–colored paneled skirt that barely skimmed a pair of the latest Mary Janes, and, cinching her narrow waist, a broad black patent leather belt. At first glance she looked to be at least seventeen, and she knew it.

"I think you may want to change into a riding skirt and boots, Wallis," her Uncle Emory said jovially as she joined him at the table. "Henry is already at the stables waiting for you. He has a new hunter he wants to show off."

Henry's eagerness to be out riding with her again sent a ripple of pleasure down her spine. She helped herself to sausages, determined not to show her own eagerness. Making Henry wait—and then arriving dressed in a way that indicated going riding with him wasn't top of her list of things to do—would be a great tease.

She spun breakfast out for as long as possible and then, with a fast-beating heart, forced herself to keep to a leisurely stroll as she made her way toward the stables.

He was dressed for riding and was waiting for her at the large barn where all Pot Springs' horses were stabled. At the sight of her shoes and skirt he quirked an eyebrow. It was a query she ignored. Making him believe she was no longer desperately eager to spend time with him on horseback was the most fun she'd had in ages.

"Uncle Emory said you had a new hunter you wanted to show me."

"I have. I think he's going to impress you."

Even though it was two years since they'd last met, he didn't give her a hug or a cousinly kiss on the cheek. Wallis didn't mind. Cousinly kisses weren't the kind she wanted to experience.

Side by side, but not touching, they walked into the barn and down its wide central walkway. Several horses' heads protruded inquisitively from the loose boxes, but Wallis couldn't see any that were familiar.

"Pa has been doing a lot of buying and selling lately," Henry said, reading her thoughts. "One of his latest acquisitions is perfect for you. A three-year-old filly with a gentle disposition. At the moment she's out being exercised."

He stopped in front of the end box. "This is the Southern gentleman I wanted to show off. His name is Thunder and he's pretty darn special, don't you think?"

Riding was simply a challenge Wallis had set herself, and now that thanks to Henry she was fairly competent at it, she had no real interest in horseflesh. Even she, though, could tell that the horse in question was special. He was black as sin with a white star on his muzzle so perfect it looked as if it had been painted.

"He has the best head I've ever seen on a horse," Henry said, "and he's as fast as the wind." He turned his head away from Thunder to look at her, saying with a grin, "Not a horse for you to ride, Wallis."

"No." There was a look in Thunder's eyes that made Wallis reluctant to even stretch her hand out toward him. "I'm not even tempted, Henry."

"But you do want to ride again this summer?"

Though the great doors at either end of the barn were open to let a cooling breeze blow through, the interior of the barn was in deep shade. Combined with the smell of hay and manure and horseflesh, it made for an arousingly intimate atmosphere.

"Yes." She held his eyes, glad there were no stable boys around to spoil the moment. "Of course I do."

He was wearing riding boots and breeches and a checked linen shirt that was open at the neck. He'd obviously already been out riding, for there were beads of perspiration on his throat. She couldn't take her eyes from them. He had to kiss her now. He *had* to.

He made a small movement preparatory to moving away from her, and, knowing she was about to lose her chance of equaling Pamela in the being-kissed-by-a-mature-man stakes, she shot a hand out, laying it against a bulging bicep.

For a split second he hesitated, heat flooding his eyes, and then in sudden capitulation he pulled her roughly against him, lowering his head to hers.

The shock of actually being kissed in such a way after dreaming about it for so long nearly made Wallis forget all she had learned from Pamela's experience with Sergei Romanov. As Henry's lips parted hers, she remembered and, sliding her arms up and around his neck, obligingly allowed his tongue to slide past hers in the way men seemed to like.

Unlike Pamela, who had found the experience very peculiar and more than a little unpleasant, Wallis found it dizzyingly arousing.

Breathing hard, Henry finally lifted his head from hers. "You're a minx, Cousin Wallis. And far too old for your years," he said thickly. "You're also a Warfield and you're not to go around letting anyone else kiss you like this. If you do, you'll get a reputation for being fast, and then you'll never get a decent marriage proposal from anyone. Understand?"

"Yes," she said, understanding very well.

"I think you should go back to the house. Spend some time with my mother. Give her all the Baltimore gossip. We'll go riding together tomorrow and then, the day after, I'm leaving on a visit to some of Pa's friends in Charlottesville."

She nodded, knowing very well why he was leaving for a

stay in Charlottesville. Uncomfortably aware of her age, he was putting distance between the two of them. That he was doing so because he found her such a very great temptation filled her with elation. That there would be very few further such kisses between the two of them didn't trouble her. He'd given her what she wanted—her first experience of a truly adult kiss— and, though she had a crush on Henry, she'd never been serious about him. The only person she was life-and-death serious about was John Jasper.

After vacation was over she tried hard to accidentally-on-purpose run into John Jasper. It wasn't easy. The Bachmans didn't live close to either Biddle Street or East Preston Street and didn't attend Baltimore's Episcopalian Christ Church, where Wallis spent her Sunday mornings.

It was in June, on her grandmother's birthday, which fell shortly before her own birthday, that Wallis got lucky where John Jasper was concerned. It was a Saturday morning and as she turned onto Preston Street, awkwardly carrying her grandmother's present—a cashmere shawl lavishly tissue-wrapped and boxed—John Jasper entered it on the opposite side of the street.

Wallis clutched the box tighter and with a pounding heart waited for him to cross the street toward her.

He did so at a negligent stroll, his hands in his trouser pockets, the June sun glinting on his tightly curling dark hair.

"Hi, Wallis," he said as he walked up to her. "Where are you going?"

When she spoke, her voice sounded so unlike her normal voice it could have come out of a squeezebox. "It's my grandmother's birthday. I'm taking her a present."

"Does she still live at number thirty-four?"

There were blue-black glints in his hair that she'd never

been aware of before, and his eyes weren't a straight brown, as she'd always thought, but a golden brown. Simply looking into them turned her knees to jelly.

"Yes." Her voice was still a squeak. She paused, took a deep breath, and said, trying to sound as laconic as he did, "How is it you know where she lives?"

"My father is on the board of one of your Uncle Sol's companies."

Whether he had intended to walk down Preston Street she didn't know, but that was what he did, walking along beside her so close she could smell the faint tang of lemon cologne. She wondered if he had begun shaving. He was a few months older than her, already sixteen. If he hadn't, and if the lemon tang wasn't from cologne, than it was from the soap he used. Whatever it was from, it was something she liked a great deal.

"Someone told me the other day you had a little dog."

His hands were still in his pockets. She wished they weren't. If his hands had been free she could have carried her grandmother's present in her left arm and let her right hand fall down so that even if he didn't take hold of it, the back of it would brush against the back of his.

"Yes. My stepfather gave him to me. He's a French bulldog. His name is Bully."

John Jasper chuckled. "I reckon that's a pretty good name for a bulldog, Wallis. Why isn't he with you?"

"My grandmother doesn't like dogs. At least, she doesn't like them in the house, and Bully wouldn't like being tied up outside."

John Jasper looked across at her speculatively. "How would you like it if I took Bully for a walk now and then? I like dogs and I'm pretty good with them. I used to have a Siberian husky. He was a great dog. He died last year, and I still miss him."

"Why didn't you get another?"

They were fast approaching number 34, and Wallis began walking as slowly as possible, not wanting to reach it, not wanting their time together to be over.

"My ma didn't want another big dog. The dog we have now is a Pekingese. He's kind of cute, but he doesn't like going for walks. He sits on my ma's knee whenever he can, and when she's not around, he sits on the sofa."

They'd reached number 34, and there was nothing for it but for her to come to a halt. She turned toward him. "You can take Bully for a walk any time you want, John Jasper."

What she didn't say, but what she intended, was that when he did so, she would go along too.

"That's great, Wallis. I can't wait."

He made no move to continue on his way, and she made no move to climb the steps to number 34's front door.

For a long moment they held eyes. Wallis's heart was beating so loud she was sure John Jasper could hear it.

"You're awful pretty, Wallis," he said at last. "Would you mind if I touched your hair?"

She shook her head, her throat so tight she couldn't speak.

He took both hands out of his trouser pockets and then slowly raised his right hand, gently touching her glossy, near-black hair.

They were standing very close now, so close that Wallis knew if anyone in number 34 saw them she would be in very serious trouble.

There was an expression in his golden-brown eyes that she recognized. It was the same heat-filled expression she had seen in her cousin Henry's eyes the moment before he'd kissed her.

She raised her face slightly, letting John Jasper know by the expression in her eyes that even though it was bright daylight; even though they were on a public, but blessedly deserted street; and even though they were smack outside her grandmother's house, if he wanted to kiss her, she wasn't going to do anything to stop him.

He made a small sound that excited her immeasurably, and then he bent his head to hers, kissing her softly full on the mouth.

Compared to her cousin Henry's kiss, it was a very chaste kiss, but Wallis didn't mind because she knew it was a far more special kiss than the one Henry had given her. For one thing, she was certain that it was John Jasper's first kiss, and for another she knew John Jasper wasn't, within weeks, going to announce his engagement to a girl from Charlottesville.

When he raised his head from hers, his cheeks were flushed and he looked very pleased with himself.

"I'll be seein' you then, Wallis," he said, belatedly shooting a glance up at number 34's windows to make sure no one had been watching. "Tell Bully I'll be coming for him soon."

"I will."

He turned away, beginning to walk back down Preston Street the way they had come, his hands back in his pockets.

As she ran up the steps to the front door, her heart singing with happiness, she could hear him begin to whistle. It sounded as if he were whistling "Yankee Doodle Dandy."

When her grandmother's black butler opened the door to her, she walked into the house with a smile on her face so wide it reached from one side of it to the other.

Her grandmother was in the drawing room, seated in her favorite rocking chair. Her Uncle Sol was standing a foot or so away from her, smoking a cigar.

Her grandmother liked cigar smoke and often asked Sol to blow it in her hair so that she could enjoy the fragrance of a Dutch Masters Palma long after he had left the room. Wallis, too, wasn't averse to something she thought of as being distinctly manly.

To celebrate the fact that it was her birthday, her grandmother wasn't wearing black bombazine but a gown of far more expensive pure silk, her only jewelry a jet mourning pin.

"Thank you, Bessie Wallis, dear," she said, accepting the present Wallis gave her. "Your uncle has something very like a present for you, too. Don't beat about the bush, Solomon. Tell Bessie Wallis what it is you have in mind for her."

Sol blew a plume of blue smoke into the room and then said in his usually stiff manner, "You will be sixteen in a week or two, Wallis. It's time to be thinking about your eighteenth-birthday debut—and how, over the next two years, you will be preparing for it."

That her uncle was already talking about her debut sent a thrill of anticipation down Wallis's spine, though she wasn't quite sure what he meant by her preparing for it, for the preparations would, surely, all be done by him.

"You've been a good scholar at Arundell," he continued, turning to one side so that he could flick ash from the end of his cigar into the empty fireplace, adding as an afterthought, "apart, of course, for mathematics."

Wallis remained wisely silent.

"I'm not sure, though, that there is anything to be gained by your staying on at Arundell until you are eighteen."

Alarm flared through her. "But what about my graduation, Uncle Sol? Everyone stays on for graduation. If I don't, everyone will think it's because . . . because . . ."

"Because I no longer wish to pay your fees?"

It was so exactly what she had been going to say that Wallis flushed scarlet.

"There will be no fear of them thinking that, Wallis. Let me tell you what I have in mind."

Sol crossed the room and crushed the butt of his cigar out in an onyx ashtray.

"Two years at an exclusive finishing school will be of far more use to you than another two years at Arundell," he said, when he again turned toward her. "It isn't as if you need another two years of schooling. You are never going to have to work for your living. Your aim, like all young ladies of your social class, must be a good marriage to a wealthy young man of illustrious background."

There was no way Wallis was going to disagree with him. A finishing school would be wonderful. To the best of her knowledge, there wasn't one in Baltimore. The nearest was Oldfields, at Glencoe—and Glencoe was quite a distance away. If her uncle had Oldfields in mind, it would mean her becoming a boarder—and being a boarder, living away from home, would be a terrifically exciting adventure. Oldfields, however, was known to be the most expensive and fashionable finishing school in Maryland, and the fees would be colossal.

She dug her nails into her palms, wishing as hard as she could that she would get the right answer to her next question. "Which finishing school did you have in mind, Uncle Sol?"

"Oldfields. I've already paid it a visit. You will be a boarder, of course, but a boarder in exceptionally genteel surroundings. The school itself is a large mansion set in several hundred acres of woodlands, and students are housed in a large wing that has been added onto the main house. There is a large ballroom with crystal chandeliers for dancing lessons. Deportment is practiced on a magnificent grand staircase. The drawing rooms are hung with silk. Altogether, I couldn't find fault with anything. If you are happy to make the transition there, I will put it in hand straight away."

The thought of the ballroom made Wallis's head spin.

"Oh yes, *please*, Uncle Sol," she said ecstatically, running toward him to give him a kiss on his cheek. It was a gesture she knew always pleased him and, as she now had genuine affection for him, one that came easily to her.

"Oldfields?" Pamela stared at her, not sharing in her excitement. "Good for you Wally, but I won't be traipsing after you there as I traipsed after you to Arundell."

They were walking back to school from the Gymnasium on Charles Street, hanging back from the rest of their classmates in order to have a little privacy.

"But why not?" Wallis was genuinely baffled. "Your father always lets you have your own way over everything. If you said that you wanted to go to Oldfields, he'd let you go there like a shot."

"That's true—but only because he doesn't care where I am, or where I go." She gave a bitter smile. "He only brought me with him when he left England because he thought he was giving my mother grief. He's never truly got over the fact that instead of giving her grief he played right into her hands, as she no more wanted me around than he did."

Wallis had known almost from the beginning of their friendship that even though Pamela lived a life surrounded by riches, she was far poorer than herself in that she didn't have even one parent who loved her and was interested in her. Now was not the moment to express sympathy, though. Not when something more important was at stake.

"Oldfields," she said again. "Why don't you want to go there? It's very exclusive. Everyone there will come from a really wealthy privileged background."

"Well, of *course* they will, Wally." Pamela rolled her eyes in exasperation. "But they won't be from *my* kind of wealthy privileged background. When it comes to a finishing school, I won't be going to an *American* finishing school. I shall go to a

Swiss finishing school, just like every other girl who will be in my debutante year—and when you hightail it to Oldfields, I'll hightail it to Switzerland."

Pamela had always said that when it came to her coming-out year, she would come out in London, not Baltimore, but it had never occurred to Wallis that Pamela would be leaving Baltimore two years beforehand. She was sensible enough to know that she would make new friends at Oldfields, but she also knew that when she did, none of the friendships would be as close and as necessary to her as her friendship with Pamela.

She stopped walking, saying with deep passion, "Even though you will be in Switzerland and then London, we will still be friends, won't we?"

Pamela's eyes held hers. "Always, Wally."

Both of them were wearing straw school hats, and Pamela's was held in place by a long hatpin. Not taking her eyes away from Wallis's, she removed the hatpin.

"To show us both how much we mean what we say, we should seal our promises in blood. Are you game?"

Wally nodded, and, as she held her breath, Pamela scored a deep line with the hatpin across her own wrist, drawing blood, and then, as Wally gritted her teeth, she took Wallis's hand and scored a deep line across Wallis's wrist.

"Now we mix our blood," Pamela said fiercely.

Wallis watched, transfixed, as Pamela pressed their bleeding wrists together.

"There." As their blood mixed there was high satisfaction in Pamela's voice. "Now we're blood *friends*—and nothing can part blood friends, Wally. Blood friends are friends forever."

Chapter Seven

On Wallis's first day at Oldfields, Edith Miller rushed up to her in delight. "Bessie Wallis! You do remember me, don't you? We were in the same class at Miss O'Donnell's on Elliott Street."

"Of course I remember you, Edith."

For the first time it occurred to Wallis to wonder if other of her classmates from her early school days were at Oldfields.

"I'm not called Bessie Wallis any longer," she said firmly. "I'm just called Wallis." She allowed Edith to link her arm with hers. "Is there anyone else from Elliott Street at Oldfields, Edith? Mabel Morgan, for instance? Or Violet Dix?"

To her vast relief Edith shook her head. "No. Mabel's mother told my mother Mabel was going to go to a finishing school in Virginia. I don't know whether Violet will be going there as well, but she probably will be. Mabel and Violet nearly always went everywhere together. Shall I show you round, Wallis? I've been here two months now, so I feel quite at home."

Wallis nodded, happy to have someone who could introduce her and speed up the process of making new friends. At Elliott Street Edith had never been a particular friend of hers, but that had only been because Edith had been quiet and mousy and she had found her dull company, not because she was unlikable, as Mabel and Violet were unlikable.

"What did you think of Miss Nan when you came for your interview, Wallis?" Edith asked as they began on a tour of Oldfield's lavishly furnished drawing rooms and study rooms. "Did you like her?"

"By Miss Nan, do you mean Miss McCulloch?"

Edith nodded. "Yes. She's the sister of the Reverend Duncan McCulloch, who founded Oldfields. She's very strict, but also very nice."

"She reminds me of Miss Carroll, my headmistress at Arundell." Wallis paused to look at a large notice very prominently displayed. It read, *Gentleness and Courtesy Are Expected of Girls at All Times*.

She quirked an eyebrow, and Edith said without a glimmer of humor, "Miss Nan thinks it very important all Oldfields girls have a well-developed sense of gentility and grace. The same notice is posted on the doors of the dormitories, and the school's two basketball teams are called Gentleness and Courtesy. I'm on Courtesy. Let's go up to the dormitories and I'll introduce you to Ellen Yuille. She's from North Carolina and very lively. I know you'll get on with her. Her father is something very big in Duke Tobacco."

Wallis met Ellen and immediately liked her. She also met Beatrice Astor, Alice Maud Van Rensselaer, and Phoebe Schermerhorn. All, like Ellen, came from exceptionally wealthy families. Wallis was soon firm friends with them.

A few weeks later she wrote to Pamela,

> . . . *some things at Oldfields are a bore, but not many—and the girls here are swell. Of the boring things, we are only allowed two at-home weekends in addition to regular vacations—it's not much, is it? How many are you allowed*

*at Mont-Fleuri? Other things are fun. I love the dancing
lessons in the ballroom and the deportment and etiquette and
flower arranging lessons. The first person I ran into when I
arrived was Edith Miller, from our Elliott Street days. She's
not quite the mouse she used to be, but she still plays by all
the rules and never risks getting into trouble. Other girls are
more lively—especially Phoebe Schermerhorn, who regularly
sneaks out of Oldfields after lights-out to meet up with a beau!*

A letter from Pamela speedily winged its way across the
Atlantic in response.

Dear Wally,

*Edith Miller was so quiet in class I barely remember her!
Phoebe sounds much more fun. Compared to Oldfields, Mont-
Fleuri is relaxed and we get to go down into Geneva nearly
every Saturday. Lots of the girls here have a secret beau and
we are all—every last one of us—in love with Hans, our ski
instructor. (Hans, of course, is only in love with me!) I'd like
to stay in Switzerland for Christmas (otherwise how will I get
a present from Hans?) only, after years of maternal neglect,
my mother is now suffering a season of guilt and insists I
join her and Tarquin in Norfolk. (I don't think the guilt will
last for long. By the time vacation is over I doubt we'll be on
speaking terms.) What would make it all worthwhile would
be an invite to Sandringham which would give me the chance
to flirt with Prince Edward again (if, of course, he is there at
Christmas). There's no chance of Sandringham, though, as
King George and Queen Mary are going to be in India nearly
all the winter celebrating their Coronation Durbar.*

Wallis didn't know whether to be pleased or disappointed
that Pamela stood no chance of being a guest at Sandringham

during the Christmas holidays. In not hobnobbing with royalty, Pamela wouldn't be able to score over her socially—and she was pleased about that. On the other hand, if Pamela became a friend of Prince Edward's, then as she was Pamela's best friend there was a chance that one day Pamela would be able to introduce her to him—and that was something that not even Beatrice Astor, Alice Maud Van Rensselaer, or Phoebe Schermerhorn could hope for.

In the first month of 1913 Pamela's royal name-dropping continued.

> *You'll never guess who my new roommate is—the daughter of the shah of Persia! She's sensationally beautiful in a dark-haired, dark-eyed kind of way (not as beautiful as me, naturally). I just love being able to say I have a friend who is a princess of the House of Persia. It sounds so exotic. You'll hate me for this Wally, but I'm sooooo glad I'm at Mont-Fleuri and not Oldfields. Mont-Fleuri is very sophisticated. Nearly every royal house in Europe sends a princess or two here, and most of them will eventually become crowned queens.*

Wallis was both impressed and exasperated. She was also—though pride prevented her from admitting it to Pamela—beginning to get bored with many of Oldfields's rules and restrictions. Oldfields girls were, for instance, forbidden to meet with boys under any circumstances. They were even forbidden to write to them or accept letters from them. It was a rule Wallis could see no sense in and consequently didn't feel honor-bound to keep.

Defiantly, and with no sense of guilt, she began writing to John Jasper.

His response was swift. At the beginning of April he asked if she would be able to meet up with him if he drove down from Baltimore.

. . . Pa bought me a Packard for my seventeenth birthday,

he wrote in a large sprawling hand.

It goes like the wind! I'm not allowed to keep it on campus at Loyola, but since Loyola is so near to home it isn't any great inconvenience. Just let me know if you're able and give me a time and place.

He'd signed it *JJ* and added three kisses.

Wallis hid the letter in her underwear drawer.

"What I want to know," she said a half hour later to Phoebe, "is how you get out of Oldfields to meet your beaux—and how you get back in again."

Phoebe shot her a broad grin. "As long as you do it at night, it's easy peasy. There's a small isolation dormitory next to the infirmary. It's only ever used if someone comes down with something infectious. It's on ground level, I've never found it locked yet, and the window is a cinch to open."

Wallis gave a sigh of satisfaction.

Phoebe quirked an eyebrow. "If you are caught, you risk being expelled."

"I won't be caught."

"Well, if you are, just don't say who gave you the idea. Who is the beau? Does he have a car?"

"His name is John Jasper and I've known him ever since kindergarten. And he has a car. A Packard."

Phoebe was slightly impressed, but more by the risks Wallis was willing to take in order to meet up with John Jasper than by John Jasper himself. A beau known from kindergarten days didn't sound exciting, and although Packards were swish and had rarity value, her own current beau drove a heart-stoppingly racy scarlet Lagonda.

On the night she had arranged to meet with John Jasper, Wallis didn't tell anyone other than Phoebe what she was going to do. She didn't want there to be a hum of speculation and a lot of nervous chatter going on in her dormitory, in case it aroused the attention of a member of the staff. If that happened, she wouldn't be able to meet up with John Jasper at all.

At ten o'clock, after lights out and when the three girls she shared a room with were asleep, she slipped out of bed and dressed speedily and quietly in the dark. Then she eased the dormitory door open and stepped out into the corridor.

There was no sign of any member of the staff. With her heart pounding fast and light and feeling as if it were somewhere up in her throat, she padded softly along the corridor and down the stairs. Once in the grand central hallway she could hear the low murmur of voices coming from the drawing room. Scarcely daring to breathe, wondering how, if she ran into a member of the staff, she could possibly come up with an explanation as to why she was dressed in outdoor clothes at such an hour, she made her way along the corridors toward the school infirmary.

For the first time it occurred to her to wonder if there was perhaps a patient in the infirmary and if the school matron would be seated by a sick bed with a nightlight on. She crossed her fingers tightly, praying there wouldn't be.

Her prayer was granted. When she reached the infirmary, it was in darkness. In mounting excitement she entered the isolation room. Her hands were slippery with sweat as she pushed the sash window upward and then, seconds later, she was standing in the chill April night air and all that was left was for her to make a quick run across the grounds to the dirt road skirting them.

Not even for a minute did she think John Jasper wouldn't be there.

Phoebe had been quite explicit in the instructions she had told Wallis to give him. "The dirt road is quite manageable in the dark. Leastways, none of my beaux have come to grief on it. Oldfields can be seen quite clearly from it, and if he halts his car so that it is directly in line with the school, you won't be able to miss each other."

Wallis had a steady nerve, but crossing the grounds by moonlight tested them to the limit. She imagined dark shapes in the darkness where she knew no dark shapes could possibly be. An owl flew unnervingly low past her. Seconds later, as the owl plummeted, a small animal made a terrified screeching sound. Wallis almost did the same thing. Phoebe had made her nighttime escapades seem a piece of cake. What she hadn't said was that the night would be filled with creatures—owls, mice, bats—that no sane person would want to tangle with.

When she finally neared the dirt road and John Jasper's voice came out of the darkness, saying low and urgently, "Wallis? Is that you, Wallis?" it took her all of her self-control not to cry with relief.

Calling out, "Yes, it's me," she ran toward the sound of his voice, determined not to let him see how unnerved she'd been. Though she would never have been so forward as to run into his arms if they had been meeting in daylight, running into them now seemed the most natural thing in the world to do.

He hugged her tightly. "Dear Lord, Wallis! I'd no idea you'd have to come so far in utter darkness to meet me. If I'd known, I'd never have let you do it."

Held deliciously close against the tweed of his ankle-length overcoat, she giggled. "It was nothing," she lied glibly. "I'm not scared of the dark, John Jasper."

She felt his lips touch her hair, and then, as she smelled the faint familiar fragrance of lemon cologne, he said gruffly, "I don't know any other girl who would have had the guts to do what you just did, Wallis."

Wallis moved in the circle of his arms in order to look up into his face. "I do," she said impishly. "Her name is Phoebe Schermerhorn and she does this kind of thing all the time."

He didn't grin back down at her. Instead, he traced the line of her cheek with his gloved forefinger, tucked a stray strand of her hair back into the woolen beret she was wearing, and said thickly, "I think I'm in love with you, Wallis Warfield."

"That's good." Her eyes held his steadily. "Because that's just what I want you to be, John Jasper."

He chuckled at her sassiness, then lowered his head to hers.

Her arms went up around his neck and she did what she had longed to do ever since they had been children in Miss O'Donnell's classroom. She hooked her fingers into his hair, feeling the tight curls spring coarsely against her palms. His mouth was hot and sweet and this time when they kissed, she instinctively allowed her mouth to open and her tongue to slide past his.

The impact on John Jasper was profound.

He gave a low groan, and Wallis was overcome with elation. If this was all it took to bring boys to their knees in submission, then she need never find herself without a beau.

"Let's sit in the car," she said huskily when he finally raised his head from hers. "I want to hear all about Loyola. Are you on the baseball team? And I want to hear all the Baltimore gossip."

For over an hour they sat in the Packard, talking, kissing,

and canoodling, and then talking some more. At last she said regretfully, "It's time I was getting back, JJ."

He nodded, trusting her judgment, well aware that she was the one who was running all the risks. "But not on your own," he said. "I'm going to walk you back across the grounds."

She was too relieved by his suggestion to argue. She took good care not to sound it. "If you want to," she said, as if predatory owls and bats and mice held no terrors for her.

The look of admiration he gave her sent fresh tingles down her spine.

Tonight something very special had happened between her and John Jasper. He wasn't merely now just a beau. He was a beau she was certain would still be her beau when she had her debutante year. A beau who, when he finished college, would ask her to marry him.

When he did so, she didn't have a shadow of doubt what her answer was going to be. Though John Jasper's family weren't as superlatively wealthy as the families of some of the girls she was now friends with, they were still wealthy enough for her Uncle Sol not to think such a match a misalliance. John Jasper was an only child and was studying law. Not only would he be a husband she was head over heels in love with, he would also be a husband able to give her the financial security she had so far had to live without.

When she was safely back in her bed, she wondered how many children they would have. A boy first, of course. Everyone wanted to have a boy first. They would be able to call him John Jasper II. Then a little girl would be nice. If they had a little girl she would call her Alice, after her mother. That meant their daughter's second name would have to be John Jasper's mother's name. She wondered what his mother's Christian name was and hoped it wasn't something awful, such as

Wilhelmina or Augusta. Then, reliving the passionate kiss she had shared with John Jasper when he had said good-bye to her outside the infirmary window, she fell asleep to dreams of wedding bells and fairy-tale white gowns.

The next morning she woke to find she had earned herself a whole new reputation at Oldfields. Not only was she now known to be hardworking and fun to be with, she was now known to be fearlessly daring. She had always been popular within her own small group; now everyone wanted to be her friend. It was a popularity that sat easily on her. Too angular and boyish in build to be as pretty as the other girls, she had long ago learned that to be noticed, she had to be different. Thanks to her mother's dressmaking skills, she had succeeded where her clothes were concerned, and now, thanks to her reckless nighttime meeting with John Jasper, she was succeeding in other ways as well.

The bubble burst a few days later when she was called out of the classroom and told that Miss Nan wished to speak with her.

As she walked with leaden feet from the classroom, she knew that behind her every girl was holding her breath, certain that she would never return to it; that Miss Nan had learned of her escapade and that she was about to be expelled.

Wallis was also utterly certain she was about to be expelled. The blood drummed in her ears as she neared the room known at Oldfields as the Holy of Holies. What on earth was her Uncle Sol going to say—and do—when he was informed of how disgracefully she had behaved? Even just thinking about it made her feel violently ill.

"Miss Nan has asked that you go straight in," the school secretary said, with a look of exquisite sorrow.

Wallis drew in a deep breath, pulled her shoulders back, and lifted her head high. If she was going to the executioner's block, then she was going to go with panache.

Her initial shock on entering the room was that there was no anger or disappointment on Miss Nan's face. Instead, like her secretary, she simply looked immensely sorry for her.

"Please sit down, Wallis."

Wallis sat down, her hands clasped tightly in her lap, her heart thudding.

"It is my painful duty, Wallis, to tell you that your stepfather has died. You will, of course, be given time off school to attend the funeral. Deep as your grief will be, Wallis, I am trusting you to conduct yourself through these difficult days with dignity. When tears are shed, they should be shed in private."

Wallis was too stunned for tears. How could Free be dead? He was always so amiable. Always so happily content. That she would never hear his chuckling laughter again or be the subject of his gentle teasing was almost impossible to take in. And what about her mother? Her mother and Free had been idyllically happy together, and they had only been married a few short years. How was her mother going to come to terms with such a devastating blow?

"Your stepfather had been ill for some time, Wallis," Miss Nan continued. "Your aunt, Mrs. Merryman, tells me it is something your mother kept from you, not wanting to cause you anxiety and worry. Mr. Rasin died in Atlantic City, where he had gone in an effort to improve his health. Your mother will be bringing his body home to Baltimore for the funeral."

She rose to her feet. "There is no need to return straight to your classroom, Wallis. Please take all the time you need for quiet reflection. Perhaps a long walk or time spent alone in the chapel?"

"Yes. Thank you, Miss Nan." The words came stiltedly and automatically.

Miss Nan walked her to the door. "Later on today, when

you have composed yourself, you will need to pack a suitcase. In the morning you are to return to Baltimore until the funeral is over. As your mother has not yet returned to Baltimore with your stepfather's body, your aunt will meet you on your arrival."

Wallis left the room in a daze. A half hour ago, confident of John Jasper's love for her, she had been the happiest girl in the world. Now all she could think about was the depth of her mother's grief and her own deep sense of loss. Free had been a kind stepfather to her, and she was going to miss him a great deal.

She didn't take Miss Nan's advice and go for a long walk or spend time in the chapel. Instead she went back to the empty dormitory, sitting cross-legged on her bed as she tried to come to terms with the latest upheaval in her life.

The next day's train journey back to Baltimore, knowing what lay at the end of it, was a miserable one. Her Aunt Bessie was at the station to meet her and, heedless of what Miss Nan had told her, tears came the minute her aunt's arms went lovingly around her.

"Hush there, pet," Bessie said, her own eyes overly bright. "We have to be strong for your poor dear mother. Her train from Atlantic City arrives on platform four in thirty minutes' time."

When the Atlantic City train steamed into the station, it did so slowly, as if its driver were well aware there was a dead man aboard, being brought home for burial.

Wallis pressed a black-gloved hand to her throat, wondering if her mother had traveled in the guard's van with Free's coffin; wondering where the coffin was going to be taken; wondering how long it was going to be before the funeral took place.

The train surged to a noisy halt, and within seconds the platform was a mass of disembarking passengers. Even in such a crush, Wallis spotted her mother the instant she stepped down from her carriage.

Dressed in widow's weeds, a black crepe veil falling to knee length, she looked so tiny and lost that Wallis's heart felt as if it were going to break.

"Mama!" She began to run down the platform toward her, pushing past everyone who stood in her way. *"Mama!"*

Alice stumbled into Wallis's arms, Bully at her heels, and Wallis could see that beneath the veil, her mother's lovely face was the color of parchment.

"Oh Wallis, sweetheart." Her voice was a cracked whisper. "I hadn't thought it was possible to be hurt so much, so soon."

The next few days were tougher than Wallis had ever thought possible. First of all there was the grim task of accompanying Free's coffin to the undertaker's, where it was to remain until the funeral. Then came the realization that she and her mother were not returning to Biddle Street until the funeral but were to stay with one of Free's sisters. Bully wasn't welcome there and so he went to stay with Bessie, which was very much where Wallis wished she and her mother were staying.

The funeral took place at the Episcopalian church where her grandmother had worshipped her whole life, ensuring that the service was dignified by her presence. All through it, as Alice wept uncontrollably, Wallis remained by her side. Afterward they returned to Free's sister's home and it was there that Alice was dealt yet another blow.

"Free's estate is entailed," her sister-in-law told her just before the will was read. "And as you and Free had no children of your own, I think his will may come as something of a shock, Alice dear."

Her words were an understatement, for the shock was so

great, Alice never fully recovered from it. Much as he had loved her, Free had been unable to leave her anything. Instead, his estate was divided equally between his three sisters. The monthly checks from his trust fund stopped and Alice—and Wallis—were again wholly reliant on Sol.

"And your Uncle Sol isn't going to fund Biddle Street," Bessie said to Wallis the morning she was to return to Oldfields. "He's just as jealous of Free as he was when Free was alive, and he doesn't want your mother living somewhere she and Free were so happy."

"But where will my mother live? She has to live somewhere! I can't believe Uncle Sol is being so cruel to her! It's not her fault she doesn't love him!"

"He's renting an apartment for her at Earl's Court, on the corner of St. Paul Street and Preston Street."

"Preston Street? Is that so he will be able to keep an eye on her?"

"I guess so, Wallis. But if the man had eyes in his head, he'd know it was unnecessary. Free's early death and the loss of her home has aged your mother overnight. She's lost all the liveliness she used to have, and I don't think she's ever going to get it back again."

Wallis didn't think she would either, and it made her heart ache in a way she found almost unbearable.

Saying good-bye to her mother when she left for the train station was one of the hardest things she had ever done, but she had no choice. Her mother took pride and pleasure in her being an Oldfields girl, and her not returning to Oldfields wouldn't bring her mother comfort. Instead it would only add to her bitter unhappiness.

She arrived back in the midafternoon, when everyone was in class. On her bedside locker was a small pile of mail. She could tell from the shape of the envelopes that most of them contained sympathy cards. The only exception was one addressed to her in John Jasper's familiar large scrawling handwriting.

From the very first sentence it was obvious that when he had written it, he had been unaware of her stepfather's death.

> *Dearest darling Wallis,*
>
> *Forgive the shortness of this letter, but I'm in a mighty hurry—not because I'm due on the field for a baseball match but because I'm about to leave with Pa for New York. He's heading off to Europe, and at the last minute has insisted I go with him. We sail on the* Bremen *in two days' time. The powers that be at Loyola won't be pleased when I don't return after my weekend home, but what the heck. Europe is an opportunity too good to miss. We're going to do the whole grand tour thing. London, Paris, Berlin, Geneva, Rome, Vienna. I shall miss you lots and think of you everywhere I go. Don't forget whose girl you are while I am away. You will be in my heart every step of the way,*
>
> Love now and always,
> JJ xxx

> *PS. Isn't Pamela at a finishing school near Geneva? With a bit of luck I'll be able to meet up with her and bring her up to date with what is happening in Baltimore.*

Wallis stared down at the letter, hardly able to believe the battering that fate was giving her. First had been Free's unexpected death—or at least it had been unexpected to her. Then had come the shattering news that through no fault of his own, he had died leaving her mother unprovided for. Now this. Instead of being able to look forward to further romantic, illicit meetings with John Jasper, he was aboard the *Bremen*, putting thousands and thousands of miles between the two of them.

She didn't cry easily, and she didn't cry now. Crying when things went wrong never got anyone anywhere. When, though, would things go right for her? When would she be able to live with the same sense of security her friends all so unthinkingly lived with? No one she had ever met lived off the charity of relatives as, until her mother had married Free, she and her mother had been forced to do—and as they were now being forced to do again.

Her mother would have a home, but only because Sol was providing her with one of his choice. She would remain at Oldfields, but only because her uncle was paying the fees. As for her debutante year, without her uncle she wouldn't be having a debutante year at all. She wanted to rage aloud at the unfairness of it all, but rage, like tears, was something she couldn't afford to indulge in. If she wanted friends like Beatrice Astor and Phoebe Schermerhorn to assume her life was as untroubled as theirs, then she had to appear to be as carefree as they were.

She rebrushed her hair and smoothed her skirt.

She was an expert at putting a good face on things. She had, after all, had years and years of practice.

Chapter Eight

Everyone at Oldfields was exquisitely kind to her over the next few days, treating the loss of her stepfather with as much consideration as if Free had been her actual father. Quicker than she could have imagined, life settled back into a happy routine. Despite the strictness of Miss Nan's rules and regulations, there was still a lot of fun to be had.

Tableaux were staged in the gym, and, when they were, Wallis was nearly always a central figure. At the end of the summer Miss Nan allowed Wallis's class to put on a vaudeville show, providing that all sketches and songs were of a high moral standard. As Wallis was tone deaf and couldn't sing a note, she opted to do a scene from Shakespeare's *A Midsummer Night's Dream*, playing the part of Titania, the fairy queen. She won high praise, for she absolutely refused to simper and played the part with great dignity.

It was, though, mousy Edith Miller as Sophie in a scene from Strauss's *Der Rosenkavalier* that brought the house down. Her singing was a revelation, pure and faultless, and to everyone's stunned amazement she imbued the part with such ardent abandon that it made the hairs at the back of Wallis's neck stand on end.

In October she went into Middleburg with Phoebe and Beatrice to have a tintype likeness taken that she could send to John Jasper. In November she escaped Oldfields again in order to go with Phoebe to a Schermerhorn costume party in Washington. Phoebe attended it dressed as a cartoon character, and Wallis, a feather from Elliott Street days in her hair, went as Pocahontas.

Not a month went by when she didn't receive two or three letters from John Jasper. Shortly before Christmas he wrote to her from Berlin.

> *Dearest beautiful Wallis,*
>
> *I'm missing you more and more with every week that goes by. If I'd known how long Pa intended staying this side of the Atlantic, I'd have let him make this trip solo. Be prepared that when I do come back, I shall have a ring in my pocket for you. I don't want you thinking of yourself as being anyone's girl but mine! In your last letter to me you asked what life was like in Germany. All I can say is that it's very odd and that the Germans in Germany aren't as easy to get on with as the Germans who live in the States. There's a very fevered atmosphere here that I don't much care for. It seems like every day there's a military procession of one kind or another. The kaiser and his sons are never seen out of army uniform, and they all wear pickelhaubes—medieval-looking helmets which have a fiercesome spike on their crown.*

He'd gone on to tell her of the operas he had seen and the galleries he had visited and had ended his letter with yet another strong hint that when he returned home he was going to ask her to marry him.

I've sense enough to know that experiencing all this
European culture firsthand is something of a privilege, but
the honest truth is I'm already tiring of it and what I want
with a deep passion is to be back home in Baltimore, seeing
you every possible moment I can. Whenever I get too down
about things, I just remember that we have the rest of our
lives to look forward to—and that because you're my girl,
I'm one hell of a lucky guy.

He'd signed off with so many kisses, they ran off the page.
Pamela's letters were very different. Instead of yearning to
be back in Baltimore, she was adamant that she never intended
to live there again.

Neither do I intend to live in Switzerland again,

she wrote in her New Year letter.

Mont-Fleuri has been great, but I've had enough of it (after
my romance with Hans was discovered, things got quite
unpleasant. Hans was dismissed as Mont-Fleuri's ski
instructor, and as everyone blamed me, my popularity took
a steep nosedive and so I've left and am now in England). I
spent Christmas in Norfolk (boring because there were no
invites to Sandringham), and am now under my mother and
Tarquin's not very watchful eyes in London. It's so much fun
here I can't imagine wanting to be anywhere else—apart
from weekends, of course. At weekends there is always a
country-house party somewhere. I can't imagine what it
must be like for you, still stuck at "Gentleness and Courtesy"
Oldfields and with nothing more exciting to look forward to
than a coming-out season in boring old Baltimore.

The letter made Wallis so cross she almost didn't reply to it. When she finally did, she didn't let her annoyance show. Pamela was still her best friend, the one person in the world who knew all about her financially precarious upbringing: her and her mother's utter reliance on Uncle Sol, the homemade dresses, the pay-to-attend dinners. It was a litany of scrimp and scrape that even John Jasper didn't know about. And none of it had ever made the slightest difference to Pamela—a duke's daughter who, with good reason, was hopeful of catching the eye of Britain's Prince Edward and who might one day be not only Lady Pamela, but Queen Pamela.

In all of the many letters the two of them had exchanged over the past two years, Wallis had scarcely mentioned John Jasper. He was too special to her for her to want to run the risk of Pamela being dismissive about him. In Pamela's league, eligible husbands-to-be had to be titled. Coming from an old Baltimore family, no matter how aristocratic, simply wasn't enough. Now, though, she wanted to make it quite plain to Pamela that where romance was concerned, out of the two of them, her life was by far the more exciting—and that meant telling Pamela that John Jasper would be putting a ring on her finger when he returned home from his grand tour of Europe. In her bold, confident hand she brought Pamela up to date with just what her relationship with John Jasper was, ending with:

> . . . and though John Jasper still has a lot more places to visit, Rome and Vienna and London—I think it's safe to say that out of this year's debutantes, I will be the first to walk down the aisle!

At Easter she had the choice of spending the short holiday vacation at either her Aunt Lelia's, at Wakefield Manor, or in

Baltimore. A vacation at Wakefield Manor with her cousins would have been livelier, but her grandmother had broken her hip, and so she opted for Baltimore, so that as well as spending time with her mother, she could also spend a lot of time with her now-housebound grandmother at 34 East Preston Street.

Pamela wrote to her that if she were going to marry John Jasper, she should cross the Atlantic and sow some wild oats beforehand. If it hadn't been for the fact that she was soon to leave Oldfields and embark on her debutante year, the invitation was one she would have found seriously tempting. The letter had continued with news that Wallis found slightly surprising.

> *I've made a very unusual kind of friend over the last few weeks, Wallis. Her name is Rose Houghton and she's a good deal older than I am, twenty-five or twenty-six. She is the granddaughter of the Earl of May and has had her hair bobbed! Her father, Viscount Houghton, died ages and ages ago. What is interesting about her is that she is a militant suffragette—and please believe me, Wallis, when I tell you that in Britain militant suffragettes are very militant! My mother loathes her, but Tarquin thinks she's splendid and, though I couldn't care less about votes for women, so do I.*

In the same post was a letter from John Jasper.

> *Dearest darling Wallis,*
>
> *We are now in Vienna as guests of a count and countess Pa made good friends with when in Berlin. Like Berlin, Vienna is built on a grandiose scale, but the mood here seems lighter and I far prefer it. As in Berlin there are a lot of military processions, but here they really are a sight to see. Austro-Hungarian uniforms must be the smartest in the world! Next stop is Geneva, where I hope to meet up*

with Pamela. After that it will be Paris and London—and
then home!

Before reading to the end of the letter and the delicious rows
and rows of kisses, Wallis laid it down on her lap. She hadn't yet
told John Jasper that Pamela had left Mont-Fleuri, and she decided that when she did, she wouldn't tell him Pamela had left
in disgrace after an illicit romance with the school's ski instructor. If there was one quality she was known for, it was loyalty,
and even though the content of Pamela's letters was becoming
more and more irritating, she had no intention of putting her in
a bad light where John Jasper was concerned.

Pamela's next letter to her was full of the arrangements for
her coming-out.

I'm to be presented at court the first week in June, and
I'm so hoping Prince Edward will be there. Were there
photographs in American newspapers of him when he greeted
the president of France at Portsmouth at the beginning of
President Poincaré's state visit here? He looked wonderfully
dishy. Every inch a fairy-tale prince. If only I could engage
him in conversation for only a few minutes I'm sure he'd be
besotted! Rose Houghton's youngest sister Lily is a talented
sculptress, and Rose let slip that Lily once sculpted a bust of
HRH. Don't you find that thrilling? I do. I now want her to
do a bust of me, but she lives somewhere romantically remote
on a Scottish island, and as I've no intention of leaving
the excitement of London for the rain-sodden Hebrides,
my chances aren't high.

Wallis tried hard not to be jealous that Pamela's coming-
out would be launched by a presentation to King George and
Queen Mary in the grand ballroom at Buckingham Palace, but

it was hard not to be when plans for her own coming-out had been thrown into such disarray by her stepfather's death.

For a coming-out year, a girl needed clothes. Lots of clothes. And the only person who could now provide the money for them was her Uncle Sol. Before very long she was going to have to ask him for the necessary money. It wasn't a pleasant thought, and so instead of dwelling on it she thought about Prince Edward instead.

She didn't know about other American newspapers, but there had been no photograph of Prince Edward and President Poincaré in the *Baltimore Sun*. In her next letter to Pamela she would ask her to send her a cutting from a British newspaper.

A few weeks later, shortly after she turned eighteen, there was different European royal news—and this time every newspaper in America carried it. The headlines were all the same: Habsburg heir assassinated in Sarajevo.

It didn't arouse much interest at Oldfields. There were only a few days to go before Wallis's class left, and the topic of the moment wasn't the Balkans, but the debutante year that lay ahead of them all. Wallis was the exception. The archduke had been the nephew of Emperor Franz Josef, and Emperor Franz Josef's capital city was Vienna, where John Jasper and his father were. The assassination would have caused great excitement there, and she wondered if he was in the middle of it all.

By the time she received a letter from him telling her that the assassination had caused an enormous fuss, that the assassin was Serbian, and that he and his father had run into a huge street demonstration of Serbian flag burning, she had left Oldfields and, in London, Pamela had been presented at court and was a fully fledged debutante.

The majority of her own debutante dances and parties wouldn't begin until the autumn, and she was already getting ready for them.

"Or I would be if I had the money for all the gowns I'm going to need," she said to Aunt Bessie. "I've asked Uncle Sol if I can have a meeting with him to discuss the necessary financing, but I'm not sure how much I should be asking for. How much do you think my clothes bill will come to?"

Her aunt's reply shocked even her.

"Taking into account the Princeton Prom, the Bachelor's Cotillion, your own coming-out ball, the coming-out balls of all your fellow debutantes, all the tea dances and celebration luncheons you will be invited to, and the fact that you simply cannot be seen in the same outfit twice, you will have to ask for at least a thousand dollars. And don't look so aghast, Wallis. Solomon Warfield can afford that amount with ease."

Wallis wasn't reassured. What her Uncle Sol could afford and what he was willing to part with were often two very different things.

She decided that her best approach was to be businesslike and to meet with him at the bank where he was president. As the victoria was now a thing of the past, she traveled downtown in her grandmother's chauffeured Pierce-Arrow.

The bank was situated in a fifteen-story building on the corner of Baltimore Street and Calvert Street, and just entering it gave Wallis a good feeling. The foyer was splendidly large, the floor marble, the walls decorated with glittering mosaic-tiled scenes depicting the founding of Baltimore. The whole atmosphere announced that here money was made—and Wallis knew that to a very large extent that money was her Uncle Sol's.

He greeted her as if she were a client, asking her to sit in the chair facing his desk.

"What can I do for you, Wallis?" he said, eyeing her with satisfaction.

Dressed in a spankingly smart raspberry-and-white striped

walking dress, she was as neat and tidy as a bright new pin. Outwardly he could see no Montague in her, for with her dark hair and strong angular jaw she didn't possess a glimmer of her mother's blond, delicately pretty, porcelainlike beauty.

That she didn't was a relief to him. He had no desire to be reminded of Alice, and he liked the very un-Alice-like way Wallis had set up this meeting with him. It showed a commonsense approach to financial dealings—and common sense, where money was concerned, was a quality he admired highly.

"We've never fully discussed my coming-out, Uncle Sol," she said, coming straight to the point. "I'm not quite sure what your plans are for me."

"I plan to give you the kind of coming-out year your father would have given you if he hadn't been taken from us at such a tragically early age. Your debutante ball will be as large and lavish as befits a Warfield. Now, does that put your mind at rest?"

Wallis smiled sunnily. It had certainly put her mind to rest where her coming-out ball was concerned, but there was something else that still had to be clarified, something her uncle probably hadn't even thought about.

"I shall need an allowance for clothes, Uncle Sol."

""Ah, yes. Of course." He took out a wallet. "How much do you anticipate needing?"

"A thousand dollars."

"A thou . . . ?" He tried to finish the word and couldn't. He took a deep breath and tried again. "A thousand? A *thousand*?"

"Yes, Uncle Sol." Wallis had no intention of being apologetic or of backing down. "Not only do I have to have an extraordinarily beautiful gown for my own debutante ball, but I have to have other gowns for all the balls I will be invited to. And those balls will be given by people like the Astors and the

Schermerhorns and the Van Rensselaers. I can't possibly wear the same ball gown twice, just as I can't wear the same outfit to more than one celebration party or luncheon—and there will be lots and lots of those."

The mention of Astors, Schermerhorns, and Van Rensselaers clinched it for her, as she had known it would. Sol had sent her to Oldfields in order for her to make friends and mix socially with girls from such families. There was no way now that, for the sake of a thousand dollars, he was going to put the friendships she had made at risk by having it look as if she were a poor relation.

"The money will be in your account by tomorrow—and mind you put it to good use. Restrained good taste is the mark of a lady, Wallis. Don't follow the crowd. Create your own style."

Wallis, who had been creating her own style for years, rose to her feet, rounded his desk, and gave him a kiss on his cheek. Then she exultantly made her way back down to the grandiose foyer, dizzy with delight at the thought of all the new gowns and outfits that were about to be hers.

Her debut gown was her first priority, and she knew exactly how she wanted it to look. Months ago she had seen a picture of the Broadway star Irene Castle wearing a Grecian-style gown of white satin combined with chiffon and trimmings of pearls. The chiffon veiled the shoulders and fell in a knee-length tunic, banded in pearl embroidery. It was elegant and distinctive—and she knew no other girl would have a gown remotely like it.

The first grand ball of her season would be the Princeton Prom in September, and for that she had her dressmaker make her a floaty gown of lavender blue organdy—going to great pains to make sure the blue was the exact same color as the color of her eyes.

Though she hadn't yet received an invite to Beatrice Astor's debut ball, she knew for a certainty that she would be receiving one and that it would be taking place at the Astor mansion on Fifth Avenue, in New York.

"It has to be extra special, Mama," she said to Alice. "What is the most extra-special material there is?"

Alice, who was enjoying Wallis's visits to the dressmaker almost as much as Wallis was, tilted her head to one side, thought for a moment, and then said: "Cloth of gold. You can't have an *entire* gown made of it. It would look vulgar—especially so considering how young you are. But a gown made with a bodice of cloth of gold would look spectacular—especially if it were delicately embroidered with flowers."

"And the skirt, Mama?"

"A full skirt made of crepe de chine in a shade complementing the gold of the bodice. Something in a sunset color."

Wallis clapped her hands in delight. In a gown such as her mother had just described, she was going to be the object of all eyes. No one—not even Beatrice—would outshine her.

All through the rest of July and the beginning of August, Wallis thought of nothing but clothes and invitations. On the twenty-fifth of July, a small two-line news piece in the *Baltimore Sun* announced that Austria had broken off diplomatic ties with Serbia.

In a letter she received from John Jasper a few days later, he told her he and his father would soon be heading home, as war between Austria and Serbia seemed imminent.

Wallis didn't give another thought to the war seemingly about to take place between Austria and Serbia. All that mattered to her was that it looked as if John Jasper would be back in Baltimore in time to escort her to the Princeton Prom.

"Where is this Serbia that is in the news again?" her Aunt

Bessie asked a few days later when accompanying her to a milliner's. "Wherever it is, according to today's *Sun*, Austria has just declared war on it."

Wallis wasn't sure where Serbia was either, and neither did she care. If Austria had declared war on it, it meant John Jasper would be home in time for the prom and that she would very soon have his ring on the third finger of her left hand.

Life had become a hectic round of dressmaker appointments and lunches with other eighteen-year-old girls, whose chatter was constantly about clothes and husband hunting. Wallis never joined in the last subject, because she had no need to. The man of her dreams was already hers, and soon, certainly before Christmas, their engagement announcement would be in the *Baltimore Sun* for everyone to read.

Even when it became obvious that war in the Balkans was going to be the catalyst for a great war, with Germany and Austro-Hungary ranged on one side and Great Britain, France, and Russia on the other, Wallis remained uninterested. The drama was all taking place on the other side of the Atlantic. It couldn't possibly affect her.

A week after Britain's declaration of war against Germany, she received a letter from John Jasper telling her that he and his father were now in London.

> . . . *and when Pa has finished meeting up with people here,*
> *we'll be booking a sailing aboard the* Mauretania *and*
> *heading home at full belt for Baltimore. I can't tell you how*
> *much I'm missing you, Wallis. The first thing I'm going*
> *to do when I have Baltimore soil under my feet again is to*
> *ask your uncle if I can have an interview with him. How*
> *does a Christmas engagement sound? Wouldn't it be swell?*
> *I love you with all my heart, sweet Wallis—and I sure as*

heck don't want anyone else escorting you to the Princeton Prom—or the Bachelor's Cotillion!

Just as the war wasn't affecting her, so it didn't seem to be affecting Pamela—or at least not adversely.

Dear Wally,

In London every eligible young man is now in uniform— and they look spiffing. Tarquin's youngest brother joined the North Somersets the instant war was declared and has just set off for France, taking with him his two best hunters, a valet, and a cook. Tarquin is hoping he'll come home laden with medals. The Prince of Wales has been given a commission in the Grenadier Guards. Enclosed is a newspaper cutting of him in uniform. Doesn't he look handsome? At my presentation to King George and Queen Mary he was standing a little to the left of Their Majesties, and though it was bad form of me, as I made my curtsey to the king I looked directly at his heir. Not only did I get a smile of recognition, I got a wink! Of course, afterwards, everyone said he'd simply got something in his eye and was trying to blink it away, but I know better! Rose Houghton has left for France in order to work as a nurse in one of the field hospitals. Her uniform is so divine I'm half tempted to go with her.

At the end of the month, as Wallis waited in a fever of impatience for news of John Jasper's sailing on the *Mauretania*, she received a letter from him filled with disappointment.

My Dearest Sweetheart,

I don't know how to tell you this, but Pa now says he has no intention of returning to Baltimore until the New Year.

The only glimmer of good news about this is that he has
booked passage for the two of us aboard a liner sailing from
Southampton January 1st.

There was much more to his letter, but Wallis scarcely read it. The devastation she felt at knowing he would not be her escort at either the Princeton Prom or the Bachelor's Cotillion was too deep. With the letter still in her hands, she fought against giving way to tears. Tears wouldn't solve the problem she now had—and that problem was an urgent one. Who was going to be her escort on her big night at the prom?

"What about Cousin Lelia's boy, Basil?" Aunt Bessie suggested. "He's very good looking. Even though he's your second cousin, you'll still be the envy of all the other debutantes."

There were forty-nine other debutantes that year, and to be the envy of them all had become Wallis's main ambition in life. That weekend she paid a self-invited visit to Wakefield Manor to speak to Basil. His reaction wasn't at all what she had expected.

"I can't possibly, Wallis," he said apologetically. "I'm dating Miriam Foxwood. If I escorted you to the prom, she'd be so mad at me I might never see her again."

To Wallis that didn't matter a jot.

"You *have* to be my escort, Basil! Every other boy I know is already spoken for!"

"Nick Rhodes isn't. He's my best buddy. And he'll be over the moon to escort you, Wallis. I just know he will be."

"Is that because in the looks department he's nothing to write home about?"

Basil grinned. "Nope. I'll introduce the pair of you; then you can see for yourself."

Though Nick Rhodes didn't send her pulse racing and her heart hammering, he was presentable enough to have that effect on other girls and, with his agreement that he would be her escort, the prom was one social event nicely sorted out. It still left the Bachelor's Cotillion, though—and the Bachelor's Cotillion was *the* important event of the season.

In the end, that problem, too, was solved by family—and in a way that amused Wallis greatly.

"Your cousin Henry would like to escort you to the cotillion," her Uncle Sol said, well pleased at the idea.

As Henry's engagement had long since been broken off, Henry was *very* suitable. Even though she no longer had a crush on him, Wallis was gleeful. Henry was exceedingly good-looking, and in white tie and tails he would be even more so. At the cotillion she was going to be the envy of every girl there. She wrote Pamela with news of all the arrangements that had been made, describing what gown she would wear to each function. Pamela wrote back with news of her own.

> *Guess who got in touch with me the other day? John Jasper! Why didn't you tell me he and his pa were now in London? It was good to see him again, even though all he did was talk about you and of how the two of you are going to get engaged the minute he gets home. Tarquin has invited the Bachmans to Norfolk. Won't it be a hoot if there is an invite to Sandringham while John Jasper is with us?*

The next letter from John Jasper bore a Norfolk postmark.

> *This is a real quaint part of England,*

he wrote when he got around to telling her about how he had met up with Pamela.

> *Pamela's stepfather may be an earl, but he's an easy to know, likable guy. When you get to meet him you'll see what I*

mean. (And you will get to meet him because we'll come back here together, either on our honeymoon or after it.) I didn't get to meet British royalty. I guess with the way things are going in the war, King George has more on his mind than vacationing at Sandringham. The British Army has called for 500,000 more men to volunteer. Did you read about the terrible bloodbath at Mons in Belgium? People are still saying it will be all over by Christmas, but I don't think so. I'm just heartily glad it's a war America isn't involved in.

Wallis, too, was glad that America wasn't at war, but gratitude for the fact wasn't uppermost on her mind. What was uppermost was that instead of being with her in Baltimore, John Jasper was in Norfolk with Pamela.

Remembering her old suspicions that Pamela found John Jasper just as heart-stopping as she did, it wasn't a comforting thought. She chided herself for her lack of trust. Pamela's ambition was for marriage to a highly titled Englishman—the Prince of Wales if she could get him. The days when she might have flirted with John Jasper were long past. And John Jasper wouldn't flirt with Pamela—not when he'd never taken interest in her when she'd lived in Baltimore.

With her mind set at rest, she focused all her attention on the whirl of social activities now filling her days. It was a debutante's duty to host a luncheon or party for every other debutante and so sometimes she had as many as three functions to attend in one day.

Outgoing and extroverted, Wallis loved every minute of her social whirl.

At the Princeton Prom she was the belle of the ball. At the Bachelor's Cotillion she was the star of the evening. In a letter to Pamela, she wrote:

. . . and the best, my debutante coming-out ball, is yet to come.

All arrangements for it had been left in her Uncle Sol's capable hands.

In December, two weeks before it was to take place, Sol telephoned her to say he would like a private word with her at 34 East Preston Street.

When she arrived there he was waiting for her in the drawing room.

"I have unfortunate news for you, Wallis," he said, even before she'd had the chance to sit down. "Knowing how strong your character is, I trust you will view things as I do and agree with me that there is no alternative to the action I have decided to take."

Wallis took a deep, steadying breath.

"And what action is that, Uncle Sol?" she asked, fearful of what was to come.

He stroked his heavy mustache with his thumb and forefinger and then said bluntly: "Because of the terrible slaughter taking place in Europe, I have decided that it would be inappropriate for you to have a large debutante ball—or, indeed, a debutante ball of any kind. With thousands of families grieving and left destitute, the present time is no time for festivities."

Wallis stared at him, hardly able to take in what he was saying. In a stunned voice she said in disbelief, "But I *have* to have a coming-out ball, Uncle Sol! How can I be a debutante without one?"

"You can be a very special debutante, Wallis. A debutante who doesn't mindlessly follow the crowd, but one who has a social conscience."

She wanted to shout that she didn't give a damn about a social conscience but knew it would get her nowhere. What she had to do now was think of a way of overcoming the blow she had been dealt.

It was the Montague side of her family who came to her aid.

"'Trust that pompous prig Solomon Warfield to have let Wallis down," her Aunt Lelia said vehemently to Alice on being told the news. "If you ask me, he doesn't give a damn about Wallis's social conscience, or his own. The war is simply his excuse to save some money."

"But what is Wallis to do, Lelia?" Alice's eyes brimmed with tears. "Free left me totally unprovided for. There's no way I can give her a debutante ball, and she owes hospitality to all the other debutantes."

"Dry your eyes, Alice. I'll give the child a coming-out ball. And I'll give her one at the Marine barracks in Washington, D.C.—which is something Solomon Warfield couldn't arrange even if he'd wanted to. Having a husband who is the commandant of the United States Marine Corps has uses."

It most certainly did, as Wallis found out when she entered a flag-festooned band hall at the Marine barracks and was greeted by a Marine guard of honor.

It was an evening quite unlike that of any of the other debutantes, for not even Astor or Schermerhorn wealth could have provided a sixty-piece Marine band, every member red-jacketed and covered in gold braid.

Even though John Jasper wasn't there to share it with her, Wallis knew she would remember the evening as being one of the happiest of her life—and one of the best things about it was that when it was over, there were only another three weeks until John Jasper sailed for home.

Every morning she expected to receive a letter from him telling her of his own fever of impatience.

None arrived.

Neither were there any letters from Pamela.

"It's because of the war, Wallis," Alice said when she mentioned the lack of overseas mail.

Wallis didn't agree with her mother's reasoning. Liners were still crossing the Atlantic just as regularly and as unhampered as they had always done. Waiting for the mail to be delivered suddenly became the most important part of her day, and when a letter bearing John Jasper's distinctive handwriting was finally delivered, she almost snatched it out of the mailman's hand.

Usually she took John Jasper's letters to her bedroom so that she would be able to read them undisturbed. This time she simply tore it open where she was standing, ecstatic at knowing that with his sailing date only days away, it was probably the last one he would ever need to write to her.

The first thing she noticed was that the letter was short, barely a page long.

My dearest, darling, most wonderful Wallis,

This is the hardest letter I have ever had to write—and I would give my life not to be having to write it. There are no excuses for what has happened—apart, of course, from the fact that I was more lonesome without you than you can ever imagine. On January 1st—the day I would have been sailing home to you—I shall be marrying Pamela at St. Margaret's, Westminster. It is a marriage of necessity—one that neither Pamela nor I want. I love you, dearest, sweetest Wallis, as I have always done, but honor demands I do the right thing by Pamela. I'm not going to ask you to forgive me, for I don't see how you possibly can. I certainly can't forgive myself. I've ruined three people's lives. Yours. Mine. Pamela's. All I can do is to make sure that the baby's life won't be ruined also. Goodbye, my dearest love. Know that for the rest of my life you will have my heart. John Jasper.

She screamed, uncaring of who might hear her. Then, with the letter crushed in her hand and her world tumbling around her ears, she raced upstairs to her bedroom. Slamming the door behind her, she threw herself face down on the bed, pummeling the pillow and drumming her feet against the mattress in a storm of anguish so intense she thought it was going to kill her.

How could John Jasper have done such a thing? How could he have been unfaithful to her in such a way? Especially how could he have been so unfaithful to her with her best friend? The double betrayal was so gross—so unspeakable—she couldn't even begin to imagine how she was going to live with it.

She thought of John Jasper and Pamela coming back to Baltimore to live and knew there was no way in the world she could endure such pain. But how was she to avoid it?

Sobbing so hard she could scarcely breathe, she forced herself to think about her options. She could go to Wakefield Manor and live with her Aunt Lelia. Or she could go to Pot Springs and live with her Uncle Emory's family.

But both Wakefield Manor and Pot Springs were close to Baltimore, and she didn't want to be close to Baltimore—she wanted to be a million miles away.

She stopped drumming her feet into the mattress and pummeling the pillow.

There was somewhere she could go; somewhere that, though not a million miles away, was still at the opposite end of the country. Her cousin Corinne's husband, Henry Mustin, was stationed in Florida. She would write to Corinne and ask if she could stay with her and Henry. Once there, Baltimore would never see her again—and she would do her damnedest to ensure that for as long as she lived, neither would John Jasper or Pamela.

Chapter Nine

In London, Pamela wasn't much happier than Wallis. It had been amusing luring John Jasper into being unfaithful. That she had been able to do so had proved to her yet again that no man could resist her if she'd set her mind on having him. She hadn't wanted John Jasper long term, of course. He had simply—because of his fierce determination to stay on the straight and narrow while away from Wallis—been a challenge; a challenge that had come with the additional temptation of being forbidden fruit. To Pamela, forbidden fruit was irresistible.

"And now look where it's got me!" she had said bitterly to Rose Houghton when she had first realized she was pregnant. "I'm a duke's daughter. How can I marry a man who has no title and who never will have a title?"

Rose, in London in order to accompany a group of newly recruited nurses to the field hospital she had been assigned to, had been unsympathetic. "You should have thought of that before you behaved as if he were the only man you were ever going to love," she'd said bluntly. "And I've got more serious things to think about than your problem, Pam—which isn't much of a problem at all, as the unlucky man in question is prepared to marry you."

Their meeting had taken place in a tea shop adjacent to Guy's Hospital.

Rose, rising to her feet, had brought it to an abrupt conclusion. "I have to get back. The nurses I'm taking to France are waiting for me. Make the best of the situation you've created, Pam. From all you've told me about him, if you give him half a chance, Mr. Bachman will make you a very good husband."

Then, with only the curtest of good-byes, she had marched out of the tea shop and back to the hospital and her waiting nurses.

Pamela, who had expected far more from Rose, had been incensed.

"I don't see why," Tarquin said to her when she complained to him about how uncaring of her plight Rose Houghton had been. "In France she's nursing men who have lost legs and arms, and sometimes their sight. You can't expect her to be massively concerned because you've misbehaved and now have to marry whether you want to or not."

"I wouldn't be having to get married if you'd find someone who'd get rid of the baby!"

Despite being a man of the world—and one who often sailed close to the wind—he blanched, white to the lips. "This isn't a conversation suitable between a stepfather and stepdaughter, Pammie. That you feel able to say such things is my fault for never having taken my role as a stepfather seriously. Over this matter, though, I am very serious. Abortions—even the most expensive abortions—lead all too often to the girl in question dying in slow and bloody agony. It is a risk I have no intention of taking where you are concerned. John Jasper isn't from some no-account family. The Bachmans are wealthy and, in Baltimore, socially prestigious. He may not be the stepson-in-law I had anticipated or the husband you had envisaged, but he's the one both of us are going to have to settle for!"

It was a conversation that had left her with no room for maneuvering, and though she hadn't admitted it to either Rose or Tarquin, there were some aspects to her forthcoming marriage she didn't find objectionable. She had always found John Jasper, with his thick thatch of curly black hair and golden brown eyes, wildly attractive, and though unlike Hans he hadn't been experienced as a lover, once he had taken the plunge he had been a very quick learner. From now on, bedtime was going to be enjoyable. There was another aspect of marriage, as well, which she knew was going to be convenient.

As she had found out to her cost, a baby could all too easily be the result of taking a lover. For a single woman, such an outcome was nearly always disastrous—as it would have been for her if John Jasper had already been married, or if he had dishonorably chosen not to marry her. Once a woman was married, though, there could be no scandal at all should she fall pregnant.

Something else that was on the plus side was that her pregnancy was not yet obvious. Her wedding would still be a big, splendid society event, and when she walked down the aisle, she would do so in a sumptuous white wedding gown with a train yards and yards long and a dozen bridesmaids in attendance.

"I don't care if it is already arranged," John Jasper said to her tightly when the wedding came under discussion. "Under the circumstances a great big wedding would be in bad taste, and it's not the kind of wedding we are going to have."

Pamela's reaction was to snap at him that it was most definitely the wedding they were going to have, but she fought the temptation. She didn't want him changing his mind about things and sailing off into the sunset, leaving her in a situation so ghastly it didn't even bear thinking about.

They were alone in the drawing room of Tarquin's London town house in Eaton Square. She was seated on a Queen Anne sofa, her pale blond hair knotted at the nape of her neck, her mauve hobble-skirted dress fashionably and daringly V-necked.

He was standing by the window, looking unseeingly out at the steadily falling snow.

"If we don't have a big society wedding, people will suspect why. I couldn't bear that, John Jasper. Truly I couldn't."

It was as near as she had ever come to pleading with him about anything, and though she hated herself for it, there was a slight catch in her voice.

He took a deep steadying breath, unwillingly accepting that what she said was true. She was the daughter of a duke. Any other kind of wedding but a grand society wedding was unthinkable. By not having one, the situation would be made worse than it already was.

He turned his head toward her, and as he met the anxiety in her eyes, his heart gave an abrupt jerk. Though he didn't love her, he most certainly had feelings for her. With one bat of her eyelashes or touch of her fingertips she could arouse a storm of desire in him that no one, not even Wallis, had ever aroused.

Even so, he had known from the very beginning that he was never going to fall in love with her the way he was in love with Wallis. With Wallis, friendship and camaraderie had underpinned the desire. With Pamela there had been only desire. Romancing her had been a sowing of wild oats. A sexual adventure. A fling. He had never intended it to be for keeps, and easing his conscience had been the knowledge that neither had she.

When it came to marriage, Pamela had intended landing a far bigger fish than a Bachman of Baltimore—and in bed had bluntly told him so.

As he remembered her hopes of becoming at the very least a countess or a duchess, guilt weighed on him heavily.

Feeling the biggest heel in Christendom, he walked across to her.

"You're right about the wedding, Pam," he said, taking hold of her hands and drawing her to her feet. "I won't pretend I'm going to enjoy a big society bash, but I'll survive it."

She had too much pride to show how vastly relieved she felt. Instead she said philosophically, "We're just going to have to make the best of the cards we've dealt ourselves, aren't we? But be warned, John Jasper. One thing I'm never going to do is to become Mrs. Bachman of Baltimore. My Baltimore days are well and truly over, and I'm never going back there. Not for you. Not for your family. Not for Tarquin. Not for anyone. Never, never, never."

She had known, of course, that it was the last thing he had wanted to hear, but she hadn't cared. She might have been left with no choice but to marry him, but nothing was going to persuade her to leave the world of London high society for a comparative backwater like Baltimore. Wally might think the city of her birth the height of sophistication, but she'd had no experience of life anywhere else, and she was wrong.

Wally.

If Pamela had been about to marry anyone other than John Jasper, she would have done everything possible to persuade Wally to ignore the present dangers of Atlantic travel and join her in London. After all, when a girl was about to be married, the person she most needed at her side was her best friend and, despite everything that had happened, that was how she still thought of Wally. She knew, of course, that it wouldn't now be how Wally felt about her.

The thought filled her with more regret than she'd thought herself capable of. She was going to miss Wally. Until John

Jasper, she'd never had any secrets from Wally. Both of them had always taken it for granted that when they married, they would be each other's chief bridesmaid or, in the case of the one of them who married first, the other's matron of honor. Now she was going to have to marry without Wally walking down the aisle behind her—and there was no way on God's earth Wally would now have her as her matron of honor.

It was all very depressing, but it wasn't in her nature to brood. Wally would meet someone else and get over John Jasper. And it wasn't as if she and John Jasper were going to be married forever and ever. Shocking though it was still perceived as being, people did, now, get divorced. Her mother, who had been a duchess, had divorced and, on remarriage, had become a countess. Though there were no doubt still some sections of society who cold-shouldered her mother and Tarquin, on the whole the cold-shouldering wasn't very obvious. King George, who was a stickler for the proprieties, still socialized privately with Tarquin, and both she and her mother had been guests at Sandringham.

There was no reason why, like her mother, she shouldn't divorce and marry an earl, or, if it took her fancy, a marquis or a duke. Prince Edward was now out of the running, of course. No royal in the history of the British monarchy had ever married a divorcée, and it was unthinkable that they ever would. Besides, her chances of becoming Princess of Wales had never seriously been in the cards. It had only been girlish romantic daydreaming and a bit of silliness between her and Wally.

She bit her lip.

She had to stop thinking about Wally. Wally wasn't going to be her matron of honor, and so she had to choose someone else who would be. And she had to choose her bridesmaids. They would know, of course, why they were being asked at so late a date, but there was a war on, and hurried marriages before men went off to the front had become the norm.

John Jasper, of course, being an American, wasn't going off to Flanders, but hopefully not everyone would think that one through.

The bridesmaid difficulty was one that her mother and Tarquin decided was best avoided. "I'll rustle up five of my godchildren," Tarquin said. "They'll look like little angels, and their mothers will be so delighted at their being the center of attention they won't speculate maliciously about the haste of the arrangements."

As there was no time for a suitably extravagant bridal gown to be made, she'd had the brilliant idea of wearing her grandmother's carefully preserved bridal gown.

When Lady Violet St. Clair had married Lord Percy Denby at St. Margaret's in 1864, the occasion had been acclaimed the wedding of the year. Queen Victoria had not been present, but the newly married Prince of Wales, together with his ethereally beautiful Danish wife, Princess Alexandra, had headed a guest list of glittering splendor. The bridal gown—a shimmering creation of palest gold lamé with an exquisite overlay of cobweb-fine Valenciennes lace lilies—had been a head-turning sensation. Pamela knew it still would be.

"All that is now needed is that my guest list be headed by royalty," she said to her mother as the exquisite gown was carefully adjusted by an expert seamstress for a perfect fit. "If Tarquin were to invite him, surely King George would come?"

Her mother, who because of the circumstances of the wedding could barely bring herself to speak to her, breathed in hard, her finely sculpted nostrils whitening.

"Even minor royalty does not accept invitations to whirlwind weddings," she said icily, flicking a beringed hand in the direction of the young woman carrying out the adjustments to indicate she should leave them.

When the door had closed and they were on their own, she said with real venom, "And no one in their right minds would invite King George to a wedding knowing there will soon be a seven-month baby to explain away! It would be social suicide!"

Totally unfazed by her mother's fury, Pamela admired her reflection in a three-way mirror. "As far as the world at large is concerned, it will be a nine-month baby. If it weren't for the war, John Jasper would be taking me to Europe until several months after the baby's birth. As it is, we're going to leave almost immediately after the wedding for New York."

"New York?" Her mother was so taken aback she forgot how angry she was. "Surely Baltimore would make more sense?"

Pamela twirled to one side in order to get a clearer view of what the gown looked like from the back, saying grimly, "Not for me, Mother."

"But people are saying that the Atlantic is no longer safe." There was something almost like concern in her mother's voice. "There are rumors that the Germans are going to make all shipping to and from Britain fair game."

"There are always rumors, but can you imagine German submarines torpedoing an American passenger liner? I can't. Adding two months to the baby's birth date when we return will be easy, and hopefully he or she will be obligingly small."

Her mother made no comment for the simple reason that she couldn't bring herself to do so. Having a daughter who should have been making a spectacular marriage marrying an insignificant American because her racy behavior had left her with no other choice was a scenario she was finding very hard to deal with.

One relief was that the wedding itself would pass without comment. There were enough titled members in her family and in Tarquin's to enable the occasion to be seen as a splendid society event. Everyone—the press included—would think the bride's wearing of her grandmother's bridal gown wonderfully sentimental. The happy couple's immediate disappearance on an extended stay in America would, because of the groom's nationality, raise no eyebrows. Pamela was right, too, in thinking that on their return the baby could easily be passed off as being two months younger than its actual age.

Everything was under control. Everything was taken care of.

She pulled on a pair of gloves the exact shade of her mauve walking dress. All that was needed now was for the ceremony to be over and the happy couple to disappear from sight en route to Southampton on whatever liner was to take them to New York—an event that, for her, couldn't happen quickly enough.

On the morning of his wedding John Jasper left the Savoy Hotel and went for a solitary walk along the nearby Victoria Embankment. The Thames was sleet-gray, the trees in the nearby Temple Gardens rimed with frost. No one was about. It was too early and too cold.

Bleakly he sat down on one of the park benches facing the river. That what should have been the happiest day of his life was, instead, going to be far from being so was his own fault and no one else's. What had happened had happened, and now he and Pamela had to make the best of things.

He clasped his hands between his knees, reflecting that marriage and motherhood were not things Pamela was likely to be very good at. Though he tried to continue thinking about Pamela, it was Wallis who filled his thoughts. He wondered what she was doing. With a constriction of his heart, he wondered how soon it would be before she had another beau.

He remained thinking about her, his broad shoulders hunched, his head bowed low over his hands until, in the near distance, Big Ben chimed the hour.

As the last of eight strokes died away he rose to his feet. Faithlessness to Wallis led him into his present situation. He wasn't now going to be mentally faithless to Pamela. From now on, no matter how hard it would be for him not to do so, he wouldn't allow himself to think of Wallis. If his and Pamela's marriage was to work—and for the sake of their unborn child, he was determined that it would—then a line had to be drawn beneath the past.

Determined to draw that line, he quickened his pace toward the Savoy, from where, in two hours' time, he would be leaving for St. Margaret's, Westminster.

"It's time for us to leave, Pammie." Tarquin looked down at his fob watch. As he put it away, he said, "Your mother and the bridesmaids left fifteen minutes ago, and John Jasper has probably been kicking his heels for going on half an hour."

"It's traditional for the bride to be late."

"Not so late that the groom has second thoughts and leaves for the hills."

Pamela picked up her bouquet of bloodred roses and slid her arm through his, grateful that her father had declined to cross the Atlantic and that it was Tarquin who was to give her away. "Much as John Jasper might want to leave," she said drily, "he won't. I don't imagine he's feeling very comfortable, though. He hardly knows a soul among the guests and barely knows his best man."

"He has his father as a support." As he led her from the room, he added, "Pa Bachman is rather a dark horse, isn't he? He hasn't said a word to me about the undue haste of the arrangements. Has John Jasper put him in the picture?"

"No—and if Pa Bachman has guessed, he's too delighted at having a duke's daughter for a daughter-in-law to raise a fuss about it."

They descended the grand staircase to the applause of the household staff who had gathered in the hall to see her leave.

Pamela squeezed hold of Tarquin's arm, saying as she reached the last step, "I do hope there are absolutely *masses* of photographers waiting for us at the church door."

"There will be, and there will be a crowd as well. Society weddings at St. Margaret's are a source of great public entertainment."

The journey from Eaton Square to St. Margaret's took only minutes, and when they arrived at the church, the crowd was so large the car had to slow to a snail's pace to inch its way through them.

Her veil, held in place by a bandeau of seed pearls and orange blossoms worn low across her forehead, fell into a train three yards long, and as she stepped from the car great oohs and aahs of appreciation went up from the crowd.

Delighted, Pamela turned and waved to them and then, as the church bells rang and her little bridesmaids were ushered into position behind her, she stepped through the ancient west door and into the church where John Jasper, the only beau Wally had ever had, was waiting for her in front of the altar.

Chapter Ten

Wallis spent the next few weeks in a sea of misery, her sense of betrayal overwhelming. She told no one of John Jasper and Pamela's marriage apart from her mother and Aunt Bessie. Both of them were outraged at his faithlessness and Pamela's lack of loyalty.

"Blood friends, indeed!" Aunt Bessie had said, her china blue eyes flashing sparks. "If that is how Pamela Denby behaves toward someone she says is a blood friend, what depths of disloyalty will she sink to with her ordinary friends?"

Wallis had made no answer. Her imagination simply didn't stretch that far.

Telling her mother and her aunt of her heartbreak had been a necessity in order for them to understand why she needed to leave Baltimore.

"And Cousin Corinne couldn't be happier about my staying with her and Henry," she said to her mother when at last she was safely in receipt of an invitation from Corinne. "Corinne says that Henry has very little free time—he's just been appointed a lieutenant commander. It means she sees too little of him, and she says my company will be very welcome."

"Your Uncle Sol will have to approve. I don't think he'll be difficult about it. I'll make sure he views letting you stay with Corinne a kind of compensation for the debutante ball he denied you."

Believing that Wallis was going to Florida for only a short visit, Sol made no demur about her making the trip. He had other, more important things on his mind. Ever since his mother had broken her hip, she had been in poor health, and now, though the rest of the family were not yet aware of it, she was failing fast. Sol, fifty years old and still unmarried, was devoted to her.

When she died, he was plunged into deep grief—grief Wallis fully shared. Her grandmother had played an important part in her life. As immovable as a rock in her views and her Episcopalian faith, she had brought Wallis up to be proud to be a Warfield, and the pride had given her a sense of self-worth. Without that self-worth, Wallis knew she would never have coped as she had with the financial and social difficulties she and her mother had always faced.

It was a large, well-attended funeral, as befitted one of the city's great dowagers. Alice, who had never been fond of the mother-in-law who so disapproved of her, wore a shoulder-length black crepe veil. It served two functions. It reminded people that though she was now Free Rasin's widow, she was also the widow of Teackle Warfield—and it successfully hid the fact that she was dry-eyed.

Wallis, dressed from head to toe in black, but minus a veil, didn't remain dry-eyed. Knowing how strongly her grandmother would have disproved of an unseemly display of emotion, she managed to remain composed throughout the church service, but once it came to the burial, tears streamed down her face, dropping uncontrollably onto her black, kid-gloved hands.

Stiff and unbending as Grandma Warfield had been, she had always given time to Wallis, and her vivid stories of Warfield ancestors such as Robert de Warfield and King Powhatan had imbued Wallis with a feeling that was precious to her: the feeling that by being a Warfield she was someone special and different.

As she packed her trunk for the long train journey to Florida, she knew she was going to miss her grandmother. She also knew that her grandmother's death was going to spare her any feelings of guilt she might have had at moving so far away from her.

Thanks to Uncle Sol, her train journey from Jacksonville onward was made in great style. Sol owned part of the railroad, and her ticket, given to her for free, was a first-class one.

The comfort was one she luxuriated in. Heartbroken over John Jasper she might be, but she wasn't going to give in to that heartbreak. Thanks to Corinne she was embarking on a new beginning, and she was going to make the very best of it that she could.

Though not knowing about John Jasper, Corinne's advice to her was welcomingly apt.

There's no need for you to remain in black for your Grandmother Warfield at Pensacola, Wallis,

she had written.

On a naval air station such as this, social events are of prime importance, and it is essential that you bring all your pretty dresses. Single young women are in short supply, and so you are going to be spoiled for choice when it comes to beaux.

To be spoiled for choice for a beau was exactly what Wallis wanted. She opened the magazine she had bought on the station platform. Very soon John Jasper and his bride would no doubt be arriving in Baltimore. Knowing John Jasper as she did, she couldn't imagine him settling down to married life anywhere else but his hometown, and, as Britain was a nation at war, there was no reason for either him or Pamela to want to stay there.

As outside her carriage window hills and bluffs gave way to the lush vegetation of the Deep South, she found herself doing what she had determined she was never going to do again. She found herself thinking of John Jasper and Pamela. When they returned to Baltimore, where would they live? The most obvious answer was Rosemont. John Jasper would love living at Rosemont.

Her chest constricted in a tight band of pain. When gossip about her got back to John Jasper and Pamela, she wanted it to be about what a whale of a time she was having in Florida—and nothing would convince them of that more surely than the news that she had become engaged.

The first-class compartment Uncle Sol had arranged for her gave her complete privacy, and, blinking back tears, she fanned out the newspapers and the magazine that she had bought to read on the journey.

All the headlines were of the war convulsing Europe—and of how imperative it was that America did not become involved in it. After reading a gruesome report of how the Germans were using a hideous gas to half-blind and panic the Allies and an even worse report of a battle for a small hill at Ypres that had resulted in 69,000 men being killed and 164,000 being wounded, she turned the page and was met with a headline about the Prince of Wales.

PRINCE EDWARD A DISPATCH RIDER AT THE FRONT

There was a picture of the prince alongside the article. He was in uniform and astride a powerful-looking motorbike. The accompanying text read:

Prince Edward, attached to the staff of Field Marshal Sir John French, Commander-in-Chief of the British Expeditionary Force, is a familiar sight as he carries vital dispatches between British and French generals. The Prince, fluent in German, has also helped in the interrogation of prisoners and a week ago inspected Indian troops sent out to the front.

Once, in talking about Prince Edward, Pamela had stressed how very German Britain's royal family were. "Nearly every aunt, uncle, and cousin Prince Edward has is German," she had said. "Before her marriage, his mother was Princess May of Teck. Teck, in case you're not aware Wally, is a German dukedom."

A prickly feeling ran down Wallis's spine. Dreadful as it was for every soldier fighting at the front, how much worse must it be for Prince Edward, when members of his close family were now also the hated enemy?

Taking a pair of nail scissors out of her traveling bag, she cut out the news item. Ever since she had been at Oldfields, Prince Edward had been her favorite pinup. She had never had romantic daydreams about him, though. Any such daydreams had always been about John Jasper. Real-life romantic hopes where Prince Edward was concerned had been Pamela's department, not hers.

Carefully she put the cutting between the pages of her magazine and then put the magazine in her traveling bag. Any hopes Pamela might have had of becoming a royal bride were now well and truly over. She waited for a feeling of intense satisfaction. It didn't come. What came was agonizing hurt and a sense of loss for the friend who had once been closer to her than a sister and was now a friend no more.

Three hours later she stepped off the train into balmy warmth and brilliant sunshine. The contrast, after the gray chill of Baltimore, was heavenly, and as she raised her face to the brassy blue bowl of the sky, Wallis felt a surge of such optimism it almost lifted her off her feet. Ahead of her lay all kinds of new experiences, and she wasn't going to let heartache prevent her from embracing and enjoying every single one of them.

"Skinny! *Skinny!*"

Corinne's nickname for her reverberated down the length of the station's crowded platform. Through a sea of alighting passengers, Wallis headed in its direction as fast as the narrow skirt of her ankle-length traveling costume would allow.

"*Skinny!*"

The sea parted and Corinne, voluptuous in a tightly fitting turquoise day dress and a hat laden with feathers of the same color crowning pompadour-styled golden hair, ran to meet her, her arms open wide.

"Oh, Skinny! Isn't this *peachy*?" she exclaimed as they hugged and kissed. "I never thought that mean old Warfield uncle of yours would let you come. Is that your porter struggling with the two big trunks? I see you've taken me at my word and brought *lots* of pretty dresses with you. I can't wait to show you the air station, Skinny. We're goin' to have such a good time together! You'll be goin' to a party every night of the week!"

A car and driver were waiting for them. With the help of the porter, the chauffeur stowed the luggage. As Wallis seated herself in the open-topped Ford next to Corinne, she gave a sigh that was almost a purr. For the first time in her life she was free of her morally strict Warfield relations. Corinne was a Montague—and all Montagues were pleasure loving and knew how to enjoy themselves. A party every night of the week was *exactly* what she needed to put the past—and John Jasper—very firmly behind her.

"Pensacola is a small town," Corinne said as they sped through sun-baked streets lined with Spanish-style colonial houses. "All activity takes place on the air station—and there isn't another station like it anywhere else in the country, though Henry says there soon will be."

Wallis felt excitement spiral in her tummy. Flying was such a new thing, no one she knew had even seen an airplane or met an aviator, and here, at Pensacola, she was going to be surrounded by planes and aviators wherever she looked.

Streets and houses gave way to a single road, curving around a glorious palm-fringed landlocked bay.

"There are so many sandy beaches, I don't think they've ever been counted," Corinne said, pleased at the effect Pensacola was having on Wallis. "There are some cabanas on the beach nearest the base. If you like, we'll go there for a swim later today."

Wallis was just about to say she'd love to go for a swim when she saw something in the sky. In a fever of delight, she grabbed hold of Corinne's arm. "Look, Corinne! Over there, on the right! Oh, my Lord! Is the aviator supposed to let the plane swoop and dive like that? Is he safe, or is he about to crash?"

Corinne gave a throaty gurgle of laughter. "No aviator is ever safe, Skinny. Flying is far too dangerous. That plane isn't about to crash, though. It's just the way planes move through the air."

Wallis watched, entranced, as the plane flew closer. The fuselage, with its array of metal struts, was open, and the helmeted goggled figure at the controls was clearly visible.

It came nearer still, the noise of the engine deafening.

"Whoever the pilot is, he's being very naughty!" Corinne shouted, as it became obvious he was going to fly directly over their speeding car.

Wallis didn't think the pilot was being naughty. She thought he was being heart-stoppingly splendid. He came in over their heads, leaning away from his controls to look down at them. Then, with a wave and a brilliant smile, he zoomed away.

Wallis waved after him until he was a mere speck in the distance.

"Though it's hard to tell when they are wearing helmets and goggles, I'm fairly sure that was Lieutenant Earl Winfield Spencer, the bad boy of the air station," Corinne said when Wallis finally lowered her arm. "You can't behave like that every time someone flies over your head, Skinny. Getting a reputation for being fast is a lot harder to do here than in Baltimore—but it is still possible. And attracting the attention of a lady-killer such as Win, before you've even set foot on the air station, is certainly the way to do it."

There was amusement in her voice, not serious criticism, and Wallis said with a rush of deep affection, "If I'd been lucky enough to have a sister, I would have wanted her to be like you, Corinne."

With one hand holding on to her hat, Corinne gave one of her husky laughs. "I guess that's mutual, Skinny. Pensacola Air Station is just ahead of us. You're goin' to love living on it, honey. I just know you are."

The air station hugged the bay, a bewildering conglomeration of long hangars, machine shops, and slipways.

"Those are derricks," Corinne said as they passed giant-sized cranes. "They're not very pretty, are they?"

They weren't, but the residential area of the air station was. On either side of a hill that sloped gently toward the bay was a scattering of white-painted bungalows. The Ford drew up outside one that was slightly bigger than the others.

"This is home," Corinne said as a maid hurried out to welcome them. "I hope you're goin' to be happy here, Skinny. Don't worry about the constant noise of airplanes taking off and landing. You'll soon get used to it."

Wallis didn't see how anyone could get used to such a roar, but she had no intention of letting it worry her.

As they stepped into an elegantly furnished sitting room, Corinne added, "There is only goin' to be the three of us for dinner this evening. Henry thought you'd be too tired after your long rail journey to want to socialize. I told him no Montague is ever too tired to socialize, but he's much older than I am, and when he gets an idea in his head it's hard to move it. Tomorrow night—and every night afterward—will be a lot more lively."

Though she had met Henry Mustin only a couple of times, Wallis liked him. He was in his midforties, an attractive man deeply suntanned from long hours spent in the open air either aboard ship—he was master of the battleship USS *Mississippi*—or, since his appointment to establish the air station at Pensacola, in the open fuselage of an airplane.

"It's a treat to have you here, Wallis," he said to her over dinner that evening. "Corinne loves it in Florida, but she misses her family. Your being here is going to be a great boost to her spirits."

"It's already a great boost to mine."

Her depth of sincerity was obvious.

He smiled across at her, liking what he saw. She wasn't a belle in the way Corinne, who was blond, blue-eyed, and voluptuously curvaceous, was. Like all Montagues, Wallis possessed a great sense of fun, but in looks she was too much a Warfield to be a head-turning beauty. Unless he was very much mistaken, she also possessed the fierce intelligence that was such a predominant characteristic of the Warfields. He wondered if she would be interested in knowing how and why the air station had come into being and rather thought she would.

As if reading his mind Wallis said, "Tell me about the air station, Henry. All I know is that it is the first of its kind."

Gratified that his assumptions had been so correct, Henry lost interest in his beautifully cooked local lobster.

"It is—and it's growing fast. When I was first posted here to help establish a center for naval flight operations, I had only six trained pilots, twenty-three enlisted men, seven seaplanes, some spare parts, and a few canvas hangars. Those numbers have already doubled and will soon, thanks to a very vigorous pilot training program, quadruple. My main task in coming here was to prove to the Navy that airplanes have a place in the fleet."

"Was there doubt, then?"

"There was a lot of doubt—but not much of it now lingers."

He eased himself back in his chair, his hands clasped across a hard-muscled belly. "You have to remember how new a thing flight is, Wallis. That airplanes could be used by the Navy simply wasn't immediately obvious—and it wasn't a Navy man who made the Navy see things differently. That was up to a civilian pilot, Eugene Ely."

"And what did Eugene Ely do?" Wallis was now so interested in the conversation that, like Henry, she was no longer paying any attention to the food on her plate.

Henry grinned, the lines at the corners of his eyes crinkling. "Eugene landed his airplane aboard the USS *Pennsylvania*, which was, at the time, in the middle of San Francisco Bay. The Navy promptly built its first aircraft carrier, and before the year was out we had our first seaplane."

Corinne, who was interested only in the social side of Pensacola and not interested in anything else to do with it, yawned.

Wallis and Henry ignored her.

"So Pensacola is really a training station for seaplane pilots—and a bit of a training station for seaplanes as well."

"You've got it in one, Wallis. With every few months we produce another first. A Pensacola pilot holds the first altitude record, and a Pensacola pilot was the first to be catapulted in an airplane from the deck of a ship."

"And a Pensacola pilot died in the Navy's first fatal air crash," Corinne added drily.

Henry's face tightened. "That, I am afraid, is also true. The pilots in training here are extremely courageous young men. Every day they are in the air is a day filled with danger."

Corinne, realizing she had brought a somber tone to the conversation, tried to lighten things. "What Henry didn't tell you, Skinny, is that Henry was the pilot who was catapulted from the ship."

"Land sakes!"

Henry laughed, pleased at how startled and impressed she was. "The danger can't be left to the young ones all the time, Wallis." He refilled his wineglass. "I was in the cockpit of an AB-2 flying boat and the ship was the USS *North Carolina*. It was, to say the least, an interesting experience."

Later that evening, just as she had gotten into bed, Corinne knocked on her bedroom door. "It's only me, Skinny. Come to say good night," she said, as she entered the room.

Swathed in a coffee-colored negligée lavishly trimmed with lace, she sat down on the edge of the bed. "You were a great hit with Henry tonight. Because I'm so much younger than Henry, all my friends are younger too, and they don't go out of their way to pretend to be interested in what he's saying in the way you did."

Wallis's eyebrows flew high. "I wasn't pretending, Corinne. I was genuinely interested. Why wouldn't I be? I thought every-thing he said was absolutely riveting."

"You did?" Corinne stared at her, not sure whether her leg was being pulled. When she realized it wasn't, she gurgled with laughter. "Gee, honey, if you effortlessly show that level of in-terest in male conversation, you must make a slave of every man who speaks to you."

"Oh, I've had my failures, Corinne." Wallis spoke lightly, but her heart ached as she thought of John Jasper. She'd be-lieved John Jasper had—in the most romantic of senses—been her slave.

"Good night, Skinny." Corinne kissed her on the forehead. "Tomorrow I'm goin' to begin introducing you to people. We'll lunch at the San Carlos Hotel. Swim in the afternoon. And Henry has invited some eligible officers to dinner tomorrow evening."

To Wallis it sounded an ideal itinerary. Certain she had made the right decision in coming to Pensacola, she closed her eyes and, exhausted after her long day of traveling, fell into a deep and blessedly dreamless sleep.

She woke to blissful sunshine spilling into the room. The knowledge that every day was now going to be filled with tropical heat sent her spirits soaring. Putting on a stylish sum-mer dress that hadn't seen the light of day for six chilly Balti-more months, she hurried out onto the verandah to join Corinne for a breakfast of banana pecan muffins and fresh tropical fruit.

"The first thing on the agenda this morning is a stroll down the hill to the beach and the flying area." There was a jug of freshly squeezed orange juice on the table, and Corinne poured herself a second glass. "From there we'll be able to see the prep-arations being made for the day's flights."

Thinking about the aviator who had flown his airplane over their car, Wallis's interest quickened. He'd had a brilliant smile, but the rest of his features had been hidden by his flying helmet and his goggles. Perhaps this morning she would get a clear view of him.

The way down to the beach led through the officers' compound, and the interest they aroused, respectful because of whom Corinne was married to, was intense.

"There's not a man on the air station who won't be angling for an introduction to you," Corinne said, pleased at the admiring looks that were coming Wallis's way.

A few minutes later, they reached the edge of the beach and a huge sign on which was written, *WARNING! NO CIVILIANS BEYOND THIS POINT.*

"On this particular beach, this is as far as we can go, Skinny."

In front of them was an array of training planes around which a large number of men were milling, some geared up ready to fly, others wearing mechanic's dungarees.

Beyond them, in the bay, gunmetal gray battleships lay at anchor.

They were a sharp reminder of the bloodbath taking place on the other side of the Atlantic, of the battles being waged at sea between the British and German fleets.

"Is all this training because America might soon be at war with Germany?" she asked, suddenly fearful of what the future might hold.

For once there was no laughter in Corinne's lazy Southern voice. "Yes. Despite the huge lobby against such a thing ever happening, Henry thinks it's a strong possibility—especially if the war continues into next year."

Icy fingers squeezed Wallis's heart. Until now the Great War convulsing Europe had seemed so far away; it had never occurred to her that it could touch her own life or the lives of people she knew. If America entered the war, it would certainly do so—and every man on the beach in front of her would be in the thick of the fighting.

With great effort she pushed the thought away, wanting to recapture the mood of a few moments earlier.

"I'd never realized how *fragile* seaplanes were," she said, as one of them set off across the still waters of the bay, struggling to gain height. "They're nothing more than fabric-covered boxes with struts!"

"Don't let any of the pilots hear you call their pride and joy a fabric-covered box with struts, honey! And if you're curious, this morning's training is all about navigation."

As airplane after airplane set off across the bay, Wallis failed to recognize the pilot she had waved to so enthusiastically on her way to Pensacola from the station. She didn't mind. Corinne had told her that Earl Winfield Spencer was a fully fledged pilot, not a trainee, and as there were no more than a couple of dozen fully trained pilots at Pensacola, it wouldn't be long before their paths crossed.

When they'd had their fill of watching the activity on the beach and in the bay, they strolled in the direction of the San Carlos Hotel to have morning coffee with a group of Corinne's women friends. Wallis's easy manner and sparky humor ensured that just as had happened on her first days at Arundell and Oldfields, although the group she was being introduced to was tight-knit, she was immediately welcomed into it with open arms.

"I knew you would be, Skinny," Corinne said to her an hour or so later as they all headed into the restaurant for lunch. "No Montague ever has a problem making friends. I think a frillier, flouncier dress might be in order tomorrow, though.

The one you are wearing is wonderfully made—I guess you're pretty good at twisting Sol Warfield's arm when it comes to your dress allowance and only go to the best of Baltimore's dressmakers—but it is a little on the plain side."

Wallis linked her arm with Corinne's.

"That's because I like plain and don't like fussy. Plain—if it's beautifully made out of the very best fabric, like the silk of this dress—suits me."

"Well, that's true. But it makes you a little noticeable, honey."

Wallis grinned. "That's the idea, Corinne. Being noticeable is something I like. In Baltimore, when I was wearing a Gibson girl skirt and blouse, instead of jewelry I wore a monocle. That made me *very* noticeable. How d'you think a monocle would go down in Pensacola?"

"I think Henry would have ten fits! He'd be terrified the next thing you'd do would be to take up smoking cigars!"

After lunch they headed back to the bungalow for a siesta, and then, when the most uncomfortable heat of the day was over, Corinne took her to the beach she had spoken of that had cabanas. Wallis was a confident swimmer, and as she rolled over on to her back to float lazily in the limpid blue water, she felt as if she had been reborn. Florida wasn't a different state. It was a different country. Though she would never have believed it possible in so short a time, her agonizing hurt and rage over John Jasper and Pamela's mutual betrayal was already beginning to ease. They were in the past and she was now in a future she hadn't, until a few short weeks ago, even imagined.

That evening she took a great deal of time when dressing for dinner. The gown she chose was one of her favorites: a tubular Poiret-influenced gown in shimmering scarlet with discreet but very effective beading. It flattered her flat-chested figure and emphasized her spectacularly dark hair.

"Glory!" Corinne said when she saw her. "You look sensational. In that color and with your hair parted in the middle and drawn back over your ears, you look Latin American!"

"No, I don't, Corinne. If I look something exotic, I look like an Indian princess. Don't forget that the Warfield side of me is descended from Pocahontas."

"Honey, with that line of chat it's no wonder you stand out from the crowd! How about a cocktail on the verandah before Henry's handpicked aviators arrive? Have you ever had a pink gin? They're delicious."

As Corinne's all-purpose maid put the finishing touches on the meal Corinne had prepared, they sat on the verandah in the evening sunlight, frosted cocktail glasses in hand.

From there they had a wonderful view of the street as it sloped down to the officers' compound. Beyond the compound lay the beach where, earlier, they had watched airplanes taking off for a day's navigational training, and beyond the beach lay the stunning vista of the bay, the water now the color of gold-shot indigo.

"I don't think I've ever seen anything more beautiful," Wallis said, almost as happy as she had been in the days before she had received John Jasper's letter.

Corinne took a sip of her pink gin. "It's certainly an amazing view, but to tell you the truth, Skinny, until you arrived I was getting a little bored with Pensacola. As Henry's wife—and especially as he is a lieutenant commander—I can't flirt with the pilots as you are going to be able to do. And at Pensacola, flirting is the best way of passing time that there is."

There was a pensive note in her voice, as if she genuinely missed being single and able to flirt. For the first time, Wallis wondered if Corinne regretted having married a man twenty years her senior. The benefit, of course, had been that Henry was already a distinguished naval officer, holding very high rank, but he was a serious-minded man and Corinne was as light-minded as nearly all Montagues. There were, perhaps, strains in the marriage Wallis hadn't previously been aware of.

"Here they come!" Corinne put her glass down on the table fronting their cane chairs. "I can always recognize Henry a mile off. He has such a distinctive walk. I'm not sure whom he's bringing with him, though. Men look all the same at a distance when they are in uniform."

Wallis didn't think the three young men with Henry looked all the same. Two of them were exceptionally tall and loose limbed. The third was Henry's height, five foot ten or so. Suntanned, broad shouldered, and muscular, he held himself well, walking with springy precision, like an athlete in perfect physical condition.

As the men drew nearer, strikingly handsome in crisp white uniforms, she caught her breath. Beneath his officer's cap, the aviator who had caught her attention had hair almost as dark as her own. The sun glinted on the gold braid signifying his rank, and even before Corinne spoke, she knew he was her aviator of yesterday.

"Dear Lord!" Amusement was back in Corinne's voice. "Henry's invited Win Spencer! That means the evening is goin' to be very lively."

Wallis made no response. With a great deal of effort she was trying to look carelessly nonchalant.

Seconds later, Henry was saying, "Wallis, allow me to introduce Lieutenants Archie Crosby, Robert Richard Allinson, and Earl Winfield Spencer."

Rising to her feet, Wallis smiled and shook hands with Archie Crosby and Robert Richard Allinson. Then, with her heart feeling as if it were beating fast and light in her throat, she shook hands with Win.

He flashed her the same smile he had flashed at her yesterday, from the cockpit of his plane. It had the same electrifying effect.

His peaked hat was now tucked in the crook of his free arm and his military *en brosse* haircut suited a face that was hard-boned, the jawline strong and assertive. Beneath a close-cropped mustache his mouth was unyieldingly straight and excitingly sensual.

It was the face of a forceful and sophisticated man; a face far removed from those of the fresh-faced boys just out of college that she was accustomed to. Even John Jasper, who, with his gypsy-dark good looks, had always been distinctive, hadn't possessed magnetism on such a scale.

As Win continued to hold her hand, and as Wallis made no attempt to remove it, Henry cleared his throat.

Well able to take a hint, Win dropped Wallis's hand, saying as he did so, "Miss Warfield and I met briefly yesterday, sir. Though from a distance a little too far to allow for a proper introduction."

Wallis felt her cheeks burn. No one before had had such an immediate and disturbing effect on her, and she could well understand his reputation as a lady-killer.

"Win was out flyin', Henry," Corinne said, putting her bewildered husband into the picture. "As Skinny and I were nearing Pensacola by car, he flew over the top of us and Wallis gave him the longest wave in aviation history."

"A history that is only a handful of years old, Wallis." Henry fell into step beside her as Corinne led the way into their home. "It's hard to imagine, seeing seaplanes taking off and landing on the battle cruisers in the bay, that it's only a little over ten years ago that Orville and Wilbur Wright conquered the air with the first successful flight of a heavier-than-air flying machine."

Silver cutlery and cut-glass wineglasses shone on the dining table's lace-covered surface, and a bowl of pink and yellow roses gave off a light, delicate fragrance. For such a small informal dinner party there were no place cards, and as it was obvious Henry and Corinne would seat themselves at opposite ends of the table, Wallis wondered whether she should seat herself at Corinne's right hand or Henry's left hand. Uppermost in her thoughts was which of the three lieutenants would then sit next to her.

"This end of the table, I think, Wally," Henry said, drawing a chair out for her.

He was about to suggest that Robert Allinson then sit next to her, but Win was too quick for him. As Archie Crosby pulled a chair out for Corinne, Win casually laid his hand on the back of the chair next to Wallis's.

Seconds later, seating himself after Corinne had sat down, he said, "Now, Miss Warfield, you will be able to tell me all about yourself without the rest of the table hearing."

His eyes were bold and black and frankly appraising.

It was an expression she had seen before in her cousin Henry's eyes and in John Jasper's eyes. Though both had been handsome young men, neither had possessed Win Spencer's overpowering masculinity, and Wallis was overcome with the sensation of entering deep and dangerous waters.

She didn't care.

Deep and dangerous waters were exactly what she wanted, and if she could keep this rugged, tough-looking naval officer interested in her, she was going to do so.

"There's little to tell, Lieutenant Spencer." She gave a teasing shrug of her shoulder. "And nothing that would be of interest to you, for I neither fly seaplanes nor want to."

He cracked with laughter. "Flying seaplanes isn't for women—though I rather think that with the right tuition you'd make a good job of it."

"I make a good job of everything I set out to do, Lieutenant Spencer."

"I imagine you do, Miss Warfield."

Though the words were innocuous enough, the way he said them brought a fresh wave of heat to Wallis's cheeks, especially as he was seated so close to her that his strongly muscled thigh was pressed hard against the soft silk of her skirt.

It was a flirtation steamily outside her experience and one that could be continued no longer now that the general chatter had lulled and they would be overheard. Mindful of how odd and impolite it would be not to pay Lieutenant Allinson and Lieutenant Crosby attention—and not moving her leg away from Win Spencer's—she smiled across at Robert Allinson.

"When did you become fascinated with flying, Lieutenant?" she asked as the two extra maids Corinne had engaged for the evening ferried dishes of scallops, shrimp, artichoke, tomatoes, and pasta in from the kitchen.

"I guess it was 'bout the same time Win did, Miss Warfield." He shot her a crumpled grin. "We were both serving aboard the USS *Nebraska* when it became obvious what a large part flying was going to play in the Navy of the future."

"So Rob tagged after me when I entered the Navy's flight training program," Win interjected, "and I've still not shaken him off my tail."

There was laughter, and then Henry said, "Win was only the twentieth naval pilot to receive his wings."

"With Rob trailing behind at number twenty-five," Archie Crosby added, enjoying the chance to have a dig at his best buddy.

Robert Allinson grinned across at her. "Take no notice of these two clowns, Miss Warfield. They're only jealous because I'm the good-looking one."

There was more good-natured laughter and Wallis joined in with it, even though it was patently obvious to her that where good looks were concerned, neither Rob nor Archie were re-motely in Win's league.

"You can see why I get so bored, Skinny," Corinne whis-pered to her as, when the meal ended, they left the dining room for the candlelit sitting room. "Flying, flying, flying. It's all they ever talk about. Henry even talks about it in his sleep!"

Wallis merely smiled. Corinne didn't have to be interested in flying in order to catch her man. She was already safely married. If Wallis wanted to keep Win Spencer interested in her, she needed to be knowledgeable enough about flying to hold an intelligent conversation with him on the subject.

Knowing herself as she did, she knew she could succeed in that aim as easily as falling off a log.

Chapter Eleven

For the next few days Wallis nearly drove Corinne mad with her questions about flying, flight training programs, and what exactly Win and his fellow officers' duties consisted of.

"Land sakes, Skinny!" Corinne threw the core of the apple she had been eating onto the sand, where it was immediately scavenged by a seagull. "You'd think you were thinking of taking up flying yourself!"

They were on the perimeter of the area forbidden to civilian personnel, watching, as they did every morning, training flights taking off and landing in the bay.

"And is Win Spencer Pensacola's senior flying instructor?" Wallis asked, ignoring Corinne's last remark.

Corinne shot her a bemused look. "He is, but don't get the hots for Win, Skinny. He's way out of your league. Married women are far more in his line—though not, I slightly regret to say, me." The laughter that was never far from Corinne's voice was there in full measure as she added, "Even Win isn't so rash as to try and bed the wife of the air station's commandant!"

They both broke into convulsive laughter and were still laughing when Rob Allinson strolled over to them.

"What's the joke, ladies?" he asked good-naturedly. "Anything you can cut me in on?"

Wallis, struggling to keep a straight face, said, "Absolutely not, Lieutenant Allinson. And why aren't you dressed for flying? I thought you all took trainees up every day."

"Today is my day for training recruits in signal and radio work, and we don't kick off for another half hour." Reluctantly he dragged his eyes away from Wallis and toward Corinne. "What are your plans for the day, Mrs. Mustin? Have you thought of perhaps taking Miss Warfield on a ferry ride over to Santa Rosa island?"

Corinne, by now once again in control of herself, said in the lazy voice that betrayed Montague connections to porticoed plantation houses in a way Wallis's rarely did, "I hadn't, Lieutenant Allinson, but it's a very good idea, though not, I think, for today."

She turned to Wallis. "Santa Rosa is a great place for picnics, Skinny, but picnics are best when a group has gotten together. I'll speak to Henry about it this evening. If we can make a party up and go over for an evening picnic, it will be great fun."

She flashed Rob a smile full of easy charm. "And seeing as it was your idea we go to Santa Rosa, you, of course, will have to be one of the party, Lieutenant Allinson."

He flushed slightly. "That's real kind of you, Mrs. Mustin. I'll look forward to it." His eyes were back on Wallis again. "Goodbye, Miss Warfield. It was nice speaking with you again."

As he walked away from them, Corinne raised her eyebrows. "Well, well. You've certainly made a conquest there. And a very suitable one. The Allinsons are a very well-connected Virginia family. An engagement there would please your mother immensely."

"I'm not looking to get engaged, Corinne."

It was, of course, a fib; every girl her age was looking to get engaged, because there was no other future for a girl but marriage, yet the only person she had wanted to become engaged to—and had believed she *was* unofficially engaged to—was John Jasper, and she hadn't yet quite gotten over John Jasper.

Being so strongly attracted to Lieutenant Earl Winfield Spencer was helping her get over him, for she was thinking less and less of John Jasper and more and more of Win.

She wondered if Win's family, like Rob's, was also well connected and couldn't imagine otherwise. Young men who had gone to the Annapolis naval academy didn't come from nondescript backgrounds.

"I said," she was suddenly aware of Corinne saying with exaggerated patience, "and I said it for the third time, have we to go to Electric Park, the local amusement park? Henry won't like it if we go without a male escort, but if I speak to him he'll rustle an officer up to accompany us so that we look suitably respectable."

The officer Henry Mustin obligingly rustled up was Lieutenant Archie Crosby. As Archie had been good company on the night of the dinner party, both Wallis and Corinne were delighted.

"Though I refuse to spend the afternoon hearing you refer to Wallis as Miss Warfield, and Wallis referring to you as Lieutenant Crosby," Corinne said as she and Wallis stepped into the motorcar Henry had provided for the three of them. "You are both too young for such formalities. Continue calling me Mrs. Mustin, Archie. If you didn't Henry would have apoplexy, but from now on I shall call you Archie, and so will Wallis."

They had a wonderful time at Electric Park. They rode the roller coaster—Wallis and Corinne screaming and clinging to the safety bar for dear life. They went on the Ferris wheel.

They threw balls at coconuts. They nervously ventured on the Shoot the Chute, Corinne and Wallis not caring that their skirts would be saturated by the time they tottered off it. They recovered their breath on a miniature mountain train ride and finished the afternoon with a sedate ride on a carousel.

"It's been the most wonderful afternoon I can remember," Corinne said, hugging Wallis's arm as they made their way back to the car. "And it's all been thanks to you, Skinny. Henry would never have allowed me to come here without him if it weren't that he knew I wanted to show you a good time and he was too busy to bring us himself."

"Would he have?" Wallis asked as Archie opened the rear door of the Ford for them.

"Would he have what, Skinny darling?"

"Brought us here himself? I just can't imagine Henry on any of the rides—he's far too dignified."

Corinne tucked stray tendrils of blond hair back into her pompadour hairstyle and readjusted her hat. "No, you're right. He wouldn't have come. Museums are more Henry's thing than amusement parks. That's the tricky thing about marrying an older man, Skinny. Your ideas of a good time don't often coincide."

On their return home Henry was waiting for them, and he invited Archie to a predinner cocktail on the bungalow's terrace. The view from its bougainvillea-draped walls led straight down the hill to the officers' compound and then, beyond the compound, to the beach and, in the early-evening light, a sea that was now no longer blue, but glass green.

Henry mixed himself and Archie a brandy and soda and, for Corinne and Wallis, pink gins. Sipping at what was fast becoming her regular predinner cocktail, Wallis kept her eyes on the compound, hoping to see Win Spencer's distinctively wide-shouldered, broad-chested figure. There were lots of naval officers walking in and out through the compound gates, but none of them was Win.

Corinne, unaware of the direction of Wallis's thoughts, sipped her drink, expecting her cousin to begin giving Henry a suitably low-key version of their afternoon at the amusement park, instead of which, twirling her cocktail glass around in her hand, Wallis said, "We saw Lieutenant Allinson on the beach this morning, Henry. He said he was spending the day training recruits in signal and radio work. What is that exactly?"

Corinne groaned and raised her eyes to heaven.

Archie Crosby grinned, more intrigued by Wallis than ever.

Henry smiled broadly and, oblivious of his wife's irritation, embarked on a lecture on the intricacies of signal and radio work.

Wallis followed what she could—which was very little, though she didn't allow Henry to know that. What she intended was to speak to Rob and to get him to explain it in a more simplified manner. She wasn't unintelligent, but the subjects she wanted to learn about were far too like math for her to be able to understand them without a struggle.

But it was a struggle she was going to engage in, for if she'd learned one thing about men, it was that they liked to talk about their jobs, about what interested them. Because she made the effort to do so, it set her out from the crowd and, because she wasn't beautiful or curvaceous like Corinne, anything that set her out from the crowd was worthwhile, no matter what the effort.

Predinner drinks—and sometimes dinner—with various officers became a daily institution, but it was Rob Allinson, Archie Crosby, and Win Spencer whom Henry and Corinne invited most often.

Whenever Wallis was in a room with Win, she was aware of a sexually charged atmosphere between the two of them, but it was an atmosphere Win was careful no one else should be aware of—and one he'd apparently had second thoughts about following through on.

Once, when no one else was in earshot, he'd held her tightly by the wrist and said, "You're a guest in the home of my commanding officer and I have a career to think of. If it weren't for that, Wallis . . ."

The expression in his eyes filled in the words he'd left unsaid, and for days afterward there had been a bruise on her wrist—a bruise that had excited her every time she'd looked at it.

Because Win, Rob, and Archie were best buddies, Wallis nicknamed them "the Gang of Three," and it soon became obvious that she had aroused deep feelings in Rob as well as in Win.

Henry had encouraged the match.

"Lieutenant Allinson is a fine young man, Wallis," he'd said. "Plus, and you can trust me about this, he has a spectacular career ahead of him."

She'd been touched by the fatherly interest he was taking in her, but as she said to Corinne, "I just don't feel romantically inclined toward Rob and know I never will."

"Which is a pity, honey, and I hope it's not because you have hopes where Win is concerned, because if Henry had any such suspicions he would, because of Win's reputation with women, cease inviting him here fast as light."

Wallis remained silent, and Corinne eyed her speculatively. "Win hasn't made a pass at you, has he, Skinny?"

It was impossible to fib, nor did Wallis want to. "Yes," she said, enjoying the look of shock on Corinne's face. "And God willing and the creek don't rise, he'll do so again!"

Occasionally, when a dinner party was in progress, Henry would be called away to attend to an emergency that had arisen, and whenever this happened Wallis noticed a change in

Corinne's attitude toward whatever guests were sitting around the table or enjoying drinks on the terrace. She became much more relaxed and more free in her conversation.

It was on one of these occasions, when Henry had been summoned to attend to a crisis and when the guests were Rob, Archie, and Win, that Win turned to Wallis and said, "Don't you ever get bored with your evening pink gin, Wallis? Would you like me to show you how to make a more exotic cocktail?"

Corinne gave a throaty chuckle. "Please, please show her. A mint julep I can manage, but someone in the house with a little more cocktail expertise would be very welcome."

Win's eyes meaningfully held Wallis's. "Let's go into the house, and if Henry has some crème de violette tucked away, I'll show you how to make an aviator cocktail."

It was the first move he'd made on her since he'd given her to understand it was something he was never going to do, and as she rose to her feet Wallis was weak-kneed with hope and anticipation.

The minute they were in the house and out of sight of everyone he pulled her against him, saying thickly, "This is against my better judgment, Wallis, but what the heck, I can't have anyone else running off with you."

His mouth came down on hers in swift unfumbled contact. It was a demanding, violent kiss, totally unlike John Jasper's kisses and her cousin Henry's kisses.

When at last he raised his head, saying huskily, "Now to cocktail making before anyone becomes suspicious," she felt as if her mouth were as bruised as her wrist had been.

He began taking bottles from the Mustins' cocktail cabinet, saying as he did so, "I need lemons, a sharp knife, and cracked ice."

By the time she returned from the kitchen with all he had

asked for, he had assembled a lineup of crème de violette, London dry gin, maraschino liqueur, cocktail glasses, and a cocktail shaker.

"Now, Wallis, sweetheart," he said. "Watch and learn."

He sliced the lemons and squeezed the juice into a shaker until it was a third full. Then he topped it up with two-thirds gin.

"Time to do your bit," he said to her. "Add two dashes of maraschino and two dashes of crème de violette."

When she had done so, he added a handful of cracked ice. Then he put the top on the shaker and gave it back to her, his hand remaining on top of hers.

There was ownership in his fingers. Utter assurance.

"Okay, Wallis," he said. "Give it a good shake."

Still with his hand over hers, she did so.

When the cocktail was mixed, he said gruffly, "We'd best be getting back. Corinne will wonder what we're up to."

Removing his hand from hers, he took the shaker from her and poured the contents into the glasses through a small sieve.

Then he handed her two glasses to take through to Corinne and Archie. As he did so, his hands were as steady as a rock. Hers, as she took the glasses from him, trembled violently.

They moved toward the French windows leading to the terrace and as they reached them, he said in a low undertone, "I'm going to teach you how to make a different cocktail every time I'm here for drinks and supper—and I'm going to teach you lots of other, far more interesting things, Wallis."

Wallis was sure he was—and she was sure of something else as well. Win Spencer might have the reputation of being the air station's lady-killer, but he was a lady-killer she was going to tame, and once she'd tamed him, she wasn't going to lose him as she'd lost John Jasper. She was going to bind him to her with hoops of steel.

Late that evening, just as she was about to get into bed, Corinne tapped at her door and walked straight in. "Just what happened between you and Win tonight?" she demanded bluntly. "There was so much electricity in the air when the two of you stepped out onto the terrace I thought sparks were going to fly!"

Wallis climbed into bed and hugged her silk-pajamaed knees with her arms. "Win showed me how to make aviators—and if we all have headaches in the morning it will be his fault—and while doing so he made it clear to me that he's fallen for me just as hard as I have fallen for him."

"Dear Lord Almighty!" Corinne sat down heavily on the edge of the bed. "I shall have to tell Henry, Skinny. And when I do, he'll speak to Win and that will be the end of it all."

Wallis hugged her knees a little tighter. "No, you're not going to do that, Corinne. I'm not as innocent about matters of the heart as you think I am. I've already lost someone I loved so much I wanted to marry him—and I thought I'd never get over him. Since meeting Win, I know I can get over him—that I've already done so. That is why Win falling for me is so important to me. If I returned to Baltimore engaged to Win, I wouldn't mind any longer about . . . about the other person being in Baltimore with the girl he married instead of me."

"Oh, sweetie!" Corinne put her arms around her and hugged her tight. "You should have told me you'd had an unhappy love affair. It just never occurred to me. Not when you're still so young. I hate to say this to you, Skinny, but you not only chose wrong the first time around, you've chosen wrong the second time around. Win Spencer isn't the marrying kind. He just likes to fool around a little and have fun—and as long as he does that with married women, it's okay. No one gets hurt. Doing it with you, though, is very different. You risk losing your reputation—and once that happens, all hopes of a suitable marriage fly right out the window."

Wallis pulled away from Corinne and looked her straight in the eyes. "Losing my reputation is the one thing I am never ever going to do, Corinne. Trust me. Win Spencer may not know it yet, but he's finally met his match. Just you wait and see."

There was a blissful intensity of happiness about the next few days that, because of the way they ended, Wallis never forgot. Although it was customary for the officers at Pensacola to work arduous eighteen-hour days, in the week that followed Wallis's cocktail-making lesson there was a miraculous period when the entire Gang of Three was off duty simultaneously. In the late afternoon, and with Henry's permission, they took Corinne and Wallis to a little sun-baked golf course lying halfway between the air station and the town.

It was a course Corinne had visited often, for golf was one of the few leisure interests she and Henry shared.

"It's simple, Skinny," she said teasingly. "You just grip the club so hard your knuckles shine white and then thwack the ball with all your might."

Rob and Archie creased with laughter, and Win shook his head in despair.

"First of all," he said, "you have to know how to stand over the ball properly." He passed a club out of his golf bag over to her and then pushed a tee into the ground with the palm of his hand. "Now what you do, Wallis," he said, placing a golf ball on top of the tee, "is this."

He stood behind her in such close bodily contact as he positioned her hands on the club that Wallis's cheeks flushed scarlet.

Only Corinne noticed.

As far as Rob and Archie were concerned, Win was simply giving Wallis a straightforward, necessary lesson in how to hold a club.

Her attempts to hit the ball had them all in fits of such hilarity that after twenty minutes of tuition, she was relegated to being an onlooker as the others embarked on a serious game.

Strolling across the green in Win and Corinne's wake, Rob said to her in a voice that was, for him, unusually serious, "You do know how much I like you, Wallis, don't you?"

She flashed him a sunny smile, hoping to defer what she anticipated was coming next. "Considering what good friends we all are, I should hope you do, Rob. And the feeling is mutual. Your friendship—and Archie's and Win's—has made my stay at Pensacola far more enjoyable than it would have been otherwise."

He came to a halt, forcing her to do the same.

A light breeze lifted his sandy hair, and his gray eyes were full of intense emotion.

"I don't just like you, Wallis. I love you. I know it sounds corny when we've never even dated—but the reason I've never asked you out on your own is because I was sure Commander Mustin would disapprove."

With all her heart—and purely for his self-esteem—Wallis wanted to tell him that far from disapproving, Henry thought him so honorable a young man that he would have been delighted by the thought of a romance between the two of them. Saying so, though, would make what she was about to say to him even harder for him to accept.

"I don't think our dating would be a good idea, Rob, even if Henry were to approve. I need good friends—and I want you to stay a good friend to me—but when it comes to romance . . ." She hesitated, looking ahead of them to where Win was just about to putt a ball. "When it comes to romance, I've already committed myself elsewhere."

He followed the direction of her gaze, and his face went very still.

"I see," he said. There was no bitterness in his voice, only bleak resignation. "I should have realized . . . I'm sorry I embarrassed you by speaking as I did."

"You didn't embarrass me." She tucked her arm in his. "We're friends, remember?" She let the sassiness that always amused him into her voice. "And remember, Rob, friendships often last for a lifetime, when romances don't."

Later, when Win and Archie were watching Rob take an expert shot, Win said to her and Corinne, "I expect you know Rob has a special mission tomorrow?"

Corinne, who never took any interest in what went on at the air station, shook her head. "What kind of special mission? He's not going to be catapulted from a ship as Henry was, is he?"

Win gave a deep chuckle. "Nothing so dramatic. He's going to attempt an altitude record. It will be interesting. No aviator has reached over ten thousand feet yet."

"But isn't that dangerous?" Wallis knew she sounded like a fool, for nearly everything the pilots did at Pensacola was dangerous. This, though, sounded more dangerous than usual.

"Oh, it's dangerous all right, but if he succeeds he'll get himself into naval history books."

The next morning the entire air station was out in full force to watch the record attempt. Some cadets had even taken the ferry to Santa Rosa Island, from where they thought they would get a better view.

Wallis had no opportunity to speak to Win. He was far too involved in the preparations taking place for Rob's flight.

From a great distance Rob, in flight gear, his helmet already on, his goggles in his hand, shielded his eyes from the sun in order to make them out from the large number of spectators thronging the beach.

"He's seen us!" Wallis began waving wildly. "Look! He's giving us the thumbs-up!"

As the crowd around them saw the gesture, they gave a loud cheer, and then Rob turned away, putting on his goggles and, after a last few words with Win, climbed into the cockpit of his plane.

As the plane bounced and bumped its way across the water and then rose into the air, the excitement of the spectators was palpable. Naval aviation was still in such infancy that every record set was of huge importance.

Rob flew a circle of the bay and then began to climb.

"How high do you think he is now?" Wallis asked Corinne as she shielded her eyes against the sun in order to still see him.

Corinne shook her head, not having a clue.

"About six thousand feet. Nothing extraordinary as yet," one of the mechanics standing close by said.

Against the brilliance of the sun, the fragile-looking plane made another large circle, creeping ever higher as it did so.

The tension in the crowd around her was now getting to Wallis. Initially she'd been feeling only intense excitement. Win had been so laconic yesterday about the test flight that, despite knowing it was dangerous, she'd been no more anxious for Rob's safety than she was any time an officer she knew took to the air.

Now, however, fear was flicking bat's wings at her, and her hands were clutched so tightly together they hurt.

"He must be at the eight-thousand-feet mark now," a man standing next to the mechanic said. "What kind of pressure do you think the struts are beginning to take?"

"It's a Curtiss AH-14. I'd have thought it would be okay for another couple of thousand feet."

Even with binoculars the plane could now barely be seen.

"Please God," Wallis whispered beneath her breath. "Please, *please* let Rob come back safely."

"He will, honey." Corinne's voice held none of its usual careless indifference to events. Instead, it was nearly as taut as her own.

Then, with relief so vast Wallis felt as if her knees were going to give way, it was possible to see the tiny plane again, and this time its long, swooping circles were bringing him closer and closer to the glass-smooth waters of the bay.

When he landed, even though the height he'd reached was still not known, huge cheers went up and then, after a period of tense waiting, Henry Mustin, resplendent in his uniform as commander of the air station, announced through a megaphone, "Lieutenant Allinson has set a naval aviation record with a height reached of 11,975 feet."

The cheers were deafening and, with the news semaphored to Santa Rosa Island, could even be heard from there.

"He's going to do a lap of honor," Corinne said, relief showing in her voice. "Tonight the air station will be afloat with champagne."

Once again the small plane bobbed and bucketed across the water and took to the air. This time Rob made no attempt to fly any higher than was normal, but he did turn inland, flying over the beach and its crowds of spectators.

Leaning out of the cockpit, he waved down to Wallis and Corinne from a height of about 150 feet, then banked, making a turn and heading for Santa Rosa.

"Thank God he achieved what he set out to achieve." Corinne took the binoculars she had been using from around her neck. "A record like this for a hydroplane is going to do his career a world of good."

"Thank God he's safe," Wallis said with deep gratitude for a prayer answered.

Suddenly, above all the victory-laden chatter going on around them, came a distant choking sound that silenced everyone in midsentence.

For a brief second Wallis, not conversant with what different sounds from an engine meant, was bewildered. Then, before her horrified eyes, Rob's plane began to plummet and spin seaward.

All along the entire beach there were gasps of disbelief, shouts of horror, screams.

It was a nosedive so steep nothing could have averted the plane's impact with the sea and its instant disintegration.

As people began running toward the part of the beach nearest the bobbing wreckage, Wallis sank onto her knees. "Oh God," she whispered, tears coursing down her cheeks. "Oh, sweet Christ!"

This time there was no answer to her prayers.

Dimly she was aware of Corinne helping her to her feet; of somehow forcing herself to move in the direction everyone else was moving in; of standing in a grief-stricken stupor on the sand as she watched Rob's lifeless body dragged from the waves.

It was a moment that would be imprinted in her memory for as long as she lived, a moment that gave her a horror of flying she was never to lose—and a moment when she realized that, in loving Win, fear for his safety would now be her daily companion.

Chapter Twelve

The aftermath of Rob Allinson's death subdued Pensacola for weeks. Henry became almost a different man. Dinner parties and cocktails on the bungalow's tiny terrace came to an abrupt end. He had always been less outgoing than his extrovert wife, but his expression became one that was permanently thunderous as he complained bitterly about the lack of safety features in the planes his aviators were required to fly. It was he who had to break the news of Rob's death to his parents, and when he returned from doing so, not even Corinne dared go near him.

There was talk of an inquest. There were endless emergency conferences and telephone calls as an official inquiry was demanded.

As for Win, he withdrew into himself in a way that frightened Wallis. As no dinner or cocktail parties were now being held at the Mustins', they met in other ways. Occasionally they went to the movies together. Sometimes they met openly as a couple at Pensacola's country club. Whenever they did, he was morose and taciturn, his grief for his friend so deep she couldn't penetrate it. To her concern, it was a grief he began to drown in drink. Cocktails, as a leisure activity, were part and parcel of life at Pensacola, but now the only thing Wallis ever smelled on Win's breath was gin, and though he outwardly never showed it, she knew that often when they met he was drunk as a skunk.

"I wouldn't worry about it, honey," Corinne said when Wallis finally expressed her concerns to her. "It's his way of dealing with his grief, and once he's come to terms with that grief, he'll be back to normal. One thing about this tragedy is that Henry now has so many other things on his mind, he's not even blinking at the fact that you and Win have begun spending time together on your own."

It was, Wallis realized, something to be deeply grateful for, but she devoutly wished Henry's acceptance of her and Win's budding romantic relationship hadn't been brought about by tragedy.

As the summer progressed, Henry and Corinne's social life returned to normal; dinner parties and cocktails on the terrace resumed; and Win returned to being his usual self—a man who said little and smiled rarely, but who, when in a good mood, was always good company.

Dating him was nothing at all like dating John Jasper. There was always an edge of danger with Win. Wallis never quite knew what his mood would be—and accepted that this was due to the immense stress of his job. As the senior instructor at Pensacola, he carried a huge burden of responsibility for the safety of his trainees. When accidents occurred—and they occurred regularly—a siren would sound, announcing to the entire air station than an emergency had taken place.

The sound always made Wallis's blood run cold, her fear always that the aviator who had run into trouble was Win.

In September when the siren sounded, it wasn't because

of one of the regular nonfatal accidents, but because the struts in a plane being flown by a twenty-three-year-old officer had loosened and the plane had crashed, killing him instantly.

Hateful as she found the thought of being separated from Win, Wallis craved a few days away from what had become the constant tension of waiting for the crash siren to sound.

"I haven't the slightest desire to be back in Baltimore again, Corinne," she said one evening when they were on their own together, "but I haven't seen my mother in far too long. You don't mind if I go back for a week's visit, do you?"

"Goose! Of course I don't mind. What about the old boy-friend, though? I thought you didn't want to return to Baltimore until you had a whacking great diamond on the third finger of your left hand?"

"I don't, but who knows how long I'll have to wait until Win comes up to scratch? And I shan't make my presence there public. I'll simply spend time with Mama and Aunt Bessie."

"Don't forget your Uncle Sol. Once he knows you're in Baltimore, he's going to want to give you the third degree about life in Florida."

A grin touched the corners of Wallis's mouth. "Don't worry about Uncle Sol, Corinne. I worked out how to handle him years ago—and when it comes to his getting an update about life here in Pensacola, he's going to get a very watered-down version, with the name Earl Winfield Spencer not being mentioned even once."

"Wallis, sweetheart! It's so *good* to see you!"

Both her mother and her aunt were at Baltimore's station to meet her at the train, and as her mother's arms closed around her, Wallis was flooded with guilt for her long absence from home.

"And my, but you look sophisticated, Wallis." Aunt Bessie looked her up and down proudly, liking what she saw. Wallis had never gone in for fripperies on her clothes, and the dress she was wearing, made by Wallis herself, was as far removed from floaty summer chiffon as it was possible to get. The material was navy linen; the tunic, collar, and cuffs were braided in white, worn over a narrow skirt daringly, and very fashionably, calf length. Her little navy hat sported a jaunty matching feather, and her shoes had the highest heels Bessie had ever seen.

Looking at her, Bessie saw what Alice didn't. Wallis had left them a girl and returned a woman—and Bessie's immediate reaction was to wonder as to the identity of the man responsible for the change.

She didn't have to wait long to find out.

Wallis might have had no intention of telling her Uncle Sol about Win—or certainly not until she had a ring on her finger—but she had no such scruples when it came to her mother and her aunt.

An hour later, as the three of them sat around the table in Alice's small apartment, drinking tea and eating slices of the lemon drizzle cake Alice had made to welcome Wallis home, Wallis wiped a crumb from her mouth and, her face radiant, her lavender eyes aglow, said dramatically, "Mama. Aunt Bessie. I have news I simply *have* to tell you. I've fallen in love with the world's most fascinating aviator!"

Bessie, always pragmatic, received the news cautiously, hoping Wallis wasn't going to emulate her mother's heedless impulsiveness when it came to matters of romance.

Alice, romantic to her core, clapped her hands in delight.

"But that's wonderful, Wallis honey." She pushed the cake stand to one side so that she could take hold of Wallis's hands and give them a loving squeeze. "Who is he? Where does his family come from? Has he spoken to Henry about his intentions? What does Corinne think of him?"

"His name is Earl Winfield Spencer. He's twenty-seven, a lieutenant, and he comes from a small town in Kansas."

"If he's eight years older than you are, that's quite a gap in age," Bessie said, leaving the small town in Kansas to one side for the moment but not liking the sound of it.

Alice flared up immediately. "Nonsense, Bessie! Twenty-seven is a perfect age for a young man to think of marriage. Teackle was twenty-six when we married."

"And you were twenty-four. Wallis is only nineteen."

"Well, we're not even engaged yet," Wallis said lightly, before her mother and her aunt could have one of their spectacular differences of opinion. "Though I hope we soon will be. Would you like to see a photograph of him?"

She took a slim leather wallet from her purse and, from behind her newspaper cutting of the Prince of Wales, removed a photograph of Win.

It had been taken when he was in full-dress uniform, and when she handed it to her mother, Alice gave a gasp of admiration.

"Why, Wallis! He's *very* handsome!"

Bessie, who had a lot of trust in the old saw "Handsome is as handsome does," took the photograph from her.

The face that stared up at her from it was certainly arresting. Because he was in full uniform and wearing a cap, she couldn't see his hair, but his eyebrows and mustache were dark enough for her to assume his hair to be black. There was a tough look to his mouth and an intense, arrogant expression in his eyes. He was a young man who obviously thought a great deal of himself, and he reminded Bessie of a cousin on her father's side who had died in his twenties—and Bruce Montague had been something of a bully.

Keeping her thoughts to herself, she handed the photograph back to Wallis. "What about his family, Wallis? You said they were Kansans."

Wallis helped herself to another slice of her mother's delicious lemon drizzle cake. "They are, but Win's father is now a Chicago stockbroker and his family line, like ours, goes back to the early 1600s."

"There now!" Alice said triumphantly to her sister. "Lieutenant Spencer is just as well-born as the Montagues and Warfields, and the only reason we're not familiar with his name is that he isn't a Baltimorean."

Bessie, who had no desire to spoil Wallis's homecoming by continuing to express doubts about the suitability of her new beau, changed the subject by saying out of the blue, "Rosemont has been sold and is going to be turned into a very luxurious hotel."

"Sold?" Wallis left the slice of cake she had just taken untouched on her plate. "But where has the duke gone to live? And what about . . . about . . ." It was so long since she'd said their names aloud, she could scarcely get them past her lips. "What about Pamela and John Jasper? I thought they would be making their home at Rosemont."

Alice flashed Bessie a look of fury. Bringing the former Pamela Denby and John Jasper Bachman into the conversation was the last thing she had expected her usually so-sensible sister to do.

Bessie ignored the look. She wanted Wallis to remember that it wasn't so long since she was head over heels in love with John Jasper, and not to be as impulsive where her new beau was concerned. "The duke has married a Californian and, according to the rumors, is building himself a mansion in the style of a Florentine Renaissance palace on top of a mountain somewhere south of San Francisco."

The shock Wallis had been given was one she was already over. It wasn't as if she were still in love with John Jasper. Win had cured her of those feelings, and she now thought of John Jasper in the light of a youthful first crush.

"So where are Pamela and John Jasper living?" she asked, not distressed by the subject, but interested. "In the very best part of town, I assume?"

Alice's eyes widened. "You mean you don't know that they never even came back to Baltimore to honeymoon? They're still in London—and with that terrible war still going on nearly everywhere in the world but America, I guess that's where they'll have to stay until the world comes to its senses."

Wallis felt relief flood through her. She had no intention of leaving Pensacola to live again in Baltimore, but at least she now knew she could pay visits home without fear of unexpectedly running into either of the newly married Bachmans.

"What do Henry, and the officers serving under him, think about the war, Wallis?" Bessie's kindly face was taut with concern. "I'm so afraid America will get drawn into it. President Wilson is enlarging the army and so, though he *says* America will never get involved, it isn't a very good sign, is it? Do you hear news on the air station that perhaps we don't get?"

Wallis wasn't sure whether she did or not, but as everyone stationed at Pensacola was a military man, the pros and cons of the war were a constant subject of conversation, and she was well versed in what was going on in Europe and the Middle East and Russia. She doubted that her aunt would want to know, though, that every man taking part in those conversations was desperate for America to enter the war so that he could see action and hopefully cover himself with glory.

Not touching on the subject of Pensacola's eagerness to be part of the war, she said, "The news at the moment—at least the news from France—is quite good. The French have dealt a massive blow to the German lines in Champagne, and the British have achieved the same result in Flanders."

Some of the tension left Bessie's face, and Wallis felt no guilt at not adding that Henry thought it likely the positions taken would be speedily retaken, with the stalemate on the Western Front continuing well into the winter.

The next afternoon she paid a visit to her Uncle Sol at his bank downtown. He was so pleased to see her that she felt quite affectionate toward him. Her spirits lifted even more when he told her that her grandmother had left her four thousand dollars in her will and that his own allowance to her would continue as before.

It was as she was walking away from the bank, down sun-dappled Calvert Street, that a familiar voice called out from the other side of the sidewalk, "Wallis Warfield! Don't dare walk on without giving me a few minutes of time!"

Across the street, a very well-dressed Edith Miller was waving furiously in her direction.

Wallis, who had always liked Edith despite the fact that she lacked spirit, waved back and waited while Edith crossed the street toward her.

"No one told me you were back in town." Edith hugged her tight. "Where is it you've been all this while? With relatives in Louisiana? Or was it Florida?"

"Florida."

"Well, you sure look well on all that Florida sun. You just wait till I tell Violet and Mabel that you are back in town. They are both married now—so is Pamela Denby, but I guess you know all about Pamela's marriage to John Jasper Bachman.

Mrs. Bachman—John Jasper's mother—is great friends with my mother, and so I get to hear all the news. They live in London, and because Pamela's mother is married to an earl, they move in the very highest of social circles."

"How very nice for the two of them." Wallis found it hard to sound suitably sincere, but with great difficulty, she managed it. Then she bade Edith a swift good-bye, not wanting to hear another word about Pamela and John Jasper.

Both of them were in her past now. She wasn't in love with John Jasper anymore. She was in love with Win—and when she returned to Pensacola, she was determined to make him even crazier about her—so crazy he would have no option but to make her a proposal of marriage.

Chapter Thirteen

Win's reception of her when she returned was ardent. He'd missed her—and he made her well aware that he had missed her badly.

Wallis was jubilant. Though her nerves had been so shredded by Rob's death and the all-too-regular sound of the bloodcurdling crash siren that she'd needed to escape the air station for a little while, she had done so with a fear she had barely allowed herself to acknowledge: the fear that on her return, Win would have transferred his affections to someone else.

That he hadn't filled her with supreme confidence in the hold she now believed she had over him.

There was only one fly in the ointment.

Win's relationships had previously nearly always been with married women. He was a man accustomed to full sexual intimacy—an intimacy Wallis had no intention of providing. To give way to the temptation—a temptation so strong she often had to exert all her considerable willpower in order to resist it—would, she knew, ensure they would never walk down the aisle together.

It was Win who solved the problem by showing her how, in the dark of the movie theater where most of their kissing and cuddling took place, she could, by sliding her hand into his pants and allowing him to guide her hand, satisfy him.

She found doing as he asked—and the stifled grunting noises he then made and that she had to cover by coughing as hard as she could—both exciting and bizarre. She had never been afraid of being daring, and being so now was all part and parcel of her campaign to bind Win to her forever—and she was also determined to perfect her new ability so that Win would get more pleasure from it than anyone else had ever given him.

Other kinds of lessons also continued. Whenever he was a guest at the Mustins', which was regularly, he kept the promise he had made to teach her how to make a great variety of cocktails.

She spent Christmas in Baltimore with her mother and Aunt Bessie, and by then she could make a White Lion, a brandy smash, a Golden Slipper, a whiskey julep, and an applejack sour, as well as a good half dozen other cocktails.

The problem was ingredients. Between them, her mother and aunt could rustle up bourbon whiskey, gin, rum (though not Santa Cruz rum, which Win insisted was the only possible sort for White Lions), Madeira wine, a bottle of maraschino, raspberry syrup, and lemons and limes.

A gentleman friend of her mother's obligingly bought Santa Cruz rum, Yellow Chartreuse, curaçao, crème de violette, and cider brandy for the applejack.

It was, the friend in question said when the holidays were over, the best Christmas he had ever had, or ever expected to have.

For a Christmas present, Win gave Wallis a bottle of heliotrope perfume. It wasn't what she wanted. She wanted a ring. She gave him a silver-plated money clip engraved with his initials. She didn't care for the perfume but wore it—and hoped that something more to her liking would come her way later in the year.

In January it was Archie Crosby who took her to one side for a private word, rather as Rob Allinson had done shortly before he had been killed.

This time, as it was now well accepted she was Win's girl, she didn't expect a declaration of love from Archie, but neither did she expect what came.

"I don't want you to get upset at what I'm goin' to say, Wallis," he said, his homely face looking desperately uncomfortable. "I like you far too much to want to upset you, but it's something I've wanted to say for a long time, and I just hoped time would take care of things and that I wouldn't have to say it."

Wallis stared at him in bewilderment. "You're not making a lick of sense, Archie."

Archie shifted his feet uncomfortably and then said bluntly, "It's you and Win, Wallis. I'd just rather you weren't getting so heavily involved with him. He's not the sort of guy you need."

Wallis's bewilderment changed to amusement. It hadn't occurred to her that Archie wanted to step into Win's shoes where she was concerned, and he had so little chance of doing so she found it funny.

Keeping a straight face with difficulty, she said lightly, "Please don't worry about Win and me, Archie. The two of us are just swell together—and you're wrong in thinking he isn't the guy for me. He is *exactly* the kind of guy for me."

Instead of letting the subject drop, Archie stubbornly held his ground. "You only see one side of Win, Wallis, because when he's with you he's always out having a good time and enjoying himself."

"Well, of course he is!" Wallis's amusement was fast fading, and she was beginning to get cross. "What's wrong with that?

You wouldn't want him to be miserable when he was out with me, would you?"

"No, of course I wouldn't. I just want you to know that isn't the real Win Spencer. Please don't get me wrong about what I'm about to say, Wallis. I like Win. Hell, as a buddy and in a tight corner he's the best there is. But he's the moodiest guy you're ever likely to meet, and I know that's a side of him you've never seen."

Wallis shrugged her shoulders. "So what? Everyone gets moody at times."

Archie gritted his teeth and then said, "When Win gets moody, he gets violent. Especially when he's had too much to drink."

Wallis's amusement returned. She knew that when the men stationed at Pensacola wanted to let rip, they didn't do it at the country club, but visited the bars in town. If Win, as an officer, had had occasion to break up the brawls his trainee pilots no doubt often got into, she didn't mind one little bit. That Win was so obviously a tough guy, not to be messed with, was one of his main attractions for her.

Seeing her uncaring reaction, Archie looked as if he were steeling himself to say a great deal more. Bored with the subject, Wallis didn't let him. Tucking her arm into his, just as she had done with Rob, she said firmly, "No more talk about Win, Archie. I don't need to hear it. Let's talk about Lieutenant Johnson's young single sister-in-law who is visiting at the moment. She's in her early twenties—just the right age for you—and a glorious redhead. Now, are you going to move in on her fast or let some other clown beat you to it?"

The subject always uppermost on everyone's mind was the Great War, which, in the spring of 1916, because of the main belligerents' vast empires, seemed to involve every country on earth except America.

"And all President Wilson suggests is that when the war is over, a league of nations should be formed in order to keep the world at peace and that the United States would be willing to join such an international organization!" Henry said explosively over the dinner table one evening when no guests were present. "How, in the name of all that is holy, is the world ever to be at peace without America pitching in? The Allies need our help so badly, it's pitiful."

"Well, we are helping in every way we can, honey." Corinne hated any talk of the war, and she certainly hated the thought of American boys going into battle on foreign fields. "We've cut all our economic ties to Germany, and we're supplying Britain with practically everything she asks for."

"Except fighting men." Henry rarely spoke harshly to Corinne, but he did so now.

To Wallis's surprise, Corinne didn't back down. Instead she said spiritedly, "That's because the war is a European thing which doesn't involve America. It's only spread over such a large part of the world because the countries involved have empires which most Americans—including me—don't approve of!"

Slapping her napkin down on the table, she rose to her feet, her eyes flashing angry sparks. "Remember what another of our presidents said, Henry? America would neither interfere with existing European colonies nor meddle in the internal concerns of European countries. Well, what was good enough for President Monroe is good enough for me—and I bet a dime to a dollar that it's good enough for the wives and the mothers of the men who, if America entered the war, would be the ones doing the fighting!"

And on that note she swept out of the dining room, leaving both Henry and Wallis staring after her openmouthed—Henry because Corinne had never before ever spoken to him in such a fashion in front of another person, and Wallis because she'd never before known Corinne to voice an opinion on a serious subject, and the fact that Corinne even knew about the Monroe Doctrine, let alone could quote it, was a surprise so startling as to be almost unbelievable.

Later, when she thought about it again in the privacy of her bedroom, she wondered if Corinne had heard someone else recently quote it. She also wondered who the person in question could be, and, for the first time, if her beautiful, golden-haired cousin was secretly spending time with an officer on the air station and wasn't being entirely faithful to her much older husband.

Spring at Pensacola was a time of great beauty. In the Mustins' yard a riot of jasmine clothed the fencing in impenetrable tangles of scented yellow blossoms. On the terrace, decorative pots overflowed with red and gold zinnias, delicate sky blue larkspur and, Wallis's favorite, pale lilac anemones with deep indigo hearts.

In the countryside, pink dogwood was everywhere, and it seemed to Wallis as if the entire state of Florida were perfumed by the heady white blossom of the orange trees.

Her relationship with Win was growing more intense week by week and month by month and, impatient as she was for a proposal of marriage, she now had no doubt that there would be one.

When cocktail-making lessons at the Mustins' began to pall—and when only Corinne and other guests were present and Henry was absent—Win began teaching her how to play poker. Considering how abysmal she was at math, under Win's expert tutelage she took to the card game like a duck to water. What thrilled her most about it was that the money she won wasn't money that came from an allowance paid by Uncle Sol, or money that came from the small amount her grandmother had left her. It was money gained by her own skill and her own efforts, and the fact that she soon became known on the air station as a poker player to be reckoned with amused Win vastly.

Something that didn't amuse him was when men paid her admiring attention. When they did so, his reaction was always instant and fierce—and on one occasion it was so fierce it scared the life out of her.

It happened on an evening when, instead of dining at the country club, they had gone into Pensacola for dinner.

A man in his early twenties, in civilian clothing, had wolf-whistled her as she and Win had been about to walk into a restaurant.

Wallis hadn't found the attention in the least insulting, but Win's reaction had been instantaneous.

With an ugly blasphemy he had spun around, closing the distance between himself and the man in swift strides. Couples strolling nearby, sensing that an altercation was imminent, had speedily scattered.

Wallis, sensing the same thing, had run after Win, shouting that the wolf whistle didn't matter.

Ignoring her, he had seized hold of the man and then, to her horror, had grabbed him by the throat and slammed his head hard against a wall.

With blood trickling down his face, the man had buckled at the knees, slumping into a huddle at Win's feet.

Women had screamed. A crowd had gathered. Win, not

troubling to see how badly injured his victim was, had brushed his uniform down and then pushed his way through the spectators to where Wallis was standing, almost senseless with shock.

All he had said, as he had taken hold of her arm, was, "We have a table booked for eight. We need to be on our way."

"But shouldn't we call for an ambulance?" She hadn't been able to see if the man was still so dazed as to be semiconscious because of the crowd that had gathered around him, but even if he wasn't she knew he must still be bleeding.

"If he needs one, someone will call one."

He'd propelled her into the restaurant and had ordered himself a stiff brandy. Minutes later the police had arrived and Wallis had been forced to admire the way Win dealt with the situation. He had made it sound as if his reaction to her having been insulted was the only possible reaction for a man of honor. While the questioning was going on, news had come that the man was on his feet and the police officers, mindful of the gold stripes on Win's uniformed shoulders, had shared a drink with them and left.

From then on she had appreciated just what it was Archie had tried to tell her. Win had a hair-trigger temper, and people crossed him, or insulted her, at their peril.

In June her conscience about not having seen her mother since Christmas pricked her so strongly she could no longer ignore it.

"I'm goin' to have to make another trip to Baltimore, sweetheart," she said to Win, hoping, because he had missed her so much the last time she had paid a visit home, that he wouldn't make a scene about it.

For a moment she thought he was going to do so. His thick black eyebrows drew together in the way they did whenever things weren't going the way he wanted.

"I won't be gone for long, darling. A couple of weeks at most."

"I'm due leave." His eyebrows were still pulled together, but this time she knew it wasn't because his mood had suddenly changed, but because he was thinking. "How about I come with you to Baltimore? Meet your folks?"

Wallis's inner elation knew no bounds. Win would never have made such a suggestion if he weren't intending asking her to marry him. If she showed that elation, though, he would know the reason for it, and she had enough savvy to know that displays of overeagerness for marriage had scuppered many an imminent proposal.

"That would be great," she said, with the same intonation in her voice as if he had suggested they go to Electric Park or Santa Rosa. "Mama loves socializing with new people, and Aunt Bessie will be thrilled to be told all about airplanes from the only aviator she is ever likely to meet."

To her mother and her aunt she wrote that she would be visiting soon—and that Win would be accompanying her—but that they were on no account to behave as if she and Win were already engaged.

> . . . *because it could just possibly spoil everything and I do so*
> *want to become a Navy wife. Just treat him as my beau—*
> *which he most definitely is—and leave all talk of marriage*
> *till after he has finally popped the question.*

Her big decision, as the date of their trip drew nearer, was whether to introduce Win to her Uncle Sol, because she had absolutely no idea what her uncle's reaction would be. Would he be pleased that she had a beau who, in traveling from Florida in order to meet her family, obviously had marriage in mind and who came from a family able to trace its lineage back to the 1600s—and who, into the bargain, was a naval officer holding a very responsible position at Pensacola? Or would he be furious that she was considering marriage to a man who was neither a member of Baltimore high society nor conspicuously wealthy?

In the end, she knew the introduction would have to be made. A sudden announcement, made from Pensacola, that she wished to become engaged to someone he had never met would mean he would, on principle, instantly oppose the match.

When the day came for them to travel north, they did so by train, sitting in a compartment, her hand tightly held in his. There were other people in the compartment, but their hand-holding couldn't be frowned on, because she was wearing a pair of kid gloves and so no one could tell that there were no rings on the third finger of her left hand.

As the train steamed out of Florida into Georgia, Wallis was sure that this was exactly how it would be for the two of them when, after their wedding, they left by train for their honeymoon destination. Which would be where?

Their wedding would, quite obviously, take place in Baltimore. Unless there were very unusual circumstances, brides always married in their hometown and at the church where they had been confirmed and at which their family were regular attendees, which, in her case, was the Episcopalian Christ Church.

She knew Win was longing to say loving words to her, but with other people in the compartment it was impossible, and he had to content himself with occasionally giving her hand a very hard, meaningful squeeze. Meanwhile, she continued to daydream and make plans.

Whom would she have as her matron of honor and her bridesmaids, and how many bridesmaids would she have? Too many, eight or ten, would be seen as being vulgar. Six would be the most acceptable number.

She knew from Win that he had a sister, Ethel. Even if Ethel was plain as a pot, she would most definitely have to be invited to be a bridesmaid. Her cousin Lelia would also, without question, be another, and, if she had a Montague cousin as a bridesmaid, then she would have to drum up a Warfield cousin. She would also need to have a couple of friends from her Oldfields days, Alice Maud Van Rensselaer or Phoebe Schermerhorn or Ellen Yuille.

As the train sped out of Georgia and into South Carolina, she mused on the difficulty of the fact that, prestigious as their families were, none of them were Baltimoreans. A bridesmaid from a high-society Baltimore family was an essential. The answer came to her instantly. Edith Miller. Edith could be her fourth bridesmaid, Ellen Yuille her fifth bridesmaid, and then she'd have to choose between Alice Maud and Phoebe as her sixth bridesmaid.

"Another half hour and we'll be in North Carolina," Win said, breaking in on her thoughts.

This time it was she who squeezed his hand. Win was a striking-looking man and, in his naval uniform, would attract all eyes when they got off the train in Baltimore.

She took little notice of the distinctive countryside of North Carolina, for she was now thinking about her chief bridesmaid or, if the person she decided on was married, her matron of honor. From age six until a little over a year ago, there had never been any question as to who that would be.

It would be Pamela.

It was a promise they had made to each other as schoolgirls and which she had never remotely imagined would ever be broken.

It had been well and truly broken now, though.

As the train continued to rattle nearer and nearer to Maryland, she wondered whom Pamela had had as her chief bridesmaid or matron of honor when she had married John Jasper.

Though she didn't give any outer indication of it, her mood changed from the happiness she always felt when with Win to one of bleak desolation. The rawness of her hurt over John Jasper had long since gone, but the hurt over Pamela's betrayal and the consequences of that betrayal—the shattering of a friendship she had thought would last for life—was as deep as ever.

Corinne, of course, would be delighted to act as her matron of honor.

Much as she loved Corinne, though, it would not be the same as having Pamela as her matron of honor.

Dimly she was aware of Win saying they were crossing into Maryland.

This time she didn't merely squeeze his hand. She stretched her free hand across her body so that she could squeeze hold of his arm. She wasn't going to let thoughts of Pamela spoil the joy she was taking in planning her wedding. She was going to put Pamela firmly where she belonged. In her past.

"When the train approaches the station, can we lower the window and lean out?" she asked. "Mama and Aunt Bessie will be there to meet us, and they'll love it if they can see us waving toward them as the train nears the platform."

"We can do anything you want to do, Wallis." He patted her hand lovingly.

Wallis's heart soared.

When Win was in a good mood, no man on earth could compare with him, and she was going to allow no one—not Uncle Sol, not another woman, no one—to take him away from her.

Just as she had predicted, her mother and Aunt Bessie were on the station platform, awaiting their arrival in a frenzy of excitement.

"Oh, Wallis darlin'! It's so *good* to see you!" Her mother laughed and cried at the same time, hugging her tightly.

"It's wonderful to see you too, Mama, but I must make introductions."

Slightly embarrassed by what she hoped Win wouldn't think was her mother's lack of good manners, Wallis laughingly extricated herself from her mother's arms and said, "Mother, may I introduce you to Lieutenant Earl Winfield Spencer? Win, my mother, Mrs. Alice Rasin."

She then introduced Win to her Aunt Bessie and, as he shook hands with them, he treated them to one of his rare broad smiles. "Please call me Win," he said. "As your daughter's beau, I'd much appreciate it."

Alice's eyelashes fluttered as if she were a girl of sixteen, not a twice-widowed matron in her mid-forties.

Bessie felt herself relaxing. She had been very much afraid that because his photograph had reminded her so much of the distant cousin who had been such a bully, she would take an immediate dislike to Wallis's beau. True, Earl Winfield Spencer had an almost overwhelmingly strong personality—and certainly didn't look the kind of man anyone would choose to antagonize—but as they had shaken hands, no sixth-sense alarm bells had rung.

As they left the station and piled into her Ford motorcar, she decided to give Win the benefit of the doubt, for it was obvious by the glances he kept shooting across to Wallis that he was deeply in love with her. As for Wallis . . . Bessie had never seen her niece looking so radiant.

She let out the Ford's clutch and put her foot on the accelerator pedal. A wedding in the family would be a welcome change from funerals. She only hoped Win would pass Solomon Warfield's scrutiny as easily as he had passed hers.

. . .

Win's initial meeting with Sol took place—at Sol's request—in his office at the Continental Trust Bank on the corner of Baltimore Street and Calvert Street.

Win already knew that Solomon Warfield was the president of the bank. Though he said nothing as they walked through the marble-floored foyer, Wallis knew he was deeply impressed.

Her uncle's office was even more opulent than the foyer, but Win, broad shouldered, ramrod straight, and in full naval uniform, looked splendidly at ease in it. It was Wallis who was nervous.

As Sol rose from behind his massive Biedermeier desk and rounded it to meet them, her voice was unsteady as she said, "Uncle Sol, may I introduce to you Lieutenant Earl Winfield Spencer? Win, my uncle, Mr. Solomon Warfield."

Sol and Win shook hands, Win unflinchingly holding Sol's piercing gaze.

It was Sol, not Win, who looked away first.

That her uncle was unused to people not being intimidated by him was obvious to Wallis, if not to Win.

"I understand you serve under Commander Henry Mustin, a relative of Wallis's mother's family, Lieutenant Spencer?" Sol said, impressed by the magnetic forcefulness of Win's personality.

"I have that honor, sir. Commander Mustin has, as you are probably aware, set many personal naval air records, and it would be impossible to serve under a more respected or gifted man."

"I'm pleased to hear that, Lieutenant. Won't the two of you please take seats?"

As they did so, he retreated to the far side of his desk and sat down, leaning back in his dark green, leather-padded office chair as if about to embark on a lengthy interrogation.

To Wallis's vast relief, no lengthy interrogation followed.

Sol merely asked the provenance of Win's family, showing satisfaction when he learned that it was both old and respectable.

He wound up the meeting by saying gruffly, "As Wallis's late father's eldest brother, I would like to do as he undoubtedly would have, Lieutenant Spencer, and invite you to dine at the family home on Preston Street."

"It is an invitation I am most happy to accept, sir."

Unspoken, but accepted by all three of them, was that the invitation—and the acceptance of it—was the prelude to a public announcement of an engagement.

As they left the building, Wallis wondered if Win would propose to her while they were in Baltimore, or would he wait another few weeks until it was her birthday? A sparkling diamond engagement ring would be the best birthday present ever.

Neither Bessie nor Alice was invited to the intimate dinner that took place a few days later. Wanting to keep in Solomon Warfield's good books, Win, exerting all his willpower, drank sparingly: a predinner dry sherry, a couple of glasses of wine with the meal, and a companionable whiskey and soda with Sol when all three had retired to the drawing room.

It all went so smoothly that Wallis wanted to punch the air with glee. Next day, however, she was brought down to earth with a nerve-racking bump when she received a message from her uncle, saying he would like to meet with her alone on East Preston Street before she and Lieutenant Spencer returned to Pensacola.

"It will be about my allowance," she said to Win. "Uncle Sol often increases it about this time of year, and when he does, he always likes to have a little time with me on my own."

It was a blatant lie, but one Win accepted unquestioningly.

This time when she entered the Preston Street house, Wallis had to steel herself to do so. Since her grandmother's death the house no longer felt like a family home of any kind to her—and she was dreading hearing the reason her uncle had summoned her.

He received her in the drawing room, dressed for his office at the bank in a two-button frock coat, his top hat on a chair nearby.

"Please be seated, Wallis," he said, making no move to sit down himself.

Wallis did as asked, clasping her hands tightly together in her lap to calm her nerves.

"Lieutenant Spencer," Sol said without preamble. "I take it you are expecting a proposal of marriage from him?"

Wallis's throat felt too tight to speak, so she nodded.

"When he does so, I take it that you intend to accept?"

Again Wallis nodded.

Something changed in her uncle's stiff, abrupt manner. To Wallis's surprise he crossed the room to sit down beside her and, to her even greater surprise, unclasped her hands, taking one of them in his.

"Teackle was my favorite brother, and, that being the case, I am fonder of you than you may imagine, Wallis. When it comes to a proposed marriage between you and Lieutenant Spencer, I feel I must point out certain things to you."

Wallis sucked in a deep, steadying breath.

"The first is that it would not be the kind of marriage I had anticipated for you. You are a Warfield of Baltimore. I had hoped you would marry into a prestigious Baltimore family. The second is that I don't think you have quite taken on board just what it means to be the wife of a naval officer. Lieutenant Spencer can be posted anywhere at any time. Where you live will be up to the Navy. It will not be something you—or Lieutenant Spencer—will be able to make a choice about. Thirdly, on your marriage my allowance to you will cease, and naval pay is notoriously low. For all these reasons, when Lieutenant Spencer makes his proposal—which from his manner at dinner yesterday evening I would judge to be very soon—I want you to think very carefully before accepting it."

Slowly, and with great relief, Wallis let out her breath. The interview hadn't been as bad as she had feared. She certainly didn't want a member of Baltimore's high society as a husband—not when John Jasper and Pamela would most likely be moving back to Baltimore as soon as the war was over and the Atlantic again safe. Nor did she mind the thought of being moved at a moment's notice from one naval station to another. She had always made friends easily, and she liked variety in her life. Win might even be posted abroad, and, as far as she was concerned, that would be even better.

What wouldn't be better was her uncle's intention to stop her allowance, but she wasn't going to let that prospect deter her from marrying Win. Naval pay couldn't possibly be as low as her uncle seemed to think. Win always had plenty of money, and he was Pensacola's senior instructor. One day he would no doubt be a distinguished naval commander, like Henry.

"Thank you Uncle Sol, for being so concerned about my welfare," she said, giving him her very best smile as she rose to feet. "I appreciate all you have said, and I promise I will bear it all in mind when—and if—Win proposes."

Her last sentence was a lie as blatant as the one she had told Win earlier. She hadn't the slightest intention of bearing anything he had said in mind—nor did she think there was going to be any "if" about Win proposing to her.

Her instincts proved her right.

A month after they returned to the air station, they enjoyed one of their regular dates at the movies. Before the lights were down, Win suddenly said he'd changed his mind about wanting to see the movie, and that he wanted to go to the country club instead.

Whatever Win wanted was fine by Wallis, but when they reached the country club he made no effort to enter it. The darkened porch was deserted, and he sat her down on one of its many cane chairs.

Then he did what she had been praying he would do almost from the first moment she had met him.

He went down on one knee in front of her.

"I love you, Wallis," he said thickly. "I've never met anyone quite like you before—and I don't expect I ever shall. I never thought I'd say this to anyone, but will you marry me, Wallis? You do love me enough to marry me, don't you?"

The tears of joy that filled her eyes were his answer.

The next second she was in his arms, and his mouth was on hers, hard and passionate and urgent.

When at last he raised his head from hers, he said, "We need to set a wedding date soon, Wallis. I can't stand not having you for much longer. It's driving me mad."

"We have to get engaged first," she said lovingly. "And even an engagement needs time to be arranged beforehand."

He looked down at her in dismay. "You mean we can't just announce our engagement tomorrow?"

"Of course we can't!" There was happy amusement in her voice. "Notices announcing it have to be put in the Baltimore papers. A grand party has to be arranged. Everything has to be done very properly and correctly."

"Goddamn it!" There was despair, not anger, in his voice. "Then what kinda time scale are we running to, Wallis?"

Wallis did some quick calculations. Desperate as she was to marry Win, she didn't want any Baltimore gossip about the engagement and wedding being such a rush job that it indicated a baby was on the way.

"It's July now. We could have our engagement in September and the wedding in November. That's not too long to wait, darling. Is it?"

From the intimate pressure of his body against hers, it was obvious that even a few minutes was going to be too long to wait—and they were on the darkened porch of the country club, not in the dark of the movie theater.

She slid one of her arms from around his neck and, with her palm pressed close against his chest, ran it slowly and seductively downward.

And then farther downward.

There were always ways of managing things when a girl was adventurous—as she was.

As Win gave a gasp, followed by a deep groan, she wondered what style of wedding gown to have. Marrying in November meant it would be a winter wedding. Perhaps white velvet? And perhaps, to turn winter into an asset, they could marry late in the day when it was dark and the church would be lit only by candles.

It would be the kind of wedding that would ensure she would once again be known for being different; the kind of wedding that no one attending it would ever forget.

Chapter Fourteen

But where,

Alice wrote to her,

*is the money going to come from for your trousseau and
wedding gown and wedding breakfast? I'm poor as a church
mouse and Bessie hasn't any money to spare.*

I'm going to speak with Uncle Sol,

Wallis wrote back in the distinctive green ink she had begun
to favor.

*He didn't give me a debutante ball. The least he can do is put
his hand in his pocket for my wedding.*

Alice's response was terse.

I wouldn't count on it, sweetheart.

Wallis *was* counting on it and, for the moment, wasn't worrying about it. Over the years she had learned how to manage her Uncle Sol in ways her mother—perhaps because of Sol's feelings for her, and her antipathy toward him—had never succeeded in doing. As far as Wallis was concerned, Solomon Warfield would pay for her wedding—and it would be a Baltimore extravaganza.

Of more immediate concern was her trip to Highland Park, a wealthy suburb of Chicago where the Spencer family lived. Arrangements were made that, in order for there to be no gossip, she would not stay at the Spencer home but would stay in Chicago itself as a guest of friends of her Aunt Bessie's.

Once again she and Win found themselves seated on a train, hand in hand and traveling north, this time not to Maryland, but to Illinois.

"Your family, Win," she asked, overcome by nervous tension. "Will I like them? Will they like me?"

A little too late it was occurring to her that as Win never spoke about his family, she knew next to nothing about them.

"Sure they'll like you, Wallis. You're a Warfield from Baltimore. How could they not?"

It had never previously occurred to Wallis that the Warfield name was known and respected in Chicago, but then she remembered that one of the few things Win had told her about his father was that he was a member of the Chicago Stock Exchange. Her Uncle Sol's financial business dealings were vast and, taking into account his position as president of the Continental Trust Bank, it wasn't too surprising that the Spencers were aware of the Warfield family's standing within Baltimore society.

She breathed a little sigh of relief and then was overcome by anxiety again. "But will I like them, Win? They won't find me too breezy and forward, will they?"

He gave a bark of laughter. "Hell, no. Your breeziness and forwardness is just what my family needs to liven them up."

In a way she found his answer reassuring, but it was also disquieting. What sort of family were the Spencers that they needed livening up?

She soon found out.

It took only one evening meal with them for her to realize that Win's family were like no family she had ever previously met—or ever wanted to meet—and that it was no wonder Win spoke about them so little.

Though they went through the formal motions of welcoming her, there was little warmth in the welcome—and that also applied to the welcome Win received. If he was aware of the rather odd reaction to his home visit, Win showed no signs of it. Unlike his parents and his siblings, he was cheery and talkative, making it quite clear that the visit was one preparatory to the announcement of an engagement between himself and Wallis.

"You must understand Miss Warfield, that we as a family will not be able to render financial assistance to the two of you," Win's mousy-looking mother said when they were seated around the family dining table and before any other subject had been raised.

Wallis was just about to reply that as far as the wedding was concerned, everything would be traditionally done and, as the bride, her family would be attending to all the expenses of it, when she realized that Mrs. Spencer was speaking about not rendering them financial assistance *ever*.

"All our sons live on their own pay," her future father-in-law said brusquely, saving her from having to make any kind of an answer to his wife. "Navy pay isn't up to much, but it will just have to see the two of you through."

It was the second time Wallis had been told that Navy pay wasn't up to much, and though she had discounted the remark the first time it had been made, she was now feeling the beginnings of real anxiety.

Win eased them a little when, while passing a dish of peas across the table to the brother nearest to him in age, Dumaresque, he said with no concern at all in his voice, "There's no need to worry about our financial future. We're never going to need family help of any kind."

Wallis was pleased to hear it, as, she was sure, were his parents.

In whatever situation as a newcomer she had been placed, Wallis had always made firm fast friends immediately. It was a talent that was innate and, when she had stepped into the large-frame turreted Spencer home, she had done so expecting that at least where Win's sister was concerned, a friendship would be struck up almost instantly.

Looking at Ethel across the table, keeping a polite smile firmly on her face as she did so, Wallis knew instantly that, for the first time, her talent for making friends had deserted her, for Ethel barely acknowledged her presence.

Though they were dining as a family, there was no feeling of family cohesiveness. It was almost as if the Spencers had all met each other for the first time. The other odd thing about them was how dissimilar in looks they were to each other. Dumaresque was Nordically blond. Egbert was dark—but far too skinny to fall into Win's brand of to-die-for good looks. The youngest brother, Frederick, looked more like a foreigner than an American. As for Ethel . . . she most certainly wasn't pretty and, as she had no sparkle or conversation either, seemed destined for spinsterhood.

Somehow, thanks to Win's attitude of behaving as if his family were nice and normal and close-knit, Wallis survived the evening, grateful that she wasn't staying under the Spencer roof, but would be returning to Chicago and her Aunt Bessie's friends.

On the ride back into the city neither she nor Win brought up the subject of how odd the evening had been. She, because she didn't want to hurt Win's feelings by letting him know how uncomfortable she had been made to feel. What Win's reasons for remaining silent on the subject were she didn't know, but she assumed it was all part and parcel of the way he had coped when there. The habit of behaving as if nothing at all were amiss was too deeply ingrained for him to break it, even with her.

It was something she understood. In a very different way, she, too, had always felt an outsider within the Warfield side of her family—and had developed her own ways of coping with that feeling. Now she saw quite clearly that where family was concerned, Win, too, was an outsider. It was yet another bond between them. Bonds that were, she was sure, becoming bonds of steel.

On their return to Pensacola she found a letter from Uncle Sol waiting for her.

You will need to be in Baltimore for the public announcement of your engagement,

he had written, once he had finished with the preliminaries of asking about her visit to the Spencers,

and the social niceties in such a situation require that you remain in Baltimore until the wedding takes place.

He went on to say much more. About how fortuitous it was that, like the Warfield family, Win was an Episcopalian. That he seemed like a man who had both feet firmly on the ground. A remark that, as Win was an aviator, amused Wallis vastly despite the earlier unwelcome part of his letter.

Looking at that unwelcome first part once again, her amusement died. Baltimore high society was a stiff and unforgiving world, and she knew that her uncle was right. She couldn't possibly remain at Pensacola during the eight weeks between her engagement announcement in the *Baltimore Sun* and her wedding. There would be engagement celebration luncheons and dinners to attend—all of which would be reported on the *Baltimore Sun*'s society page. Not only that, there was her trousseau to be bought and her wedding gown to be made, neither of which could be achieved in a small town like Pensacola.

From September to November was only eight weeks and, as a Navy wife, both she and Win would have to become accustomed to such separations—some of which would undoubtedly be of a much longer duration. Preparing for an extravaganza wedding in just a few short weeks would mean she'd be so busy the time would simply fly past.

All she had to do now was to break the news to Win. His face had immediately darkened, as she had known it would. Before he could go into a black mood over the necessity of her remaining in Baltimore between their engagement and wedding, she said soothingly, "Baltimore is Baltimore, darling. The conventions have to be followed. And aren't you glad you're getting a high-society Baltimorean for a wife, rather than someone for whom such things don't matter?"

He was. He had never been shy about letting her know that it was her impeccable background that, in the beginning of their relationship, had made her stand out from the crowd. Because he was an ambitious Navy officer, when it came to marriage the right kind of wife was of vital importance, and Win knew that Wallis's confident social skills and cultured elegance were going to be great assets to him.

The loving kisses and cuddles Wallis so enjoyed followed his agreement that it was essential she remain in Baltimore after their engagement had taken place and until they married.

For the next few weeks, until she left Pensacola for Baltimore, Wallis's head was a whirl of wedding plans. Velvet was an unheard-of material for a wedding gown—even a winter wedding gown—but velvet was what she was determined to have. As to the candles that would so romantically light the church, plain tallow ones simply would not do. She would have to speak to the minister, the Reverend Edwin Barnes Niver, and arrange for the candles to be of scented beeswax. Then there were the flowers to think about: the flowers for her bridesmaids' bouquets and her bouquet and the flowers that would decorate the church. And what color would her bridesmaids' gowns be? And what style? There was so much to think about and to decide that she felt dizzy, and, though she didn't let Win know, she couldn't wait for the day when she would return to Baltimore and be able to make proper preparations for what she was sure was going to be the biggest day of her life.

In mid-September she once again made the train journey north, this time unaccompanied by Win, who was so devastated at the prospect of being parted from her that at one point, as she mounted the steps of the train, she thought he was going to drag her down from them and forcibly take her back to the air station.

Minutes later, safely aboard, she leaned out the carriage window, and, holding on to her hat with one hand, she waved with the other until Win—and Pensacola's dusty little station—were lost to sight.

Then she seated herself in a corner of the carriage, opened

her purse, took out a notebook and pencil, and, impervious to the passing countryside, began making lists.

"Your Uncle Sol has taken care of the engagement announcements," Alice said to her, delighted to have Wallis back home for the next eight weeks. "They will appear in all the Baltimore newspapers at the end of the week, September sixteenth—and the wedding date, November eighth, is to be included. Now the first thing we have to do is to sort out your trousseau and wedding gown—and how they're going to be paid for."

"No, it isn't, Mama. The first thing I have to do is to formally invite the cousins and friends I've chosen to be my bridesmaids. Then I have to see Uncle Sol."

"Better you than me, honey," Alice said with deep feeling. "The times I've had to go cap in hand to that old goat are more than I care to remember—and all too often I came away with either an empty cap or one that was only half full!"

Wallis had no intention of visiting Uncle Sol at the Continental Trust Bank. Their meeting would take place at the Warfield family home on East Preston Street to remind her uncle—if he so needed it—that she was a Warfield and that her wedding was a public family Warfield occasion and had to be funded as such.

"The expenses you speak of, Wallis. What are they?"

Even though he was in the comfort of his home, Sol was dressed formally in a frock coat. Wallis couldn't help wondering if he was determined to be the last man in Baltimore to own one.

"My wedding gown, the matron of honor's gown, the bridesmaids' gowns, and, of course, their hats. With your permission I would like to wear my grandmother's tulle veil, so no expense there."

Solomon Warfield made a sound in his throat that could have meant anything.

Undeterred, Wallis continued counting off the things that would need paying for. "Flowers. Flowers for the bridal bouquets and for the church and for the decoration of the tables at the wedding breakfast."

"Where," Sol asked, "do you intend this wedding breakfast to take place?"

"I thought the Stafford Hotel. It has a magnificent ballroom and a wonderful orchestra."

She paused in order for her uncle to make comment on her choice of venue, but as he did not, she continued with her list of wedding expenses.

"Then there is the honeymoon. I thought the Greenbrier Hotel at White Sulphur Springs. West Virginia countryside is so beautiful in the fall when all the trees are brilliant orange and sizzling red."

Uncle Sol had taken up his usual stance in front of the fireplace, his legs apart, his hands clasped behind his back.

"Dare I ask, Wallis, if you have calculated the financial total of all these expenses? You didn't mention champagne, but I am assuming champagne will play a large part at the wedding breakfast, nor did you mention the number of guests you intend to invite."

"I guess the expenses will come to about two or three thousand dollars, Uncle Sol, perhaps more. As to the guests, the number, including relatives from both sides of both families—and friends—comes to just over three hundred."

He regarded her steadily from beneath bushy grizzled eyebrows.

"Who, Wallis, do you intend to take the place of your late father and to give you away?"

"Why, you, Uncle Sol." That he would do so was so obvious,

his question startled her. There wasn't, after all, anyone else who could give her away. Her other two Warfield uncles were Sol's younger brothers and had never played the part in her life that Sol had.

Seated on the slippery leather sofa she had never been comfortable on, even as a child, she waited for him to return to the nub of their conversation: the amount he was going to pony up for a grand Warfield wedding.

The silence between seemed to stretch into the eternities.

At last he said, "Firstly, I shall of course walk you down the aisle in Christ Church in order to give you away in marriage to Lieutenant Spencer. For me not to do so would, as I am pleased to see that you agree, be unthinkable. Secondly, I shall not be paying so much as a dollar toward the expense of a wedding as lavish as the one you are planning. Such a wedding would have been suitable if you had been marrying into a distinguished, socially prominent Baltimore family of the kind I had always hoped to see you marry into. As it is, your wedding to Lieutenant Spencer should be a tastefully small affair—especially as it is a time of war—with far fewer bridesmaids, a more modest venue for the wedding breakfast, and a guest list of no more than eighty."

Wallis could hardly believe her ears. Keeping control of her temper with difficulty, she rose to her feet and walked toward him.

Not until there were only inches left between them did she come to a halt.

Looking him straight in the eyes, she said tightly, "Uncle Sol, I am a Warfield. I am entitled to the kind of a wedding that Warfields are accustomed to having—to the kind of wedding my father would have given me if he were alive."

Sol eyeballed her straight back. "Teackle isn't alive," he snapped back with a crudity so shocking she felt as if she had been slapped across the face. "And on the subject of the financing of your wedding to Lieutenant Spencer I have said my last word. A small wedding and I will pick up the tab. The kind of wedding you are planning—and you are on your own, Wallis. I shall pay for nothing."

Of all the many unpleasant encounters she'd had with her uncle over the years, this was most definitely the worst. That he meant to stand by every word he'd said was so obvious she didn't even attempt to argue with him—and she sure as hell wasn't going to plead.

She said through gritted teeth, "I'm going to have a wedding worthy of a Warfield—and if I have to pay for it myself, I shall do so out of the legacy my grandmother left me."

Sol sucked in his breath. "That money was not left to you to spend frivolously. That *any* money left to you would be spent in such a manner was something your grandmother always suspected—which is why her legacy to you, in comparison to her total estate, was so small. You have too much Montague in you for your own good. Like your mother, when it comes to financial matters you haven't a lick of sense."

Wallis's eyes narrowed into slits as she fought the urge to push him backward into the fireplace. Instead she hissed, "I thank God every day I have some Montague mixed in with my Warfield blood, and when this wedding is over I shall never set foot in Thirty-Four East Preston Street ever again!"

Spinning around on her heels, she stormed away from him, out of the room, out of the house, slamming the door behind her so hard it was a miracle it didn't rock on its foundations.

White-hot fury roared through her veins as she made her way back to her mother's. She was going to have the wedding she had planned. A grand extravaganza of a wedding. And one day Solomon Warfield was going to eat the words he had so cruelly spoken to her, for, much as she loved her mother,

Wallis knew she had too much Warfield blood in her to be like her mother.

Iron determination followed hard on the heels of her fury. The day would come when her Uncle Sol would eat his heart out to be publicly recognized as being her relation—and when it did, she wouldn't even give a nod in his direction.

Chapter Fifteen

In her letter to Win, telling him of how exciting it was waiting for the Baltimore papers to publish the news of their engagement, she didn't mention one word of Sol's refusal to pony up for the costs of the wedding.

Win didn't know about the legacy she had received from her grandmother—not because she had been keeping the money secret from him, but because nothing financial had ever been spoken of between them. The question of finance was most definitely not a romantic topic, and the first time it had vulgarly been brought into a conversation had been by his parents—and Win had immediately indicated how out of line he had felt it to be.

That she was paying for their extravaganza wedding was a secret she was determined to keep.

Alice Maud Van Rensselaer was unable to accept her invitation to be a bridesmaid, as she was to be a bridesmaid at a cousin's wedding on the same day, but when Wallis resorted to Phoebe Schermerhorn instead, Phoebe accepted the invitation ecstatically. Ellen Yuille was also happy to accept, and it went without saying that both the cousins she had invited to be bridesmaids and Win's sister also accepted with alacrity. To be the attention of all eyes as a bridesmaid at a Baltimore high-society wedding was an opportunity not to be missed.

Edith, when she received her invitation, was completely bowled over.

"It was so unexpected, Wallis," she said, her plain face rosy with pleasure when they met up for lunch at the Baltimore Country Club. "I never realized you thought of me as being such a close friend. What is your fiancé like? Is he very handsome?"

Wallis opened her purse and took out a photograph of Win in his full-dress naval uniform. "Judge for yourself," she said proudly, handing Edith the photograph across the dining table.

Edith looked down at Win's devil-may-care image, and the roses in her cheeks deepened. "Oh, he's *very* handsome, Wallis." There was wistful envy in her voice. "I wish I had a beau like that. I did, once, but he came from a family with no money, and Papa said he was a fortune hunter and that he would prove it. He told my beau that he could marry me, but that on our marriage he would cut me off without a penny."

"And?" Wallis asked, already knowing what the outcome of the story would be.

"And Papa was right." Edith looked so sad Wallis was tempted to rise from the table and put her arms around her. "My beau lost interest in me immediately."

For the first time in her life it occurred to Wallis that there could be drawbacks to being as wealthy an heiress as Edith. How, if you were one day to inherit a vast fortune, could you be sure that the person you loved and who said he wished to marry you really loved you in return, or just wanted to marry you for your money?

Edith handed her the photograph back, and as Wallis slid it into her purse, the newspaper clipping of Edward, Prince of Wales, fell out onto the table.

Edith looked startled. "Do you still keep the prince as a pinup, Wallis? I know you did at Oldfields, but I'm surprised Lieutenant Spencer allows you to still do so."

Wallis shot her a sunny smile. "Lieutenant Spencer is *not* privy to the contents of my purse, Edith." She smoothed the cutting and looked down at it. "Truth to tell, I don't know why I still keep it. Habit, I guess."

Edith, putting her sadness behind her, giggled. "You'll never guess what I have in my purse."

The purse was lizard skin with a solid gold clip fastener. Edith snapped the clip open, took out a photograph, and laid it by the side of Wallis's newspaper cutting.

It was the most sensational photograph of Prince Edward that Wallis had ever seen and had obviously been mass-produced for a royalty-loving public. He was in full-dress uniform—though of what regiment Wallis couldn't tell. Gold braid was draped in double loops on the right-hand side of his chest; on the left was pinned a row of glittering medals with two huge medals of a different kind pinned beneath them, both of which looked to be diamond encrusted. In his right hand the headgear he carried looked like a huge black fur ball, and his left hand was resting on a sword.

In the posed, studio shot, the prince wasn't looking directly toward the camera. His glossy fair hair was parted crisply on the left, and his fine-boned face was as resolute as if he were about to ride into battle to slay a dragon and rescue a princess.

As they looked at the photograph, not only was Edith no longer thinking of the beau who hadn't wanted her when he'd known she would come to him penniless, but Wallis was no longer thinking of Win.

"The headgear he is holding is called a busby and is made of bearskin," Edith said helpfully. "And I have another photograph just like this at home, so if you would like this one, I can give it to you if you would like."

"That's very kind of you, Edith. I would like that very much."

In all the years she had known Edith, Edith had never surprised her in any way, but she was surprising her now. She picked up the photograph. "How is it you are suddenly so knowledgeable, Edith? And how come you have not only one photograph, but two?"

"Pamela sent me them." Ignorant that John Jasper had once been Wallis's beau, Edith never had the slightest compunction about bringing Pamela's name into their conversations. "The prince is serving in France at the moment, but when he is home on leave Pamela and John Jasper are part of the circle of friends he likes to spend time with. She knows what an admirer of his I am."

Wallis let out a long, slow breath. Hearing John Jasper's name linked with Pamela's no longer had any power to hurt. She no longer even ever thought about him.

Pamela, though, was different.

She missed the very special kind of affinity she and Pamela had shared. She was close to Corinne—but there were things she could never tell Corinne, such as the way she had kept Win sexually satisfied throughout their courtship. As for telling Edith such a thing . . . The very thought made her want to burst into laughter. Edith would be so deeply shocked; she'd probably die of it.

She could have told Pamela, though.

She had always been able to tell Pamela anything.

Edith broke into her thoughts, saying with a dreamy expression in her pale blue eyes, "I wonder who Prince Edward will marry? I suppose it will be a princess. Princes always marry princesses, don't they?"

Wallis didn't know but presumed they did. She'd certainly never heard of one who hadn't. She liked the thought of it, though. It would be so much more romantic—just like the story of Cinderella.

"Pamela once had high hopes of becoming the Princess of Wales," she said, tucking the photograph safely in her purse. "She was certain that if she could meet him socially often enough, he would fall for her big-time."

"Oh, but that must have been ages ago—when we were at Oldfields. She won't have thoughts like those now she's a happily married lady with a darling little baby boy."

Not wanting to put thoughts she knew Edith would find distressing into her head, Wallis merely smiled and changed the subject to that of bridesmaids' dresses and bouquets. Inwardly, though, she was wondering just how Pamela must be feeling, having lots of opportunities to charm Prince Edward. She couldn't now become the Princess of Wales, but she could become the Prince of Wales's mistress. Knowing Pamela as she did, Wallis was certain that if given such an opportunity, Pamela would take it—John Jasper or no John Jasper.

The thought didn't fill her with outrage. Instead she felt something close to amusement. John Jasper didn't deserve a faithful wife when he had treated her, Wallis, so badly. As for Pamela—Pamela had always been outrageous. It was one of the reasons Wallis had always found her such good company.

She suddenly became aware of Edith asking, "When is it I have to go to Madame Lucile's for my first fitting, Wallis?"

"In a month's time. Phoebe is coming down from New York that weekend and Ellen is coming up from Virginia, as is my cousin Lelia, so you will all be being fitted for your bridesmaids' gowns at the same time."

Every week was now huge fun—though Wallis took care

not to sound as if it were when writing to Win, in case he got the impression that he wasn't being very badly missed. It was hard, though, to pine, when there were so many family celebratory luncheons and dinners to attend.

Many were luncheons and dinners she had known would be given for her, but some, such as a lifelong friend of her mother's, Mrs. Aubrey Edmunds King, giving a splendid luncheon for her, and Aunt Bessie's sister-in-law, Emily McLane Merryman, giving a luncheon for her at Gerar, her home near Cockeysville, were quite unexpected.

Montague relations held parties for her in Virginia; distant Warfield relations held a party for her in Washington, D.C.; and Edith's mother hosted a lavish tea for her at the country club. Along with all the celebrations came wedding presents. An elaborate silver cutlery service and a matching silver tea service, all in the Repoussé pattern of the famous Kirk silverworks; an engraved large silver fruit bowl; china settings and crystal; exquisite bed linens and table linens and so many vases and ornate picture frames Wallis couldn't imagine how they would all fit into the small bungalow at Pensacola that she and Win would be moving into.

There were many fittings for her bridal gown, and the fittings for the bridesmaids' gowns turned into a giggly, girly affair with Madame Lucile, Wallis's dressmaker of choice, dispensing champagne—though only when the gowns were once again safely under wraps.

The only thing marring Wallis's happiness was that Win, in one of his many letters to her, wrote that despite President Wilson's being recently reelected on the slogan *He Kept Us Out of War,* Henry, and every other high-ranking military man, believed that war was coming.

It was a prospect that elated Win.

It didn't elate Wallis.

She didn't want to marry and possibly become a war widow in the space of a year or so.

"Don't look on the black side, honey," Alice said chidingly when she confessed her fears to her. "If President Wilson says we're not going to war, we're not going to war—and even if we did, there'll be no one can look after himself better in a tight corner than Win. He'll be here soon for the wedding and you're just goin' to look the most beautiful bride that ever walked down an aisle."

In the late afternoon of November 8, Wallis stood perfectly still as her mother and Corinne slid her wedding gown over her head. The white velvet and the pointed bodice encrusted with seed pearls gave the gown a lyrically lovely medieval look.

"Now for Grandmother Warfield's tulle veil," Alice said, so overcome by how beautiful her daughter looked that tears glistened on her eyelashes.

With infinite care the veil, attached to a delicate coronet of orange blossoms, was secured to Wallis's glossily dark hair.

Her bridesmaids, already dressed and carrying their bouquets, crowded into the room to look at her.

"It's a gown fit for a queen." Phoebe wasn't being merely flattering; she meant every word. The gown, with its court train falling from Wallis's shoulders, most definitely had a royal look about it, helped enormously by the regal way her friend effortlessly held herself.

"Here's your bouquet, Skinny." Corinne handed her her wedding bouquet of white orchids and lilies of the valley.

"It's five o'clock, honey." Alice wiped away the tears of happiness and pride that were threatening to fall. "Only an hour to go. Win's friends will already be escorting family and friends into the pews."

"All the ushers are naval flight officers," Edith whispered to Phoebe. "And they will all be in full-dress uniform."

Phoebe gave a shiver of delight. With war the topic of the moment, men in military uniform had taken on extra glamour. Being as fabulously rich an heiress as she was, her parents would never allow her to marry a naval air officer, but she was determined to have one as a secret beau.

As her bridesmaids crowded around her dressing table to primp and preen for the last time, Wallis, anxious about a host of details her bridesmaids didn't have to worry about, said to Alice: "I hope the church flowers are arranged just as I asked. Aunt Bessie has checked them, hasn't she?"

"She surely has, and she says they are magnificent. The altar is banked with Annunciation lilies, just as you insisted on, and there are bowers and sprays of white chrysanthemums decorating the aisles and every pew. Bessie says the scent is glorious."

"It's time we were goin'." The prompt came from Corinne. "Your Uncle Sol is waiting for you downstairs and getting mighty fidgety."

"You are quite certain about this, honey, aren't you," her mother whispered to her as the bridesmaids crowded out of the room and down the stairs. "Because if you've any doubts and want to call it off, both Aunt Bessie and I will stand full square behind you—not that we think you should be calling it off," she added hastily. "We both think Win the most charming man imaginable."

Wallis kissed her on the cheek. "Don't worry, Mama. I don't have any doubts. Not a single one."

Her mother and Aunt Bessie left for the church first, followed by the bridesmaids.

Sol, grim-faced, offered her his arm.

Having determined to let nothing of the bad feeling that now existed between them show publicly and spoil what she was determined was going to be a perfect day, Wallis slid her free hand into the crook of his arm and, holding her lavish bouquet in her other hand, walked with him out of the house to the horse-drawn carriage waiting for them.

Insanely, her last thought as she stepped into the candlelit church wasn't about whether Win would be standing at the foot of the altar waiting for her, or whether she would be able to make her responses correctly, or whether her voice would be so choked with emotion that she wouldn't be able to be heard, but of how much she wished Pamela were waiting inside the church to share her big moment with her.

Instead, as the organ struck up the first chords of the wedding march, it was Corinne who led her bridesmaids down the aisle in front of her to where Win was waiting, flanked by Dumaresque, who was acting as his best man.

Before their families and friends and the crème de la crème of Baltimore high society, they exchanged their vows, and Win, his eyes burning hers in a way that made her blush, slipped a plain gold band onto the third finger of her left hand.

Wallis was certain that at that moment, there wasn't a happier woman in the entire world.

As they walked back down the aisle together, returning joyful smiles every step of the way, she saw the *Baltimore Sun*'s high-society columnist busily taking notes and knew that a lengthy—and very detailed and admiring—account of her wedding would be in one of the forthcoming issues.

"Oh, my! Isn't this just magnificent!" she heard Corinne say to the world at large as they exited the church to find Win's fellow officers ceremonially lined up, their swords raised and crossed for them to walk beneath.

After that came a storm of rice and rose petals, and then Wallis stepped into the white satin-lined wedding carriage that was to take her and Win to the Stafford Hotel where, despite her Uncle Sol's stern disapproval, their lavish wedding reception was to be held.

Win's hand gripped hers tightly. "How does it feel to be a married lady, Mrs. Earl Winfield Spencer?" he asked as everyone they passed on the sidewalks waved and, whether they knew them or not, shouted out good wishes.

"It feels blissful, Win. Nothing could be better than this. Nothing at all."

He flashed her a dazzling white smile. "Wait until tonight, Mrs. Spencer. Then you'll see how blissful things can really be."

Between her thighs she felt damp heat. She was looking forward to the night with far more eagerness than she knew was proper. However, maidenly modesty had been cast to the winds months ago when Win had first guided her hand below the waistband of his trousers. Pretending to it now would be downright foolishness, and she was quite sure that though Win wanted a virginal bride—and was getting one—he didn't want a bashful one. *Bashful* was a word not in her vocabulary. What she was, though, was curious—and very, very expectant.

The reception was being held in the Stafford's magnificent ballroom, and as she and Win entered there was a roar of thunderous applause from their guests and the orchestra struck up with a waltz.

Laughing with happiness, Wallis handed her bouquet to Corinne and allowed Win to lead her out into the middle of the floor. Then, as the applause continued, the two of them circled the ballroom in each other's arms to the sumptuous strains of a Strauss waltz.

It was the gayest and merriest of wedding receptions. Win's naval friends lent the occasion extra glamour. Phoebe captured the handsomest of the officers for a beau within minutes of the dancing starting and looked as though she intended to be a very naughty girl before the night was over.

When it came to the cutting of her multitiered wedding cake, she and Win did it with a sword, and when it came to the champagne toasts, there were so many of them Wallis knew that if she wasn't very careful she would become tipsy.

Win certainly became tipsy and, by the end of the evening, was drunk—though Wallis doubted very much if many other people would be aware of it. Win was skilled at keeping an outwardly steady appearance when heavily under the influence of alcohol. It was a requirement he said was a necessity in a naval air officer.

Finally it was time for her to change out of her wedding gown and into her elegant French blue going-away dress. She threw her wedding bouquet into her sea of guests, where it was caught by one of her old school friends and then, through yet another storm of rose petals, left the Stafford Hotel with Win for the Shoreham Hotel in Washington, D.C., where they were to spend their wedding night.

Once in the car, Win put a hand immediately on her breast, and then, even before beginning to fondle her, fell against her, eyes closed.

Acutely aware of the chauffeur's interest, Wallis felt only relief.

There would be enough time for fondling—and much more—once they were in the privacy of their hotel bedroom.

The distance from Baltimore to Washington, D.C., was short, which was why they had chosen it for their first-night destination. In the morning they would start their honeymoon by driving to White Sulphur Springs and its famous Greenbrier Hotel.

As their car drew up at the Shoreham, Wallis gently shook Win's shoulder to rouse him. "Win, darling. We've arrived. We're at the hotel."

He came to instantly, and again she knew his ability to do

so from a drunken stupor must have come from long practice. Amused, she stepped from the car, slid her hand into the crook of his arm, and, as bellboys took care of their luggage, walked into the hotel lobby to proudly sign her married name in the hotel register.

The room they had been allocated wasn't the bridal suite. It was the Greenbrier that would be producing that luxury. It was, though, a very tastefully decorated room with an enormously big and high brass-headed double bed.

"At last," Win, said, unbuttoning his white naval jacket and throwing it carelessly over the nearest chair. He drew her toward him and slowly began unbuttoning the river of buttons on her going-away dress.

"I've waited so long for this moment, Wallis." His eyes were hot, his voice thick with desire. "So very, very long."

So had Wallis, but she didn't think it was something a bride should blatantly admit.

"I love you, Win." Her voice was soft and husky as her dress fell to her waist, leaving her high small breasts covered only by a flimsy lace-edged camisole.

The room was seductively lit by antique oil lamps, and the flickering light cast her body in a soft glow as he slid down first one camisole strap, then the other.

For a long time he looked at her, and then he lowered his head, taking first one pale pink nipple into his mouth, sucking on it and rolling it around with his tongue, then doing the same with the other.

Wallis gasped. Kissing and cuddling had previously always aroused her, but now she felt as if a bolt of electricity had shot through her, traveling straight down to her vagina.

When Win finally raised his head, he said, his voice no longer thick only with desire, but slurred by the liberal amount of champagne and spirits he had drunk, "Take the rest of your clothes off, Wallis. I want you now. Straightaway. I don't want to waste another moment."

Neither did Wallis. Without even first taking her honeymoon negligée from her suitcase, she stepped out of her dress and took off the rest of her underclothes. At the other side of the bed Win unsteadily scrambled out of his dress shirt, his trousers, his underwear.

They both tumbled into the flock-mattressed bed at the same time, hurtling into each other's arms.

Wallis was well aware of what was to happen next, but had no idea of how it would feel. With excitement at boiling point and with an urgent delicious ache between her legs, she returned Win's passionate kisses and then, as he rolled on top of her and she opened her legs to accommodate him, he did what he had done in the car.

He passed out.

"Win?" His dead weight was so heavy she could hardly breathe. "Win! Wake up, darling. Please!"

A snore was her only reply.

With great difficulty she eased herself from beneath him.

Then, as his snoring became ever more deep and rhythmic, she moved a little away from him, folding her arms behind her head and looking up at the ceiling.

This wasn't the way she had anticipated spending her wedding night, but she reckoned that after a score of champagne toasts, it was probably the way nine out of ten brides spent it.

She closed her eyes. Tomorrow night would be different.

Tomorrow night they would be at White Sulphur Springs in their bridal suite.

Tomorrow night Win would be romantic and tender and everything would be utterly, utterly perfect.

Chapter Sixteen

The train journey to White Sulphur Springs was idyllic. For most of the way they had a compartment entirely to themselves, and Win kissed and cuddled her in a way that set all her senses on fire in anticipation of the coming evening.

The wooded Allegheny Mountains were at their best in the fall, and the higher the train climbed into West Virginia, the more spectacular the scenery became, the late-autumn leaves a constantly shifting panorama of red and orange and gold.

The Greenbrier was a luxurious hotel in a prime position, but the minute they entered it Wallis knew that, because of the time of year, they were going to be among only a handful of guests. November was not a favorite month for vacationing.

She squeezed Win's hand lovingly. They hadn't come to the Greenbrier to socialize, and the fewer guests there were, the more privacy they would have.

When the bellboy had deposited their luggage in their room and had closed the door behind him, Win's handsome tip in his pocket, Wallis let out a deep satisfied sigh. "It's a splendid room, Win. The bed is even bigger than the one we had last night at the Shoreham."

Win wasn't listening to her. He was looking down at a notice that lay beneath the glass top of their dressing table.

"Goddamn it!" he said explosively, "West Virginia is a dry state! The hotel doesn't sell liquor!"

Although Wallis enjoyed predinner cocktails, they weren't a necessity to her, and Win's outraged indignation amused her.

"Then we're just going to have to manage without, darling," she said, walking up behind him and sliding her arms lovingly around his waist.

He whipped around, thrusting her away from him so violently that she stumbled, saving herself from falling only by catching hold of the back of a chair.

"We're like hell going to manage without!" His face was flushed with rage. "Don't bother unpacking. We're not staying."

Wallis's head reeled as she gripped tight hold of the chair. "But Win, darling . . . We *have* to stay. You must be able to get a drink of something somewhere."

He didn't bother replying to her. Instead he strode to where their suitcases had been deposited and, seizing hold of the one that was his, yanked it up onto the bed, vicious anger in every line of his body.

Wallis had never before been the object of male anger bordering on violence. Uncle Sol had often been angry, but he had never given physical vent to it. As for her late stepfather, she couldn't remember Mr. Rasin uttering even a cross word.

She ran her tongue across her bottom lip nervously as Win began rifling through his suitcase, tossing clothes left and right onto the bed. Common sense told her that in the mood he was in she should be afraid of him, but she wasn't afraid.

She was too stunned by shock to be afraid.

It was as if, in the space of half a second, she'd stepped from one world into another, one that was entirely different and horrifyingly unwelcome.

"Ah!" Triumphantly Win retrieved a hip flask from the bottom of his case. Unscrewing the top of it, he took a deep swallow and then turned toward her, his good mood restored. "There's enough gin here to get up to flying speed till I can find another source of supply."

Dazedly Wallis eased her grip on the back of the chair. It was as if the ugly scene of a few seconds ago had never taken place. Had it, perhaps, simply been occasioned by honeymoon nerves? Had Win wanted to be shored up by a little alcohol before taking her to bed for the first time? It wasn't something she had previously thought even slightly likely, but she found the idea of her courageous aviator husband being a little shy on the first night of his honeymoon endearing.

When he put the flask down and opened his arms, she walked across the room and straight into them.

"We need to change and go down to dinner, Wallis," he said, his mouth against her hair. "The sooner we've dined, the sooner we'll be back here."

It was reasoning that made complete sense, and with her honeymoon mood fully restored, Wallis changed into one of the glamorous new gowns that formed part of her extensive trousseau.

All through dinner her buoyant mood persisted. Everything was back on keel again; everything was going to be just as she had imagined it would be.

The first dent in her renewed confidence came when they reentered their bridal suite to find a bottle wrapped in brown paper waiting for Win on the nightstand.

He tore the paper off and she saw that it was a bottle of gin.

He gave her a wink. "A little cash given to the right person will always produce liquor in a dry state, Wallis. Every waiter worth his salt has his own bootlegger—and this looks like pretty good stuff."

He unscrewed the cap and took a deep swallow, and then, happy with the bottle's contents, he wiped his mouth with the back of his hand.

Remembering what the result of the champagne toasts had been the previous day, Wallis felt her tummy muscles tighten.

Remaining virginal on the first night of married life was one thing. Remaining virginal for two nights did not, to her, seem like a good idea.

"Let's go to bed, darling," she said, willing him to put the cap back on the bottle.

He took another drink and then turned off the gaslights so that the room was lit only by moonlight. This time when she had undressed, Wallis slid the cream silk, lace-edged night-dress she had bought especially for her wedding night over her head.

When Win lay down beside her, he was stark naked with a strong erection. Having become familiar with the feel of his private parts over the long months of their courtship, the sight of him naked wasn't the unnerving experience it would other-wise have been. Fleetingly she wondered how less forward brides dealt with the shock of seeing their husbands naked for the first time. As Win's mouth closed on hers, it occurred to her that they probably never did see their husbands naked; that all lovemaking, perhaps lifelong, took place in rooms not only devoid of artificial light but devoid of moonlight as well.

"I love you, Wallis." Win's voice was hoarse and urgent. "Not being able to have you has been driving me crazy for months." His face was now buried in her neck, his fingers in places she had never previously allowed.

What in imagination she had thought would be excitingly erotic was, in reality, decidedly uncomfortable.

Telling him so would, she knew, not be a very good idea.

Parting her legs, he tried to enter her.

Wallis dug her nails into her palms and shut her eyes tight against the pain.

The sensation she had waited so long for, the sensation when he would slide inside her, never came.

"Goddamn it, Wallis!" The frustrated anger that had been in his voice when he had discovered the hotel didn't serve alcohol was back in full measure. "You must have a hymen like a brick wall!"

Bewildered, disappointed, and hurting like hell, Wallis tried to keep control of the situation. "Try again, darling. It really doesn't hurt that much, and I want you so badly, darling. Truly I do."

Win did try again—so forcefully Wallis had to bite the back of her hand to prevent herself from screaming.

Win didn't have any experience with virgins, but he did know when something was wrong. When a man had a hard-on like an iron bar, a normal hymen was no real barrier to it. Which meant there was nothing normal about the difficulty he was meeting with.

The language he used in his frustration was language Wallis had never heard used before. As he rolled angrily away from her, tears of hysteria began building up in her throat.

"What's wrong, Win? Why can't we do it? What can I do to help?"

It was a problem that in the immediate present Win had only one answer for.

"I'm going to get out of bed and you're going to kneel down in front of me and instead of using your hand, you're going to take me in your mouth. D'you understand?"

Numb with pain and an overwhelming sense of failure, Wallis nodded and clumsily did as he asked.

With his hands heavy on the top of her head in order to keep her head forced down, it wasn't romantic or tender and it was a long, long way from being perfect.

For the rest of their honeymoon, though, it was what she had to resort to, for no matter how often Win tried to relieve her of her virginity, she was as much a virgin when she returned to Pensacola as she had been when she had left it.

The only person she could talk with about the problem was her mother—and the only advice Alice felt able to give her was to go to a doctor.

It was something Wallis simply couldn't bring herself to do. She didn't want a doctor at Pensacola knowing about her shameful intimate secret, nor did she want a Baltimore doctor knowing about it. The only doctor she was prepared to see was one who didn't know her and whom she could see under another name—and how that could be arranged she didn't know.

Outwardly, of course, both she and Win behaved as if there were nothing at all wrong with their marriage. In reality, there was so much wrong with it, Wallis often locked herself in the bathroom and, huddled on the floor with her hands over her face, wept with sheer misery.

Win's two main failings were failings she now knew he'd always had—and about which both Rob and Archie, without being disloyal to Win, had tried to warn her. He drank far more than she had ever suspected, and he didn't have only a quick-fire temper—he had a violent temper. Under normal circumstances both defects would have been bad enough. As it was, the sexual difficulties they were encountering in their marriage meant that both his drinking and his temper were growing more and more out of control.

He shouted at her for the least little thing. He jeered at her that she wasn't a proper woman—but he didn't lose his interest in her as a woman. In a bizarre way, his inability to possess her only made him want her more—and there was only ever one outcome. It was one that Wallis—out of sheer necessity—was becoming extremely proficient at.

Win had always been violently jealous, but now his rage wasn't aroused only if he thought anyone was flirting with her; it was also aroused if he thought she was flirting—and whenever he mistakenly thought she was, he became physically abusive toward her.

Her arms and upper body were marked by bruises she grew expert at hiding.

"Not my face, Win!" she would plead whenever he succumbed to violent, frustrated rage and hit out at her. "Please, not my face!"

Well aware of how fast gossip would spread on the air station if Wallis began appearing in public with black eyes and a split lip, Win took care not to land any of his punches where the result would be visible. After all, he had his career to think about. Wallis was a relative by marriage of Commander Mustin's, and he knew that if there were no visible signs of his abuse, Mustin would never know what took place in the privacy of his and Wallis's home, for if Wallis had one quality in massive abundance, it was her pride.

As far as the world was concerned, he knew she was determined their marriage would be seen as being a success, which, bizarrely, in many ways it was, for she soon had the reputation for giving the best dinner parties on the air station and was certainly the liveliest and most popular hostess Pensacola had.

In part this was because Wallis couldn't help being lively and good fun. As a Montague, being so was in her blood and in her bones. Social success was also compensation for her miserable failure to be a proper wife to Win. The knowledge that she wasn't enabled her to understand the violence that had become a standard part of their life together. It was simply something she had to put up with and accept. There was no other alternative.

By early 1917 her life as a Navy wife had settled into a well-established routine. Though the bungalow she and Win had been allocated was small—so small it could have fitted easily into the drawing room at 34 East Preston Street—it was also pretty. On a little verandah that looked out over a glorious view of the bay, scented roses and oleanders grew in tubs. Inside, every wall was painted white. It was the very first thing Wallis had insisted on having done. The gay chintz curtains at the windows were curtains she had made herself, and though the bungalow was too small for live-in household help, household help was cheap on the air station and, like every other wife living there, she had both a cook and a maid.

There was a strict rule on the base that no pilot was allowed to drink on the days he was scheduled to fly. Wallis was well aware that Win—and several other aviators—broke this rule by toasting the flag before a flight, having another to "boost their courage," and a third to "settle them down," but at least they never risked getting noticeably drunk, and when Win wasn't drunk, he tended not to be so violent.

Saturday nights were when he always let his hair down, doing so at the only nightspot Pensacola possessed: the San Carlos Hotel.

"You're a lucky woman, Skinny," Corinne said to her one evening as they and other friends were grouped around one of the tables and Win, having grabbed a cane and a straw boater that weren't his, was fronting the orchestra as an impromptu song-and-dance man. "Win is such a live wire. He must be great fun to live with."

Wallis did what she always did on such occasions. She

laughed agreement, grateful that Corinne didn't suspect that fun, where she and Win were concerned, was in very short supply.

"Another huge intake of cadets is coming in tomorrow," Win said to her one morning in early February. "How the hell I'm expected to get them all up and running as pilots in the necessary time, I sure as hell don't know. It's going to be a physical impossibility."

Wallis was pinning her hair into its habitual glossy chignon. She paused in what she was doing. "What do you mean by 'in the necessary time,' Win?"

Win shrugged himself into his uniform jacket and began buttoning it up. "Before America declares itself to be at war. Haven't you noticed how fast things are changing on the base? When you first came here there were only a handful of officers. Now there are fifty-eight officers and over four hundred enlisted men, with more arriving on every train."

He gave her a kiss on the cheek. "Don't forget we're due at Brad and Fidelia Rainey's this evening for a game of poker."

At times like this Wallis could imagine them as a normal, happily married couple. They were moments she treasured.

As she walked him to the front door, he said, "By the way, word is Henry is being transferred to Washington to be executive officer of the USS *North Dakota*. If he is, Corinne will be going with him."

When the door had closed behind him, Wallis leaned against it, her eyes closed.

If Corinne were to leave Pensacola, she would lose the best friend she had there. Worse, if war was declared, there was no telling where Win would be sent on active service. Wherever he was sent, what would then happen to her? Would she be expected to remain at Pensacola, or would the Navy expect her to return to her family home in Baltimore for the duration of the hostilities? If they did, she wouldn't be able to do so.

Uncle Sol would most certainly not welcome her beneath his roof—nor did she want to be beneath it. Her Aunt Bessie was now in Washington, D.C., acting as paid companion to an elderly rich widow, and her mother, in order to be close to her, had moved into a small apartment nearby.

The uncertainty of her future made her feel sick with an anxiety that was all too familiar. It was how she had felt as a child when she had not known if she was going to be able to go to the same school as all her friends. The same crippling anxiety she had felt when her mother had left her alone in the house in the evening and she had lived in terror of her not returning. The anxiety she had lived with all her life of not knowing if Uncle Sol would fund her as, if her father had lived, he would have funded her. Nothing had ever been able to be taken for granted: not the education that all her Warfield cousins had received without even thinking about it, not her and her mother having a roof over their heads; not her debutante year. Even her wedding had not been taken care of in the way most brides' weddings were traditionally taken care of.

The knot in her stomach turned to real pain, and she wondered if she was developing an ulcer. It wouldn't be surprising, considering the tension she lived with on a daily basis, never knowing when a harmless word or action would trigger Win off in a rage that would result in his physically hurting her.

She looked at her watch. On most afternoons she played bridge with other naval wives, but she wasn't in the mood for bridge today. What she needed at the present moment was escapism—and her favorite method of finding it was going to the movies.

She walked back into the bedroom and picked up a jacket

and her purse. The Isis Theater in Pensacola showed a different movie every week and had become one of her favorite places of retreat. A peanut vendor had his stall just outside the theater and, armed with a bag of hot peanuts, she would sometimes go there two and three times a week, even though it meant watching the same film over and over again.

Often she went with Fidelia Rainey, but as Fidelia was hosting the poker game that evening, Fidelia would be busy making food preparations—food always accompanied a Pensacola poker game, for it was generally only the men who played while the women grouped in another room, talking and nibbling at whatever delicacies had been prepared for them.

By the time Wallis left the bungalow that evening with Win, she had recovered her high spirits. The movie had been a Charlie Chaplin comedy and had immediately put her in a good humor. Poker was also her favorite way of spending an evening. When Win had taught her the game, he had taught her well, and she had a natural aptitude. It was now taken for granted by Pensacola's regular poker players that if Win was playing, Wallis would be playing also, though not always at the same table.

"There's no point to it, Wallis," he had said practically. "What's the sense of you losing dough to me or me losing dough to you? This way we have a double chance of leaving the tables we're at a darn sight better off than when we sat down at them."

Over the months since they had been putting this game plan into action, Wallis had lost a lot of the popularity she had originally had with Win's friends' wives. They didn't play poker and they didn't like the fact that while they were in one room, embroidering or knitting and talking about domestic concerns, Wallis was in another room making their husbands roar with laughter at her sassy remarks and, more often than not, empty-ing their pockets for them.

That she wasn't as popular as she had once been didn't bother Wallis—not if the alternative was to sit talking about babies and recipes all evening. Men had always liked her and she, in turn, preferred men's company to that of most women. Corinne was an exception, of course, as was Fidelia Rainey.

"It's wonderful to see you, Wallis," Fidelia said with genuine warmth as she and Win entered her home. "Archie is here. He wants to play at whatever table you're at, and so you'd best look to your laurels. When it comes to poker, Archie is a hotshot, as you well know."

It was a good evening. Interspersed with the seriousness of the game at hand, Wallis kept her fellow poker players enter-tained with her account of the movie she had seen that after-noon. Whereas the other two tables played in nearly complete silence, there were periodic gales of laughter from Wallis's table, but then there always were, especially so when Archie was also seated at it.

As they said their good nights and began walking the short distance to their bungalow, she patted her purse in satisfaction. "I did very well tonight, darling. What sort of an evening did you have?"

"When we get home, I'm going to show you." He spoke through gritted teeth, and her stomach tightened. Something—probably someone—had put him in a bad mood, and if she wasn't very careful, she would be the one paying for it. At times like these she had discovered that silence was often the best method of keeping out of trouble, and so she merely gave his arm a loving squeeze and said nothing.

The second they stepped over the threshold of their bun-galow he slammed the door behind him with such force the walls shook.

Seizing hold of her by her upper arms so hard she knew the imprint of his thumbs and fingers would be on her flesh for weeks, he dragged her in the direction of the bathroom.

"You think I don't know what's going on between you and Archie?" he yelled. "You think I'm stupid?"

He kicked the bathroom door open with his foot. "I bet it's not so impossible for you to fuck when it's Archie doing the fucking, is it?"

He kicked her legs away from beneath her, but not so that she was facing his crotch, but so that she had her head over the toilet bowl.

"No!" In terror she knew immediately what he was about to do. "No, Win! There's nothing going on between Archie and me! Nothing! Noth—"

Seizing hold of her head, he thrust it down into the bowl so that her entire face was below the waterline.

She struggled against him with all her strength, certain he was going to drown her, certain her last moments had come. Just when she thought she couldn't survive a moment longer, he released his hold of her.

Gasping for breath, her hair saturated, she collapsed on the floor by the side of the bath.

"And that's where you're going to stay!" he yelled down at her.

Swinging away from her, he took the key out of the bathroom door, yanked the door closed, and turned the key in the lock from the outside. Then, seconds later, Wallis heard the front door open and then slam shut.

It was after midnight, and where he had gone she neither knew nor cared.

She was alive. He hadn't drowned her. For the moment, that was enough.

Juddering with shock, she struggled to her feet and reached

for a towel. Then, as her legs still wouldn't support her, she slid back down against the side of the bath and feebly began drying her face and toweling her hair.

Then, and only then, did she give way to dry, choking sobs. How had her life turned into this hideous nightmare? She needed to be able to talk to someone about it, but there wasn't anyone. She certainly couldn't distress her mother or her Aunt Bessie by telling them what a charade her marriage was, and if she told Corinne, Corinne would tell Henry and Win's career would be over fast as light. If that happened, Win really would kill her.

As the hours ticked past, the bathroom grew colder and colder. She wrapped a dry towel around her shoulders, dreading what the next day would bring. What she needed was a girlfriend she could confide in, and she certainly couldn't confide in anyone at Pensacola or any of her Baltimore friends.

There was only one person in the world she needed at a time like this, and that person was Pamela—and Pamela was thousands of miles away, married to John Jasper and very probably the mistress of Edward, Prince of Wales.

Chapter Seventeen

"At long last it's official! President Wilson has seen sense and announced that America is at war with Germany!" It was April 2, 1917, and in great excitement John Jasper burst into the master bedroom of his and Pamela's London home, copies of the *Times* and the *Daily Dispatch* in his hand.

Pamela was still in bed, a bank of lace-edged pillows behind her, a breakfast tray in front of her.

"About time," she said cuttingly, spreading marmalade on a thin slice of toast. "Britain has been at war for two and a half long bloody years."

"I shall join up, of course." He tossed the newspapers onto her breakfast tray and strode across to the large windows that looked out over Green Park. "I'm going immediately to the American embassy—I imagine the queue of Americans volunteering for active service will stretch all the way outside the embassy and halfway, if not the whole way, down the street."

Pamela ate her slice of toast and picked up the *Times*. The headline read:

USA ENTERS WAR TO SAVE DEMOCRACY

The article beneath it began with the words:

April 6. America is at war. At 1.18 this afternoon President Woodrow Wilson, sitting in a tiny room in the White House, signed the declaration of war passed by Congress this week. The war resolution went through the Senate by 90 votes to 6, and the House passed the same measure by 373–50, following an emotional debate that lasted 17 hours.

It was a long article and Pamela, whose newspaper of choice was the *Daily Dispatch*, didn't bother reading to the end of it. Lifting the breakfast tray to one side, she swung her legs from the bed.

"I'm not sure I want you to join up and go off to war."

He turned away from the window to face her, his winged eyebrows raised. "What? After all the cracks you've made these last two and a half years about America not pitching in?"

"America not pitching in and *you* not pitching in are two very different things."

She slid her arms around his waist, her head against his chest, not looking him in the eyes. "It's professional soldiers America will be sending to Flanders—not volunteer conscripts—and I don't want to be receiving a black-edged telegram telling me you're dead."

John Jasper closed his arms around her. Their marriage was such an odd assortment of highs and lows, turbulently passionate one moment, icily cold the next, that he never knew what emotion he was going to meet with from her, and this latest one—deep concern for his safety—came as a welcome surprise.

It wasn't going to change his mind about joining up, though. If America was at war, he, as a young and fit American, was going to stand up and be counted, and he knew Pamela was wrong in assuming only professional soldiers would be being sent to Europe. The total strength of America's regular army was only 5,000 officers and 123,000 men, plus the part-time soldiers in the National Guard. His country would need him, and he had no intention of letting his country down.

"I'm glad you feel that way about things, Pammie," he said thickly, amazed at how much emotion she was now capable of arousing in him. "But I could never live with myself if I didn't do my bit."

Pamela kept her head on his chest. It was true that she didn't particularly want John Jasper to die in a mud-filled trench—or anywhere else, for that matter—but it wasn't the real reason she was trying to coax him out of volunteering for active service. The real reason was that in January, when the Prince of Wales had been home on leave and on the night before he had returned to France, she had finally achieved her ambition of becoming much more to him than just someone he was socially friendly with. Her new relationship with him was one she was hoping to solidify on his next leave and she knew that, as a soldier, the prince might have second thoughts about embarking on a full-blown affair with a woman whose husband was risking his life at the front.

"What about Oliver?" she said, contriving to sound as if she were on the verge of tears. "If you should be killed, how will I ever explain to him that his papa didn't *have* to go to France—or wherever else you might be sent—but that you *chose* to go?"

He put a finger beneath her chin and tilted her head to his.

Swiftly Pamela banished the expression of frustrated crossness she knew was in her eyes, replacing it with one of loving, tear-filled concern.

He said tenderly, "How will I ever explain to Oliver—when he is older—if I *don't* go?"

She knew by the determined set of his jaw that nothing she could say was going to make him change his mind. As far as

John Jasper was concerned, his honor was at stake, and John Jasper, as she had come to know very well since even before their marriage, was an extremely honorable man.

That he was made living with him quite exasperating at times. It was an accepted code of conduct among British aristocracy that marriages were made for sensible reasons, such as allying one great family with another or combining one vast estate with another, and that after a son and heir had been born—and his paternity not doubted—not only could the husband seek excitement and romance elsewhere, but so also could the wife.

Discreet bed-hopping was an acknowledged pastime at all country house parties, and hostesses obligingly sited the rooms of guests in close proximity to the rooms of whomever they were known to be having an affair with. What was never done, of course, was to conduct an affair openly. Though the inner circle would gossip about who was currently sleeping with whom, for it to become public knowledge would be to court social death.

It was a game that everyone she and John Jasper mixed with knew the rules of—and that John Jasper adamantly refused to play. He might not have wanted to have had to marry her, but now that he was married, he was quite blunt about his intention of being a faithful husband—and of expecting her to be a faithful wife in return.

To her own very great surprise she had found being so no huge strain. There were very few men in society as handsome as John Jasper, and she knew from her premarital experience that as a lover, he rated very highly; so high, in fact, that she'd had no desire to look elsewhere for satisfaction in bed. And then, in January, had come a temptation she had found completely irresistible.

. . .

It had occurred when she and John Jasper had motored up to Norfolk to visit her mother and Tarquin at Tarquin's country home near Sandringham and had arrived to find a party in progress.

"Prince Edward is here," her stepfather had said, greeting her fondly. "Like you, he's an unexpected guest, but he's returning to London later tonight and off back to Flanders first thing in the morning. The poor boy wanted to spend the last few hours of his leave in a lively manner, not something achievable at Sandringham."

Her interest had been immediate. Since the war, chances to socialize informally with Edward didn't happen often enough, and she had been determined to make the most of what was a very unexpected opportunity.

"Is Portia here?" she'd asked as John Jasper headed for the drawing room.

Some months ago there had been rumors that Prince Edward was romantically interested in Portia Cadogan, one of Earl Cadogan's daughters.

"No." Knowing she would want to refresh her makeup in the bedroom she and John Jasper always stayed in, Tarquin had walked her to the foot of the central staircase. "The party only came into being when Edward drove up an hour or so ago and asked if I could throw one together. It's not been easy, and you and John Jasper couldn't have arrived at a more opportune moment." He'd hesitated, then added, "And as I know you're interested, Portia Cadogan is now being squired around by Edward Stanley, a friend of Edward's from his days at Oxford."

Pamela had pressed her fingers to her mouth and had then pressed them against his. "You're a wonderful bearer of good news, Tarquin." Her eyes had danced with elation. "I'll be down in five minutes' time to make an impression on him."

The luggage she and John Jasper had brought with them was in her bedroom almost as soon as she and her maid were.

Swiftly, knowing she had no time to lose if she was to capture Edward's attention before some other scheming little minx did so, she'd had the quickest bath of her life and had her maid remove the most daring of the evening gowns she had brought with her.

It was made of crystal beaded sea green chiffon; the color echoed the mesmerizing color of her eyes. The neckline plunged both front and back, fitted like a second skin over her hips, and then fell into a narrow swirl of panels that floated around her legs as she walked. She'd added pearl earrings and a waist-length rope of pearls, sprayed herself with L'Heure Bleue, and had made her way to the drawing room, pondering what she knew of Edward's recent personal life.

Now that he was twenty-three, the only female his name had been linked with—apart from Portia Cadogan—had been Lady Coke, who was at least twelve years his senior.

"It can't be a love affair," she had said to John Jasper when gossip about Edward and Lady Coke had first been whispered to her. "She may be lively company, but she's ancient. Nearly old enough to be his mother."

"Perhaps a bit of mothering is what he wants," John Jasper had said. "From what I've heard, he never received much as a child. It's my guess that's all there is to his relationship with Marian Coke. She's far too smart to make Tommy look ridiculous by having an affair with someone so much younger than herself—even if the someone in question is heir to the throne."

It was one of those moments when John Jasper surprised her. She hadn't realized he was on such friendly terms with Thomas, Viscount Leicester.

When they first married she had imagined that his being an

American would put him at a disadvantage socially, but that hadn't proved to be the case. John Jasper exuded good breeding and was immediately well liked by everyone she introduced him to. He was also usually right about things, too, and she very much hoped he was right in believing that Prince Edward's relationship with Marian Coke stopped at the bedroom door, for it meant that where romance and Edward were concerned, she was still in with a chance.

At her stepfather's opulent country house, that chance had finally arrived.

She'd walked into the drawing room to find fifteen or so people gathered there, all friends of Tarquin's and all people already known to the prince. "Alexander's Ragtime Band" had been playing on the gramophone, the carpet had been rolled back for dancing, and champagne had been flowing.

To her startled surprise, she had seen that Edward was in uniform. It had been a stark reminder that next morning he was to return to the front and a world of horrors so far removed from the evening now being enjoyed as to be unimaginable.

"Not that he's often near enemy shellfire," she'd heard someone say to Tarquin under cover of the music. "He tries hard enough, poor bugger, but the king insists on his only doing staff work. He must be the only sod out there disobeying his remit by going up to the front line every chance he gets."

The poor sod in question had been talking to her mother when she had walked up to him and dipped a curtsey.

That he'd been absolutely delighted to see someone of his own age, rather than his host's age, and someone he had been meeting intermittently ever since he'd been a child, had been thrillingly obvious to her.

"Pamela," he said, startlingly blue eyes lighting up. "How splendid. Now I have someone to dance with!"

Though she had been calling him Edward to his face ever

since childhood, she now, whenever they met, always very correctly waited for him to invite her to do so.

"It's ragtime, sir," she'd said, laughter fizzing in her throat. "Are you sure we shouldn't wait for something a little more respectable to be on the gramophone?"

"Bosh!" The lines of strain on his fine-featured face had been unmistakable. He might be restricted to staff work, but the nightmare of the bloodbath he was so shortly returning to had imprinted itself on him as clearly as it had every other serving officer she had met. "Tarquin won't object if we dance to ragtime." He put a hand beneath her elbow. "Can you do the Turkey Trot? Don't you love all these American dances? They're so outrageously hectic that when you're dancing them you forget everything."

She'd known from past experience that at any occasion where there was dancing, Prince Edward always courteously danced at least once with every woman present, no matter what her age or looks. A quick glance around the room had shown her that age- and looks-wise she had no competition and that, having arrived at the party late, she was fortunate in that all Edward's duty dances had already been danced.

"Another ragtime number!" he'd shouted across to the friend of her mother's who was tending the gramophone.

The sound of Irving Berlin's "Everybody's Doing It Now" filled the room.

For the next forty minutes the two of them had danced almost unceasingly, following the Turkey Trot with the Bunny Hug, the Grizzly Bear, the cakewalk and then, finally, a foxtrot.

Perspiration had been beading his brow when at last he had come to a stop. "Champagne for you, and a pint of lemon barley water for me, I think," he had said breathlessly. "Then, as I need to cool down, how about we take a turn around the garden?"

That their doing so would be noted by everyone and commented upon endlessly afterward because the occasion was so informal, because so few people were in attendance, because the party was one he had instigated, and because his nerves were fraught at the thought of his imminent return to the front had been something he had been uncaring about.

Pamela had been more than uncaring. She had been ecstatic.

With a glass of champagne in her hand and not even glancing in John Jasper's direction, she had allowed Edward to escort her from the room.

The night had been pleasantly mild, the moon high.

Immediately as they were free of the house, his buoyant mood had collapsed as if pricked by a pin.

"You've been a lifesaver tonight, Pamela," he'd said bleakly, putting his half-empty glass of barley water down on one of the terrace's glass-topped tables.

"Because of tomorrow? Because of going back to France?" Insensitive as she normally was to what was going on in other people's heads, she had known that on this occasion it was vitally important that she successfully do so.

"No, and if that sounds bizarre it's because ghastly though it is out there—so unspeakably ghastly I don't have words to describe it—I want to be there with my fellow officers, doing my bit. Or as much of my bit as the powers that be are allowing me to do."

In the moonlight his hair had been the sleekest, palest blond imaginable, the despair in his eyes, as they had met with hers, absolute.

Swiftly she had laid her champagne glass down on the table and lightly touched his arm with her hand.

"Tell me," she had said tenderly, certain she was living through her finest moment.

He had taken hold of her hand, grasping it tightly. "I'm just not my own man, Pamela." His voice had been full of the plea to be understood. "As heir to the throne I never will be. There isn't one major decision in life I can make for myself. Everything is laid down for me for years and years ahead. When the war ends—and it will end with Britain and her allies being victorious and the Hun pounded to a pulp—it's set in concrete that I will have to marry, whether I want to or not. Then there will be an endless treadmill of the kind of royal duties that would send any sane man screamingly off his head. The terrible truth, Pamela, is that I'm not cut out to be royal. I hate all the endless dressing up. All the fussy ceremonials."

It had been a confession Pamela had been totally unable to deal with.

She had thought of how she always took all her worries to Tarquin and had said hesitatingly, "What about your father? Does he understand how you feel?"

He'd given a humorless laugh. "My father is a bully who has never understood how *anyone* feels. He even shouts at my mother—and before you ask me if I've spoken to the queen about the way I feel, I haven't. Attempting to talk to my mother would be like attempting to talk to an iceberg."

That King George and Queen Mary's relationships with their children left a lot to be desired was something she had understood from Tarquin a long time ago.

She had moved comfortingly closer to him and he had drawn her into his arms, burying his face in her neck.

"Pamela, darling!" His voice had been choked with need. "You've no idea how wonderful it was to see you enter the room this evening and for me to know I had someone to be with who would understand me and make me feel better."

Remembering that he was reputed to be cripplingly shy

with women, she had moved her head fractionally, making it easier for him to kiss her.

He had done so with hungry passion, and when he had moved a hand so that it slid inside her plunging neckline and cupped her breast, she had given a small triumphant sigh and had inwardly cursed that he was to leave for London within an hour or two and then—for who knew how long?— for France.

As if reading her thoughts and with his hand still on her breast, he had said urgently, "It's nearly eleven and I have to leave for London. You will write to me, Pamela, won't you? And you will be waiting for me when I return?"

It had been like asking the pope if he were a Catholic.

"Yes," she'd said, keeping glee out of her voice only with the greatest difficulty. "Of course I'll write to you, and of course I will be waiting for you when you next have leave."

With her head resting on his shoulder, they had walked back to the house hand in hand and hip to hip.

Within minutes of their reentering the drawing room, Edward had thanked Tarquin and her mother for their hospitality and with a last longing look in her direction had bidden everyone farewell. Then, seated at the back of a big black car, his aide at the wheel, he had disappeared into the night en route for Buckingham Palace.

John Jasper said again, "How will I ever explain to Oliver— when he is older—if I *don't* enlist, Pammie?"

She blinked, bringing her thoughts back to the present with difficulty.

"I don't know, John Jasper." Any other answer was impossible when it was so obvious that if he was given an opportunity to fight for his country, he would do so.

Later, when he had left the house for the American embassy, she had continued with her own plans for the day in the hope that they would help her forget the monumental step John Jasper was now taking.

At lunchtime she was at the Ritz, meeting up with Cynthia Asquith, whose father, until a few short months ago, had been prime minister. Cynthia knew everything about everyone, and Pamela wanted to know more about Edward's long-standing friendship with Lady Coke.

"Marian Coke?" Cynthia had adjusted the fox fur around her shoulders and arched an eyebrow that had been plucked almost into extinction. "What is it you want to know about her, Pamela?"

Pamela had taken a sip of deliciously ice-cold Chablis and said, trying to sound as if her interest were only casual, "I know her name has been linked with Prince Edward's for quite a time now, but it seems so unlikely I did wonder if the rumors were true."

"That they are lovers?" Cynthia had flashed her a malicious little smile. "It is hard to imagine Marian Coke in the role of an experienced instructor in the art of love, isn't it? And besides, I always thought ladies of the night were roped in to give that kind of *éducation sentimentale*. Marian, however, certainly used to be Edward's closest confidante, though whether she still is I really don't know. Have you heard that Henry Daventry died in Gallipoli? And that Charles Lister, after many woundings, has died in Egypt?"

From then on the conversation had become a depressing roll call of friends, and friends of friends, who had died, and Pamela had been relieved when their lunch together had come to an end.

. . .

There was a letter from America waiting for her on her arrival at home. The handwriting was Edith's. She picked it up from the silver salver in the hall and then, en route to her bedroom, where she intended to read it in undisturbed peace, she called in at the nursery to spend a few obligatory minutes with her son.

Now nearly two, Oliver was not yet old enough to be interesting, at least not to her. It was John Jasper who, from the minute Oliver had been born, had barely been able to tear himself away from the nursery.

"It's because Mr. Bachman is American," she had said apologetically to Oliver's nanny when she had complained about having to endure such unusual parental presence in her domain. "They don't behave the way we do."

She entered the large sunlit nursery to find Oliver playing on the floor with a pile of brightly colored wooden bricks.

His face lit up at the sight of her. "Mama!" he shouted, scrambling eagerly to his feet and running toward her on chubby legs.

She bent down to kiss him on his cheek, hoping he wouldn't clutch at the waterfall of lace on the bodice of her dress, or try to grab hold of her pearls as he had done on a previous occasion.

Nanny, ever vigilant, relieved her of her anxieties by hurrying over and scooping him up in capably beefy arms.

"There, there, Master Oliver!" she said chidingly. "We don't go rushing at Mama in such an ungentlemanly way! We say, 'Hello, Mama. How are you?'"

"Hello, Mama," Oliver said obediently, the excited light in his eyes no longer there. "How are you?"

"I'm very well, thank you, Oliver." Pamela, oblivious to how much her son wished to be in her arms, not his nanny's, gave him another kiss on his cheek, this time a good-bye one, her thoughts already elsewhere.

Despite the best efforts of German submarines, domestic mail still arrived regularly from America, and Edith was a diligent correspondent. More often than not the content of her letters was boring, but occasionally she had news of Wallis, and it was for this reason that Pamela kept the correspondence going.

Telling her maid that she wouldn't need her for at least another fifteen minutes, she seated herself at her dressing table and, with a pearl-handled paper knife, opened the envelope.

> *Dear Pamela,*
>
> *I do hope that you and John Jasper and your darling little boy are all well. There are hardly any of the old crowd now left in Baltimore. It seems like everyone has married and moved away. Violet Dix has just had another baby. I can't get used to calling her by her married name. She's put on an awful lot of weight. I don't think you would recognize her. The papers are full of how we will soon be declaring war on Germany, but there is still a lot of opposition to doing so.*

Pamela glanced at the date the letter had been written. It was the sixteenth of February, a good six weeks ago.

> *My mother received a courteous letter from Wallis's Aunt Bessie, asking for Baltimore news. You know that both she and Wallis's mother are no longer living in Baltimore, don't you? Mrs. Merryman is acting as paid companion to a rich widow and Mrs. Rasin is also living in Washington. There are rumors (which I don't believe) that she is working as a hostess in a club called the Chevy Chase.*

Pamela, who found it quite easy to believe the rumors, grinned. Wally's mother had to be at least in her mid-forties, and she found the idea of her giving Solomon Warfield a heart attack by working as a hostess highly entertaining. Where joie de vivre was concerned, it seemed as if Alice was never going to run out of it.

Edith's letter droned on about parochial Baltimore matters and, not seeing Wallis's name mentioned again, Pamela skipped most of it.

Pushing the letter to one side, she took a small key out of her purse and opened the central drawer of her dressing table. It was where she kept her jewelry. Some of the jewelry had been her mother's. Some had been given her by her father or by her stepfather. Other pieces had been presents from John Jasper. He always gave her a small item of jewelry on her birthday and, when Oliver had been born, had given her a wonderful strand of perfectly matched pearls.

She withdrew a small box stamped with the name of London's most exclusive jeweler and clicked it open. Inside, on a bed of velvet, lay an emerald brooch. A brooch, as an item of jewelry, was relatively modest, but there was nothing modest about the pear-cut emerald in its white-gold setting. It winked and glittered up at her with a thousand fires in its heart.

A gift from Edward, it had been delivered by messenger within hours of his return to France.

As she hadn't been able to show such a gift to John Jasper, it had meant that whenever they were out together she couldn't wear it. Remembering that John Jasper would soon be in France, or Egypt, or wherever else it was that Americans would be sent to fight, she closed the lid and put the little box to the very rear of the drawer.

If this was Edward's gift to her at the tentative beginnings of their affair, what kind of gifts was she likely to receive once, when he was next home on leave, it got torridly under way?

She looked down at the letter Edith had sent her. She certainly couldn't, when she responded to it, tell Edith that she was about to become the great love of Prince Edward's life, or that she had already received a magnificent emerald brooch from him.

She could have told Wally, though.

She had always been able to tell Wally anything.

At the thought of how much she missed Wally, her chest felt uncomfortably tight. It was nearly two and a half years since she and John Jasper had married, and she knew that by now she should be well over the friendship that her marriage had destroyed. She wasn't over it, though, and didn't think she ever would be. She was always going to miss Wally. There was, quite simply, no one else quite like her.

Chapter Eighteen

Though Pamela received several short letters from Prince Edward, there was never any mention in them of when he would next be home on leave.

I simply don't know when it will be,

he wrote in one letter,

> *but not, I think, for ages and ages. The king thinks it's bad for public morale for me to be seen in England when the situation out here is so poor, and though I hate doing so— because of how very much I want to see you again—I have to agree with him. So there it is. It's rotten luck and I hate thinking about it, but it simply can't be helped.*

In another letter, he wrote:

Millions and millions of thanks, Pamela, for all your great kindness to me when I was last home. I can't possibly write all I want to say to you or thank you properly, but I know

*you will understand. Being discreet is terribly hard and I
wouldn't be able to write to you at all if it weren't for your
assurances that no one ever sees your private mail but you.*

Every letter he wrote fell far short of being a love letter, but
they also left her in no doubt that she was constantly on his
mind and that when he did next get leave, she would be the first
person he would rush to see.

For Pamela, the most frustrating aspect was that she couldn't
brag to anyone about the way Prince Edward had fallen for her,
for fear that if he should hear she had been doing so, he might
beg off. The only person not in Edward's circle that she felt she
could safely brag to was Rose Houghton.

In May, Rose made a brief trip to England in order to escort a
fresh intake of Guy's Hospital nurses across to France. It had become a habit that whenever she did so, the two of them would
meet up for midmorning tea and toast in the tea shop adjacent
to the hospital.

"So we see quite a lot of Prince Edward whenever he has
leave and particularly when he visits Sandringham," Pamela
said to her, trying to sound as casual about it as she could. "My
stepfather's country home is only a few miles away, and he
served with King George when the king was Prince of Wales
and in the Navy."

"Yes." With her elbow on the gaily checked tablecloth,
Rose rested her chin on the back of her hand, her eyes holding
Pamela's with an expression she couldn't quite read. "You've
told me about your stepfather's friendship with King George
before."

Slightly cross that Rose wasn't more impressed at how close
she and John Jasper now were to the royal circle, Pamela said
spiritedly, "Just because you aren't interested in royal doings
doesn't mean other people shouldn't be."

Rose pursed her lips and then said, "Other people wouldn't be if they joined the VADs or the Red Cross, saw for themselves the unspeakable hell taking place across the channel, and did what the girls I'm taking across to France later today are going to do. Or worked eighteen hours out of twenty-four in an attempt to alleviate the suffering of the wounded and the dying."

Pamela refused to feel shamefaced. "We can't all be heroines," she said, infusing her voice with what she hoped sounded like deep regret. "Some of us have children."

It was a remark Rose let pass, but Pamela knew what she was thinking. High-society mothers never took on the task of the day-to-day care of their children. If she had wanted to train as a nurse, she could have, just as others in the same position as herself had done.

Their midmorning tea and toast wasn't turning out to be a great deal of fun and, not for the first time, Pamela wondered why Rose's friendship mattered to her so much. They didn't have a thing in common. Rose was an idealist. Before the war that idealism had been devoted to the Votes for Women cause. On the outbreak of war she had immediately trained as a nurse. She rarely indulged in high-society gossip and, though ever since their first meeting they had kept intermittently in touch, Pamela still knew very little about her, other than that her father, Viscount Houghton, had died when she was a child, her mother, now remarried to a French nobleman, lived in Paris, and Rose and her three sisters had been brought up in Hampshire by their grandfather, Lord May.

What had intrigued her at the beginning of their friendship was the knowledge that Rose's youngest sister had once sculpted a bust of Prince Edward, which had indicated to her that the Houghtons had close royal connections.

Rose had quickly disabused her of the idea. "Lily paints

portraits as well," she had said, "but she doesn't need her subject to sit for her. Not all artists do, you know."

Pamela hadn't known, and the knowledge immediately made the Houghtons less interesting. She hadn't crossed Rose off her list of acquaintances, though. What mystified her was why, when their interests and values were so vastly different, Rose hadn't crossed her off *her* list of friends.

"I have to be getting back to the hospital." Rose looked down at the watch pinned upside down for easy readability on her nurse's uniform. "And it's my turn to pay the bill."

She caught the waitress's eye and, as the middle-aged waitress wrote out the bill, picked up the gaily wrapped parcel she had entered the tea shop with. From its shape it looked to be a book and was obviously a present.

"It's for my grandfather," she said as Pamela quirked an inquisitive eyebrow in its direction. "It's his seventy-fifth birthday in a few days' time. I had hoped to get down to Snowberry to give it to him myself, but my turnaround time is so short I'm going to have to post it."

"If you are due to leave for France this afternoon, you don't have time to be going to the post office. Let me do it for you."

"Will you?" Rose looked relieved and began taking more money from her purse.

Anticipating why, Pamela said exasperatedly, "For goodness' sake, I can pay the postage without you having to give it to me, Rose."

Taking the book from Rose's hand, she rose to her feet. "Keep yourself safe," she said as they left the tea shop. For once the sincerity in her voice was deep and real. "Don't do a Nurse Edith Cavell and get yourself shot by the Germans."

"Nurse Edith Cavell was a heroine," Rose said crisply as

they reached the street and paused for a moment before parting. "I'm not."

Pamela, who totally disagreed with her, was far too elated at what she now intended to do to say so.

Having given Rose a good-bye kiss on the cheek, she watched her hurry off to the hospital, the mid-calf-length navy cloak of her uniform lifting gently around her in the breeze.

Then, instead of making her way to the nearest post office, she stepped into the street and hailed a cab.

Forty-five minutes later she was seated in a train steaming southeast through London's grimy suburbs. Rose's neat handwriting on the wrapped book gave Snowberry's full address, and though she knew she would have to hire a cab once she left the train at Winchester, Snowberry's nearest town, she didn't anticipate it would be too difficult to find the village in which Lord May's family home was sited.

As smoke-blackened terrace houses gave way to more superior housing, it suddenly occurred to her that she'd never told Rose the news she'd been bursting to tell her: the news that Edward, Prince of Wales, was infatuated with her.

She shrugged. It was too late to tell her now—which was maybe all for the best. Rose certainly wouldn't have gossiped to anyone about it, but she might very well have been disapproving. Usually Pamela couldn't care less if people disapproved of her, but she didn't want Rose doing so. For reasons she couldn't define, she wanted Rose to think well of her.

She also wanted Rose to be less of a mystery to her, which was why she was en route to Snowberry. That and the fact that with no Prince Edward on hand to pursue an affair with and John Jasper at officer's training camp, life had become extremely dull. Visiting Snowberry would, at the very least, give her day an element of interest.

. . .

"Snowberry Manor, Little Hemingfold," she said to the driver of the first cab she came to after walking out of Winchester's train station.

She had thought he might not know where Snowberry was, but he simply asked her to step inside the cab and within a very short time they were passing through unbelievably beautiful countryside.

Pamela had never been a country girl. The bulk of her childhood had been spent in Baltimore, and when she had returned to England for her debutante coming-out she had lived with her mother and Tarquin at Tarquin's town house in London.

The only countryside she was familiar with was that around Tarquin's country home in Norfolk—a landscape she found unbelievably flat—and the hunting country of Leicestershire.

Everyone who was anyone hunted, and her stepfather was no exception. Because of her years spent in Baltimore, her riding skills were too mediocre for riding at full tilt across open country, leaping ditches, hedges, and fences, but the social side of hunting was vibrant, and in the years before she had married John Jasper she had rarely missed a season.

This countryside was far more pleasantly rolling and lush than that of Leicestershire. The well-tended fields were interspersed with woodland, and everywhere there were clouds of foaming white May blossoms.

They passed through several small villages and then, after trundling through a particularly pretty village and climbing the hill leading out of it, the cabdriver turned right, swinging through a huge gateway.

The long driveway beyond it was lined by giant elms and, at the end of it, its mellow walls covered in ivy and honeysuckle, was an exquisitely beautiful Elizabethan manor house.

Diamond-leaded windows winked in the early-summer sunshine, chimneys soared from huge buttressed chimney stacks, and gables rose at odd, intriguing angles.

"Will you be wanting me to wait for you, miss?" the cabdriver asked as he came to a halt in front of an iron-studded oak door that Pamela was sure had been in place long before the Civil War of the 1600s.

"I don't think so." She opened her purse to pay him. "But wait until someone opens the door to me before leaving."

Moments later the door was opened by a butler who looked to be nearly as old as the house.

The cabdriver trundled away down the magnificent drive and Pamela said brightly, "Mrs. John Jasper Bachman for Lord May."

She was met with a look of bewilderment and added, "I am a close friend of his granddaughter, Miss Rose Houghton, and Miss Houghton has asked me to pay her grandfather a visit."

"If you would wait here, Mrs. Bachman, I will inform his lordship of your arrival."

Creakily he disappeared out of the hall and down a corridor.

A few moments later, Pamela heard another elderly voice say spryly, "A friend of Rose's, William?" and then, seconds later, Lord May was walking up to her as arthritically as his butler, saying genially, "Welcome to Snowberry, Mrs. Bachman. William tells me Rose is a friend of yours?"

"Yes. At the moment she is in London on one of her twenty-four-hour turnarounds in order to escort another batch of nurses across to France. She had hoped to be able to visit you, especially as it is your birthday soon. As doing so was an impossibility and she was anxious that you received the present she had got for you for your birthday, I said I would bring it down on her behalf."

She held out the carefully wrapped parcel.

"But how wonderful!" Lord May's face was bewhiskered with a mustache as white as William's hair. "D'you hear that, William? This young lady has traveled all the way from London to give me a present from Rose."

As he was talking he was escorting her out of the large stone-flagged entrance hall and into a massive drawing room stuffed with comfortable-looking sofas and chairs. On one occasional table was a half-completed jigsaw puzzle; on another chess men were set out in midplay. At the far end of the room stood a baby grand piano, its gleaming black surface crowded with photographs in silver frames.

"Sit down, my dear, and tell me all the up-to-date news about Rose. Would you like tea, or would you prefer a glass of sherry?"

Pamela would have far preferred a pink gin but kept the thought to herself. "A glass of sherry would be lovely," she lied, her attention caught by a bronze bust standing on a pedestal in a corner of the room.

Ignoring the invitation to sit, she walked across to it, staring at it in rapt fascination. The likeness to Edward was spellbinding; the sculptor—or sculptress, for she knew it must be the bust Rose's sister had done of Edward—had even caught the look of melancholy that often filled Prince Edward's eyes when he thought himself unobserved.

"What a superb bronze of the Prince of Wales," she said, accepting a glass of dry sherry from William.

With a glass of sherry also in hand, Lord May crossed the room to stand beside her. "Yes. Quite a magnificent likeness, don't you think? My youngest granddaughter sculpted it five or six years ago."

The pride in his voice was both well deserved and touching.

Pamela put a hand out and lightly touched the bronze, shiny straight hair—hair that, in life, she had now felt beneath the palm of her hand. Wondering what Lord May would say if he knew how intimately close she was to Prince Edward, she said, "Rose told me her sister had sculpted a bronze bust of the prince. I never thought it would be so breathtakingly like him, though. Not when he hadn't sat for her."

Lord May chuckled. "He had no need to sit for her. Not when she knew him so well."

Rose hadn't actually *said* her sister had never met Prince Edward, but that was certainly the impression she had given.

Trying to keep what was now burning curiosity out of her voice, she said casually, "Did she? I hadn't realized."

Lord May turned away from the sculpture and, a little unwillingly, Pamela also turned her back on it.

"There was a time, Mrs. Bachman," he said to her confidingly, "when David was always down here. That was when he was at naval college. You can't get from Windsor to Dartmouth without passing within a mile or so of Snowberry."

He was politely waiting for her to sit down before sitting down himself. With legs weak from shock, Pamela sat.

David?

David?

It was common knowledge in society that within his family circle Prince Edward was known by the last of his many Christian names, but no one else that she knew had been given the liberty of using it. He certainly hadn't yet invited her to use it.

She wondered if, in private, Lady Coke was allowed to call him David.

And why had the Houghtons been allowed to call him David? It didn't make sense. Not when Rose wasn't part of Edward's inner circle of friends and had given no indication of ever having been so.

Lord May seated himself comfortably in a nearby chair and began opening his birthday present.

"A biography of Admiral Nelson!" he said, withdrawing the

book from its wrapping paper. "How typical of Rose to know *exactly* what I would most want. And now let's chat about Rose. How did the two of you come to be friends? Are you friends with Iris and Marigold as well?"

"I met Rose at a supper party. I've never met Iris and Marigold—or Lily."

Lord May chuckled. "Not many people have met Lily. She lives on a Hebridean island with her husband and two girls and rarely leaves it. Iris lives very close. Her husband's estate, Sissbury, abuts Snowberry for a good half mile. She's a homebody, though, and rarely visits London. Marigold, of course, you will know of, even if you haven't met her."

"Will I?" Pamela was startled and desperately in need of another drink.

Lord May nodded his head in the direction of the mass of silver-framed photographs standing on the piano. "There are several photographs of Marigold you may like to look at. I particularly like the one taken when she played the part of Mary, Queen of Scots in Mr. Barker's film of that beautiful, but tragic queen. There's also another of her taken when she played the part of one of Henry the Eighth's wives in Mr. Barker's film about Henry. I can never remember whether the part she played was that of Anne Boleyn or Catherine Howard."

Will Barker was a producer and director as famous in England as D. W. Griffith was in America, and Pamela, more weak in the knees than ever, rose to her feet and crossed to the piano.

She and John Jasper had seen all of Will Barker's epic feature films, and Lord May was quite right in that, though she had never met Marigold, she certainly knew of her, though by the name Marietta des Vaux, not Marigold Houghton.

Reading her thoughts, Lord May said obligingly, "When Marigold embarked on her career as an actress, her husband insisted she use a professional name and not her married name.

Marigold didn't mind. Rose had already set a precedent for that kind of thing."

"What kind of thing?" Pamela felt dizzy. "Is Rose not Rose's real name?"

Lord May stood from his chair, saying as he crossed the room to join her at the piano, "Yes, it is. But as you are a close friend of hers, you will know how militant a suffragette she was until the war halted such activity. The militant young women of the movement didn't go in much for marriage and, when they did, they made a stand by not relinquishing their maiden names." He lifted up a photograph Pamela hadn't yet looked at. "That is what Rose did when she married Hal."

The photograph was a wedding photograph, and the radiant bride was Rose.

The surprise was so great, Pamela gasped.

Realizing how much he had taken her aback, Lord May said sympathetically, "You look as if you could do with another drink. I don't think you enjoyed that sherry very much. How about a pink gin? It's Marigold's favorite tipple."

With vast relief she answered that it was her favorite tipple, too. Then, wondering how many other surprises he had up his sleeve, she said before he left her side, "Who is Rose's husband, Lord May? Is he, as Marigold's husband is, a member of the peerage?"

"Hal?" Another deep chuckle rumbled up from his throat. "No, and even if he were given the chance of a peerage I doubt he would take it. He's as radical in his views as Rose, but then, if you've read his editorials, you will know that."

"Editorials?" Pamela was beginning to wish she hadn't delayed him in ringing for William. She'd never felt more in need of a stiff drink in her life.

"Hal," Lord May said with relish, "is the editor of the *Daily Dispatch*."

Pamela opened her mouth to speak, but no words came. How could she have known Rose for so long and not known she was married—and to whom? How, with a sister nearly as famous in eight-reeler feature films as Mary Pickford, could Rose not have told her who her sister was? Most important of all, why had Rose never mentioned what close terms Prince Edward had once been on, not only with her, but also with her entire family?

David.

You had to be very close to the Prince of Wales to be invited to call him by the name his family used. The general mystery she had always felt surrounded Rose had now deepened into one particular mystery. What kind of friendship had her family and Prince Edward enjoyed? And why did Rose no longer even acknowledge that it had once existed?

The only person who could answer the last question was Rose herself—and she had no way of knowing when she would next be seeing Rose. It could be within weeks or not for months.

As Lord May personally chauffeured her back to Winchester and the train station, she wondered what Wallis would make of the conundrum. Wallis had always loved talking about Prince Edward and, if she had known of it, would be jealous to death of the relationship Pamela now had with him.

Wallis.

There had to come a time when Wallis would no longer intrude on her thoughts, but she couldn't imagine when that time would be.

"It has been a splendid afternoon," Lord May said, bringing his stately Talbot motorcar to a halt outside the station. "I quite understand why you and Rose are friends."

"Do you?" It was more than Pamela had ever understood.

He gave her a beaming smile and said, solving at least one mystery, "You remind her of the naughtiest of her sisters. You remind her of Marigold."

Chapter Nineteen

Pamela found the next few months deeply boring. John Jasper was now in an officer's training camp somewhere in the south-west of England, gung ho at the prospect of being speedily sent to France in order to join up with an American battalion under the overall command of Major General "Black Jack" Pershing.

Black Jack is a veteran of the Mexican and Philippine wars,

he had written to her.

*If anyone can give the British and French the support
they need in order to finally bring this world war to a close,
it's him.*

Pamela had liked the nickname "Black Jack." It summed up a handsome, piratical figure. When she had next written to John Jasper, she had asked how old General Pershing was. John Jasper had replied that Black Jack was in his fifties, and she had immediately lost interest.

By the end of June the first wave of American troops had

reached France. The *Daily Dispatch*—which Pamela read with added interest now that she knew its editor was married to Rose—had as its headline:

HEROES' WELCOME FOR US TROOPS IN FRANCE

After an all-too-brief leave home, John Jasper was sent to Flanders in order to join one of the American battalions. His first letter to her, hastily scrawled in pencil, had been typically positive.

> *Black Jack is a superb commander, Pammie. Though the British and French don't particularly want an American army—they simply want men—he's digging his heels in and not allowing us to be dispersed under British and French commands. We are the U.S. Army in Europe—and he's making sure everyone knows it.*

It was interesting information but did nothing to relieve her boredom. Edward's brief letters to her weren't much better, though as he had now taken to addressing her as "My Angel," they did send a shiver of anticipation down her spine.

Even though his letters weren't subject to the same kind of censorship as other mail from the front, he still carefully never mentioned names or places or dates. He did, though, ask her for a photograph. *It will cheer me up enormously*, he wrote in handwriting that sloped very heavily to the right, *and will do me worlds of good.*

With John Jasper no longer at home to see her doing so, she began wearing the emerald brooch when out to dinner with friends. "It's a gift from an admirer," she said whenever it was commented on, half hoping that two and two would be put together and half fearing it would be, in case too much early speculation should work against her and not for her.

In July she received another letter from Edith, this time with news of Wallis in it.

> *Wallis's last letter to me was from Squantum, near Boston, not Pensacola,*

Edith had written in painfully neat handwriting.

> *Her husband has been put in command of the naval air base there. Wallis says he is desperately disappointed at not being posted overseas on active service. All three of his brothers are serving in Europe. Dumaresque, who was best man at their wedding, has joined the Lafayette Escadrille (a squadron of the French air service) and his two younger brothers, Egbert and Frederick, are members of the U.S. expeditionary forces in France. At Pensacola they lived on the base, but Wallis says Squantum is too new a base for there to be such facilities, and their home is a hotel apartment in the Back Bay section of Boston. She didn't say she was lonely, but I imagine she is, for I can't think of any old Oldfields girls who were Bostonians. Wallis says she spends most of her time visiting places of historical interest in order to fill up her day.*

Pamela had smiled wryly, amused by the fact that Wally was quite obviously just as bored as she now was.

In October she received a letter from Prince Edward that filled her with dismay.

> *Dearest Angel,*

he wrote in his distinctive handwriting,

*I hardly know how to break this news to you, but the next
letters you receive from me will be from even further away
than France.*

She went immediately to the one person who *did* know of
Edward's infatuation for her and of the steady stream of letters
he sent to her.

"What does he mean?" she demanded of her stepfather.
"Where is he being posted? Egypt? Palestine? Why can't even the
Prince of Wales mention place names in his correspondence?"

Tarquin clipped the end of a cigar and lit it.

"Because although his mail isn't subject to censorship,
there's a principle at stake and he's adhering to it, and because at
the moment the situation with regard to the Italians is critical."

"Is that where he's going? Italy?"

They were in the drawing room of Tarquin's town house in
Eaton Square. Her mother wasn't in residence and wouldn't be
until Tarquin left London for their home in Norfolk. That they
no longer spent time in each other's company was something
Pamela uncaringly accepted.

Tarquin blew a plume of blue smoke upward.

"If you read your newspapers, Pamela, you will know that
the Italian line is close to collapsing and Russian resistance has
already collapsed. It means German troops are bolstering up
the Austrians, and if British and French reinforcements aren't
sent immediately to her aid, Italy runs the risk of being knocked
out of the war. That being the case, the Fourteenth Army Corps
is to be sent south immediately, and it was suggested, at the
highest level, that if Prince Edward accompanied the corps it
would boost morale in Italy enormously."

Pamela, uncaring of the Italians, flung herself petulantly
down on the nearest chair. "Then there's no telling when his

next leave may be! Oh, this bloody, bloody war! How much longer is it going to go on for?"

"It's going to go on until we win it—and with American help, that could now be quite soon. A year. Maybe less."

At Christmas John Jasper was home on leave, not looking remotely like the John Jasper who had kissed her good-bye six months earlier. That he had seen horrors beyond telling was imprinted in the deep lines that now furrowed his face and the flat, shuttered expression in his eyes.

For once Pamela had shown sense. She had asked no questions, and when he had used frenzied, violent lovemaking in an effort to blot out the hell he had just left and would soon be returning to, she had responded with a depth of passion even she hadn't known herself capable of.

"Don't get yourself killed, John Jasper," she had said fiercely when the time came for them to say good-bye. "I couldn't bear it. Truly I couldn't."

They had clung together, his head bent low over hers, his mouth touching her hair, her cheek pressed hard against the roughness of his army jacket. For once there were no thoughts of Prince Edward in her mind and, in his, no regrets for having been forced into a marriage he had not wanted.

The fears she felt for John Jasper, fighting in the front line where the average rate of survival for an officer was less than three months, were not fears she felt for Prince Edward. Despite his keenness to be in the thick of the fighting, because he was heir to the throne, the powers that be ensured that his exposure was limited. It was something he had complained bitterly about in one of his letters to her.

All this heir to the throne bosh drives me wild,

he had written.

I've got three brothers and if I should be killed, Bertie would
simply become the next heir. If Bertie were to be killed,
it would be Henry and, if Henry were killed, it would be
George.

Pamela hadn't spent time with either Henry or George, but she had been in Prince Albert's company, and a less likely Prince of Wales and heir to the throne than Bertie she couldn't imagine. Unlike Edward, but like his father, he possessed no charisma. This lack was made worse by a stammer so bad it made any kind of public speaking an impossibility.

The letters she now began receiving from Edward from Italy were far less guarded about where he was and what he was doing than his letters from France had been. In one of the first ones she received, he wrote of the situation in France, which, despite the arrival of American troops, was as night-marish as ever.

. . . It's not even a stalemate now that small squads of Hun
stormtroopers are infiltrating the British front line wherever
it has been smashed, creating breaches which the German
Eighteenth Army then pour through. As for the situation
here in Italy . . . If it weren't so tragic, it would be a joke.
The Italians have suffered a massive defeat, and British and
French help is proving to be too little, too late. The only thing
keeping me cheerful are your letters—and your photograph,
which I carry with me everywhere. For now, my angel,
I must close if I want to catch the King's Messenger bag.
Good night, Pamela darling. Tons and tons of all my very
best love, E.

Sometimes, when she put his letters away in a secret compartment in a jewelry box she had bought precisely for that purpose, she wondered if he also wrote to Marian Coke. It wasn't a pleasant thought. If he did, though, she was quite sure he wouldn't be using endearments such as "My Angel!" and "My Darling Angel!" to her.

Edith's letters arrived as intermittently as ever. In one she wrote that her brother was now one of the cadets training under Lieutenant Earl Winfield Spencer.

> *Though not at Squantum, but on a new naval air station on North Island, near San Diego. I haven't heard from Wallis in quite a while, but Humphrey (my brother) says she has had a nasty fall and is sporting a black eye!*

Remembering the monocle that Wallis had worn in order to attract attention when they were at Oldfields, Pamela wondered if Wallis was sporting an eye patch to cover her injured eye and if, on an evening, she wore an eye patch covered in sequins.

At the beginning of 1918 she received two pieces of stupendously good news. John Jasper had been injured, though not seriously.

> *But seriously enough for me to be in an army hospital. Be warned that I'm going to have a permanent limp, but at least I still have my leg, which is more than most of the other poor buggers here have.*

Unsaid was that he was also now far from the front line and that she no longer ran the daily risk of receiving a black-edged telegram.

The other piece of good news was from Prince Edward.

Dearest Angel!
I've been given six weeks' home leave in order to make a
tour of the defence plants. I'm certainly going to make sure
that there will also be time for a little rest and recreation in
London. I haven't danced now for over half a year, so get your
dancing shoes out and ready! Tons and tons of love, E.

Excitement spiraled so high, Pamela felt drunk on it. By the time his leave was over everyone in his circle would know she had usurped Lady Coke as being the most important woman in his life—and she was determined to remain so not for a few mere months, but for years.

Mistresses were not something Edward's father had ever indulged in. A more straitlaced and, in Pamela's eyes, more boring man than King George would be impossible to find. Edward's grandfather, King Edward VII, though, had been a very different kettle of fish, a renowned womanizer. His list of mistresses had been long and varied. Many of his affairs had been fleeting, but a handful of mistresses, especially as he had grown older, had stayed the course, and his relationship with his last mistress, Mrs. Keppic, had been regarded by high society as being almost a marriage. Even his long-suffering queen had regarded it as such, sending for Mrs. Keppic when her husband lay dying so that he could have the comfort of having the woman he so dearly loved at his bedside.

That was the kind of mistress Pamela intended to become, but unlike Alice Keppic she wasn't going to wait for Edward's middle-aged years before enjoying such a prominent position. She was going to become a royal mistress now and remain so right until, and after, Edward became king.

She clutched the letter elatedly in her hand. John Jasper wouldn't like the situation, but he would simply have to come to terms with it, as George Keppic had. It was traditional for an

Englishman to regard it as an honor if his wife became the mistress of the reigning monarch or his heir. The benefits to him careerwise, financially, and socially were always enormous, and if she couldn't convince John Jasper of those benefits, she would leave it up to Tarquin to convince him.

She needed new gowns. War shortages had affected high fashion, and material was at a premium. The last time she had visited the Ritz there hadn't been an enviable frock to be seen. Even worse, a hideous number of the frocks had been black, signifying mourning for a husband, brother, or father.

She shuddered, pushing the memory away, concentrating instead on how she could be clad in something suitably floaty and glittery and eye-catching when she again stepped into Prince Edward's arms.

His next letter to her was brief and to the point.

When we first meet again, can we do so out of the public eye?

With her heart hammering, Pamela had replied that there was nothing she would like better and, realizing he was leaving it up to her to arrange a discreet venue, suggested that, in her stepfather's absence, they dine à deux at his town house in Eaton Square.

"You are a very naughty girl, Pamela," Tarquin said to her when she told him of the arrangement she had made. "And I'm damned if I'm leaving town just so you and Prince Edward can enjoy an illicit romantic tryst. However, as I certainly don't want you doing so in your own home when your husband is lying wounded in a military hospital, I shall absent myself accordingly, but tell His Royal Highness that I expect him to begin making his own arrangements."

Pamela flung her arms around his neck and gave him an

unrestrained kiss on the cheek. "Thank you, dearest Tarquin! You really are the most wonderful stepfather!"

"I'm the most appalling stepfather. The only person I know who has less morals than myself is you."

She giggled, well aware he was speaking the truth. "That's why we've always got on so well," she said, removing her arms from around his neck. "My naughtiness amuses you."

She picked up the fox fur she had carelessly dropped on a sofa when entering the room. "The one thing I don't understand is why someone as puritanical as King George regards you as a friend."

"He wasn't always so puritanical, and I remind him of his Navy days when he was able to kick up his heels. He's become a bore, I agree, but he is a king and the glamour of kingship is very alluring, Pamela. I like being in its presence. Which is why I'm quite happy to help you further your romance with Prince Edward. For a man of twenty-three I suspect he's relatively inexperienced. Handle him with care and don't frighten him off. This is a chance that won't come again."

Edith's next letter came so hard on the heels of her last one that Pamela's first thought was that someone must have died. Without taking it to her bedroom to read, she opened it immediately, seeing with alarm that Edith's pin-neat handwriting had degenerated into a hasty scrawl.

Dearest Pamela,

You will never ever guess the news I have just received from Humphrey! He says the entire air station at North Island is agog with it! Apparently the reason Wallis's husband wasn't sent on active service overseas is that his superior officers have known for a long time that he has a DRINK PROBLEM!

Humphrey says Lieutenant Spencer's alcoholism has never been a secret on the base, but that as he is such a popular character and, despite his drinking, such a good administrator, it has been something overlooked until now, when the truth about a far worse vice has been revealed.

Dear Pamela, my hand is shaking as I write this. Lieutenant Earl Winfield Spencer is a WIFE-BEATER!!! Wallis and Win were due to attend a dinner at Commander L. E. Summers' home and when they didn't arrive for it, the commander sent an officer to the Spencers' home. Mrs. Summers, who had a headache, accompanied him in order to get a breath of fresh evening air. When they arrived they could hear Wallis sobbing and had to force a way in. She was alone in the house and TIED TO THE BED!!!

Humphrey says that if it hadn't been for Mrs. Summers seeing Wallis's condition—her monster of a husband had beaten her black and blue before leaving her in such a helpless state—the incident would have been hushed up, but Mrs. Summers was so incandescent with rage that now everyone knows about it. Mrs. Summers says there was old bruising as well as new and that this HIDEOUS INCIDENT was not an ISOLATED ONE!

No one now believes Wallis was telling the truth about her black eye. It is quite obvious she received it at the hands of her husband. However, Humphrey says Wallis is being tight-lipped and he thinks she is probably FURIOUS that everyone now knows about her husband's treatment of her. Wallis always did have a lot of pride, and it isn't as if she can leave her husband, for where would she go? I feel desperately sorry for her, but can't write and tell her so because I know she would HATE it that I know how VILE her husband is to her. You were always her very closest friend and I do so wish you still were, for she obviously has absolutely no one

to confide in and no one from whom she is willing to accept
sympathy.

Yours in haste, Edith

Pamela sat down on the nearest chair, anger at Wallis's plight pulsing through every vein in her body. She knew, even better than Edith, that Wallis had no family who either could, or would, help her. Certainly Wallis's Uncle Sol wouldn't do so. He would simply view a broken marriage as being a slur on his fine family name. As for Wallis's mother and her aunt, if her mother was working as a paid hostess in a Washington club, then she certainly wasn't in a position to help her, and, as Bessie Merryman had given up her Baltimore home in order to become a rich widow's companion, she couldn't provide an escape for her either.

If she had still been in America and if they had still been best friends, then she most certainly would have been able to help. She would have taken the train to San Diego and, if Wallis hadn't been willing to pack her own bags, would have packed them for her. Then she would have taken Wallis back to Baltimore—or Washington or New York—and funded her and stood by her while she got a divorce and rebuilt her life.

But she wasn't still in America, and they weren't still best friends.

The siren signaling a Zeppelin raid wailed ominously into life, and as members of her household staff scurried toward the kitchen in order to take shelter under its massive scoured worktable, she made her way into the dining room to take a similar precaution, though under polished mahogany and in dignified isolation.

" . . . And so I'm going to squire you to Maud Kerr-Smiley's party tomorrow night, and then afterward, darling Pamela, we will finally have some time on our own together."

. . .

For the first time since their last meeting, Edward's contact with her wasn't by letter, but by telephone. Even more thrillingly, he was less than a quarter of a mile away, at Buckingham Palace.

Maud Kerr-Smiley was the wife of an MP, Peter Kerr-Smiley, and someone she knew socially, though not very well. That Edward had chosen to spend the early part of their reunion evening at a party given by Maud surprised but didn't faze her. It didn't really matter where the early part of the evening was spent. It was their dinner à deux later—and what would happen after it—that was important.

She spent the entire day preparing for the evening with the single-mindedness of a soldier preparing for battle. She was lavish with the perfumed oil she poured into her bathwater. When she patted herself dry, she smoothed a mixture of glycerin oil and rose water over every inch of her body. The silk, lace-trimmed lingerie she chose to wear was the most exquisite she possessed, and the gown her maid helped her step into was a Poiret-inspired creation of flame-colored chiffon embroidered with crystals.

Her hair had always been her crowning glory and was the reason that, though it was now fashionable to do so, she hadn't yet had it bobbed. Carefully her maid combed the torrent of golden waves softly back over her ears and into a heavy knot at the nape of her neck. Pamela clipped pearl drop earrings to her ears, surveyed herself in the mirror, and liked what she saw.

Her cat-green eyes were emphasized by beautifully arched eyebrows. She had lightly smeared Vaseline on her eyelids, and her eyelashes were enhanced by the latest cosmetic: cake mascara. She wore a light dusting of powder on her flawless pale skin, and her lipstick was the exact flame color of her gown.

As she sprayed herself lightly with a perfume perfect for the mood she hoped to invoke in Edward, she sensed, rather than heard, his chauffeur-driven car arrive.

Putting down her perfume spray, she pressed a hand hard against her stomach to still the butterflies fluttering there.

A few moments later the front doorbell rang.

Her butler, who had been primed to expect a royal guest, answered it and, moments later, was announcing, "His Royal Highness, Prince Edward."

It was then Pamela realized that after their long correspondence, she hadn't a clue as to how she should address him. Normal etiquette was to address a royal prince initially as "Your Royal Highness" and then afterward as "sir."

In their letters she had, at his request, addressed him as Edward and he had addressed her as "My Angel," "My Darling Angel," or "Darling Pamela," which would make now addressing him formally seem very odd.

Nevertheless, "Your Royal Highness" was what she decided was her safest bet.

He corrected her instantly. "Edward," he said, taking her into his arms before she even had the chance to curtsey, and giving her a deep passionate kiss.

She had forgotten how slightly built he was and that in height he was only five feet five, or, at most, five feet six. While responding to him with ardor, she was conscious of only two things. One was that she should have worn shoes with much lower heels, and the second was that despite being his "Angel," she still wasn't being invited to call him David.

The Kerr-Smileys lived in nearby Belgrave Square, and when they arrived Peter Kerr-Smiley was at the front door to receive his royal guest, while his wife was at the foot of the staircase, ready to lead Prince Edward into the drawing room where all her other guests were awaiting his arrival.

That Prince Edward had brought a guest of his own with him was unsurprising to the Kerr-Smileys, but that his guest was Mrs. John Jasper Bachman, not Marian, Lady Coke, was a surprise so huge that both of them had to struggle hard to hide it.

It was a moment Pamela reveled in. Even better was the moment when she and Edward stepped into the drawing room together and an entire roomful of high society's finest instantly registered the nature of her relationship with him.

Edward hated formality, and the party soon became quite riotous. Lots of champagne was being drunk—though not by Edward, who, Pamela had long ago realized, was surprisingly abstemious. There was, however, lots of laughter and lots of dancing. Edward was a very good dancer—and so was she. His good manners decreed that he also took care to dance with his hostess, but immediately afterward he returned to her side, whispering in her ear: "Let's show everyone how to do a proper tango, Pamela darling."

To a storm of applause they did so, and it was then that the Zeppelin-raid sirens sounded.

The room immediately fell silent, with no one knowing quite how to react and no one wanting to show nervousness in Edward's presence.

"Trust a bloody Zep to try and spoil my first night home," Edward said lightly, breaking the tension. "As I'm sure Maud doesn't have enough tables to shelter us all, I vote we just carry on enjoying ourselves."

The tension eased. Another record was put on the gramophone. Dancing began again, albeit a little nervously, and as it did, there came the sound of urgent knocking on the front door.

"Someone's looking for shelter," Peter Kerr-Smiley said,

heading out of the room to find out to whom his butler was about to open the door.

"Considering the number our fighter planes have brought down, I'm surprised the Germans are still persisting with Zeppelin raids," Edward said confidentially to Pamela as they took a rest after their energetic tango. "They cause panic, of course, and that's where they score as a weapon of war, but they are very unstable. Once an incendiary bullet, fired from either a fighter plane or ground-based antiaircraft gun, pierces a Zep, it ignites the hydrogen gas it's filled with and it immediately becomes a giant ball of fire. I've never seen one crash to the ground in flames, but it must be a spectacular sight."

Pamela was too busy thinking of where the present Zep, if ignited into a ball of flame, might land, to make a reply to him.

It was then that Peter Kerr-Smiley reentered the drawing room with an olive-skinned, well-dressed man, and a petite, very pretty woman swathed in fur.

"Orphans seeking shelter," Peter Kerr-Smiley said to the room in general as he led his two uninvited and very unexpected guests across the room in order to introduce them to his royal guest of honor.

By the time they reached Edward, the woman had shed both her hat and her coat. Without the coat she looked even more petite and delicately boned. She also looked to be no more than twenty-two or twenty-three, and whatever fright she had felt at finding herself in an exposed position in Belgrave Square with a Zeppelin raid in the offing, she had quickly recovered from it. She had bright, dark, laughing eyes. Her bobbed hair was dark, too—so dark that beneath the light of the chandeliers it shone blue-black.

"May I introduce Mrs. Dudley Ward, sir?" Peter Kerr-Smiley said to Edward.

Mrs. Dudley Ward dipped a charming curtsey, and Pamela

sensed Edward's body stiffen. It was as if he had been struck by an unseen physical force.

She looked swiftly toward him, but even as Peter Kerr-Smiley was introducing Mr. Buster Domingues, Mrs. Dudley Ward's escort, to him, Edward's entire attention was rooted on Mrs. Dudley Ward, whose laughter-filled eyes were holding his without the least trace of shyness or awe.

"Would you do me the honor of dancing a quickstep with me?" she heard Edward say to her and registered that when Mrs. Dudley Ward replied to him, her voice was as husky and as fragile-sounding as her looks.

As Edward danced away from her, Mrs. Dudley Ward in his arms, Pamela was sickeningly aware of three things.

The first was that Mrs. Dudley Ward was inches shorter than Edward even in high heels.

The second was that she was as exotically dark-haired as Marian Coke and Portia Cadogan, the previous two women in his life.

The third was that Edward was dancing with Mrs. Dudley Ward not out of politeness, as he had danced with Maud Kerr-Smiley, but because he had been instantly, immediately, overpoweringly smitten by her.

She gritted her teeth, praying that when the dance ended he would return Mrs. Dudley Ward to her escort and would then speedily return to her side and stay there for the rest of the evening.

The record came to an end.

Another record was put on the gramophone, this time a foxtrot.

Without having released his hold of her for a second, Edward again began dancing with Mrs. Dudley Ward and, seemingly incapable of taking his eyes from hers, he did so for the next dance—and the next.

People began shooting amused glances in Pamela's direction. When the sniggers began, Pamela knew there was only one way for her to avoid total humiliation.

With her head held high she left the room and then, a black velvet cocoon coat around her shoulders, left the house, uncaring that the sirens were still wailing.

If Prince Edward had stayed the night with her at Tarquin's town house he would, she was quite sure, have afterward been bound to her for as long as she had wanted him to be.

Because of a German Zeppelin, that was not now going to happen, and her rage was incandescent.

"Piccadilly," she said tautly to the cabdriver she waved down, not wanting to even think about the perfectly set table for two in her stepfather's town house and the silk-sheeted bed in its vast bedroom.

All she craved, as the all-clear sounded, was her own home and privacy in which to give vent to her fury at the way fate, in the petite shape of Mrs. Dudley Ward, had cheated her of her dream of becoming Edward's mistress.

Chapter Twenty

Wallis's dreams had long lain in ashes. San Diego was idyllic, but her marriage had become a hell on earth. Though Win now held the prestigious position of commanding officer of North Island naval base, it wasn't a position he had wanted.

What he had wanted—what he still wanted—was an overseas combat assignment. His frustration at not being given one increased his heavy drinking, his dangerously erratic mood swings, and the frequency of his violent attacks on her.

His only saving grace was that he now never drank while on duty and that his superiors viewed his achievements at North Island with satisfaction. He was training not only pilots but mechanics and, as the war ground on, had added Marines and military personnel and raw recruits from Los Angeles to the training program.

That he habitually worked a twelve- to fourteen-hour day was a mercy for which Wallis was deeply grateful, for the instant he was off duty, his drinking and his rants would begin. His chief rant was that he was still in America when the brother closest to him, Dumaresque, was engaging in aerial dogfights over France and covering himself in glory. Hard on the heels of that rant would be his explosive fury that though she was adept at ensuring he was never sexually frustrated by her inability to engage in full normal intercourse, it meant there was no way he could father the sons he craved.

Wallis used every device she could think of in order to avoid triggering his temper. Now that Win was a commanding officer, their home was spacious, and she would retreat into another part of it and bury herself in a book or with a piece of sewing. If one of his black moods was on him, her efforts not to antagonize him never succeeded for very long. On one never-to-be-forgotten day he had indulged in his habit of tying her to the bed and then, while she was completely helpless to try to stop him, had taken every one of her family photographs and ripped them to pieces in front of her.

That his behavior was beyond anything that could be considered normal and that he was a deeply troubled man was knowledge she had done her best to hide and keep to herself. It was something the Mrs. Summers incident had made well nigh impossible, and when someone had had the nerve to mention it to her, she had laughed it off, saying that Mrs. Summers's remark that she had found her beaten "black and blue" was a figment of the elder woman's imagination, that she had not been found sobbing, and that her being found as she had been was simply a bedroom bit of private fun between herself and Win. As to why she was found alone in the house—it was, she had said, because Win had briefly left it in order to buy a bottle of wine.

Whether her version of her humiliating experience was believed she had no way of knowing, but no one ever mentioned it to her again or alluded to it in her presence. Privately, she tried to get what pleasure she could out of being wife to a man holding prestigious rank, knowing if she ever publicly admitted to his abusive behavior he would lose his position as the air station's commanding officer and that there would then be no compensations in her married life at all.

His behavior precluded her from making close friendships. What she did have was lots of people she was friendly with and, as the wife of the commanding officer, the kind of hectic social life that suited her outgoing, extrovert nature.

Whenever high Navy brass visited the station, which was regularly, there were always cocktail parties and dinners in their honor, and she loved being the hostess and, as her mother had done at her pay-to-attend dinners, ensuring that everyone had a good time. At such events Win had to at least make a show of being a considerate husband, but it was never more than a show, and whenever he had the opportunity he would make a snide remark to her that, though no one else present understood it, was a veiled and cruel insult.

As well as gaining pleasure from her innate hostessing skills, she also gained pleasure from the home they now lived in. Their house in San Diego stood on the corner of a quiet intersection, and the windows of the thirty-four-foot living room looked out over splendid views of Balboa Park. With a vaulted, sixteen-foot ceiling, it was a room filled with light, and Wallis decorated it as she had their home at Pensacola: with white walls, pale oak furniture, and gay chintz curtains and cushions.

Everything, if it hadn't been for the secret at the heart of their marriage and Win's attitude toward her because of it, would have been perfect. In early 1918 Wallis finally plucked up the nerve to make an appointment with a Los Angeles gynecologist, doing so with black humor under the name of her childhood bête noire, Violet Dix.

Once in the gynecologist's examination room, she knew why she hadn't braved such a visit sooner. Being seated in a chair with her legs in stirrups while the doctor slid what looked to be a pair of stainless steel salad tongs into her vagina and then opened them was an experience she vowed then and there she would never repeat.

Even worse, it was all to no avail.

"If your problem were simply that of a hymen that needed minor surgery in order to break it, it would be a common problem easily resolved," he said to her when she had put the items of clothing she'd had to remove back on. "You are, however, suffering from an abnormality I have had no previous experience with and with which I would be very reluctant to interfere. I strongly suspect, Mrs. Dix, that you have no womb and that no amount of extensive surgery would enable you to ever bear a child."

Frozen-faced Wallis thanked him, paid him, and left his consulting room.

She had never been very maternal or interested in children and, other than for Win's sake, didn't particularly want to bear a child. What she did want to do was to function as other women did in the bedroom and to put an end to Win's sneers that she wasn't a proper woman.

By the time she reached the train station, she was too deep in thought to be aware of how crowded and busy it was. Was the fact that she was unmaternal because of her lack of a uterus and a womb? Shouldn't she have guessed long ago that there was something basically wrong with her internal organs when, at Oldfields, she was the only girl who didn't have what was referred to discreetly as "monthlies"? The school nurse had told her it was nothing to worry about; that lots of girls, if they were athletic as she, captain of the Oldfields hockey team, was, didn't menstruate and, as she was spared all the considerable inconvenience of "monthlies," she was to think herself lucky.

She had thought herself lucky and, until now, had never given her very active, period-free life another thought.

She boarded a train for San Diego, thinking about it now very deeply.

Did whatever was different about her account for her flat-chested, angular figure? Certainly there was nothing remotely rounded or femininely voluptuous about her, and that there wasn't had never troubled her. She had liked looking different and had always played up to it. At one time, when she was about seventeen, she had even taken to wearing men's shirts and bow ties.

She had never felt unfeminine, though.

She had never overly preferred the company of girls to boys; rather the reverse. Even since she had been old enough to be interested in boys, she had always been very popular with them—and had wanted to be so.

The knowledge brought with it vast relief. Despite her markedly masculine appearance, she most certainly wasn't a man. Where sexual desire was concerned, she was very much a woman. Importantly as well, her visible genitalia were completely normal. She wasn't a freak. She was simply a woman possibly without a uterus and womb and with a hymen no one, not even a gynecologist, wished to tamper with.

Well, if that was the case, so be it. She could live with it. Even without penetration she could still give sexual satisfaction and, if Win had been a more tender and considerate lover, knew she would be capable of receiving it as well.

She would, though, never be able to give Win the son he so deeply craved.

As the train continued to steam toward San Diego, she felt an emotion for Win she had never felt before.

She felt pity.

It wasn't his fault he had drawn such a short straw when he had married her. That he should give vent to his frustration in violent rages was almost understandable—and from now on she was going to do her best to understand it. In many respects, they had such a lot going for them. Win was a man's man, popular with those beneath his command. He was certain he was in line for further promotion—which meant she would have even more prestige socially. Their lifestyle gave endless opportunities for the kind of entertaining and hostessing that she so enjoyed and that she excelled at.

The two of them simply had to make the best of things. As the train finally steamed into San Diego's tiny station she determined that she, at least, was going to do so. Somehow, some way, even though drink had made Win portly instead of slim-hipped and even though his once well-defined jawline was now as jowly as that of a man several years his senior, she was going to rekindle her feelings for him. For what she had unwittingly cheated him out of, she owed him that at least.

Full of inner resolve, she took the bus that led out to the air station. Win never got home till late in the evening, and so she would have time to make an especially nice dinner for the two of them. She would leaf through her cookery bible, *Fannie Farmer's Boston Cooking-School Cook Book*, and find something she was certain he would enjoy.

As she got off the bus and walked the short distance to their pleasingly large house, its yard a riot of oleander and roses, she felt almost lighthearted. She now knew the worst and had decided how she was going to live with it. All that was needed to make it work was just a tiny bit of reciprocation from Win.

Though it was still only late afternoon, she knew the instant she closed the front door behind her that the house wasn't empty and that Win was home.

There was no noise, though. No clinking of a bottle against the edge of a glass. No sound of him moving about.

With tension mounting, she shed her jacket and gloves and

walked swiftly through the sitting room, calling out, "Win! Win, darling! Where are you?"

She found him in the dining room. He was seated at the table, his face ashen, a telegram in his hands.

Slowly, with a look of stupefaction on his face, he raised his head to hers.

"Dumaresque," he said starkly. "He's dead. Shot down in a dogfight with a Fokker triplane."

Deeply shocked, she put a hand on the table's shiny surface to steady herself.

Dumaresque had been the only person in his family Win had truly cared about, and his death was going to hit him hard. Even worse for him would be the manner of Dumaresque's death. For Dumaresque to have died in action while he, Win, had been thousands of miles away, safely training pilots in navigational skills, would in his eyes be such a slur on his manhood she doubted if he would ever get over it.

Even as the thought came to her, he crushed the telegram fiercely in a white-knuckled fist.

"Win, darling . . ." She rounded the table in order to put an arm around him, to offer him some kind of comfort.

Brutally he pushed her away. "Don't 'Win darling' me!" he snarled, stumbling to his feet. "Dumaresque is dead and so are hundreds of thousands of others! And where am I? I'm a useless object sunning myself in California!"

With her heart thumping painfully in her chest, Wallis said briskly, "Of course you're not useless, Win. Organizing air stations the way you do is helping win the war on a scale much larger than would be the case if you had been sent overseas as a pilot. The job you do is vitally important and you are very good at it—"

"I'm a fucking failure!" Sobs caught in his throat as he barged past her to the door leading into their sitting room. "I should have been out in France with Dumaresque. I should be out there now, hunting in the skies for the bastard who brought him down in flames!"

In mounting alarm she hurried after him, but he was already at the cocktail cabinet, one hand around the neck of a bottle of gin.

He swung around to face her. "Get out!" he screamed, tears streaming down his face. "Get out! *Get out! GET OUT!*"

She didn't need telling for a fifth time.

Scooping up the jacket and gloves she had just shed, she beat a hasty retreat, running in her haste to be out of the house. With the front door closed safely behind her, she paused, panting for breath. What was she to do now? Trawling through Fannie Farmer's cookbook for something extra delicious for dinner was completely out of the question. What she had to do was to steer clear of Win until he had drunk himself into an unconscious stupor. Only then would it be relatively safe for her to return.

In Pensacola, the movie theater had been a retreat for her countless times in the past, and the movies was where she now headed. There, in the dark, she would work out how she was going to deal with what she knew was going to prove to be yet another destructive blow to her marriage.

The movie was an English film that had been released just before the outbreak of the war. It was historical, all about Henry VIII and his six wives. Wallis had too much on her mind to pay it much attention, but one thing she did notice was that the actress taking the part of Catherine Howard reminded her very strongly of Pamela.

Afterward Wallis was to always remember the day Win received the news of Dumaresque's death as the day when, instead of their marriage being given a second chance as, when returning from Los Angeles, she had intended it would be, it became the day their marriage finally reached the point of no return.

He became inseparable from his flask of gin, often disappearing to the beach at night to drink for hours on end in lonely, bitter isolation. To make things even worse, there were other Spencer family tragedies. His mother was killed in an automobile accident. His sister Ethel committed suicide. Even to Wallis, who always struggled to be pragmatic, it seemed as if the Spencer family had been born under a particularly dark star.

Where the darkness of her own life was concerned, the one sliver of hope she clung to was that when victory finally came and the war was at an end, Win would no longer be burdened by the shame he felt in not having seen front-line active service.

By the end of the summer it seemed as if the war were about to come to a victorious conclusion. The Germans were being pushed back to the old Hindenburg Line, the position they had held before the spring offensive. The battlefields began to be littered with abandoned German weapons, and the numbers of German prisoners taken soared into the thousands.

September brought with it fresh, sweeping victories. All along the Western Front, from the Scheldt River in the north to Sedan in the south, the Germans were finally in retreat.

In October, American troops under the command of General Pershing crashed through the German line on the River Meuse, hammering the final nail into Germany's coffin. From then on, there was no doubt about the outcome.

On the eleventh of November Wallis woke to the news that an armistice had been signed and that the war in Europe had ended. The jubilation at the air station was manic. People ran from their homes screaming and yelling and whooping with joy and relief. Whistles blew. Bells rang. Guns were triumphantly fired.

In San Diego there was dancing in the streets. The next day Win led his men in a confetti-blitzed parade through the city. A sixty-piece U.S. Navy band marched behind them, and bringing up the rear were flag-waving Boy Scouts, the California Women's Army Corps, and a whole host of city dignitaries.

For Wallis it provided a rare moment: a moment when she could justifiably be proud of Win. Despite his off-duty drinking binges and the rumors on the base as to his treatment of her, he had, through a mixture of sheer energy and talent, created the North Island naval air station virtually from scratch, just as he had the air station at Squantum.

It was a big achievement and she knew that if he could only curb his drinking and his temper, there was no telling what heights he might reach within the Navy. Knowing exactly how her Montague and Warfield relations would react if she told them she wished to divorce Win, she determined yet again to soldier on with her difficult marriage. Quite simply, it seemed to her she had no other choice.

Chapter Twenty-One

With the war now at an end, everyone she knew, apart from herself and Win, was looking forward with fierce optimism to the future. Optimism was not a quality Win had ever possessed, and the end of the war brought with it, for him, a feeling of utter worthlessness. Being in command of a naval air training station when a war was in progress had been one thing. There had been an adrenaline-filled sense of urgency about it. There was no sense of urgency at all in being in command of a naval air training station when the war to end all wars had been fought and won.

"What is the damned point of it?" he said savagely time and again to Wallis. "All I'm now doing is pushing a pen all day long—and there's no promotion in the pipeline. It's men who've seen active service who are getting the promotions."

With every passing day his sense of failure and disappointment increased. At home he retreated behind a wall of silence so complete that there were times when Wallis would have been grateful for the cutting remarks he had once been so free with. Now he rarely spoke to her at all.

She compensated for the hostile silence she lived with at

home by spending as much time as possible outside it. There were congenial people on the air station with whom, in the plush surroundings of San Diego's Hotel del Coronado, she played bridge, bezique, and backgammon. She went to the cinema once or twice a week with Fidelia Rainey and then came a lifesaving event. Henry Mustin was posted to San Diego in order to assume command of the air detachment of the Pacific Fleet. A month later, Corinne joined him.

"So give me all the gossip, Skinny," she said as they sat in a quiet corner of the del Coronado, sipping chilled martinis. "What's griping Win? Henry says he's like a bear with a sore head—and doin' himself no favors because of it."

Wallis had given a lot of thought as to how much she was going to tell Corinne. Because Corinne was not only family but also the nearest thing to a best friend she had, her instinct was to tell her everything. If she did, though, Corinne would tell Henry—and the outcome of that would not be good for Win's career.

She said, choosing her words carefully, "He's not happy, Corinne. I never could convince him that being in command of Squantum and then North Island was far more important to the winning of the war than serving as a pilot at the front. When Dumaresque was killed in action, he felt guilt, shame, every negative feeling you can imagine."

Corinne took a sip of her martini and then said, "Negativity isn't a quality the Navy looks for when promoting men. I hate to say this honey, but Win is his own worst enemy. Especially where booze is concerned."

Wallis flinched. For Corinne to speak so bluntly about Win's drinking problems meant those problems were also known to Henry and, if they were known to Henry, it meant they were also known to the Navy brass who held the power to promote—or not to promote—Win.

"Win never drinks on duty, Corinne."

Corinne quirked an eyebrow. "If all Henry's heard is true, the amount Win drinks off duty means he doesn't have to drink on duty. His off-duty drinking is enough to keep him tanked up all the time."

It was too true for Wallis to deny. She bit her lip, hoping rumors as to other aspects of Win's behavior hadn't also reached Henry Mustin's ears.

Corinne swirled an olive on a cocktail stick around in the remainder of her drink. "Both Henry and I feel partly responsible for your marriage to Win, Skinny. You met him in our home, and both of us knew Win was a man with a very short fuse. I guess we just couldn't imagine him giving rein to his temper where a woman was concerned. Something it seems we were wrong about."

Wallis opened her mouth to vehemently deny that Win had ever been abusive to her, but it was a lie too far and the words wouldn't come.

Corinne put her drink down and took hold of Wallis's hand, gripping it tightly. "No one else is goin' to give you this advice, but then I'm not anyone else. Nothing is ever goin' to get any better between you and Win. He's a man with a whole pile of problems—all of them of his own making. Leave him. Get a divorce and start afresh. If you don't, he'll crush your spirit, Skinny. And you can trust in one thing—though the rest of the family will react to the word *divorce* as if the world has come to an end, Henry and I won't. We know too much about Win. You'll have us rooting for you even if you don't have anyone else."

Grateful as she was for Corinne's support, Wallis still continued trying to make her marriage work. For her to become a divorcée would break her mother's heart. Not only that, it would signify failure on a very public scale, and, ever afterward, her reputation would, she knew, be viewed as being tarnished. It was Corinne's attitude toward Win that brought matters to a head.

After months of treating Wallis as though she didn't exist, he slammed into the house late one afternoon, incoherent with rage. "You've told her!" he screamed, sweeping their collection of cut-glass crystal from its display shelf onto the floor in an avalanche of glittering, shimmering shards. "Mustin's never going to put a good word in for me now!"

"I haven't told Corinne anything, Win! I swear to God I haven't!" Desperately she tried to get out of the room, but whichever way she darted he was right in front of her. Broken glass crackled beneath the soles of her shoes as he made a lunge, seizing hold of her wrists.

She knew what was going to happen next. He was going to drag her into the bedroom and hog-tie her to the bed as he had done countless times before. Then he would leave her there for hours while he went off on a drunken bender.

As always, she struggled like a wildcat, but he was a big man.

"Bitch!" he shouted at her as he lashed first one of her wrists to the headboard, and then the other, following the expletive with a string of other, far viler ones.

Wallis had heard them all before, but as Win stormed out of the bedroom and then out of the house, she vowed she wasn't going to go through the rest of her life listening to them. She was going to follow Corinne's advice. She was going to divorce Win and start her life afresh.

In late spring of 1919, when Win was away on a week's training exercise, she took the train to Washington to speak with her mother.

"Honey, you just can't do a thing like that." Alice stared at her as if unsure as to whether she had heard right.

"Yes, I can, Mama. This last time when he tied me to the bed, he didn't come back for thirty-six hours! I nearly died of thirst, and I've never been so hungry in my life."

Alice began twisting her hands together. "Some men aren't easy to live with, darling, and I guess Win is a shade worse than most. You can't divorce him, though. No Montague has ever been divorced. It's just something completely unheard of."

"There's a first time for everything, Mama. Win doesn't love me anymore—and because of the way he treats me, I don't love him anymore either."

"In marriages between well-bred people, love doesn't always have a lot to do with things."

"Maybe it doesn't, but those aren't the rules you've lived by, Mama. You always married for love and were fortunate enough to always stay in love. I haven't been. There's another reason, too, why I think divorcing Win is the right thing for me to do."

The blood left Alice's face. "Dear Lord, Wallis! You're not in love with another man, are you?"

"No, Mama." She paused, wondering how, without causing her mother unnecessary distress, she could best explain that she could never have children. In the end she decided that vagueness was the best policy. "Because I've never fallen pregnant, I went to see a gynecologist, Mama. He says I'm not quite as other women are internally and that I'll never be able to have a baby. For that reason alone, I think Win should be free to marry again. That way he'll stand every chance of having the son he so wants and that I can't give him."

Alice's china blue eyes widened and her mouth began to tremble at the corners. "No babies?" she whispered, the unspeakable prospect driving everything, even the word *divorce*, from her mind. "Not ever?"

Wallis closed the distance between them, taking her mother in her arms. "No, Mama," she said huskily, Alice's tears wet against her cheek. "Not ever."

Alice had wept and, when she had recovered from her weeping, had said with a stubbornness Wallis almost admired: "It makes no difference to the shame a divorce would bring on both Montagues and Warfields, Wallis. If you won't listen to me, perhaps you'll listen to Bessie."

If the situation hadn't been so painful, Wallis would have laughed at the idea of her mother telling her she should listen to Bessie when she knew it was something her mother had never done.

Bessie, though, was almost as pragmatic as a Warfield and not in a million years could Wallis imagine her much-loved aunt insisting she remain in a marriage where she was treated so appallingly. It was an assumption that proved to be ill founded.

"You may separate," her aunt said to her, her homely face distressed, "but you cannot possibly divorce, Wallis. It would be an action your reputation would never recover from. As for your argument about not being able to give Win the sons he wants . . ." Her voice trailed off and a look of deep pain crossed her face. "Not everyone can have the children they would like to have, Wallis. Even if Win were to marry again, there is no guarantee there would be children and, even if there were, no guarantee that one of them would be a boy."

The gentle reminder that she, Bessie, had never been fortunate enough to have children wasn't lost on Wallis, who felt deep shame at not having been more sensitive to her aunt's widowed and childless situation.

"I'll make coffee for us all," she said, bringing the conversation to an abrupt conclusion and aware of her aunt's and her mother's deep relief.

It was a relief that only made her feel more ashamed, for she had no intention of taking their word as law. They were Montagues, but as well as being a Montague, she was also a Warfield, and the only person whose word was law for a Warfield was Uncle Sol's. If she could persuade her Uncle Sol to give her his support where a divorce from Win was concerned, her mother and her aunt would begin to think differently about things.

"A divorce? *A divorce*? Are you mad, Wallis?" Solomon Warfield was puce with indignation. "Have you completely lost your mind?"

"No, Uncle Sol." Wallis dug her nails deep into her palms. "Win is a violent alcoholic and—"

"What do you expect when, instead of marrying a young man from Baltimore high society you marry a naval officer whose family comes from Kansas?" Spittle formed at the corners of Sol's traplike mouth. "You did what you've always done, Wallis. You did exactly as you wanted. Spencer was your choice and now you're going to have to live with it. There'll be no divorces in the Warfield family. Not while I have breath in my body."

Determinedly Wallis stood her ground. "I'm only twenty-three, Uncle Sol. I'm young enough to start my life afresh and—"

"HOW?" Sol's bellow nearly took the roof off 34 Preston Street. "How, in the name of all that is holy, do you intend to keep yourself? You have no money. The little your grandmother left you, you spent foolishly on a quite unnecessary extravaganza of a wedding. You have no marketable abilities. When it comes to math, you can't add up a column of ten figures without coming to three different totals! *I* am certainly not going to fund you! My days of doing that are over! I'm telling you now Wallis, once and for all, I WILL NOT LET YOU BRING THIS DISGRACE UPON OUR FAMILY NAME! Warfields don't divorce. They never have and, God so help me, they never will!"

With Uncle Sol's furious words ringing in her ears, she had made the long, long trip back to San Diego. With so much adamant family opposition, she didn't see how she could divorce Win. What her uncle had said had been too painfully true. She had no family money on which to rely. As a Warfield, she hadn't been brought up to earn her own living. None of the girls she had ever associated with at Arundell or at Oldfields had ever gone to university or given a passing thought to becoming financially independent. For girls brought up as she had been brought up, life was simple. After school and finishing school they became debutantes and, when their debutante year was over, they made highly suitable marriages. She had ticked three out of the four boxes—and she had also married. The problem was, she hadn't done so suitably.

She'd been too swept off her feet to care that Win wasn't from a prestigious Baltimore family. She hadn't cared that his family wasn't wealthy on the scale that her Uncle Sol or her friends' families were. She hadn't cared about his reputation for having a temper, because it had never occurred to her that his temper would ever turn on her. She hadn't cared about anything but being the first debutante of her year to marry and the excitement and glamour of having a husband who was one of only a small handful of pioneer aviators.

It was an impetuosity for which she was paying the price. She had, as her Uncle Sol had remarkably refrained from saying, made her bed and now she had no choice but to lie in it.

Win's first words to her when they were together again were, "I've been detailed to take charge of a detachment of aviators training at March Field in Riverside. It's still California, so there's no sense in you uprooting yourself from here."

It was the longest sentence he'd said to her for months. Through the open door leading into their bedroom she saw that his case was already packed.

She leaned against the doorjamb, dizzy with relief at the prospect of having the house to herself; of being able to live in it free from fear.

He swung on his heel, striding into the bedroom, snatching up his suitcase.

"Don't think just because I'm not here keeping an eye on you that I won't know if you start getting up to tricks with anyone," he said viciously as he walked back toward her. "You start fooling around and I'll know about it the second after it's happened."

She hadn't the slightest intention of fooling around with anyone, but she didn't say so. She couldn't. Her throat was too tight for her to speak.

Without a kiss good-bye or a word of affection he slammed out of the house.

Silence enfolded her like a warm embrace. She had no idea how long he was going to be away, but she knew one thing. Every minute they were apart was a minute she was going to treasure.

Within days, her always full social life picked up speed.

"Don't sound so surprised by it," Corinne said, deeply amused. "Win isn't comfortable company for anyone anymore. People would much rather have you at their dinner parties without Win than with him."

"Is that why Rhoda and Marianna Fullam never went out of

their way to be overfriendly to me, and are now inviting me to accompany them to nearly every event they attend?"

Rhoda and Marianna were the daughters of Rear Admiral Fullam, and the set they moved in was very high-flying. Thanks to them, Wallis now found herself attending polo matches at Del Monte and beach parties in La Jolla and had even, via Rhoda, met and had her photograph taken with Charlie Chaplin at the del Coronado.

"Rhoda and Marianna absolutely adore you, Skinny, but for them, Win is a fly in the ointment. You can't blame them. No one wants to socialize with someone who is always in a black mood and who drinks not to have a good time but to get seriously drunk."

It was the Fullam sisters who early the following year first leaked the news to her that Britain's Prince Edward was scheduled to spend a full day in San Diego while en route to Australia aboard the battle cruiser HMS *Renown*.

The news was so cataclysmic, Wallis was terrified it was nothing but wild speculation. Corinne silenced her fears.

"No, Skinny. It's true and the news will be made public before the end of the week. The governor and the mayor will head the welcoming party, and they'll be accompanied by dozens of local and military officials."

"Will Henry be one of them?"

"I certainly hope so. I don't think wives will be included in the welcoming party, though. Our turn to be presented will come later. There's bound to be a grand ball so that the very maximum number of people will be able to get a close-up view of him."

Over the next few weeks, more and more details were made public of the plans being made. There was to be an official Navy luncheon aboard the battleship *New Mexico*. This piece of news sent Wallis's heart racing. Throughout the latter part of the war Win had been in command of San Diego's North Island air station. Surely that meant he would be recalled from March Field in order to attend the luncheon aboard the *New Mexico*? And surely it meant she, too, would be presented to the prince?

With Win no longer around to take exception at her doing so, she got out all her old pinup photographs of Prince Edward and propped them up on her dressing table. What would he be like in the flesh? Would he be just as heart-stoppingly handsome? Would he be the embodiment of all her romantic daydreams?

Corinne passed on any news she received from Henry almost the instant she heard it.

"The prince will arrive here on April seventh and will be accompanied by his cousin, Lord Louis Mountbatten," she said to Wallis over the telephone. "After he has been officially welcomed and has had lunch, there will be receptions aboard the *Aroostook* and HMS *Renown*, followed by a grand parade through the city streets that will culminate in the stadium, where it is expected he will give a speech. In the evening there is to be a Mayoral Ball at the Hotel del Coronado, followed by a banquet. An invitation for Win and yourself will be with you any day, so get shopping for the most splendid evening gown you can find!"

Splendid evening gowns were in short supply in San Diego, and so she took the train to Los Angeles, returning with a pearl-embroidered gown of turquoise slipper satin that sheathed her greyhound-slim body like a sheet of ice. With it she would wear high-buttoned white satin gloves, white satin shoes, and, around her throat, a choker of pearls that had belonged to her grandmother.

In an agony of suspense she waited for the official invitation card to arrive. When it did, it was an invitation to the Mayoral

Ball only, and there was no mention of the banquet that was to follow the ball.

"You'll receive a separate invitation to the banquet," Corinne said to her reassuringly. "Henry and I have already received ours, and so have the Raineys."

Win made a terse telephone call informing her he would be arriving in San Diego on the morning of the seventh. That he wasn't arriving in the city until the actual day of Prince Edward's visit was a clear indication to her that he hadn't been invited to the luncheon aboard the *New Mexico*.

She didn't need to wonder why. That his drinking was finally beginning to ruin his career was something too starkly obvious.

Another day went by without the invitation to the banquet arriving.

Then another day went by.

"Win and I are not going to be invited to the banquet," she said at last to Corinne, her voice bleak. "I guess Win's certainty that he's being sidetracked is just all too true."

Corinne, who as well as having been invited to the Mayoral Ball and the banquet had also been invited to accompany Henry to the luncheon aboard the *New Mexico*, said awkwardly, "I'm sorry, Skinny. There's nothing I can do. The invitations aren't something Henry has any control over."

"I know that, Corinne." Wallis managed a smile, determined not to let her mortification at not being invited to the banquet show. She would pretend that not being included among the crème de la crème didn't matter to her. To behave any differently would only draw extra attention to her and Win's exclusion.

As the day of the prince's visit drew nearer, she was seized by a single, overpowering anxiety. What if Win drank too much at the Mayoral Ball? In showing himself up, he would show her up, too. If Win became visibly unsteady on his feet, he would be forcibly escorted from the ballroom—and she would have to leave with him.

The prospect of such humiliation kept her awake at night. She also lay awake wondering how she could arrange to be presented to Prince Edward at the ball. There would never be another opportunity for such a thing to happen. The evening of April 7 was going to be a once-in-a-lifetime occasion.

She stared up at the ceiling, wondering if Rear Admiral Fullam might be in a position to introduce her to the prince. She would speak to Rhoda and Marianna and ask them to have a word with their father.

And whatever else happened, the minute Win stepped through the door on the morning of San Diego's big day, she was going to have to keep him away from his bottles of gin. This was one occasion in his life when he simply could not be seen to be inebriated in public.

The first words he said as he came in through the door were, "It's all a huge fuss over nothing. Who cares if a British prince stays overnight in San Diego? What has he ever done in life but be born with a silver spoon in his mouth? It's bullshit and I'm not having any part of it."

Wallis sucked in a deep, steadying breath. For a man of Win's rank, attending the Mayoral Ball wasn't something that was a matter of choice. If he didn't go, his absence would be noted and would be another black mark against him.

With great difficulty she forced lighthearted gaiety into her voice. "You can't miss the biggest event San Diego has ever had, Win. There are going to be over a thousand people there, many of them coming from as far away as San Francisco."

"More fool them." He shrugged himself out of his jacket and ripped off his tie. "This country is a republic. Fawning over royalty sticks in my craw."

Her stomach muscles began tightening in painful knots. If she persisted in trying to persuade him differently, he would lose his temper completely and she would then run the risk of finding herself trussed up like a chicken, with no way of freeing herself.

With her mind racing she tried to think of her best plan of action.

"We've had an emergency at March Field and I've had no proper sleep for twenty-four hours," he said, striding away from her in the direction of the bedroom. "Don't wake me. Especially don't wake me in order for us to go to the del Coronado."

The bedroom door slammed shut after him.

Slowly she let the breath ease from her body.

Win might feel very differently about going to the del Coronado when he woke, but it wasn't something she could depend on. Her best plan of action was to now make alternative arrangements for getting herself there. She would beg a lift from Corinne and Henry. Arriving with the commander of the Air Detachment, Pacific Fleet, would put her in an excellent position when it came to contriving an introduction to the Prince of Wales.

When it came time for her to dress for the ball she entered the bedroom on tiptoe, no longer eager for Win to wake. Going to the ball without him would be far preferable than going to it with him. By deciding that the ball in Prince Edward's honor was "bullshit" and that he wasn't going to attend it, he had unintentionally done her the biggest possible favor.

Hardly daring to breathe, she carried her evening gown, gloves, shoes, and jewelry out of the room and dressed in the sitting room.

When the Mustins' car drew up outside the house, she didn't wait for anyone to knock on the door. She simply opened it and closed it behind her as quietly as a burglar leaving the scene of a crime.

"Skinny, you look sensational," Corinne said as Henry's driver opened the rear passenger-side door for Wallis and she slid into the car next to her. "I've told Henry that Win will be joining us later." She squeezed Wallis's hand tightly to indicate that this was the story she had given Henry and that it was a story Wallis should stick to. "Wouldn't it be just swell if Prince Edward fell in love with an American girl tonight? Can you imagine it? An American future queen of England? Wouldn't it just be the most sensational thing you could possibly imagine?"

As the car sped off in the direction of the Hotel del Coronado, Wallis was immediately reminded of Pamela and of the way Pamela had daydreamed for years of winning Prince Edward's heart and of becoming the Princess of Wales and, one day, queen.

As she looked out of the car window at the dusky light now clouding the sky, turning the water of San Diego's magnificent bay from blue into deep indigo, she wondered what Pamela's relationship with the prince now was. Edith's latest letters hadn't mentioned her. They had been too full of the fact that she was now finally engaged.

"Let me tell you how splendid the lunch was aboard the *New Mexico,*" Corinne said as the twinkling lights of the Hotel del Coronado came into view. "Prince Edward was charm personified. He went out of his way to speak to every single person who was there. I dipped the curtsey I'd been practicing ever since we received our invitation and he smiled *right at me.* He's unbelievably handsome, Skinny. Every inch a fairy-tale Prince Charming."

As they neared the creamy white Victorian chocolate-box confection that was the hotel, it seemed to Wallis that it, too, had come from the pages of a child's fairy story. The rose-tinted roofs of its turrets and cupolas were a deep wine red against the smoky light of the early evening sky. Its sea of verandahs had gingerbread trims that were straight out of something by Hans Christian Anderson. It was the perfect venue in which to meet a prince who would one day rule an empire.

She had been to the del Coronado many times but never on an occasion so splendid. Chandeliers blazed with light. Jewels glittered on evening gowns so fabulous they made Wallis's mouth water. Dress uniforms sported magnificent displays of medals. Wallis had never before seen so many gold stars. In the ballroom the orchestra was playing Irving Berlin's "A Pretty Girl Is Like a Melody," and when Fidelia Rainey's husband asked her if she would like to dance, she accepted unhesitatingly.

Several dances—and several partners—later, she caught sight of Rhoda Fullam. Rhoda, resplendent in purple taffeta, weaved a way toward her.

"What time is Prince Edward due to arrive, Rhoda?" she asked.

"Nine. Isn't this just too magical for words? Papa is hoping very much that the prince will dance both with me and with Marianna."

Wallis caught her breath. The prospect of actually *dancing* with Prince Edward hadn't even occurred to her. All she was struggling to do was to be presented to him.

"For some reason Win's name and mine haven't been included on the official presentation list," she said, trying to sound as if it were an oversight that could have happened to anyone. "I wondered if your father could have a word with whoever is in charge of the presentations? Win isn't here, as yet, and may not be able to get here, but I would hate to miss out on such an opportunity just because of a silly error."

Rhoda's eyebrows pulled together. "But why would there have been such an error, Wallis? I don't think Papa could do as you ask, because I'm sure the names of everyone who is to be presented were submitted and approved weeks ago."

Wallis was sure they had been as well, but she wasn't going to let such a detail stand in her way.

"Please, Rhoda. A word from your father to whoever is in charge of presentations would do the trick, I'm sure of it."

As they were talking, Rear Admiral Fullam was standing only a few yards away from them, and with a slightly irritated shrug of her shoulders, Rhoda walked over to him. Wallis, not wanting to look too pathetically eager to hear what the result of Rhoda's request was going to be, moved away.

She didn't move too far away, though. She didn't want Rhoda to be unable to find her again.

Suddenly a ripple of tension ran through the ballroom.

"He's here!" The whisper ran from mouth to mouth like wildfire. "The prince has arrived!"

There was such a crush in the vast room that Wallis didn't see his entrance. As she stood on tiptoe, straining for a glimpse of him, Rhoda squeezed a way toward her, saying, when she reached her, "My father obviously has a soft spot for you, Wallis. He says he'll make sure you're included in the list of those to be presented."

With great difficulty Wallis resisted the urge to punch the air in glee. Instead she said warmly, "That's swell, Rhoda. It's a favor I won't forget."

The band, which had stopped playing as Prince Edward had entered the room, picked up their instruments again and began a foxtrot. As people again took to the dance floor, their necks craning in their efforts to keep the prince in their line of sight, Wallis saw him in the flesh for the first time.

It was a moment she was never to forget.

Though he was twenty-six years old, he looked younger. There was a boyishness about him that made it hard to believe he had spent the four nightmare years of the Great War as an army officer, always seeking to be where the greatest danger was. Everything else about him was just as his photographs had led her to believe, and as the people who had met him had described.

He wasn't very tall. His cousin, Lord Louis Mountbatten, who had accompanied him into the room and was standing beside him, was far taller and, being broad-shouldered, far more imposing.

But he didn't have Prince Edward's charisma, nor did he remind her of medieval drawings of St. George, about to slay the dragon.

Physically he was the absolute, utter antithesis of Win. His masculinity had nothing bullishly threatening or aggressive about it. It was impossible to imagine him giving vent to senseless rages or coarse, offensive behavior. As she watched him in conversation with Governor Stephens and Rear Admiral Fullam, she noticed how he gave each man his full, undivided attention, even though she was quite sure he was impatient to take to the dance floor.

She drew as near to where he was standing as she possibly could, watching with a fast-beating heart as senior officers and their wives began to be invited to step forward to be presented to him.

He spoke a few words to each person he shook hands with. Every one of them received a smile of immense charm.

Among the long line of those being singled out to be presented was Fidelia Rainey and her husband. Then it was Marianna Fullam's turn to dip a deep royal curtsey.

Wallis dragged her eyes away from the prince and toward Rear Admiral Fullam, willing him to look in her direction.

He did so, giving her an infinitesimal nod of the head to

indicate that she should join the next group of naval wives waiting to be presented.

Wallis drew in a deep steadying breath.

As she did so, Corinne came up behind her like a whirlwind, seizing hold of her arm.

"Come with me *now!*" she hissed, her face bloodless. "Win is here and about to create a scene that will ruin his career in five seconds flat!"

"I can't, Corinne," she hissed back. "Rear Admiral Fullam has arranged for me to presented to the prince. I have to join the next group and—"

"And nothing!" Uncaring of the attention they were beginning to attract, Corinne spun her around. "Win is here, looking for you. He's falling-down drunk and spoiling for a fight, and if he sees you being presented to Prince Edward he's in bad enough shape to try landing a punch on the royal jaw. Now behave like a sane woman and come with me *now*. With a bit of luck he'll then be satisfied with dragging you off home and no great harm will be done."

Wallis looked once more toward Prince Edward, knowing that a moment she would have treasured for the rest of her life was now not going to happen. Win had ruined it, as he had ruined so many other things in the life they shared.

With a heart feeling as if it had turned to ice, she allowed herself to be hurried out of the ballroom by Corinne. There had been many moments when she had vowed that her marriage to Win was over and that she was going to leave him—and she had never done so.

Now, though, was different.

Now it really was the end between them, and she was going to allow nothing and no one to persuade her otherwise.

Chapter Twenty-Two

She didn't act precipitately. She had done so too often in the past and always it had been to her disadvantage. Win was living in expectation of a new posting, and, when it came and if it was somewhere far distant, a decision by her not to accompany him would cause no raised, scandalized eyebrows. Lots of Navy wives didn't accompany their husbands on their postings, especially if the posting was abroad.

Six months after Prince Edward's visit to San Diego, Win was detailed to return to Pensacola as senior flight instructor. It wasn't abroad, but it was the other side of the country, and when she told Win she wouldn't be going back to Pensacola with him, he seemed almost as relieved as she was at the prospect of a separation that, in Navy terms, wouldn't seem odd to anyone.

The following spring he was appointed as assistant to Rear Admiral William A. Moffett in the U.S. Department of the Navy in Washington, D.C. It was the kind of posting that, in social terms, required him to have a wife at his side, and he was brutally blunt in his demand that she join him there.

For Wallis, Washington was a very different prospect than

Pensacola had been. Both her mother and her Aunt Bessie were living in Washington and, once there, she would have family nearby when the breach between herself and Win was made public.

Their married quarters were a small flat in a residential hotel called the Brighton. It wasn't somewhere Wallis intended to stay.

"I know you don't approve, Mama," she said to Alice, perfectly composed about the decision she had made in the ballroom of the Hotel del Coronado and which she was now about to put into action, "but I can't live with Win another single day. His posting here in Washington isn't the kind of posting that suits him. It isn't active enough for him, and, because he's bored pushing a pen all day long, his rages when he's at home are even worse than they were in San Diego."

She wasn't embroidering the truth. Win's rages had become the talk of the Brighton as he screamed invectives at her, lashing out at her with his fists, and then, as a coup de grâce, smashing up whatever furniture first came to hand.

"There have been so many complaints by other residents that we've been asked to leave, but I'm not leaving with Win, Mama. Every minute with him is a minute when my life is at risk. Can I come here and live with you, Mama? Please?"

Alice wrung her hands despairingly. "If you do, honey, word will get back to Baltimore, and what will people say when they know you've left your husband? Your reputation will be ruined, and I have so little room here and . . ."

Silently Wallis unbuttoned her dress and stepped out of it.

At the sight of the bruises and weals that the dress had been hiding, Alice gasped, her eyes wide with horror.

"Now will you let me come and live with you, Mama?"

With a choked sob Alice threw her arms around her. "Of course I will, Wallis darling. Why didn't you tell me how cruelly you were being treated? If I were a man I'd punch Win Spencer's lights out and make sure all his superior officers knew exactly what kind of a beast he really is."

Without troubling to point out to Alice that she'd been telling her for a long time how cruelly she was being treated, Wallis gave her a grateful kiss and then went out to the taxi she had crossed town in and, after paying the driver, carried the bags she had brought with her into her mother's small apartment. They contained all her clothes and all her personal possessions. Come hell or high water, her life with Win was finally and irrevocably over.

Win's career, if not over, was soon visibly on a downward spiral. He was obliged to leave the Brighton Residential Hotel and, no longer having a wife living with him, he moved into the Army and Navy Club. Via the grapevine Wallis heard he was constantly quarreling with his superiors, and when he abruptly told her over the telephone that he had received yet another posting, Wallis wasn't at all surprised. This time his posting was the kind that would put thousands of miles between them.

In February 1922 he was commissioned captain of a gunboat, his destination Hong Kong.

"That sounds to be a posting just up your street," she said pleasantly when he told her. "No more deskwork. You'll be happy as a clam."

"No, I won't," he snapped back. "The *Pampanga* is a leaky old tub that should have been scrapped years ago."

It was Henry who told her what Win's task was going to be. "The *Pampanga* is one of several vessels that form the South China Patrol of the Asiatic Fleet. China is being torn apart by rival warlords, and the *Pampanga*—and other small ships like her—constantly patrol the coastline and estuaries. Their main

mission is protecting American businesses and missions—
every day there is news of priests and nuns being killed—and
to help any American personnel who need rescuing. It's a task
Win is perfectly suited for."

Life in Washington—without Win—perfectly suited Wallis.
Several friends from Arundell and Oldfields lived in the city,
and through them she entered the heady world of diplomatic
society. Wherever she had gone and whatever situation she had
found herself in, she had always been popular, and Washington
was no exception. She never told anyone that she had left her
husband and was trying to figure out the best way of getting
a divorce on very little money. Because she was a Navy wife
whose husband was serving in China, it was taken for granted
that she was on her own because China was too dangerous a
place for her to be.

Until now, though she was a natural-born flirt and as far
back as she could remember had always preferred male company to female company, she had never been unfaithful to
Win. It was a situation that changed within hours when Phoebe
Schermerhorn—now the wife of Conrad Zimmerman, a high-
flying Washington lawyer—introduced her to thirty-five-year-
old Felipe Espil, first secretary at the Argentinean embassy.

Felipe—a rich, smooth, Rudolph Valentino look-alike—was
the biggest catch in the city.

"He originally came here ten years ago as an attorney,"
Phoebe said to her as, arms linked, they had entered one of the
French embassy's glittering white-and-gold reception rooms.
"That he is now first secretary to the Argentinean ambas-
sador will give you some indication of just how ambitious
and talented he is. His reputation as a lady-killer is fearsome.
One smoldering glance from eyes so dark they appear to be

black, and even the most respectable matron becomes a quivering wreck."

"You too?" Wallis asked, anticipation tingling along her nerve ends.

Phoebe gave a throaty laugh. "'Fraid not. Conrad keeps me on a tight leash, and as he's an absolute dear and I'm crazily in love with him, I don't allow Señor Espil to work his Latin American magic on me."

Wallis wondered if Felipe Espil would be able to work his magic on her. More to the point, as she threaded her way through the crowded room accompanied by Phoebe, she wondered if *she* was going to be able to work any magic on *him*.

In Washington society, the most important thing was precedence.

Ambassadors, of course, were the kingpins of any diplomatic gathering, but a first secretary tipped soon to be an ambassador himself ranked a close second. As the wife of a Navy officer, she came so low in the pecking order that only her friendships with people like Phoebe ensured that she was invited to events such as tonight's reception. All that would change, though, if Felipe Espil began escorting her to parties and functions.

Even though she had still to lay eyes on him, her determination that he would do so was fierce. In Baltimore, because her impeccable Warfield ancestry wasn't accompanied by Warfield money, she had been denied unequivocal acceptance into high society—an acceptance that should have been hers by right. She wasn't going to let the same thing happen to her in Washington. In Washington she was going to fight tooth and claw to ensure she didn't have to rely on the kindness of friends in order to move in the highest possible social circles.

"There he is," Phoebe said suddenly, squeezing hold of her elbow-length-gloved arm. "Over there. Talking to Senator Grumbridge."

Wallis looked—and sucked in her breath.

He was gorgeous. Tall and slim with olive skin and finely chiseled features. His brilliantined hair was night-black, his eyebrows satanically winged.

Even before they made a move toward him, she was more dazzled than she'd ever been before in her life.

"Want an introduction?" Phoebe asked.

"Oh yes," she said, letting her breath out slowly. She gave a quick glance around the rest of the room, satisfied that the gown she was wearing was sufficiently different to set her apart. It was of black chiffon—the only black gown in the room, for black was rarely worn by anyone other than widows. Her angular, boyish figure was the height of fashion, and the low-waisted sleeveless dress with its deep U-shaped neckline flattered her far more than the same style did the other women in the room.

Where their gowns were lavishly decorated with beading or fringing—and sometimes with both—her gown was starkly plain except for the spectacular bunch of artificial red cherries she had pinned to one shoulder.

Satisfied that if not the most beautiful woman in the room, she was certainly the most eye-catching, and not being afraid to let her confidence show, she allowed Phoebe to lead her in Felipe Espil's direction.

As Felipe sensed their approach, he brought the discussion he was having with the senator to a halt and turned toward them. His eyes met Wallis's. They were just as dark and as mesmerizing as Phoebe had led Wallis to believe—and they immediately gleamed with admiration.

"Mrs. Zimmerman." Dutifully he paid attention to Phoebe first, taking hold of her hand and raising the back of it fleetingly to his mouth. As he released it, he said in a richly accented voice, "You're acquainted with Senator Grumbridge, I believe?"

"Yes"—Phoebe smiled toward the senator—"but I don't

think either of you have had the pleasure of meeting an old school friend of mine, Mrs. Spencer."

Felipe gave Wallis the benefit of his full attention, the admiration in his eyes now blatant. He raised her hand to his well-shaped mouth, and for Wallis, as she waited for the hot imprint of his lips on her flesh, time stood still.

He didn't kiss the back of it. Instead he held it so that her fingers were upright, her palm facing him. Then, uncaring of whoever might be watching the two of them and his eyes still holding hers, he kissed the tip of each finger very slowly and very meaningfully.

Desire confounded her. Given privacy, she would have done whatever he asked of her.

Phoebe said, "Wallis is from Maryland."

"Ah, a Southern belle." With what Wallis sensed was deep reluctance, Felipe let go of her hand. "They are reputed to be God's greatest creation, are they not?" White teeth flashed in a smile. "I now understand why."

In an adjoining room a small orchestra was playing dance music. "A foxtrot," Felipe said. "My favorite. Would you do me the honor, Mrs. Spencer?"

The minute his arms closed around her and they began to dance, Wallis had the overwhelming sensation of having come home. This man—wealthy, well bred, sophisticated, and cultured—was her destiny. John Jasper had been an innocent schoolgirl infatuation, a first love she would always remember, but whom she certainly no longer sighed for. Win had been a horrendous mistake: a man neither wealthy, well bred, nor cultured, and certainly not someone who could reinstate her into her rightful place in high society. There were no such drawbacks to Felipe Espil, who was, Phoebe had told her, well on his way to becoming an ambassador.

"I'm here tonight in a semiofficial capacity, Wallis," he said, dancing beautifully. "It means I cannot devote all my attention to you in the way I would like. Perhaps tomorrow evening you would have dinner with me and I can make up for this?"

By the time the foxtrot ended she was quite certain it hadn't been a case of *coup de foudre* only for her, but that he, too, had fallen headlong in love the moment they had met.

"You're the fastest worker I've ever come across," Phoebe said later when they were again on their own. From her tone of voice it was quite obvious she didn't know whether to be admiring or shocked. Wallis didn't mind which she was. She was on the verge of a whole new exciting adventure, and once she had her divorce, who knew where it would end?

The next evening they dined together at one of the most prestigious restaurants in Washington. It was a clear sign to Wallis that even though she was a married woman, there was going to be no clandestine aspect to the relationship they were now embarking on. As they held hands across the table, she let herself imagine a perfect future. Divorce from Win. Marriage to Felipe. And the whole of Baltimore saying, *Of course, you remember Wallis? She's now the wife of the Argentinean ambassador in Paris.* Or perhaps it would be London. Or even—the thought made her physically dizzy—Washington.

Over a sublime bottle of Château Margaux she told him her husband was a lieutenant in the Navy and that he was stationed in China.

"And are you looking forward to his return?" Felipe had asked.

"Yes" she had answered, a smile curving her mouth, "but only because it will speed up divorce proceedings."

Later, he had suggested they drive to his Georgetown apartment and get to know each other still better over coffee and liqueurs.

Not until they were there and Wallis was seated on an elegant, brocade-covered sofa did she broach the subject that had to be surmounted before he took her to his bed.

"There's something you have to know about me." Despite her extreme self-confidence, her heart was beating fast and light. "I'm physically very unusual inside, Felipe. Not at all like other women."

He was seated opposite her at the far side of a glass-topped coffee table. As his eyebrows flew high in stunned shock, she swung her legs to the thickly carpeted floor. "My hymen is impenetrable—but it isn't the end of the world, Felipe. I can still give great pleasure in bed."

"I'm sure you can, for you are a flower of the South." He leaned toward her, his hands clasped between his knees. "And you are also, you say, a citadel that can't be stormed?" Prurient interest shone in his near-black eyes. "Will you allow me to discover this intriguing uniqueness for myself, *mi querida*?"

He unclasped his hands and, rising to his feet, drew her to hers.

"I knew you were different the instant I saw you at the party, Wallis *amor*." His voice was husky as he lifted her into his arms. "Only you, in all the room, were not a pale, insignificant butterfly. Only you had what my Jewish friends call *chutzpah*."

The next few months were idyllic. As Felipe's accepted escort she attended functions and parties that not even Phoebe or any other of her Washington friends could have had her invited to. Felipe taught her the correct protocol on meeting important dignitaries and how to be at ease with them. He insisted she read not only the *Washington Post* and the *New York Times* every day, but also the *International Herald Tribune*, Britain's *Times*— which kept her up to date with the latest news on the Prince of

Wales, who was terrifying the British public with his reckless-
ness as a steeplechaser—and the French *Le Figaro*.

"It will help you brush up on the language," he had said
when she had mildly protested that her schoolgirl French was
possibly not up to *Le Figaro*. "Languages are important within
the diplomatic community. The German you studied at Oldfields is passably adequate, but you must begin learning Span-
ish." He had flashed her a warm, intimate smile. "If you do
not, how will you know what the words mean that I whisper
in your ear?"

Among his many passions were opera, ballet, and antiques.
Always able to show deep interest in the interests of the current
man in her life, Wallis became suitably knowledgeable—and
though opera and the ballet never became more than pleasantly
enjoyable, searching out and recognizing valuable antiques
became an addiction that would last her entire life.

Her blatant association with Felipe was comfortably accepted by everyone in Felipe's social circle—who couldn't have
cared less who he was romancing—and a little more uncomfortably so by Wallis's friends from Oldfields and by her cousin
Corinne.

It wasn't accepted at all by her mother and Aunt Bessie.

"You're a married woman!" Alice would let fly at her time
and time again. "Your Grandma Warfield will be spinning in
her grave!"

Aunt Bessie had been far less hysterical, but deeply concerned. "When this affair is over you're not going to have a rag
of reputation left to you, Wallis. Win will divorce you . . ."

"Which is what I want!"

". . . and you'll never find an honorable man who will marry
you. You'll end up a lonely divorcée."

"No, I won't," she had responded feistily. "I'll end up an ambassador's wife!"

Chapter Twenty-Three

In June, and without Felipe, she attended Edith's wedding to a scion of one Baltimore's most prestigious families.

"Such a shame Pamela Bachman couldn't attend," Edith's mother whispered to her confidentially at the reception. "She is a great friend of the Prince of Wales, and Edith would have so liked her to be here. Unfortunately the Bachmans aren't arriving home until next month. Such a pity."

Wallis sucked in her breath. "Pamela and John Jasper are coming back to Baltimore to live?"

"No. I don't believe John Jasper would be comfortable in Baltimore, not since his mother died and his father remarried." Mrs. Miller's finely sculpted nostrils flared in distaste. "Such a foolish thing for a man to do—taking as his second wife a woman young enough to be his daughter."

Wallis wasn't remotely interested in John Jasper's father's marital arrangements. "Then if Pamela and John Jasper aren't going to be living in Baltimore, where are they going to live?"

"Washington." Mrs. Miller's attention was already focused elsewhere. "So nice speaking to you, Wallis. Please give my best regards to your uncle when you next see him."

As she glided away Wallis stared after her, poleaxed. High society in Washington was a small, elite circle. There would be no way she and Pamela and John Jasper would be able to avoid meeting each other, and when they did, how was she going to feel?

The high spot of the reception—the cutting of the cake—was about to take place. Wallis was oblivious. Her question to herself was one she couldn't answer. She wasn't still in love with John Jasper. Over the last few years she had barely given him a thought. Would she feel differently, though, when she saw him again? And what about his feelings for her? He had still been in love with her when he'd had no alternative but to marry Pamela. Would he still be carrying a torch for her, and if he was, how was Pamela going to feel about it?

A storm of applause and cheers went up as Edith and her bridegroom cut the bottom layer of a towering twelve-tier cake.

Wallis's thoughts were still centered on Pamela and John Jasper.

Why had they settled on Washington as a place to live? Why not New York? Washington was a city of diplomats, journalists, politicians, lawyers, and highly placed Army and Navy officials. Was John Jasper perhaps a lawyer now? Or a journalist? If he was, it was something Edith, in her letters, had never mentioned.

Five weeks after Edith's wedding, at a party at the Argentinean embassy, she looked across a crowded chandelier-lit room and saw Pamela and John Jasper enter it. John Jasper was looking down at Pamela, laughing at something she had said. Her elbow-length-gloved hand was tucked lightly in the crook of his arm. It was rare for married couples to show such pleasure in each other's company when out in public, and Wallis felt as if a bolt of electricity had hit her.

There was no jealousy in her shock, only a stunned surprise she hadn't been anticipating. What wasn't a surprise was what a breathtakingly good-looking couple they made. John Jasper's hair was still as night-black and thickly curly as it had been when she had last seen him, and Pamela had had her mane of buttercup-blond hair cut into a sleek, fashionable bob. Her silver-satin evening gown was halter-necked, the narrow bias-cut skirt skimming a figure of serpentine slimness.

A senior diplomat at the embassy had crossed the room to greet them, giving Wallis precious time in which to unravel her turbulent emotions and decide on how she was going to play this very difficult reunion.

A few moments later, when she still hadn't decided what course to take, Pamela decided it for her. As John Jasper engaged in conversation with the Argentinean, she looked around the room the way people do when hoping to see a familiar face.

Her eyes met Wallis's, then widened, and then, almost instantly, a huge smile nearly split her face in two.

"Wally!" she cried out, immediately leaving John Jasper's side and almost breaking into a run in her eagerness to reach Wallis's side. "Wally! How *wonderful*! I didn't know you were in Washington. Is your husband stationed here?"

She hugged Wallis, uncaring of the startled looks from those standing nearest to them.

As Wallis continued struggling as to how to react, Pamela stepped away from her in order to look into her face, her own face suddenly apprehensive. "You're not still mad at me over John Jasper, are you, Wally? Neither of us meant to hurt you. John Jasper didn't love me, and though I'd always had a secret crush on him, I didn't think for a moment anything serious would come of it. I was just having fun. When I found out I was having a baby I thought the world had come to an end and

I know it sounds crazy, but the one person I really needed then was you."

The familiar sea green eyes were urgent. Pleading.

Wallis stood very still. Pamela had betrayed her in the worst way any woman could betray another. They had been best friends. Blood friends. She had trusted Pamela totally, and Pamela had broken her trust in a way she had believed was irrevocable.

She opened her mouth to tell Pamela so, but the words wouldn't come. The stark truth was that time had moved on. She had thought she would never get over the loss of John Jasper in her life, but even before she had married Win she had been able to think of John Jasper without pain.

It was the loss of Pamela that had mattered to her the most, and now here Pamela was, pleading for the two of them to be friends once again. She tried to imagine what kind of friendship it might be, this second time around. On her part it would, she knew, be far more cautious. She bit her bottom lip, wondering if that mattered, and decided that it didn't.

With a shaky smile, she said, "I've needed you lots and lots of times, Pamela—and I'm not still mad at you, though I was at the time. I was so mad I would have torn your hair out given the chance."

Pamela laughed. "Since I had it bobbed there's not much to pull out." She tucked her arm companionably in Wallis's. "Come and say hello to John Jasper. He's going to find this difficult, but he'll survive it, and after this party is over, we'll go somewhere quiet where we can catch up on things. I expect Edith has written to you over the years. She's certainly written to me and will probably never forgive me for missing her wedding by a mere month."

"It was at Edith's wedding I learned that you and John

Jasper were coming back to the States to live and were going to settle in Washington." They were weaving their way through the throng of bejeweled and bemedaled guests. "What I want to know is why Washington, when New York is so much livelier?"

"Because diplomats live in Washington, not New York, and John Jasper has been posted here after serving for five years as a junior-grade diplomat at the American embassy in London. Typical of Edith to have left that little bit of information out of her letters. What did she write about?"

Laughter bubbled up in Wallis's throat. It was just as though they were at Oldfields again; just as though the years of hurt silence between the two of them had never been. "She wrote mainly about your friendship with Prince Edward."

"Ah!" There was satisfaction in Pamela's voice. "But she wouldn't have told you everything, Wally, because she never knew everything."

They were within a couple of feet of John Jasper now, and at their approach the Argentinean who had been talking to him gave a polite nod in their direction and moved away, and John Jasper had no option but to turn and face them.

He had changed in the nine years since she had last seen him. When they parted he had been a boy with an appealing good nature and the striking looks of a Roma Gypsy. Now he was twenty-six, and though the Gypsy-like handsomeness remained, it was overlaid with a patina of confidence and sophistication that was quite devastating.

He said stiffly, "It's good to see you again, Wallis."

Suddenly the muscles around Wallis's mouth wouldn't work. This was the man whom, if he had not gone on an extended European tour with his father, she would most certainly have married and, if she had done so, would have been happy with. It was impossible to think of anyone—even Pamela—not being happily married to him. She had thought she was over him, that meeting him again wouldn't matter to her. Now she knew that if the circumstances had been different he would matter to her just as much as he had done when she was a schoolgirl at Arundell.

The circumstances that were different were not that he and Pamela were married, but that despite his not being in love with Pamela when he married her, he loved her now. His doing so was something she had known the instant she saw them enter the room together.

From now on, she and John Jasper would be friends. Friends who had a shared history neither of them would ever quite forget.

She flashed him a warm smile. "It's good to see you again as well, John Jasper."

The relief in his gold-flecked eyes at the way the difficult moment had been overcome was intense.

"Isn't this nice?" Pamela slid a hand through the crook of Wallis's arm and another through the crook of John Jasper's. "Who would ever have thought that when we met up again it would be in the Argentinean embassy in Washington, and not in London or Baltimore? Who are you going to introduce us to, Wally? Not counting the ambassador, who is the most sought-after person here?"

Wallis's smile deepened. "Don Felipe Espil, the ambassador's first secretary," she said. "If you are going to be seeing a lot of me, you will also be seeing a lot of Felipe."

It wasn't until the next morning that she and Pamela were able to exchange confidences in private. "We're staying at the Crowne Plaza until we find somewhere suitable to live," Pamela had said to her when they said their good-byes at the embassy. "Come round tomorrow and we can do some real catching up. John Jasper won't be there. He'll be too busy settling into his new posting."

When Wallis arrived at the Crowne Plaza, she wasn't surprised to find that Pamela and John Jasper were occupying the best suite of rooms the hotel provided.

"And we are still cramped for space," Pamela said after Wallis had dutifully admired it. "That's because John Jasper just won't see sense where Oliver is concerned. Instead of leaving him at his prep school—where he was perfectly happy—he has insisted on disrupting his education by bringing him with us, which means, of course, we now have extra domestic staff to accommodate."

"Is he here now?"

Wallis rarely took an interest in children, but this child was different; this child had disrupted the entire course of her life.

"No. His tutor has taken him to view the city's historical sites. They'll be gone all day. Make yourself comfortable, Wally. This is going to be a very long session of catch-up. Top of my list of questions is, where is your husband? I take it he's not in Washington, or you and the suavely charming Mr. Espil wouldn't be on such obviously friendly terms."

Pamela was seated on a blue-and-gold brocaded chaise longue, her legs tucked beneath her in the way Wallis remembered her always sitting. Careless posture was something Wallis had never felt comfortable about. She'd been too drilled as a child by her grandmother to always sit with a ramrod straight back to be able to sit as casually as Pamela did.

"Win is in China. He's in the Navy. I expect Edith told you that."

"She did. She also said she didn't think the two of you were very happy together."

Defensiveness about her marriage was too ingrained for Wallis to drop all attempts at it immediately. "Edith never visited us, so how could she possibly know whether we're happy or unhappy?"

"Gossip, I expect." Pamela cocked her head to one side. "Come on, Wally. This is me you're talking to—and Edith told me enough for me to know that it can't possibly be a happy marriage."

The moment Wallis had waited so long for, the moment when she could speak truthfully about the horrors of her marriage to Pamela, was so momentous that a tremor ran through her.

Seeing it, Pamela said swiftly, "Let me pour you a fresh coffee, Wally. Would you like a brandy with it? The Crowne Plaza isn't mindful of Prohibition. The first thing the manager asked when we arrived was whether we'd like a brown-wrapped bottle of very good stuff."

"Thanks, Pamela." Wallis's gratitude was deep. "A glass of very good stuff is just what I need."

Pamela uncurled her legs and leaned forward in order to reach the coffee percolator standing on a low table between her chaise longue and Wallis's easy chair. After pouring Wallis another cup of coffee, she left the room to go into a bedroom, coming back a few minutes later with two glasses of brandy.

Only when the glass was in her hand did Wallis say, "I fell in love with Win for his rugged good looks and his courage as an aviator and married him without truly knowing him."

"And he has a temper?"

Wallis nodded, aware now that gossip as to Win's abusive behavior toward her had somehow reached Edith, and that Pamela already knew of it.

She cupped the glass in her hand, warming the brandy. "His friends warned me about it beforehand, but being a fool I simply thought it enhanced his tough-guy image. I never thought he'd start using me as a punching bag."

"Bastard," Pamela said succinctly.

Wallis took a sip of her brandy and then said, "There were reasons, Pamela. There are things about me which would probably drive nine out of ten men into similar behavior."

Wallis took a deep breath, aware that the moment had come for her to divulge her biggest secret.

"Rubbish. Nothing can excuse a man from lashing out at a woman. He's manipulated your brain if that's what you believe."

"I'm still a virgin, Pamela."

Pamela's eyes widened and her jaw dropped. "But why? Do you mean Win is *impotent*?"

"No, I wish he were, because if he were the situation wouldn't matter to him so much."

Pamela stared at her blankly. "I'm sorry," she said at last. "You've got me completely foxed."

Unsteadily Wallis put her brandy glass down on the low glass-topped table. "I have internal abnormalities that mean I can't engage in normal intercourse. I've seen a gynecologist and nothing can be done. It's just something I have to live with."

Pamela opened her mouth to speak, failed, and tried again. "Then how . . . ? Forgive me, Wally. But what do you *do*?"

Wallis gave a wry smile. "Other things. Use your imagination, Pamela. A climax doesn't depend on penetration—and men can be given pleasure in other ways. Sometimes they actually prefer the other ways."

Pamela shook her head in disbelief. "I thought I was the one who was going to take you by surprise when I told you some of the things that have happened to me since we last met, but you beat the band, Wally. Wasn't Queen Elizabeth Tudor supposed to have been a perpetual virgin? And aren't you very distantly related to her? A quote from Ben Jonson said she 'had a membrana on her, which made her incapable of men, though for her delight she tryed many.'"

"If you're going to begin quoting Elizabethan playwrights, I'm outta here, though if Elizabeth Tudor suffered from the same affliction she has my sympathy, and no, I don't think I am very distantly related to her, not even via my Montague line. What are the things you are going to surprise me with? Don't forget that thanks to Edith I already know how chummy you are with the Prince of Wales."

Pamela pulled a face. "Thanks to a certain Mrs. Dudley Ward I'm not as chummy as I once was. Let's go for a walk and I'll tell you all about how I nearly enslaved him and how Freda pipped me to the post." She rose to her feet. "Do you know in all the time I lived in Baltimore I never visited Washington once? As we are only a mile away from the Washington Monument, what say we go and take a look at it?"

Wallis never minded visiting historical sites, and there was nothing she wanted more than to hear inside gossip about the Prince of Wales.

It was a typical hot and humid August day, but they were both wearing cool low-waisted dresses with calf-length floaty skirts and, once outside, straw cloche hats pulled forward far enough to shield their eyes from the worst of the sun's glare.

As they strolled down K Street in the direction of the National Mall, Wallis said, "I came within a hairsbreadth of being presented to the Prince of Wales when I was living in San Diego."

"What went wrong?"

"Win." She didn't elaborate. Pamela had by now gotten the picture where Win was concerned, and Wallis didn't want to talk about him more than was absolutely necessary.

Pamela gave a throaty chuckle. "I came within a hairsbreadth of being much more than merely presented. At the time America entered the war, at a party given by my stepfather and at which he was a guest, Prince Edward fell for me hook, line, and sinker. The war was at its height and he was nearing the end of his Christmas leave. From then on, first from France and then from Italy, I received the most adoring letters imaginable and I knew, absolutely *knew*, that on his next leave home, when I became his mistress in the fullest sense of the word, he'd be mine for as long as I wanted him to be."

Wallis was now too worldly to be shocked at how easily Pamela would have been unfaithful to John Jasper—and she also sensed that adultery wasn't going to be the outcome of the story.

"And?" she prompted as they crossed a busy intersection.

"And on the first evening of his next leave we went to a party in Belgrave Square. It was given by someone I didn't know. Maud Kerr-Smiley, the wife of an MP. I didn't mind, as I didn't see how the early part of the evening could affect the later part of it—and it wouldn't have if it hadn't been for a Zeppelin raid."

Though she had been chuckling at the beginning of her story, there was now an edge of bitterness in her voice.

"I don't understand. Was the house bombed?"

"No, but it might as well have been."

They turned right onto Constitution Avenue.

As Pamela remained silent, Wallis didn't prompt her again. She simply waited until Pamela felt like continuing with the story of how the Prince of Wales had fallen into another woman's arms.

At last Pamela said, "Everyone was dancing when the maroons went off . . ."

"Maroons?"

"Big guns that signaled a Zeppelin raid was imminent. Freda Dudley Ward and the gentleman friend who was escorting her were crossing Belgrave Square and sought shelter at the nearest house, which, fate being what it is, just happened to be the Kerr-Smileys' house."

They sidestepped a woman walking two poodles.

"Maud's husband introduced Freda and her companion to the prince, and the instant he set eyes on Freda he was a lost soul."

"But why?" Once again Wallis was bewildered. "Is she stunningly beautiful?"

"No, though she's pretty enough. The advantage Freda has over me is that she's dark-haired—Edward nearly always goes for women who are dark-haired—and even in high heels she's *tiny*."

Wallis blinked.

Pamela laughed and gave a shrug of a silk-clad shoulder. "If you've seen him in the flesh, then you'll know how slightly built he is and that he's no more than five feet five—if that. I'm five feet six and that evening I was wearing heels. If anything was the nail in my coffin where Edward was concerned, it was those high heels. He immediately asked Freda to dance—she barely reaches his shoulder—and he's been dancing with her ever since. Tarquin says he's absolutely besotted by her and now he never looks at another woman."

"What about you? Does he still speak to you?"

"Whenever we meet at parties or dinners he simply behaves as if all his adoring letter writing to me had never happened. Which is, I suppose, something to be grateful for, because if he had begun ignoring me completely, John Jasper would have wanted to know why. Have you been following his tours of the empire? In Buenos Aires a choir of fifty thousand children greeted him with 'God Bless the Prince of Wales,' all of which they had laboriously memorized in English, and in Delhi he made a speech in Hindustani that *he* had laboriously memorized, and in South Africa he shook so many hands that his right hand swelled to the size of a balloon and he had to shake hands with his left."

"I read about his ticker-tape reception in New York and that the running boards of his car were trampled away by crowds determined to get nearer to him."

"It's the same wherever he goes, Wallis. He is without doubt the most eligible man on the planet." She gave a wry laugh. "And I let him slip through my fingers. Anyway, that's enough about Edward. I want to know all about Felipe. You're obviously going to get a divorce from Win, and when you do, do you think Felipe will step up to the plate and propose?"

As they neared the green open spaces of the National Mall, Wallis told her that where Felipe was concerned, she certainly had hopes.

"Though he's a Roman Catholic and I'm an Episcopalian, which makes things a bit tricky."

"You could always convert."

Wallis shot her a wry grin. "For a man who looks like Rudolph Valentino, it's something I'll certainly consider."

They both cracked with laughter—laughter that filled the entire day along with secrets and confidences.

Pamela told Wallis that before his infatuation with her, the only person publicly known to have been important in Prince Edward's life was Lady Coke. "Who is nearly old enough to be his mother," she had added. "And knowing Marian Coke—as I now do—I'd be surprised if there was any bedroom hanky-panky in their relationship. However, I do have a very strong suspicion that there was someone else in his life before Marian."

She told Wallis about the Houghton family and of the bust Lily Houghton had sculpted of Prince Edward when he was seventeen and a cadet at Dartmouth Naval College.

"The thing is, Wally," she had said as they had stepped out of the elevator at the top of the monument, "according to Lord May, the Houghton girls' grandfather, who is slightly gaga and probably told me a great deal more than he should have, not only did Edward visit them every time he traveled between Dartmouth and Windsor Castle, but there was no 'Your Royal Highness' or 'Sir' business with them. To them he was David, the name by which he's known within his family, and that, Wally, is *extraordinary*. Even when Edward was writing to me as his 'Dearest Angel' he never invited me to call him David—and Marian Coke says she was never given that privilege either."

"So which of the Houghton sisters do you think he was romantically involved with?"

Pamela had looked out at the dizzying view and said without a shadow of doubt: "Lily, the youngest. The one who sculpted his image and whom I've never met. Rose is far too schoolmistressy for someone as unacademically minded as Edward, and of her two other sisters, the one who is now the film star Marietta des Vaux would have scared him to death, and the other is far too plain."

Ever after that conversation, whenever Wallis saw a movie featuring Marietta des Vaux, she thought of the Houghton family and wondered if Lily Houghton really had been the first love in Prince Edward's life.

Felipe had chided her for listening to gossip he doubted could possibly be true.

It was John Jasper who convinced her that it was. "Mention Prince Edward in front of Rose and she not only goes very silent, she also goes very still. It's a most odd reaction in a woman as straight-talking as Rose. Of all the friends Pamela made in England, Rose Houghton was the one I liked the best."

He also said to her one day when they found themselves alone together for a few moments at a party, "I never meant to hurt you, Wallis. I behaved very dishonorably. The devil of it is, I can't regret doing so because though Pamela can be exasperating and self-absorbed to the point where I want to shake her till her teeth rattle, there's something very special between the two of us."

"I know." She had touched his hand with deep affection. "I was hurt. It would be a lie if I said I wasn't. I got over it, though. Now all I want is for us to be friends."

"We'll always be friends, Wallis." There was a throb of deep sincerity in his voice, and then he lightened the moment by adding wryly, "That is, of course, unless you hit me over the head with a pencil box again!"

Chapter Twenty-Four

With Pamela and John Jasper in Washington and with an ever-widening social circle, Wallis had never been happier. Everything, especially her love life, was perfect. Felipe was a tender and imaginative lover, and, in a city where such things mattered, as first secretary to the Argentinean ambassador he had entrée to Washington's most glamorous receptions and balls.

Always, when he attended such events, she was by his side. Coupled with the high-society parties Pamela and John Jasper gave—and at which she was always a guest—it was a heady mixture, and Wallis loved every minute of it.

When Henry Mustin was also posted to Washington, bringing Corinne with him, the only thing marring what would have been utter perfection was that she was no nearer to obtaining a divorce. There were two reasons. The first was that in far-off Hong Kong, Win was being mean-mindedly uncooperative about a divorce, and the second was that she simply didn't have the kind of money that a divorce would cost.

As she laughed and, with Felipe, loved her way through 1923, her lack of a divorce didn't seem to matter much. Washington wasn't hidebound Baltimore. That she was a married woman enjoying a blatant affair outraged some society matrons, but as no one wished to ostracize Felipe or the Bachmans, no one ostracized her. Standards that had been set in concrete before the war were set in concrete no longer. It was now the Roaring Twenties. Pleasure was everyone's first priority, and it was a priority that suited Wallis perfectly.

At the end of the year, just as she was making plans for a family Christmas with her mother and Aunt Bessie and a party-filled New Year with Felipe and Pamela and John Jasper, she received a telephone call asking her if she would meet with Harry W. Smith, a chief clerk at naval headquarters. Though she asked for more information, no further information was forthcoming.

"So, who *is* Harry W. Smith?" she asked Corinne. "I can't not go in case it's something to do with the allowance I'm still given as a Navy wife."

Corinne raised her hands expressively to show that she hadn't a clue.

Henry said he hadn't a clue either, but when Wallis told him of just whereabouts at naval headquarters the meeting was to take place, he said, "Whatever his reason for seeing you, it isn't going to be about your allowance, Wallis. The address you've been given is that of naval intelligence headquarters."

Sure that some kind of farcical error had been made, Wallis set off for her appointment a few days later, more amused than anxious.

It was an amusement that soon turned into incredulity.

Harry W. Smith didn't beat about the bush as to why he wished to see her. Steepling his fingers together, he said, "It is naval custom to occasionally use trusted Navy wives as unofficial couriers, Mrs. Spencer. You would, of course, have to be

given intelligence clearing, but a highly placed officer has indicated you are suited for such a task and, as your husband is at
present stationed in Hong Kong, you are also ideally placed."

Wallis's head whirled. Was Henry the "highly placed officer," and what did he mean about her being "ideally placed"?

"I'm sorry," she said, trying not to betray how deeply bewildered she was, "but I have no idea what being a courier entails."

"In your case, Mrs. Spencer, it would entail carrying classi-
fied documents to highly placed personnel in both Hong Kong
and mainland China, doing so under the cover of joining your
husband—though whether you actually do so is immaterial."

"I thought China was too unsafe for Navy wives to be
sent there?"

"It is." His steepled fingers interlocked and he rested his
chin on them, steel gray eyes holding hers. "It is the dangerous situation out there that necessitates the use of couriers.
At the present time all telegraph messages transmitted to the
U.S. Navy in China are being intercepted and read, and the
ciphers broken. It is a difficulty that has to be circumvented.
If you accept this challenge, Mrs. Spencer, you will have to
travel from Hong Kong to Shanghai and Canton—possibly
even to Peking. In a country that is in the grip of a brutal civil
war, such travel will not be easy, and your safety cannot be
assured."

Wallis struggled as to how to make the right kind of reply.
The thought of physical danger didn't daunt her. What daunted
her was the knowledge that Felipe would be highly unlikely to
remain faithful to her if she left for China—especially since she
would be sworn to secrecy.

Harry W. Smith unlocked his fingers and leaned back in his
chair, his gimlet-sharp eyes never leaving hers.

"Once in Hong Kong you wouldn't be traveling out to
Shanghai alone, Mrs. Spencer. Mary Sadler, the wife of Rear

Admiral Frank H. Sadler, will be traveling with you and, when your mission is completed, there is an old friend from your Pensacola days, the former Katherine Bigelow, who is at present living in Peking and would love you to spend time with her and her second husband, Herman Rogers."

Slowly Wallis said, "I'm honored that I've been thought trustworthy enough to act as a courier, but I intend to institute divorce proceedings against my husband very shortly and, when they are finalized, to remarry. A lengthy mission to China just isn't possible for me."

He hadn't argued with her. He had merely walked her to the door and bidden her a clipped good-bye.

She'd returned home deeply bemused. It wasn't every day a woman was asked to act as an intelligence agent. She wished she could tell Felipe about it. That she couldn't, and couldn't tell anyone else about it either, was something she was going to find intensely annoying.

When she arrived home, Corinne was waiting for her.

"Hi, Skinny," she said to her even before she had put her handbag down. "There's something I need to tell you." She stubbed a half-smoked cigarette out into a cut-glass ashtray. "You're not goin' to like what it is."

Wallis took off a hat that perfectly matched her navy silk dress. "Tell me the worst. It can't be so bad."

"It is."

At the tone of Corinne's voice, Wallis frowned. "What is it about? Henry hasn't been taken ill, has he?"

"No. It's not about Henry. It's about Felipe. There's no easy way of saying this, Wally. He's seeing someone else. He's dating Courtney Letts Stilwell, and according to Courtney he's asked her to marry him."

For a second Wallis felt as if her heart had ceased to beat, and then realization as to the absurdity of what Corinne was telling her kicked in. "Never in a million years, Corinne. Courtney Letts Stilwell has been divorced *twice*." There was amusement in her voice. "Felipe is a Catholic. He might, with a lot of persuasion, overlook one divorce, but he'd never overlook two!"

Corinne didn't share her amusement. "Courtney Letts Stilwell is a wealthy woman, Skinny. You might find that counts for a lot where Felipe is concerned."

At the certainty in Corinne's voice, Wallis's own certainty began to ebb. With legs that were suddenly weak, she sat down.

"When are you due to see him again, honey?"

"Tomorrow night. There's a party at the Brazilian embassy."

"Don't confront him at the party, Skinny. Even if what Courtney is saying isn't true, Felipe would never forgive you for creating a public scene."

Wallis's violet blue eyes flashed fire. "If it's true, Corinne, it's something *I'm* never going to forgive. Not *ever!*"

When Felipe called for her the next night in his six-cylinder Buick, she was as tightly wound as a coiled spring. Alice was present and so he didn't kiss her in the house, but the instant they were together in the car he did so.

As her hand curved around the back of his neck and her mouth parted beneath his, she was taut with fear as to what the next few moments were going to bring.

Sensing her tension, he lifted his head from hers. "What is it, *mi querida*? Is something wrong?"

Her heart began beating in sharp, slamming little strokes she could feel even in her fingertips. "I don't know. I hope not."

He shot her a down-slanting smile that turned her knees to water. "Then if you don't know, it cannot be too serious."

He put the Buick into gear and eased it away from the apartment block.

Her hands tightened on her beaded evening purse. "Corinne passed on some gossip to me yesterday that she says is quite widespread."

"Washington is a city of gossip," he said, his voice lightly dismissive. "What is the latest rumor going the rounds?"

Feeling like a vertigo sufferer on the edge of an abyss, she said, "That you've proposed marriage to Courtney Letts Stilwell."

The Buick veered violently to the left. He righted it, a nerve pulsing hard at the corner of his jaw.

Her whole life felt as if it were on the line as she waited for him to rant at the stupidity of the gossipmongers, to vehemently deny that he'd ever been anything more than socially polite to Courtney Letts Stilwell.

He didn't do so.

Instead, gripping the steering wheel so tightly his knuckles were white, he said explosively, "*Jesucristo!* Can people never mind their own business in this town?"

He swerved the car to the side of the road, slamming his foot down on the brake. "It was something I wanted to speak to you about in a reasonable way, Wallis. That you should have heard like this . . . It's despicable. Absolutely unforgivable."

"Are you telling me that it's *true*?" She was over the edge of the abyss now, falling into a bottomless pit.

With the Buick at a halt, he turned around in order to face her. "We couldn't have gone on together indefinitely, *mi querida*. I'm thirty-five. I'm getting to be a bit too old to remain a bachelor any longer."

"Then marry me, not Courtney! It's me you love, isn't it?"

"You are married, Wallis. How could we marry? You would have to get a divorce, and I'm a Roman Catholic . . ."

"Courtney Letts Stilwell has been divorced *twice*!" Wallis

was blind, deaf, and dumb with pain. "Why her? Why her and not me?"

He ran a hand over slickly sleek straight hair. "Courtney comes from a famous political and military family . . ."

"I come from one of the oldest families in America! William the Conqueror was one of my ancestors! I'm related to the Dukes of Manchester *and* the Earls of Sandwich! You're not marrying Courtney Letts Stilwell because of her family background! You're marrying her because she's wealthy!"

He flinched, and she knew her guess was right. Something inside her snapped and broke. Where matters of the heart were concerned she'd been let down too hard, too often. That she was now being let down again, simply because she didn't have the wealth her Warfield cousins enjoyed, was something so hurtful she couldn't even begin to deal with it.

"Bastard!" she sobbed, her hand shooting out clawlike toward his face.

He tried to duck but wasn't fast enough.

Her nails made contact with his cheek and raked downward in a bloody trail.

"*Perá!*" he screamed disbelievingly as he scrabbled in his pocket for a handkerchief to stanch the blood. "*Puta!*"

Wallis wasn't listening. Blinded by tears, she stumbled from the car and, with the door swinging open behind her, began running as fast as her narrow-skirted evening gown would allow.

He didn't come after her, and she didn't need a fortune-teller to tell her that he never would.

A cab turned into the street, and she flagged it down. The address she gave the driver was Pamela's. Sinking back against the cracked leather seating, she prayed she would find Pamela at home, certain that if she didn't she'd be tempted to throw herself into the Potomac from the highest bridge she could find.

At the elegant town house Pamela and John Jasper had moved into, an English butler opened the door to her. "Good evening, Mrs. Spencer," he said cordially. "I will tell Mrs. Bachman you are here."

When she was told who had unexpectedly arrived, Pamela, who was in her bedroom dressing for the evening, didn't ask that Wallis wait in the drawing room for her. Severing the in-house telephone connection, she ran, still shoeless, out onto the landing and from the top of the wide sweeping staircase called down, "Come on up, Wally! John Jasper isn't in. I'm due to meet him at the Brazilian embassy party in half an hour. Are you on your way there as well?"

Wallis didn't answer her. With a fresh lot of tears falling down her cheeks, she began mounting the stairs, and the instant she was on a level with Pamela and Pamela saw her face, Pamela's gaiety vanished.

"Dear Lord, Wally. What's happened?"

"Felipe has asked Courtney Letts Stilwell to marry him." Her voice was hoarse from crying, her face sheet white.

Pamela sucked in her breath, told her maid she no longer needed her, and, as the girl swiftly left the bedroom, closed the door on her so that she and Wallis were alone.

"When?" she asked succinctly. "Why? How did you find out?"

"I don't know when. Why is much easier. Because she comes from a socially prominent military and political family, and marriage into it will help further his career—and plus she's indecently wealthy."

She sat down on the toile-covered ottoman at the foot of Pamela's bed, a sodden handkerchief clutched in her hands.

"Corinne says gossip about his proposal is widespread, but I didn't have an inkling. So how long have I been a laughing-stock, Pamela? Do you know?"

Pamela shook her head. "I haven't heard a whisper, Wally. If I had, I would have told you."

"I wanted to marry him so much! Far more than I ever wanted to marry John Jasper or Win. Why is it nothing ever goes right for me, Pamela? Why can't I have someone love me the way John Jasper loves you?"

Pamela sat beside her and, as Wallis wept and wept, hugged her close. At last, when Wallis had wept herself into a state of exhaustion, she said gently and with great reluctance, "I have some news of my own that you're not going to want to hear, Wally. John Jasper has been recalled to London. We leave Washington at the end of the week."

The thought of living in Washington without Pamela, when Felipe would be squiring Courtney Letts Stilwell around the city, was a horror too far. "Oh God," she said in despair. "Oh Christ. Oh hell."

"What will you do, Wally?" Pamela asked, knowing exactly what Wallis felt unable to face. "Will you leave Washington and go back to Baltimore?"

For a long moment Wallis made no reply, and then she said slowly, resolution replacing despair, "No. I'm never going back to Baltimore." She wiped the tears from her face. "I'm going somewhere much farther away. I'm going somewhere I'll never run the risk of seeing Felipe with Courtney Letts Stilwell. I'm going to China."

Chapter Twenty-Five

There was a longer time gap than she had wanted between her agreeing to take top-secret documents to China and leaving for China.

"You need to be fully briefed, Mrs. Spencer," Harry W. Smith said to her. "That will entail you staying for several weeks with Captain Luke McNamee, chief of naval intelligence, and his wife, Dorothy. They live in Georgetown. I'm sure you will be very comfortable there."

Despite knowing that she was under close scrutiny, Wallis enjoyed her stay with the McNamees. Dorothy McNamee was a painter and lively, intelligent company. As Luke McNamee gave her a crash course in Chinese politics, telling her how the People's Party under Sun Yat-sen was heavily influenced by Russia and deeply divided by violent internal conflicts, and of how the government in Peking that it was trying to overthrow was just as deeply faction-riven, Dorothy told her of the living conditions she would meet with.

"For an unescorted woman, the violence that can erupt on the streets at any time is the worst danger," she warned. "You will need to carry a small pistol with you for self-protection.

Sickness is the next huge danger. Even in British-controlled Hong Kong, raw sewage is a problem and outbreaks of typhoid are frequent. Then there are the extremes of temperature. In China the summer heat is unbearable and in winter the cold is crippling."

Wallis was uncaring. All that mattered to her was that she wouldn't be at risk of going to a party and seeing Felipe with Courtney Letts Stilwell.

In mid-July she boarded the troop carrier USS *Chaumont* at Norfolk, Virginia, and, along with a handful of other Navy wives, set off for the Far East.

It was a long, slow, hot voyage. Her accommodation—a cabin in the bowels of the ship that she shared with two other Navy wives—was cramped and airless. The troops on board grew more unruly with every day that passed, and by the time the ship eased its way into the Panama Canal—after a sweltering forty-eight-hour wait to do so—fistfights were frequent.

Once in the Pacific, things grew worse, and as courts-martial began taking place, Wallis and the handful of other women on board kept to their cabins. Six weeks later, at Manila in the Philippines, they thankfully transferred to a far more comfortable ship, the *Empress of Canada*.

At last, and for the first time, Wallis began to enjoy the journey that was now nearly over. Five days later, on the fourth of September, one of the women she was sharing a cabin with shook her awake, saying, "You need to be on deck, Wallis. Hong Kong is in sight."

The next couple of hours, as they steamed closer and closer to their destination, were magical. First they passed scatterings of deserted islands, the offshore breezes heavy with the fragrance of the wildflowers growing on them, and then three-masted junks began appearing, to be joined by sampans as Victoria Peak, Hong Kong Island's most famous mountain, grew ever clearer, its topmost slopes gray and mauve and silver in the early morning sunshine.

For the women she was traveling with, Hong Kong was as far as they were going. Only Wallis carried a special intelligence-authorized naval passport that would enable her to travel to war-torn Shanghai and Peking.

Win was waiting on the dockside to greet her, as the McNamees had told her he would be. Tanned and wearing his summer-white officer's uniform, he looked almost handsome once again.

"I've been told to take care of you until you have seen certain people here and to look after you until you leave for Shanghai," he said, shaking hands with her as if she weren't still his wife, but someone he had never met before. "I must say I've never known anyone like you for springing surprises, Wallis." There was grudging respect in his voice. "This time, though, you may well have bitten off more than you can chew."

"I appreciate your concern, Win, but my life is my own now to do with as I please."

"As is mine." All around them coolies were transferring steamer trunks and suitcases into rickshaws and taxis. Her own suitcase was relatively modest, and without waiting for a coolie to do so, Win picked it up and led the way toward a parked, open-top car.

"There's something you need to know before we go a step further, Wallis." Beneath his mustache his mouth was set in the grim, uncompromising line she knew so well. "There's going to be no reconciliation between us. I'm involved in a relationship with a married woman. I don't want it making things more complicated than it already is."

"Don't worry. As you well know, I want a divorce. If you've got someone else in your life now, perhaps you'll stop being obstructive about giving me one."

He heaved the suitcase onto the rear seat of the car, opened the passenger-side door for her, and said, his manner changing, "Things could have been very different between us, Wallis. I can't help wishing that perhaps they had been."

Though she had as little desire for a reconciliation as he had, there was a lump in her throat as she said sincerely, "So do I, Win."

She seated herself in the car, thinking back to their wedding day and of how happy they had been, and of how their wedding night had turned that happiness to ashes.

It was her physical disability that had ruined their marriage, just as, eventually, it had ruined her relationship with Felipe. Felipe might never have accused her of not being a proper woman, as Win so often had, but she had been wrong in thinking her disability didn't matter to him. When it had come to marriage it had mattered a great deal.

It hadn't been Courtney Letts Stilwell's family background and wealth that had ensured he had proposed to Courtney and not to her. It had been Courtney's already proven ability to bear children.

As Win drove away from the dockside and they entered a narrow bustling street where bicycles, taxis, rickshaws, and cars were all vying for space, she wondered if, because she couldn't be physically loved as other women were loved, she was destined to go through life never being truly loved at all.

It was a bleak prospect, and tears stung her eyes. She blinked them away, fast.

Self-pity was not in her nature, and she wasn't going to begin giving in to it. She was in a country exotically strange and fascinating and she had an assignment to carry out, so important it had even earned her Win's respect.

The street began to widen slightly and she glimpsed a small shop window piled high with jade jewelry. Her mouth watered.

Perhaps when her business in Hong Kong was completed and before she left for Shanghai, she would be able to do some shopping. A jade necklace was just the balm her hurting heart needed.

"For a novice, you bought beautiful quality jade," Mary Sadler said admiringly when Wallis asked for her opinion on the necklace she had bought. "You can tell the quality of jade by its translucency and coldness to the touch—and this is both very translucent and very cold."

It was November and they were aboard a Canadian ship, the *Empress of Russia*, their destination far-distant Shanghai.

Reluctantly Wallis laid down the magazine she had been reading. It was one she had found in the ship's lounge and was several months old. What had attracted her to it was its front-cover wedding photograph of Prince Edward's younger brother, Bertie, and his bride, Lady Elizabeth Bowes-Lyon, and she had just been reading of how the bride, on her way into Westminster Abbey, had laid her bouquet on the Tomb of the Unknown Warrior.

"China is so vast it's hard to comprehend," Mary said, handing the necklace back to her, "but at least Hong Kong to Shanghai can be traveled by sea and in relative comfort. Shanghai to Peking has to be traveled by train, and though the Blue Express is relatively luxurious—a little like the Blue Train through France to the Riviera—it has become so dangerous the luxury can't be enjoyed."

Wallis dragged her thoughts away from the new Duchess of York's memorably touching gesture.

"How so?" They were seated in deck chairs, blankets across their knees.

Mary quirked an eyebrow. "Luke McNamee didn't tell you?"

Wallis slid the necklace back into her handbag. "He told me I could expect to be caught up in violence at any time. He didn't specifically mention the Blue Express."

"Naughty of him, but then if he had, you might have had second thoughts about agreeing to go on to Peking."

"It's not too late for second thoughts." Wallis's voice had wry humor in it. "So what is the problem with the train, Mary? Is the food bad beyond description?"

"In spring, last year, one group of passengers didn't have the chance to find out. Bandits stopped the train while they were asleep, overpowered the guards, and then forced everyone aboard off it."

"If they were intent on robbing them, why didn't they rob them on the train?"

"They weren't intent on robbing them. They captured them in order to hold them for ransom."

A chill, not caused by the stiff ocean breeze, ran through Wallis.

"What was the outcome?"

"The women—one of them was Lucy Aldrich, John D. Rockefeller Junior's sister-in-law—made such slow progress over what was mountainous ground that the bandits released them, leaving them to find their own way back to civilization. In the end, five million Chinese dollars were paid for the release of the men. Since then, although no further Europeans have been kidnapped, bandits boarding the train and demanding what they call 'tribute' has become a regular occurrence. If you've been given a pistol, and I assume you have—and that you've been taught how to use it—keep it where you can easily get to it."

Mary knew so much about everything and was so calm and unflappable, Wallis wished that her journey to Peking were going to be taken in her company.

"Not a chance, I'm afraid," Mary said when, two days later, she voiced this hope over dinner in the *Empress of Russia*'s dining room. "I'm joining Frank in Shanghai and not moving even a yard toward Peking. You won't want to either when you've experienced life behind the safe walls of the International Settlement."

"How safe are the walls?"

"Very. The walls are massive and manned by American, British, French, Italian, and Japanese infantry. Outside is chaos. Shanghai is a city jam-packed with refugees, brothels, opium dens. There can't be a more dangerous city on the face of the earth. Inside is another world—one of cosmopolitan sophistication. The Majestic Hotel and the Astor House Hotel—where we will be staying—have every Western comfort imaginable."

She reached for her wineglass. "The Astor House Hotel's Winter Garden ballroom is the most beautiful I have ever seen. As for the shopping . . ." She took a sip of wine and raised her eyes to heaven. "In the Yellow Lantern, the curio shop just off the hotel's lobby, you can find every kind of Oriental antique imaginable."

"And silks and embroideries?" Wallis's interest was intense.

"It's an Aladdin's cave of them, plus it's the place to go if you are looking for more jade—or for pearls."

Wallis thought she might very well be looking for both jade and pearls. Her Navy allowance was slim, but on the previous two ships she had sailed on, the *Chaumont* and the *Empress of Canada*, she had indulged in her love of poker and her winnings had been substantial—as had her winnings on the *Empress of Russia*. It wasn't a way of getting by that her Episcopalian grandmother would have approved of, but it was one she had relied on steadily ever since Pensacola.

. . .

Once Wallis was installed in the Astor House, her first port of call was the nearby British consulate. It was a measure of how important her mission as a courier was regarded that she was greeted not by a minor official, but by the consul general.

"I understand from Mrs. Sadler that your journey from Hong Kong was without unpleasant incident," he said affably as she handed over to him top-secret documents that had been by her side since leaving Washington. "However, I must stress to you that Shanghai is a city consumed by hatred for all Westerners—as, indeed, is the whole of China. Resentment for the way the country and its people have been exploited by foreigners over the last two hundred years is a major reason for the bloodily violent political upheavals now taking place. Within the International Settlement, as long as you are everywhere escorted, you are relatively safe. It is not, however, safe for you to continue on to Peking. The risk of capture by bandits is too high and there would be enormous consequences if the documents you would be carrying fell into their hands. For the moment I must ask you to remain in Shanghai. When the railway line to Peking has been secured, you will then be able to carry on with your instructions from Washington."

Wallis was quite happy to stay in Shanghai; the civil war raging outside the walls of the International Settlement gave the entire city an aura of danger and excitement. The Astor House was less than a block away from the International Settlement's protective walls, and she could often hear bursts of gunfire and hear shouts and screams as the British-controlled police force clashed with Communist Chinese protesters.

As the weeks passed, letters began to arrive for her from the States. One, in her mother's handwriting, arrived black-edged, and she opened it with her heart in her mouth, terrified she was about to be plunged into grief for the loss of her dearly loved Aunt Bessie.

To her vast relief her mother was merely marking the anniversary of a death.

Corinne's husband, Henry Mustin, had died of pneumonia the previous year.

. . . And I can't get over what a terrible, terrible tragedy it was,

her mother wrote in her spidery handwriting.

*Diving into an ice-cold sea to rescue a cadet who had fallen
overboard was such a brave thing to do and though he
didn't die in the water, but died in his bed of pneumonia,
he wouldn't have caught pneumonia if it hadn't been for his
heroic action. Corinne is distraught and I don't blame her.
Good husbands don't grow on trees.*

Wallis made a wry moue. She knew that last sentence all too well.

There was a hastily written postscript at the bottom of the page.

*PS I've got myself a new beau. His name is Charles Gordon
Allen and he is a legal clerk in the Veterans' Administration.
He says you can obtain a divorce on the grounds of
separation if you can show you've been separated for three
years and live in Virginia for a year while the divorce is being
processed.*

She had immediately written a letter of condolence to Corinne and then, wanting to think about both Henry and her mother's new beau, left the hotel intent on a good long walk to clear her head.

She hadn't been close enough to Henry to be heartbroken by his death, but she had been fond enough of him to be deeply affected by it. As for Charles Gordon Allen, she knew her mother well enough to know that her mother wouldn't have written to her about him unless she was thinking of marrying him. His being a legal clerk made him sound dull and stuffy, but perhaps someone a little dull and stuffy was the stabilizing influence her laughter-loving mother needed.

When she reached the Bund, she stood at the point where the Suzhou Creek poured its silt into the Hungpu River's clouded yellow waters. If a divorce on the grounds of three years' separation was as easy to come by in Virginia as her mother's new beau said it was, then it was something she was going to consider very seriously.

She didn't want to return to America just yet, though—and couldn't until she'd fulfilled her mission by traveling on to Peking. Once in Peking she would stay with Katherine and Herman Rogers and enjoy China for a little while. It already fascinated her, and on a whim she turned away from the busy river in search of a rickshaw. Though advice on every side was not to stray outside the high walls of the settlement, Wallis had never been given to heeding good advice. The narrow, crowded streets fascinated her and she wanted to see them from outside the walls as well as from within them.

Her rickshaw driver spoke a little English, and when she told him she wanted to be taken on a tour of the city outside the International Settlement's walls, he bowed his head, saying, "Yes, missee. Certainly, missee."

As he trundled her away in a direction she had never ventured before, Wallis felt the adrenaline punch she always felt when doing something reckless or, when playing poker, betting for particularly high stakes.

The streets teemed with people. Delicately built Chinese women carried babies on their backs, old people pushed hand-carts, and shop vendors touted their wares, their goods spilling out of tiny dark shops onto the street. The air was pungent with the smell of spices and dried fish and the deafening cries of hawkers.

She saw a spectacular display of silks and shouted to the rickshaw boy to stop. Minutes later she was in a dark cavern of a shop piled high with not only silk, but satins and intricately worked brocades.

Ever since her stay in Hong Kong, she had become an expert at beating down the price of anything she had set her heart on. In Shanghai, haggling was an art form, and, now a master of it, she indulged in it with gusto. When she emerged from the shop twenty minutes later, she did so carrying bolts of sumptuous silk that would keep her in evening gowns for as long as her heart desired.

Standing in the noisy street, waiting for the boy to stow her shopping in the compartment beneath the rickshaw's passenger seat, she became aware that she was being watched.

Shielding her eyes against the sun's glare, she scanned the tiny doorways of the shops on the far side of the street. Each had a pigtailed owner sitting outside, and because she was a Westerner, each and every one of them was looking toward her, their expressionless eyes revealing nothing of their thoughts.

They were the kinds of looks she had attracted since her first day in China and to which she was accustomed. They had long since ceased to make her feel uncomfortable, but she was feeling uncomfortable now.

Squeezed between an open-fronted shop selling porcelain

and pewter and another piled high with lacquerwork and camphor wood was a doorway that belonged to neither shop. Seated so far back in its semidarkness that Wallis hadn't at first seen her was a woman so ancient she appeared at first sight to be mummified.

Her eyes weren't mummified, though.

Meeting them, Wallis felt a sensation akin to an electric-shock knife through her.

"Me ready now," the rickshaw boy said. "We go now, missee. Chop-chop."

Wallis didn't move. "That woman," she said. "The one seated between the pewter shop and the lacquerwork shop. What is she selling?"

The rickshaw boy looked across the street. "She sell only future, missee. No ivory. No lucky elephants. We go now?"

"The future? You mean she's a fortune-teller? A soothsayer?"

The boy shuffled his feet. "She not for *waiguoren*—not for foreigners. Plenty fortune-tellers for *waiguoren* in settlement."

Wallis continued to lock eyes with the old woman across the road. If ever anyone needed her future told, she did.

"Take me across to her," she said. "I want her to tell me my future."

The prune-black eyes in the yellowed, wizened face were drawing her with such compulsion that even if the rickshaw boy had refused to do so, she would have negotiated a way between the taxis and carts thronging the street.

In great reluctance he stepped from the rickshaw's shafts. "This big mistake, missee," he said unhappily. "This woman not just astrologist. This woman has strange powers."

"Good." Wallis was already aware that the woman possessed a strange power; it was that power that was propelling her across the road as fast as her high-heeled shoes would take her.

The rickshaw boy tried to keep in front of her, his straw-slippered sandals slapping against the soles of his feet.

"Will she be able to speak English?" Wallis said suddenly, aware that if the woman couldn't, the whole thing would be a waste of time.

"No." The boy's voice was contemptuous. He spat, narrowly missing Wallis's left foot. "She old woman. Me settlement rickshaw boy. Me speakee English."

As they stepped up to the darkened doorway, Wallis hoped his English was going to be sufficient for whatever lay ahead.

The woman didn't ask her what it was Wallis wanted of her; she simply rose to her feet and led the way down an increasingly dark passage and then into a small room.

There was no window, and the darkness was intense. Just as Wallis was about to turn around and head as fast as she could back toward the brilliant sunshine of the street, a match was struck and a lantern was lit.

The room still didn't give Wallis confidence. Beneath the lantern was a large round table covered in a heavy velour cloth. There were black leather-seated lacquerwood chairs around it that looked as if they had once been very grand but were now abjectly shabby. A Chinese screen hid one corner of the room completely from view. On one of the rear walls stood an elmwood hand-painted cabinet, its shelves thick with books and chipped porcelain.

Close up, the woman looked even older than she had from across the street. If Wallis had been told the woman was a hundred years old—or even older—she wouldn't have been remotely surprised.

A clawlike hand indicated that she should sit.

She sat.

The woman then withdrew from the cabinet a heavy book, a scroll of blank paper, pen, ink, and a compass. Then she seated herself at the opposite side of the table to Wallis and, in Chinese, spoke to the rickshaw boy, who was still standing.

The rickshaw boy said to Wallis. "Madam Xiuxiu want hour, day, month, year your birth, missee."

"The nineteenth of June, 1896," Wallis said, and then paused. What hour had she been born? She knew it had been late evening, but what had been the exact time? Once, when as a little girl she had asked her mother this question, her mother had replied in high amusement, "Honey, I was far too busy at the time to think of looking at the clock!"

Madam Xiuxiu waited, not moving a muscle of her corpse-like face.

"Is the time important?" she asked the rickshaw boy.

He nodded.

What was it her Aunt Bessie had once said? That she'd been born right on the half hour and that by midnight she'd been bathed and gowned in flannelette and was lying in her mother's arms. All that couldn't have taken place if she'd been born at half past eleven, so she must have been born at half past ten.

"Half past ten in the evening," she said, wondering what would happen next.

What happened next took a long time. With the compass Madam Xiuxiu drew a large circle on the blank scroll of paper, and then she drew a narrow circle near the edge of the outer circle, and then a smaller inner circle.

Wallis had no need to ask what she was doing. She had seen a Chinese birth chart at the Astor House and it had looked totally incomprehensible, which was exactly how Madam Xiuxiu's chart was beginning to look.

It was hot and airless in the room, and as Madam Xiuxiu worked, filling the circle with symbols and figures and occasionally resorting to her Bible-like book for help, Wallis began to regret having been so impulsive, certain that the chart was not going to tell her the kind of things she wanted to know.

"Your life path is influence by the number four," the rickshaw boy whispered to her.

Wallis was unimpressed. A fortune-teller at a fair could just as easily have given her a lucky number.

"Your sun is in Gemini and your moon in Libra," he said a little later. Then, a little later still, "Mercury is your . . ."— he paused, struggling for the correct English word—". . . your *strong* planet, missee."

After what, to Wallis, seemed an interminable length of time, Madame Xiuxiu passed the finished chart across to her. Wallis looked down at it, and it was as incomprehensible as she had known it would be.

She opened her purse in order to pay and be gone.

Madam Xiuxiu shook her head. Indicating that Wallis should remain seated, she rose to her feet and moved into a position behind her. Then she placed scrawny birdlike hands on the top of Wallis's head.

Common sense told Wallis that their weight was infinitesimal, but it didn't feel like that. It felt as if a huge burning weight were resting on her head. It was a heat that was all engulfing. Her body tingled with it from her scalp down to the tips of her toes.

Dimly, as if from a distance, Wallis heard Madam Xiuxiu begin speaking, her voice a mesmerizing singsong.

The rickshaw boy's voice, as he began to translate, seemed to Wallis to be coming from a vast distance away. Part of her brain told her that he couldn't possibly be translating into English word for perfect word, but that was how she heard him, and the words seared themselves into her heart and her memory.

"You are a woman of great destiny."

Behind his words, Wallis could hear Madam Xiuxiu's voice and that, too, seemed to be coming from far, far away. Though she had not been aware of any candles or bowls of incense being lit, the room seemed full of scented smoke and she felt giddy to the point of near insensibility.

"The man who will love you," his voice went on, "will love you with every atom of his being. Kissed by the sun, he will be the ruler of kingdoms and you will be his shadow queen. The love you will share will echo down the centuries. Jewels beyond your wildest dreams will be yours, but there will never be a child."

That was it. Nothing followed.

Wallis's head spun. She felt as disoriented as if she had been chloroformed. Dimly she became aware that the wizened face and mummified body was no longer standing behind her but was facing her across the velour-covered table.

Wallis tried to force her brain to work. Had Madam Xiuxiu ever stood behind her? Had she imagined the entire last few minutes? Had the Chinese woman put her under some kind of hypnosis? How else could she have heard Chinese translated into perfect English by a rickshaw boy who previously had only ever spoken in pidgin English?

More to the point, where was her rickshaw boy? Terror at the thought of being left alone with Madam Xiuxiu seized her, and then, as if on cue, he said at her elbow, "We go now, missee. We go now, chop-chop."

It wasn't the voice or the perfect English she had heard a minute or so ago.

With a swimming head, Wallis rose unsteadily to her feet.

From a web of wrinkles the old woman's eyes bored into hers.

Disoriented as she was, innate courtesy prompted Wallis to say good-bye. All that escaped from her throat was a choking sound.

Wanting only to escape, she spun on her heel and blundered from the room and down the dark passageway into the blazing sunlight of the street.

Only when she was safely back in the rickshaw, being trundled briskly in the direction of the International Settlement and the Astor House, did Wallis remember that Madam Xiuxiu had not asked for payment and that she, Wallis, had not proffered any.

Not until hours later was she able to think of her experience calmly. Whether the words she had heard had actually been said or had been part of some kind of hallucination she still didn't know, but she knew she would never forget them.

In the blessed solitude of her small suite at the Astor House, she began running water into a pleasingly large bath, throwing a generous handful of scented bath crystals into the water, and then pouring in bath foam.

While the bath was still filling she made herself a Shanghai cocktail, mixing a measure of Jamaican rum with a teaspoon of anisette and half a teaspoon of grenadine and then, having cut a lemon in half, adding a quarter of the juice.

Giving the cocktail shaker a vigorous shake, she thought of the Chinese woman's first words to her. *You are a woman of great destiny.* Despite the extraordinary physical reaction she had experienced when the words were being spoken, she had no intention of taking them at face value. The Chinese loved dressing things up in flowery language. No doubt every person who visited Madam Xiuxiu was told that he or she was a person of great destiny.

She poured the contents of the shaker into a glass and, taking the glass with her, went into the bathroom to turn off the taps.

What had followed that opening sentence had been far more to the point. That she would meet a man who would love her with every atom of his being.

Putting the cocktail glass down on the edge of the bath, she stepped into the water, sliding down into its scented depths until she was submerged in foam up to her shoulders.

That she would meet such a man was the deepest desire of her heart.

As for Madam Xiuxiu's next two sentences, she discounted them as she had discounted Madam Xiuxiu's first sentence. *Kissed by the sun* was meaningless, unless Madam Xiuxiu meant he would be olive skinned, as Felipe had been. He certainly wouldn't be a ruler of kingdoms. That expression was again the extravagant way the Chinese spoke, as was her being described as a *shadow queen*.

She loved the phrase about their love being one that would echo down the centuries, and as for there never being a child . . . Madam Xiuxiu had certainly been right on that score and, as she had been so right, perhaps she was right about other things as well.

Wallis set her now empty glass back down on the edge of the bath. Her immediate future was one that was already decided. She was going to Peking and, once there, was going to stay with the Rogerses. Then she was going to return to America, stay in Virginia, and apply for a divorce from Win on the grounds that they had been separated for three years. That this wasn't the actual truth wouldn't matter.

She would write to Win, asking him to write her a letter in which he would mention a false date on which their separation had started. As he was now emotionally involved elsewhere, it was something she was quite sure he'd be only too happy to do.

After that, according to Madam Xiuxiu, she was going to meet a man who would love her with every atom of his being and shower her with jewels beyond her wildest imaginings.

Her mouth curved in a deep smile.

It was a future so enticing, it couldn't come quick enough.

Chapter Twenty-Six

"But why Warrenton, Skinny?" Corinne said to her on a summer's day in 1926 as they sat in the small garden of the Warren Green Hotel, Warrenton, Fauquier County, Virginia. "After the excitements of Peking I would have thought that on coming home you would have wanted to continue living somewhere there was a lot of action. There's none at all here."

"Too true." Wallis's voice was wry. "Until you visited today, the highlight of my week was a game of gin rummy with a fellow guest old enough to be my grandfather and a walk down the main street to buy a book."

Corinne, who by now was wearing her widowhood lightly, cracked with laughter. "Then why? A whole clutch of the girls you were at Oldfields with live in New York. Your mother lives in Washington. If your heart was set on Virginia, you could have moved in with Cousin Lelia at Wakefield Manor."

"A short visit with Lelia would be fine, but I'm here to get a divorce, and one of the requirements is for me to be resident in Virginia for a year—which would be to risk outstaying my welcome."

Corinne quirked an immaculately plucked and penciled

eyebrow. "Is that what happened with the Rogerses? You were their guest for over a year."

Wallis raised her face to the hot afternoon sun. "No, I didn't outstay my welcome with them. They were wonderful to me. I wanted to get on with my life, though, and that meant returning home and getting a divorce from Win."

"And Warrenton, not New York or Washington, is the place to do it?"

"If I want it to be uncomplicated and cheap, yes. My mother's new beau is a legal clerk at the Veterans' Administration Building in Washington. He told my mother how I could get a divorce in Virginia on the grounds of Win's desertion. That wouldn't be possible in Washington, which only recognizes adultery as grounds for a divorce—and whereas the cost of getting a divorce nearly anywhere else is far more than I can afford, here it's only going to cost me three hundred dollars."

"And is Win goin' to play ball?"

Wallis turned her head and shot her a wide grin. "He already has. He sent me a letter, which is now in the hands of my lawyer, in which he's stated that he left me three years ago and has no intention of ever returning to me. All I have to do to be a free woman is to sit out a year of boredom here."

"Well, Skinny, it is at least the right side of the Blue Ridge Mountains for easy trips to Washington—and the next few weeks won't be boring. Not with a couple of weddings about to take place."

She said the last sentence with a cat-that-got-the-cream expression on her face, and Wallis's eyes widened.

"You don't mean . . . ?"

"I most certainly do." Corinne's smile was radiant. "In a couple of weeks' time I shall be marrying Lieutenant Commander George Murray."

Wallis's eyes widened even further. "The George Murray who was at Pensacola when I first went there to stay with you and Henry?"

"The very one, and he's even handsomer now than he was then."

"Congratulations, you lucky girl." There was a lump in Wallis's throat. In finding another well-bred and very suitable man so soon after Henry's death, Corinne really had been lucky. Though she had dated during her stay with Katherine and Herman, she had met no one who made her heart beat even a little faster and certainly wasn't likely to do so in a backwater like Warrenton.

"You said a couple of weddings. Who else is about to make a trip down the aisle?"

This time it was Corinne's turn to be wide-eyed. "Land sakes! You mean you don't know?"

"No. Why should I? I've been away for over a year and haven't touched base with old friends and family yet."

"Maybe not, Skinny, but this is one bride you should have touched base with. It's your mother."

Wallis wasn't at all surprised that her mother was marrying for a third time, but she was almost robbed of breath that Alice hadn't yet told her of it when Corinne, and doubtless all the rest of their Montague relations, knew about it.

"Well, if that don't beat the band!"

Her expression was so comical that Corinne burst into full-throated laughter. "Guess it must have slipped Alice's mind," she said when she was finally able to speak. "For your mother, getting married is beginning to become quite commonplace!"

Wallis hooted with laughter.

Some of the hotel's elderly residents who were seated nearby gave them disapproving looks, but Wallis and Corinne didn't care. They had missed each other's company over the last year, and they were Montagues. Unrestrained laughter came as naturally to them as breathing.

"But honey, I was just waiting for you to visit me. Telling you I was about to become a bride again just wouldn't have been any fun in a letter."

Wallis laughed and gave her mother a bear hug. "Tell me all about him," she said when she finally released her. "All I know is that he's a legal clerk at the Veterans' Administration."

Alice giggled. "Well, I guess that's all there is to tell about Charlie. He's not much of a live wire, but we're very comfy together."

"That's swell, Mama. I hope you'll be as happy with him as you were with Mr. Rasin."

"I will," Alice said placidly. "God willing."

Mindful of her residency requirements, Wallis didn't leave Warrenton too often. Most times when she ventured into what she was beginning to think of as the outside world, it was to go to Washington to visit her mother or her Aunt Bessie. Occasionally, though, she took the train to New York and visited friends from Oldfields with whom she had kept in irregular touch. When Christmas approached and she received an invitation from one of them to spend it in New York, it was an invitation she eagerly accepted.

> Anywhere would be better than trying to be festive at the
> Warren Green Hotel,

she wrote to Pamela.

> It's the nearest thing to a morgue I ever hope to be in. Plus, I
> like New York, even when it's feet deep in snow. If it weren't

for your suggestion that the minute my divorce is a done deal
I come and stay with you and John Jasper in London, I'd be
looking for a way of staying in New York permanently.

That she wasn't going to do so was because she knew how
much more interesting life would be in London. Pamela and
John Jasper mixed among the very highest of high society.
There was even a chance Pamela would be able to introduce
her to Prince Edward.

Who is beginning to cause anxiety in the British press,

Pamela had written in her last letter.

After all, he is thirty-two, and the general opinion is that he
should be married and providing the country with an heir
presumptive. It is his becoming an uncle which has brought
about this latest avalanche of concern. Have there been
photographs of the Duke and Duchess of York's baby girl in
American newspapers? There's nothing adventurous about
the choice of name, Elizabeth Alexandra Mary. Elizabeth
after her mother—and, at a stretch, Queen Elizabeth
Tudor—Alexandra after her great-grandmother, and Mary
after her grandmother. It's easy to imagine Bertie a doting
papa, but a little harder to imagine Edward in the same role.

It was the kind of letter that made Wallis long to be in London, gossiping with Pamela about the royal family, and all she
had to do until she was doing so was to endure Warrenton for a
few more months. One blessing was that at least her Christmas
wouldn't be boring, for there was no telling whom she might
meet at a Christmas dinner party in New York.

"Ernest Simpson," the man seated next to her at dinner

said, in an accent that sounded very English. "I arrived too late to be formally introduced to anyone. Do you like it that the drapes haven't been drawn and we can see the snow falling in the moonlight? Christmas without snow would be a very poor affair, don't you think?"

"Wallis Spencer—and yes, I do like seeing the snow fall."

He was an attractive-looking man: square-jawed, dark-haired, and mustached. Superficially he looked very much like Win, but unlike Win his eyes weren't arrogant and sexually appraising, and he didn't possess Win's air of barely suppressed violence.

He looked like a man perfectly at ease with himself, and she immediately felt perfectly at ease with him.

"Are you British?" she asked. "Your accent sounds very much like that of a friend of mine who lives in London."

"Then I hope he, or she, isn't a Cockney." There was amusement in his voice. "I'm a former member of the Coldstream Guards. It's the oldest regiment in continued existence in the British Army. I'm afraid a Cockney would have rather a hard time of it fitting in."

"What is an Englishman doing in New York? Do you work here, or are you a tourist?"

"I work here. Though my father is English, my mother is American, and I was born in America and educated here. At Harvard."

"Of course. Where else?" There was teasing laughter in her voice and, recognizing it, he chuckled.

"Sorry. That kind of thing matters to so many people, always mentioning it has become a habit."

"As with the Coldstream Guards?"

His eyes crinkled at the corners. "As with the Coldstream Guards."

She liked that he was able to take being teased so well and that he didn't take himself too seriously.

The rest of the table were being noisily jovial, but Ernest Simpson showed no desire to join in the general hilarity, and she had no desire to, either. Talking to each other was proving to be far more enjoyable.

"What kind of work do you do in New York, Mr. Simpson?"

His eyes were dark blue. They didn't have the same effect on her that John Jasper's eyes once had, or that Win's and Felipe's eyes had had on her the first time she had looked into them. They were nice eyes, though, and, having once looked into them, she found herself happily continuing to do so.

He said, "I'm a partner in the family firm."

"Which is?"

"Simpson, Spence and Young. We buy and sell ships—and do so on both sides of the Atlantic."

Wallis's interest quickened. "You have offices in London?"

He nodded. "Do you know London? Though I was born and brought up in New York, I've always far preferred it."

"I've never been—but I'm going to go and stay with friends in London before next year is out."

"I'm hoping to begin managing the London side of things before too very long, and so perhaps we'll meet up there? I know the city very well and would enjoy showing you around it. As you're a New Yorker, it would be presumptuous of me to offer to show you around New York."

"Oh, I'm not a New Yorker, Mr. Simpson." Wallis took a belated sip of her wine, already knowing she was going to see a great deal of him long before either of them should find themselves in London and deeming that it was time she laid her cards on the table. "I'm a Baltimorean, although no longer living there. At the moment I'm living in Warrenton, Virginia."

Though he politely tried to hide it, he was surprised, as she had known he would be.

"I'm sitting out a year's residency there in order to get a divorce."

"How extraordinary." Relief that she didn't have a husband in tow showed in the dark blue eyes. "I'm in the throes of obtaining a divorce myself. I think you should call me Ernest, don't you? I also think I should begin showing you round New York. As a New York–born Englishman it's the least I can do for a girl from Baltimore."

The next morning they walked in Central Park together down paths hard with glistening, compacted snow. In the afternoon they visited the Metropolitan Museum, discovering, with pleasure, that they both shared the same taste in art. In the evening they dined at the Brevoort, which was conveniently close to her friend's home in Washington Square. When he said good night to her, he kissed her warmly and gently.

It wasn't the kind of overture to a love affair—something Wallis was certain they were on the verge of—that she was accustomed to. John Jasper, Win, and Felipe had all—in different ways—been hot-blooded and passionate. Though she had swiftly come to regret it where Win was concerned, Wallis knew herself well enough to know that sexually she was drawn to tigers.

Everything about Ernest's quiet, undemanding personality indicated he was far from being a tiger. Later, lying in bed and thinking about the calm, peaceful, and enjoyable day they had spent together, she concluded that it didn't matter. A sexually undemanding man would be far likelier to accommodate himself to her physical disability than a demanding one. After the turbulence of the last few years, she needed a relationship that would be a haven of tranquillity, and even though she had known Ernest for barely twenty-four hours, she knew that being with him would always be restful and, because he was intelligent and cultured, never boring.

From that night on, life settled into a very agreeable pattern. She began spending far more time in New York than her Warrenton residency requirements allowed, but no one seemed to notice, and her divorce petition continued to move slowly but steadily toward a satisfactory conclusion. Making it easier for them to be together more often, Ernest often traveled to Warrenton, and though Warrenton didn't provide them with the diversions of New York—museums and art galleries and elegant restaurants and Broadway shows—Wallis still enjoyed being with him.

Because of her experience in circumnavigating her physical disability, Ernest was as happy in bed with her as Felipe had been. If her pleasure wasn't as great as it had been with Felipe, it was still satisfactory. She and Ernest were, in the words her mother had used about her third husband, "comfy together." It wasn't the world-shattering passion the Chinese astrologer had predicted for her, but she was now sure that the words imprinted so deeply in her memory were the result of hypnotism and her own deeply hoped-for wishes, not words that had actually been spoken.

In late spring her Aunt Bessie, now financially well off thanks to a legacy from her late employer, asked her if she would like to accompany her on a lengthy trip to Europe, all expenses paid. Even though she was putting her residency requirements at risk, it was an offer Wallis couldn't bring herself to refuse.

Ernest was appalled.

"But Wallis, sweetheart, that means we'll be separated for the whole of the summer, perhaps for longer!"

She curled her arm lovingly through his.

"Please try to understand," she said coaxingly. "I'll never be given such an opportunity again, and if I don't accept, I doubt if Bessie will make the trip. Not alone. I owe her a great deal and she's relying on me to say yes."

Ernest, who had met Aunt Bessie and liked her a great deal, ran a hand defeatedly over his close-cropped, neatly trimmed hair. "I'm going to be understanding about this trip only on one condition, Wallis."

Wallis, knowing what the condition was going to be, leaned her head against his shoulder so that their eyes couldn't meet.

"My divorce is already finalized and yours will be finalized by the end of the year. When it is, I want you to marry me. I love you too deeply to care about whether we can have children or not. All I want to do is to spend my life with you. I've never been as happy as I have been these last few months."

Apart from the early days of her relationships with John Jasper, Win, and Felipe, Wallis had never been happier either, and she knew that unlike the others, Ernest would never be un-faithful to her and that he most certainly wouldn't be physically abusive to her. The problem was that though she loved him, she wasn't in love in an overpowering, being-swept-off-her-feet way, and settling for anything less was something she couldn't yet quite bring herself to do.

When she knew that her true feelings weren't showing in her eyes, she turned toward him, sliding her arms up and around his neck. "I love you, too, Ernest." Her voice was husky with truth. Seeing the flare of hope in his eyes, she added swiftly, "I'm just not sure that I'm ready to marry again yet. My marriage to Win was such a nightmare, and though I know things would be very different between the two of us, I'm just not ready to tie the knot for a second time. At least not yet. Ask me again when I'm back from Europe and when my divorce has been granted—and don't in the meantime stop loving me, Ernest. You've become the center of my life. You do know that, don't you?"

He nodded, his arms tightening around her as he fought his disappointment. "Happiness is too precious not to take it when it's there for the taking, Wallis," he said thickly. "By the time you get your divorce I'll be installed in Simpson, Spence and Young's London office. I know you have friends in London. As we'll be living there after our marriage, we could marry there. We'll be happy together, darling. I know we will be."

Wallis was beginning to feel more and more certain that Ernest was right. He would bring stability into her life, stability her life badly needed. Her intention had always been to move to London after her divorce, and the thought of living there as a married woman, with a home of her own, was tempting.

And so I'm cruising the Mediterranean with Aunt Bessie,

she wrote to Pamela a few weeks later.

> *At the moment we are berthed at Naples. From here our itinerary is Palermo and then Trieste, where we leave the ship. Aunt Bessie's intention is that we then travel by either train or hired car back across southern Europe, stopping at Monte Carlo, Nice, Avignon, and Arles until we eventually reach Paris.*
>
> *As for my love life—I'm in a quandary and wish to goodness you were around for me to talk it all out with. Ernest has asked me to marry him—something I knew he would eventually do from the evening I first met him. He's kind, sensitive, intelligent. His mother is American and he was brought up here, but he's British, both legally and by inclination. He's financially secure (after the way I had to*

*live on my Uncle Sol's charity in my Baltimore days and how
since I've had to rely on a small Navy allowance and poker
winnings, you can't imagine how happy those words make
me). I like being with him. He makes me feel safe—and that,
I think, is the problem. I'm not used to feeling safe and secure
and to tell you the truth, Pamela, I find it a little boring. I've
gotten so used to excitement that now I'm living without it,
I miss it. (Did I tell you that when I traveled alone from
Shanghai to Peking, the train was boarded by bandits?
They were terrifyingly scary but thankfully weren't on a
kidnapping spree.)*

*So there it is. I can stop drifting. Marry Ernest and live
happily and unexcitingly, ever after. Or I can not marry
Ernest and wait on fate. So far, though, fate has not been
overwhelmingly kind and I'm not growing any younger.
I'm thirty-one, and what is the likelihood of a prince on
a white charger carrying off a thirty-one-year-old
middle-aged damsel?*

In the early autumn, when they were in Paris, Bessie said
she was ready for home, but that Wallis could stay on in Paris
for a little while if she wanted to.

Wallis did want to. Ernest had now taken over the running
of the family firm in London, and in every letter she received
from him he was urging her to join him there and to marry
him. Becoming Mrs. Ernest Simpson was something Wallis
still hadn't made up her mind about, and Corinne hadn't helped
matters when, in her last letter to her, she'd written,

*Remember the old jingle, Skinny? "To change the name and
not the letter, is a change for the worse, not for the better."
As Spencer and Simpson have the same initial, I thought I'd
better warn you!*

That her time for hiding in Paris had run its course came out of the blue. Walking down the boulevard toward her hotel, she paused at a newsstand and bought a copy of the early edition of the *Paris Herald*. Turning it over, she was stunned to read that her Uncle Sol had died the previous day. Back at her hotel, a cable from Alice was waiting for her.

Uncle Sol dead. Heart failure. Funeral Friday. Mama

Though there was no way she could be in Baltimore in time for the funeral, she knew then and there that it was time to go home. Their relationship had never been easy, but he was the only father figure she had ever known. She owed it to him to show her respects by returning home.

Forty-eight hours later she was aboard a liner heading for New York.

"I'm nervous about the will, honey," Alice said as she and Wallis set out for 34 East Preston Street to hear the reading. "If it weren't that you're about to become divorced, I'm sure as God made little green apples Sol would have left the bulk of his fortune to you." Wallis had never seen anyone literally wringing their hands, but her mother was wringing them now. "He was too furious with you for bringing shame on his family name. No Warfield has ever been divorced and he just couldn't stomach it, Wallis. He said the very word stuck in his craw."

"Stop worrying, Mama. How could Uncle Sol *not* have left me any money? You're wrong, though, in thinking there was a time when he might have left me all of it. Devout Episcopalians are duty bound to leave generously to charity. What I will get is a smidgen—but a smidgen of such a large amount will, for me, be a fortune."

The reading of Sol's last will and testament took place in

34 East Preston Street's parlor. Her Uncle Emory was seated in the rosewood rocking chair from which her grandmother had ruled the household. His wife was seated on the slippery leather couch that Wallis, as a child, had been unable to sit on without, much to her grandmother's exasperation, sliding off it. Her grandmother's voice rang in her memory as if it were yesterday. *Bessie Wallis, can't you be still for just a minute? Bessie Wallis, how will you ever grow up to be a lady unless you learn to keep your back straight?*

Everywhere she looked there were memories. The little petit-point-covered stool beside the rocker where, for hours on end, she had sat listening to her grandmother tell stories about Robert de Warfield and Pagan de Warfield and of how she must never forget that Warfields were descended from England's William the Conqueror.

There were Warfield cousins in the room she barely recognized. Henry, once so handsome, now not even looking distinguished. He carefully avoided her eyes, not wanting to reveal what his hopes were where Sol's vast fortune was concerned.

Glasses of sherry were handed around.

Sol's lawyer cleared his throat and in a thin reedy voice began the reading.

The total amount of the estate was over five million dollars. Wallis, remembering how, in the days before her mother had married Mr. Rasin, her uncle had said if she would leave her mother and promise to never see her again, he would make her his heiress, clasped gloved hands tightly in her lap. Despite the huge amount of money now to be apportioned, the decision she had made then, when a vulnerable young girl, was not one she regretted.

There was tension in the room as it became apparent that the bequests to family being read out were nominal, not generous. Wallis was aware of several pairs of eyes sliding in her direction as the possibility dawned that this was because the bulk of his estate was being left to her.

After what seemed an eternity of waiting, the reedy voice intoned: "To my niece, Bessiewallis Spencer, wife of Winfield Spencer, I bequeath the interest from fifteen thousand dollars' worth of shares in railway stock and the Alleghany Company and the Texas Company."

The lawyer paused, and Wallis licked dry lips as she waited for him to continue. Uncle Sol referring to her as Bessiewallis didn't bode well, as he knew it was a name she hadn't answered to since she was a very young child and that she disliked it intensely. The rider *wife of Winfield Spencer* was more promising, for it indicated that the will had been made before she had begun divorce proceedings against Win and, if that was the case, her mother's fears that her divorce would have affected what Sol was going to leave her would be proved groundless.

"This sum," the lawyer continued, "to be paid to my niece in quarterly installments, so long as she shall live and not remarry."

He paused, this time for a little longer.

Wallis waited expectantly.

"The remainder of my estate," the lawyer said, "I leave for the formation of a home for aged and indigent gentlewomen in memory of my mother, Anne Emory Warfield, a room to be set aside therein for my niece, Bessiewallis Spencer, if ever she should need it."

It was a second or two before Wallis could comprehend the enormity of the blow and the insult her uncle had dealt her. Whatever his bequests to her may have originally been, the will that had just been read had clearly been made after she had begun divorce proceedings against Win. The amount left to her, and the terms under which it had been left, cut fierce and deep, but it was the public insinuation that she would one day have need of his house of charity for impoverished gentle-women that made her proud Warfield blood boil with such rage, she thought she was going to explode.

Her mother made a stifled sound of anguish beside her.

A Warfield cousin sniggered.

Wallis rose to her feet, her back straight, her head high. Aware that she was now most certainly going to marry Ernest, she left 34 East Preston Street knowing she was doing so for the last time. In another few weeks it would be Christmas, and by then she would have her divorce. Once it had been finally granted, she would write to Ernest, telling him she would be happy to become his wife, and then, before sailing to join him in London, she would enjoy six months of freedom as a single woman by staying with the Rogerses, who, having left Peking, were now living in a villa in the hills above Cannes, in the south of France.

It was a break that would mark the end of her former life and the beginning of a new life—and whatever that new life might bring, Wallis knew for a certainty that she would never, ever fulfill her uncle's expectations by becoming an inmate of the Anne Emory Warfield Home for Impoverished Gentlewomen.

Chapter Twenty-Seven

"John Jasper! You'll never guess!" Pamela rushed into the drawing room of their home in Hanover Square, Wallis's letter to her in her hand. "Wally's marrying an Englishman, and she's going to do so in London!"

It was the first week of January 1928.

John Jasper put down the newspaper he'd been reading. "I hope he's not a bounder," he said cautiously. "Does she know his background?"

Pamela, who though still curvaceous was also now a little plump, perched on the arm of his chair. "His father is English, his mother American. He went to Harvard, was a second lieutenant in the Coldstream Guards, and is now running the London branch of his family's ship brokerage firm. He's also been married before, but then so has Wally."

"Where is Wallis now? Is she still in Virginia?" John Jasper's interest was sincere.

"Warrenton? No. She left there the minute her divorce was finalized. She's in the south of France, staying with the friends she stayed with in Peking."

"And her soon-to-be second husband?"

"Ernest?" Pamela glanced down at the letter. "He's here in London. The wedding isn't going to be until June. I don't think their being apart until then is going to worry Wally unduly. After all, they don't *have* to be apart, do they? Wally could be staying in London with us if she wanted. She's had an open invitation to do so for ages."

She slid off the arm of the chair and crossed the room to where an Art Deco cocktail cabinet stood discreetly beside one of the room's many large windows. "I rather suspect, darling, that dear Wally isn't *passionate* about Ernest." Though the sun was hours from being over the yardarm, she began making herself a pink gin. "I suspect he's a safe port in a storm, not a grand romance. If Ernest had been the Argentinean diplomat she'd been so madly in love with, she wouldn't for one *minute* have allowed him to remain on his own in London while she stayed with friends in the south of France."

John Jasper put his newspaper down and looked pointedly at the glass in her hand. "It's only eleven in the morning, Pamela."

"I know, darling." She perched again on the arm of his chair and with her free hand ruffled hair as black and curly as it had been when he'd been eighteen. "But I'm celebrating the news that Wally's found herself another husband. Why don't you join me? You're not going to the embassy today. We're going into deepest Hampshire to celebrate Rose Houghton's fortieth birthday, or had you forgotten?"

"No," he said, not taking her up on her suggestion, "though why she has to celebrate it in the depths of the country instead of in London, I can't imagine."

"Because it's basically a family party and we should think ourselves lucky to be invited to it. Family matters to Rose, and her grandfather is now so infirm he never leaves Snowberry, which is why the party is being held there."

Aware that peace and quiet in which to read had been

shattered for good, John Jasper rose to his feet. "There won't be many people there we know," he said. "All Rose and Hal's other close friends are either socialists or press barons."

Pamela giggled. "Sometimes, darling, like Hal, they're both."

John Jasper chuckled. Pamela sometimes infuriated him almost beyond endurance, but she never bored him. A family party to be celebrated in the depth of the countryside in the middle of winter wasn't something he was particularly looking forward to, but unlike most of Pamela's friends, Rose was a steadying influence on her, and their friendship was one he had always encouraged.

Where Rose's husband Hal was concerned, he had his own reasons for maintaining as close a contact with him as possible. Hal was an English press baron of enormous, if controversial, reputation and John Jasper was an American diplomat. It was in the interests of both of them to maintain a relationship in which they could, when the need arose, speak frankly to each other.

"You'll need to wear a fur coat," he said as Pamela remained seated on the arm of the chair, the pink gin in her glass now at a disconcertingly low level. "The temperature is always a couple of degrees lower outside London."

Pamela regarded him in amusement, loving the fact that he'd lost none of the Roma-like good looks that so set him apart in any social gathering. "The party is going to be held indoors, darling. Not in the garden."

He began to walk out of the room, intent on informing their chauffeur what time they would be leaving London. As he reached the door, he said drily, "I've become accustomed to the lack of heating in English country houses, Pamela, and believe me, in whatever part of Snowberry this party is to be held, you're going to need a fur!"

Pamela waited until the door had closed behind him and

then slid off the arm of the chair and headed once again in the direction of the cocktail cabinet.

Against all the odds, she and John Jasper were happier together than any other married couple she knew. She hadn't always been faithful to him, of course. Being faithful would have been behavior thought far too odd in the high-society circle they were a part of, but whenever she had been naughty, it had always only ever been a fling, not a grand passion. She suspected that John Jasper, too, had had a little fling on occasions but that, like hers, they had always been of short duration and never of any importance.

She dropped three dashes of Angostura bitters into her glass, swirled them around, and then added a measure of gin. John Jasper had said that in all probability there wouldn't be anyone at the party whom they would know, which was quite true as she and Rose didn't have friends in common. Rose's sister Marigold, known to the world as Marietta des Vaux, might very well be there to add a shot of movie-star glamour, and she'd been longing to meet Marigold for as long as she could remember. There was someone else who just might be there as well, and that was Prince Edward.

In all the years she had known Rose, she had never gotten to the bottom of Prince Edward's relationship with the Houghton family. Rose always behaved as if no relationship had ever existed, but Lord May hadn't done so when, during the war, she had traveled to Snowberry in order to give him his birthday present from Rose. "There was a time," he had told her then, "when David was always down here."

John Jasper had dismissed it as the ramblings of an elderly man with a faulty memory, but she wasn't convinced. She drained her glass. If Edward put in an appearance later today at Snowberry, John Jasper would have to do something he hated. He would have to admit that he was wrong.

. . .

Later that afternoon she had to acknowledge that there was one thing John Jasper hadn't been wrong about. Unless you were fortunate enough to be standing, or seated, immediately in front of the roaring log fire in Snowberry's drawing room, Snowberry was freezing cold.

The next thing that registered was that Rose's birthday party was going to be a very small, very staid affair. Her grandfather, Lord May, was seated nearest to the fire and, despite being in such a prime position for warmth, had a tartan rug over his knees. There was a handful of county types there, the men advertising their good breeding by being chinless and their wives by looking disconcertingly like the horses that, in Pamela's hearing at least, were the sole subject of their conversation.

It was hard to believe that any of them were Rose and Hal's personal friends, and Pamela concluded that they were simply neighboring estate owners who had been invited because Lord May would have wished them to be invited, and that Rose had invited her and John Jasper in order to liven things up a little bit.

Also livening things up was Marigold, who, with her flame-red hair and husky unchained laugh, was glamour personified. Her husband came as rather a surprise, being at least two decades her senior and silver-haired.

John Jasper, knowing how little interest Pamela took in parliamentary affairs, said to her in a quiet aside that Marigold's husband had until recently been the Speaker in the House of Lords. However distinguished he obviously was, Pamela felt Marigold's fame and glamour would have been better served if her husband had been John Barrymore or Douglas Fairbanks.

"My sister, Iris," Rose said, introducing her to a woman who looked as if she would be more at home wearing thick stockings and brogues, rather than the silk stockings and high heels she was trying to look comfortable in.

Pamela could tell immediately that however pleasant Iris was—and her smile indicated she was very pleasant indeed—she was also uninteresting and was probably also uninteresting to her husband who, when Rose introduced him, shot her the kind of hot, speculative look that indicated he would like to get to know her much, much better.

The introduction over, Rose moved away and one of the county set immediately claimed Iris. Over Iris's husband's shoulder Pamela saw a petite, stunningly beautiful woman enter the room. She wasn't dressed for a birthday celebration. Her floral, midcalf-length cotton dress was nondescript and a little faded. It didn't matter. It only seemed to emphasize her aura of gentle serenity. In a room where nearly every female head of hair was marcel-waved, hers was a blue-black cloud that looked as if all she had done was lightly run a comb through it. Apart from a small wristwatch she was wearing no jewelry and, obviously unaware of doing so, she put everyone, even her famous movie-star sister, into the shade.

The man who walked into the room hard on her heels was equally striking. His hair was a burning red and he was wearing a kilt in the manner of a man who had been doing so ever since he could walk. Pamela didn't have to ask who they both were. As the woman crossed the room swiftly to where Lord May was seated and unself-consciously sank down on her knees beside his chair, taking hold of his hand, it was blatantly obvious that the woman was Rose's youngest sister, Lily, and that the good-looking Scot accompanying her was her husband.

"So you're a movie-star friend of Marigold's, are you?" Iris's husband said leeringly.

Gratified by his assumption, she was tempted to say yes.

Knowing that if she did, he would corral her in a corner of the room and she'd never be able to get away from him, it was a temptation she overcame.

"No," she said, still looking beyond his shoulder at the now-empty doorway. "Would you excuse me? I need to retrieve my handbag."

Without giving him the chance to detain her, she walked smartly away from him, uncaring that her clutch bag was very visibly tucked beneath her arm. Lily's attractive husband was laughing at something Marigold was animatedly telling him. John Jasper was deep in conversation with Hal. Rose was no-where to be seen, presumably in the dining room, checking on the buffet table and the birthday cake.

Not wanting to be waylaid by anyone else either boring or lecherous, Pamela headed out of the drawing room in order to find somewhere she could enjoy a quiet cigarette unmolested.

Snowberry was Elizabethan and its vast hall was stone flagged. In summer it was no doubt pleasantly cool, but now the hall was even chillier than parts of the drawing room had been. Pamela hugged her arms, wishing she had taken John Jasper's advice and had kept her fur coat on.

A glorious grand staircase of ancient oak, its newel posts and balustrades intricately carved, led up from the hall. She walked to the foot of it and leaned against one of the newel posts, about to take her cigarette case out of her bag.

"I wouldn't stay there for long," a girl's voice said pleas-antly from somewhere above her. "The newels are carved with dragons and gremlins and make a very uncomfortable prop."

Pamela turned and looked upward. At the top of the first wide sweep of stairs, a landing divided the magnificent stair-case into two. Seated on the top step of it was a fair-haired girl who looked to be about fifteen or sixteen.

"You're right." Pamela was glad to at last have someone

promisingly interesting to talk to. "I've got a crick in my back already. Who are you? Are you a member of the family?"

"Ariadne Sinclair," the girl said, making no move to stand and walk down the stairs to join her. "I don't visit Snowberry often. My family home is on Islay. It's in the Hebrides," she added helpfully.

"Yes, I know." Pamela was intrigued by the girl's hair coloring, which was neither red, like her father's, nor night-black, like her mother's. "Aren't you coming down to join the party?"

"No. I'm not allowed. Mummy says I wouldn't enjoy it as even though Auntie Marigold is here—and she's always terrific fun—so are a lot of people Mummy said I would find boring. Not you, of course," she added hastily.

"Of course not." Pamela was beginning to enjoy the conversation hugely. "And your mother was right. It is a pretty boring party. Some music would liven it up."

"Oh, there will be music later. Aunt Marigold loves to dance. She's taught me to Charleston and do the Black Bottom."

It was Pamela's turn to have a wide grin on her face. The prospect of doing the Black Bottom with Ariadne's good-looking father was one to look forward to.

"When it's my sixteenth birthday we'll be having a *ceilidh*," Ariadne said, obviously enjoying their conversation as much as Pamela was. "Have you ever been to one?"

"Not a genuine one, held in Scotland." As she spoke, Pamela was trying to figure out who it was Ariadne reminded her of. She had her mother's delicately boned features, but so did the other person, whoever he, or she, was. "I can manage a Dashing White Sergeant," she added, struck by the unusual summer-sky blue of Ariadne's fair-lashed eyes and her entrancing feylike quality.

"The nice thing about Scottish dancing is that it's a group

thing." Ariadne rose to her feet. "I'd better go back and make sure my little sister isn't getting into any mischief. With a bit of luck you'll be dancing very shortly. Avoid my Aunt Iris's husband. He's a dreadful lecher. He has hands like an octopus!"

"I will."

As Ariadne ran lightly up the next flight of stairs, Pamela wondered if her parents were aware of the hand-groping liberties their delightful daughter had obviously been well able to fend off. Like her Aunt Marigold, Ariadne Sinclair was obviously someone it would always be fun to be with.

She turned, about to walk back into the drawing room, and sucked in her breath.

Opposite her, in an unlit alcove and on a pedestal, was the bronze bust of Prince Edward that Ariadne's mother had sculpted.

Pamela didn't have to walk closer to it to know that when she did so, she would see exactly the same curve of cheekbone and lip that made Ariadne so distinctively pretty. Prince Edward's indefinable feylike quality—which Lily had so skillfully captured—was a quality her daughter also possessed.

With a trembling hand Pamela took her cigarette case out of her bag, lifted a cigarette from it, and lit it. Edward was thirty-four, and Lord May had told her that Edward's visits to Snowberry had been made when he was a naval cadet, which meant, if the bust was anything to go by, that he'd been between sixteen and eighteen at the time.

She inhaled deeply. Ariadne had told her that she would soon be celebrating her sixteenth birthday—and sixteen from thirty-four was eighteen, subtract another nine months for the length of a pregnancy and it meant Edward would have been seventeen when he had been visiting Snowberry and when Lily had conceived Ariadne.

She blew a plume of blue smoke into the air. No wonder Rose had always played down any kind of a connection between her family and Edward. No wonder, either, that Lily was now keeping her daughter as well hidden from view as the bust she had sculpted. If it had remained in its usual position in the drawing room and Ariadne had also been in the room, the likeness between her and the bust was so marked it would have attracted comment—and the comment among any neighbors who had known of Prince Edward's youthful visits to Snowberry might have hardened into suspicion.

Delighted with the secret that was now hers—and knowing that out of loyalty to Rose she would never be able to share it with anyone—she made her way back to the drawing room. There was dance music playing now, and she wanted to capture Rory Sinclair as a partner before anyone else did.

"This wedding of Wallis's sounds as if it's going to be a very mean little affair," John Jasper said to her six months later as they left Hanover Square by car for the Chelsea register office. "Who else is going to be there, apart from us?"

Pamela adjusted a raspberry-pink hat that perfectly matched her Parisian-designed dress. "Hardly anyone. Ernest's father, but not his mother. They are separated and can't even bear being in the same country together. Mrs. Simpson lives abroad but whenever she visits England, Mr. Simpson promptly leaves it as if the air has become contaminated."

She adjusted her five-string pearl necklace so that it lay a little more perfectly over the neckline of her dress. "Maud Kerr-Smiley, Ernest's sister, will be there. Her husband won't be as they are recently separated." As their chauffeur headed toward the Chelsea Embankment, she shot John Jasper an impish glance. "The Simpson family don't have a very good record where happy marriages are concerned, though I can't see Ernest getting up to any mischief and causing Wally grief, can you?"

"God! After what she endured with that louse of a first husband, I sincerely hope not!"

She slid her gloved hand into his. "Peter Kerr-Smiley Junior will be there. He's acting as Ernest's best man—or he is if grooms at register-office weddings have best men. There may be a couple of Ernest's ship-broking colleagues there. And there will be us. That's all."

"No family from America? Not even her mother?"

The car was now speeding along the embankment, the Embankment Gardens on their right, the glittering, busy Thames on their left.

"Not a one. No Alice, no Bessie, no Lelia Barnett, and no Corinne Murray and no Edith, either. Wallis would *hate* anyone from Baltimore to know she was marrying in a London register office."

They arrived there only seconds before the bride and groom. Wallis was wearing a blue taffeta coat over a pale lemon silk dress, her glossy dark hair parted in the middle and drawn back tightly into a low figure-of-eight chignon.

Pamela squeezed John Jasper's arm, whispering to him as they entered the small room where the service was to take place, "Don't you think that ever since her stay in Peking, Wallis has begun to look a little Chinese? It's the hair. It's as sleek as only Chinese women know how to make it."

The service was over almost before it had begun.

"I do solemnly declare," Ernest said, "that I know not of any lawful impediment why I, Ernest Aldrich Simpson, may not be joined in matrimony to Bessie Wallis Warfield Spencer."

Pamela raised her eyes to heaven, knowing exactly how

much Wallis must be hating hearing her full Christian name. Moments later, after Ernest had made his vows, she was also having to speak it.

"I call upon these persons here present," she said, her American drawl very pronounced in contrast to Ernest's very clipped English, "to witness that I, Bessie Wallis Warfield Spencer, take thee, Ernest Aldrich Simpson, to be my lawful wedded husband."

Ernest then slid a ring onto the third finger of Wallis's left hand and, as Wallis said drolly afterward, "the deed was done before I'd even had a chance to realize the service was under way!"

Later, at the champagne wedding brunch held at the Grosvenor Hotel where Ernest's father had permanent rooms, Pamela said, "I hope you'll be very happy this time around, Wally."

"So do I." Wallis shot her a wry smile. "Marrying Ernest may be about the only sensible thing I've done in life so far. He's very kind—which after Win will be a welcome contrast—and I'm very fond of him."

"Fond, but not in love?"

They were in the bedroom her father-in-law had put at Wallis's disposal. Wallis, who had gone there to refresh her makeup before leaving for the honeymoon Ernest had planned for them in France, slid her powder compact back into her handbag. "Being in love has never done me any favors, Pamela. Not with John Jasper, not with Win, and certainly not with Felipe. I'm tired of fighting the world alone and with no money. Ernest and I will rub along very well together. For once I'm utterly sure I've done the right thing."

Her mood changed and she laughed, looking finally like a radiant bride. "Ernest has bought a Lagonda touring car for our drive through France. It's the most ridiculous color. Bright yellow. Can you imagine Ernest buying a bright yellow car? Isn't it a hoot?"

She gave a final look in the mirror and then picked up her handbag. "So here I go, Pamela. No longer Mrs. Spencer, but Mrs. Simpson. It's a very ordinary name, isn't it? I doubt that anyone in the world but me is ever going to remember it!"

Chapter Twenty-Eight

Wallis learned a great deal about her husband on their honeymoon—all of it pleasing. Their sexual relationship had been worked out during their courtship, so there were no surprises there, apart from Ernest's physical needs being even more low-key than she had believed them to be. Sometimes it was hard for her to believe that they were husband and wife, not brother and sister. It didn't trouble her. She liked being with Ernest. He was the only person she knew who could be both interesting and restful at the same time.

Once in France she discovered that not only was Ernest's French fluent, but he had an all-embracing knowledge of many other subjects as well, including art, church architecture, and French history. As they pottered around cathedral towns such as Rheims and Chartres, he was able to bring the past alive for her in a way any professional tourist guide would have envied.

In Paris they walked narrow cobbled streets hand in hand for hours, visiting the Louvre, Sacré Coeur, Notre Dame, the Eiffel Tower. In the Place Vendôme he told her of how the column in its center was a replica of the original.

"The original was torn down in 1871 by revolutionaries led

by the painter Gustave Courbet," he said knowledgeably, adding with a grin, "The revolt failed and Courbet had to pay for the replacement. It must have cost him every last franc he ever earned."

He knew other little-known facts as well. That Paris, as well as New York, had a Statue of Liberty, though one on a much smaller scale. Wallis thought he was teasing her and, to prove that he wasn't, he drove her out to southwest Paris where, on an island next to the Pont de Grenelle bridge, it stood, a brave reminder that the New York statue had been a gift to America from France.

At midday they lunched in small bistros at gingham-checked tables. In the evening they dined more splendidly, seated on velvet-covered banquettes at white-napered tables lit by candles.

If Wallis wasn't heedlessly in love, and if Ernest's love for facts and figures was sometimes a little tedious, she was content—and contentment was something she was quite happy to settle for.

"I need help decorating and furnishing the Mayfair flat Ernest has found for us," she said to Pamela on her return. "I can't spend a fortune, but I do want to make it suitable for entertaining the fine folk you'll soon be introducing us to."

Pamela rolled her eyes. "Where do you want to start? Perhaps George and Nada would be the best bet."

They were lunching at the Ritz. It was somewhere Ernest found too expensive, except for the celebration of a special occasion, and whenever she and Pamela lunched there it was always amicably understood that Pamela would be the one picking up the bill.

Wallis took a sip of deliciously chilled Chablis. "Who are George and Nada?"

"George is the second Marquess of Milford Haven and

Lord Louis Mountbatten's brother. His mother was a grand-daughter of Queen Victoria, and one of his aunts, Alexandra, was married to the last emperor of Russia. Nada is the daughter of Grand Duke Michael Mikhailovich Romanov. Between them, George and Nada know everyone there is to know. Nada," she added, "is *extremely* naughty—and not only with men."

Wallis sensed Nada's lesbian leanings the first time she met her. As she in no way shared them, they didn't trouble her, and all through the autumn of 1928 and the spring of 1929 she and Ernest were soon regular house party guests at the Milford Havens' country estate, Lynden Manor, near Maidenhead in Berkshire.

Thanks to George and Nada they soon had other high-society friends as well. Friends such as Cecil Beaton, who had taken the most wonderful photographs of Prince Edward's younger brother, Prince Albert, and his family, and Lady Sibyl Colefax, who enthusiastically helped her when it came to choosing color schemes for the spacious drawing room and dining room in which she intended entertaining with all the flair her mother had shown in those far-off days of pay-to-attend dinners.

"I want colors that will show off my Chinese treasures," she said to Sybil, adding with a face-splitting grin, "and my clothes. I've had the Chinese silk I bought in Hong Kong and Shanghai made up into mandarin-necked jackets and dresses and luscious evening gowns with side splits at the ankle."

"Then we'll go for muted and subtle," Sybil said, aware of how much the elegant severity of Chinese-style clothes would suit her new friend. "Let me have a look at the carpet you bought in Peking. It's going to make a wonderful centerpiece for the drawing room—and we'll need to shop for a really elegant vitrine in order to show off your jade and ivory lucky elephants."

Not only was Wallis and Ernest's home full of artifacts that set it apart, but her style of entertaining was different and interesting, too.

"Don't play down being American," Pamela had said to her. "Play it up. Serve the kind of food your mother used to serve. Maryland crabcakes, fried chicken, white cloud cake—and put the cocktail-making skills Win taught you to good use. Cocktail parties are the easiest and swiftest way of widening your social circle."

Wallis had always found the London cocktail parties she had attended with Ernest to be little more than a fill-in hour before the real entertainment of the evening began. The cocktails had always been unimaginatively restricted in choice, food had rarely been served, and, when it had been, it had always been uninspiring.

Right from the first she decided that her cocktail parties were not merely going to be the precursor to other events, but events in themselves, and that she was going to conduct them with Virginian open-house hospitality so that, at cocktail hour, people would feel free to call on her and Ernest without having been formally invited to do so.

Pamela had raised her eyes to heaven at the idea, saying it would never catch on. She was proved wrong. With a nub of people such as herself and John Jasper, Tarquin, the Milford Havens, Cecil Beaton, and Sibyl Colefax regularly to be found in Wallis and Ernest's flat at cocktail hour, word spread that Wallis was great fun, that her cocktails were cocktails that couldn't be found anywhere else, not even at the Ritz or the Savoy, and that to drop in on her and Ernest before continuing on to a dinner engagement, the opera, or the theater was *the* thing to do.

Not all the new people in their lives were English. John

Jasper introduced Benjamin Thaw, the first secretary of the U.S. embassy in London, and his sultrily exotic half-American, half Latin-American wife Consuelo, into their ever-expanding social circle.

Consuelo's distinctive, head-turning beauty was a beauty one of her younger sisters, Thelma, shared. First married when she was seventeen, divorced when she was twenty, Thelma was now married to a British aristocrat, Viscount Furness, who was known to all and sundry as "Duke." Despite her friendship with Consuelo, Wallis still barely knew Thelma. By early 1929 it was something she realized she was going to have to change.

"Thelma," Consuelo said at one of Wallis's early evening parties, "has finally ousted Freda Dudley Ward from Prince Edward's life. Isn't that spiffy?"

She and Benny were continuing on to the opera, and she was wearing a black-and-gold evening dress embroidered with coral beads and crystals. Her nails and lips were a searing matching coral and she was sitting, unasked, upon John Jasper's knee, one arm carelessly around his neck.

"He's absolutely mad for her," she continued, gratified that she had caught everyone's attention, "and let's face it, who can blame him? She's far more fun than Freda, who was always trying to keep him on the straight and narrow."

Wallis was kneeling at the coffee table that held everything she needed for cocktail making. She paused in what she was doing, saying to Ernest, "Darling, will you turn the music down a little, so that we can more easily hear what Consuelo is saying?"

Ernest obligingly turned down the peppy strains of "Cecilia" by Johnny Hamp's Kentucky Serenaders.

Wallis continued with what she had been doing, pouring two and a quarter measures of American rye whiskey into a cocktail shaker and adding a measure of sweet red vermouth, saying as she did so, "Are you sure Freda is really a thing of the past, Consuelo? People have thought it before and been proved wrong."

Consuelo gave a dismissive wave of her long cigarette holder. "What would you say if I told you that when he goes on his South African tour in February, he's arranged to meet up with Thelma in Kenya? He's never made those sort of arrangements for Freda when he's been on any of his trips abroad."

Once again Wallis stopped what she was doing.

John Jasper cleared his throat. "Are you, or are you not, making me a Manhattan, Wallis?"

"I am." Wallis added ice and a dash of bitters to the mix and began shaking it.

Benny Thaw said, "It's a shame Thelma isn't single. Rumors from the palace are that the king's health is so poor he isn't expected to live for much longer. If Prince Edward were able to marry Thelma and make her Princess of Wales, she'd be queen before you could spit—and I rather like the idea of having a queen for a sister-in-law."

"Cecilia" came to an end, and Ernest deftly removed the record and replaced it with "A Precious Little Thing Called Love," sung by George Olsen.

Pamela, who was privately concluding that Consuelo had been sitting on John Jasper's knee for quite long enough, said, "Even if she were single, she'd be a divorcée, and there's no way a king of England can be married to a divorced woman, because as well as being the king, he's also head of the Church of England—and the church doesn't recognize divorce. So eat your heart out, Benny. Your daydream is never going to come true."

Wallis strained the contents of the cocktail shaker into a martini glass and added a cherry for garnish.

As she did so, her eyes met Pamela's. Whenever Edward was under discussion, Pamela never mentioned the letters he had written to her from France and Italy during the war. Wallis knew there were two reasons. The first was that Pamela valued still being part of Edward's "set" and didn't think he'd take kindly to it if she gossiped about the letters he had written to her. The second was that Pamela enjoyed having secrets and was never happier than when she was keeping one.

It wasn't something Wallis had realized in the days when they had been at Arundell and Oldfields together. Then, Pamela had always said that being best friends meant they would never have any secrets from each other, but her affair with John Jasper had shown Wallis that what Pamela said and what she did were often two very different things.

Whether Pamela had anything she was keeping secret from her now Wallis didn't know, but she did know that none of their mutual friends—not even Georgie Mountbatten, who was Edward's cousin—knew how close she'd once come to becoming Edward's mistress.

"My Manhattan, Wallis," John Jasper said, using his feigned exasperation as an excuse to remove Consuelo from his knee and get up from his chair.

As he walked across to her, Wallis gave him a smile of apology. "Sorry, John Jasper, I was trying to come to terms with the fact that if Prince Edward were suddenly to become king, Thelma would be *maîtresse-en-titre*."

"Which wouldn't matter if, as king, he had also had a queen and an heir—or at least the prospect of an heir. Something he not only doesn't have, but doesn't even show the slightest interest in having." He took the martini glass from Wallis's hand. "Even for a republican, that seems to me a dodgy situation for a monarchy. Especially one that rules a third of the globe."

. . .

All through the year and into 1930, rumors as to King George's health continued to be rampant. Wallis found it surreal to think that when he died and when Prince Edward became king, his mistress would be a woman whose sister she regarded as being a close friend. Even after over a year of being friends with George and Nada, she could never quite believe that George was Lord Louis Mountbatten's brother.

Her memory of when she had seen Louis Mountbatten standing by Prince Edward's side in the grand ballroom of the Hotel del Coronado was still vivid. Then, even being presented to him and shaking his hand would have been one of the high spots of her life. Now his brother and sister-in-law bandied his name across her and Ernest's dining table so casually it made her head spin.

Common sense told her she was being foolishly snobbish, but the fact that she was friends with minor royalty gave her a great deal of pleasure. One reason was that she knew how much pleasure her grandmother would have gained from it. Another was that she knew how furiously jealous the people who had once sneered at her for living off her Uncle Sol's charity would be. If Violet Dix or Mabel Morgan were in London now they would, she knew, be selling their souls in order to be invited to a cocktail party at which the marquess and marchioness of Milford Haven would be present.

What she had yet to achieve, though, was the presence of Thelma at one of her cocktail parties, for with Thelma would also—eventually—come Prince Edward.

She was in the back of a taxicab, thinking of a way of achieving this objective, when the cabdriver opened his glass partition and said: "Yer might loike to know, madam, that the Prince of Wales's car 'as just driven up alongside of us."

Wallis spun her head to the right. There was only one passenger in the limousine, and beneath a homburg hat his delicate profile was immediately recognizable. He was staring straight ahead of him, his expression somber.

"'E's no doubt thinkin' about the king," the cabdriver said with a knowing nod as the limousine pulled away from them, heading in the direction of Buckingham Palace. "'E's pretty bad, by all accounts. My missus 'as bin sayin' prayers for 'im all week."

Wallis leaned back against the cracked leather seating. She had now seen Prince Edward twice, both times fleetingly and both times at a distance. It had been ten years since she had seen him at the del Coronado and yet, despite his now being thirty-seven and despite his having a world of worry on his slender shoulders, the boyish handsomeness that was his trademark was undimmed.

For what seemed like an age, Pamela had been promising her she would arrange things so that she would be introduced to him, but so far, despite Pamela's best efforts, it hadn't happened. Her hands tightened on her snakeskin clutch bag as she wondered if it ever would.

When the occasion finally arose, it came completely out of the blue on a dank January day thick with fog. She had woken with a heavy head cold, and when the telephone rang she was uninterested in who it was that was calling.

"It's Mrs. Bachman, Mrs. Simpson," the butler who formed the nucleus of her and Ernest's small household staff of five said.

"Please tell her I will call her back."

He nodded and went back into the hall.

Seconds later he was again at her side. "Mrs. Bachman says it is extremely urgent, Mrs. Simpson."

Hoping there hadn't been an accident or other real emergency, Wallis forced herself into movement.

As soon as she heard the tone of Pamela's excited voice she knew the matter of urgency hadn't been connected to anything grave.

"Wally, darling! I have the most wonderful news. . . ."

"Sorry, Pamela," she said, cutting across her, "but I've come down with a dreadful cold and I'm really not in the mood for whatever it is you're about to tell me."

"You're going to be in the mood for this—and you're going to have to get over your cold pretty damn quick." Pamela's voice wasn't merely excited; it was jubilant. "I've just had a telephone call from Consuelo. She and Benny were due to spend the weekend as guests of Thelma's at Burrough Court, Duke's hunting lodge at Melton Mowbray. Prince Edward is going to be at his hunting lodge, Craven Court, which is only a mile or so away. Thelma is expecting Edward to be spending nearly all the weekend at Burrough and has arranged a small party for him. Nothing big, just a handful of people. As Duke won't be there—he's in Africa, on safari—Thelma needed Consuelo and Benny there to act as chaperones, and now Consuelo can't go."

Wallis sneezed, wiped her nose, and said, "All very interesting, Pamela, but what do Thelma's romantic weekend arrangements have to do with me?"

"Everything, Wally! Absolutely everything! Benny's mother has fallen ill, and Consuelo is leaving for Paris later this morning to look after her. She phoned me in a panic to ask if I knew who was likely to be able to stand in for her and Benny at short notice, and I immediately said that you and Ernest would absolutely love to do so. She will be phoning you any second, so good-bye, darling, and good luck!"

Before Wallis could even draw breath, the connection was

severed. She was just about to call Pamela back in order to ask her to repeat everything she'd said, so she could make sure she'd hadn't misunderstood her, when, beneath her hand, the telephone rang again.

"Wallis, sweetie." Consuelo sounded slightly breathless. "Thank goodness you're at home. I need the most awfully big favor. Thelma is entertaining you-know-who at Burrough, Duke's place in Leicestershire, this weekend. Benny and I were to be chaperones—so silly, but you-know-who insists on the outward proprieties—and I now won't be there as Benny's mother is ill and I have to do the done thing and rush to her side—which very inconveniently happens to be in Paris. Benny is still going to Burrough, but Thelma needs a married couple for the chaperoning lark and so if you don't mind, darling. . . ."

Wallis said she didn't mind, put the receiver down, and succumbed to blind panic. At long, long last she had achieved what she had wanted to achieve for so long. She was not only going to be introduced to the Prince of Wales, she was going to be informally in his company—and for an entire weekend.

It was the kind of engagement for which days of preparation were needed, and she had only hours. Almost incoherent with haste, she phoned Ernest at his office, begging him to come home immediately so that he could ensure she made no mistake when it came to packing their weekend case. Melton Mowbray was deep in fox hunting country, and any weekend spent there would primarily be a hunting weekend. Neither she nor Ernest rode to hounds, and if the dinner table talk was going to be all about hunting—which she was sure it would be—how were she and Ernest going to take part in it? When it came to the clothes to take, she needed Ernest's advice. To be not dressed appropriately for such a weekend would be an embarrassment that would haunt her to the end of her days.

"You need something in tweed for the daytime." When

Ernest arrived home he was flushed with elation at the prospect of meeting his future king in such an intimate setting. "Didn't you buy a blue-gray tweed dress with a cape when we were in Paris? That and a couple of evening dresses should serve splendidly. I've spoken to Benny and he's going to meet us at St. Pancras so that we can travel to Melton together."

His dressing room was between their bedroom and the bathroom, and as he was talking he was rifling through his wardrobe for clothes suitable for both a horse-centered weekend and a prince-centered one.

"By the way, darling," he said, placing two dress shirts with stiff fronts into his case, "I forgot to tell you that Prince Edward's brother, Prince George, is going to be at Burrough as well."

"Dear Lord, are you telling me I'm going to have to do two curtseys?"

"I'm afraid so. Left leg as far as possible behind the right and a nice little dip. You'll do fine, darling. Now how many collars and white ties do you think I should pack?"

Wallis's nerves weren't helped by her cold. "I'm sorry, Benny," she said when he met them at St. Pancras station, "but after waiting a lifetime for this kind of opportunity, it's come at a bad time. I think I'm coming down with flu."

"Then I won't kiss you. Just put extra powder on your nose and no one will guess you're under the weather."

They boarded the train, and in the privacy of their first-class compartment, Wallis said, "I've been practicing curtseys, Benny, but I think they could do with a little polish. You've attended enough court functions to recognize a curtsey properly done. I'm going to do one now, and I want you to tell me what you think."

The train had begun moving and Benny said, amused,

"You're an American, Wallis. You are not obliged to curtsey either to the Prince of Wales or to Prince George."

"Maybe not, but I'm going to. And you have a choice, Benny. You either help me perfect one or I get off this train at the next station!"

Benny's attempts to give a demonstration of a curtsey in a swaying, lurching carriage were hilarious, and Wallis laughed so much that by the time they reached Melton Mowbray she had almost forgotten how dreadfully flu-like she was feeling.

Though it was only five in the afternoon, it was both dark and foggy. A car was waiting to meet them, and as they drove the short distance to Burrough Court, her inner tension mounted.

Being introduced to the Prince of Wales in a house party situation was far different from what it would have been if she had been introduced to him a decade ago at the Hotel del Coronado. Then, she would have been merely one young woman in a long line of young women and would have had no more hope of conversing with him than she would have had of flying to the moon. This evening she would not only be conversing with him, she would be dining with him and quite possibly even dancing with him. It was enough to make anyone feel sick with nerves.

"You're the first to arrive," a pleasant-faced young woman said when Burrough Court's splendid oak-studded front door had been opened to them and they had entered the house. "I'm Averill Furness, Thelma's stepdaughter. Thelma has been delayed on the road by the fog, and the Prince of Wales and Prince George are with her. Hopefully they'll be here soon. I'll have your bags taken up to your rooms. Meanwhile, please come into the drawing room, where tea is waiting to be served."

Benny, who had been a guest at Burrough Court many times, was completely at home. "Many thanks, Averill," he said, shrugging himself out of his overcoat and allowing it to be taken from him by a member of the domestic staff. "I hope there's a log fire roaring away. The train from St. Pancras was damnably chilly."

Relieved that she had a little more time to compose herself before coming face to face with Prince Edward and, as his brother would be arriving with him, executing not one, but two curtseys, Wallis allowed her tweed cape to be taken from her shoulders and then, with Ernest close behind her, followed Benny and Averill into the drawing room.

"A log fire is always a pleasure," Benny said as they seated themselves comfortably on deep-cushioned sofas, "but to tell the truth, it isn't an essential here. When Duke bought Burrough it was just a small, two-storied hunting lodge. He added the wings on either side, giving the house the shape of a square U, insisted that every guest bedroom should have its own bathroom, and had central heating put in—a luxury not to be found in many British country houses. When it comes to central heating, Britain is still way behind America."

"That's because we're hardier than you Americans." Averill was clearly happy to be in his company. "All we need to keep warm are fur coats and good old English wool."

Benny cracked with laughter, and Averill flushed with pleasure at having made him do so.

Wallis shot a quick look in the direction of Averill's left hand, saw there were no rings on it, and wondered if Benny realized that Averill didn't mind in the least Consuelo's being in Paris.

A round table between the sofas and in front of the fire had been set for tea. A maid came in with a tea tray, removed a silver teapot from it, and placed it on the table where Averill could easily reach it.

"Milk or lemon, Wallis?" Averill asked, beginning the task of pouring.

Wallis fought down a sneeze. "Lemon, please."

There came the distant sound of car tires on gravel. Wallis's stomach muscles clenched. In another few minutes the Prince of Wales would be entering the room. Would he be all she had imagined he would be, or would he, in the flesh, be a disappointment?

She heard the front door being opened and the sound of laughter and voices. Then the drawing room door opened and in came a radiant Thelma, a royal prince on each arm, a military-looking gentleman following behind them.

"Hello darlings," she said gaily, her coal-black hair sleekly marcel-waved and wearing—much to Wallis's relief—a dress of lightweight smoky-violet tweed.

The princes, too, were wearing tweeds, in their case suits patterned in startlingly loud checks.

Benny and Ernest rose to their feet and Wallis, weak-kneed, rose to hers.

Thelma led Prince Edward forward. "Sir," she said, "allow me to introduce Mr. and Mrs. Ernest Simpson. Mr. Simpson is half American and half British, and a British subject. He was educated in America, at Harvard. Mrs. Simpson is American."

Wallis could feel Ernest's tension as he gave his future sovereign a stiff bow. Then it was her turn to make an obeisance.

With her mouth dry and her heart pounding, she put her left leg behind her right leg and dipped a deep curtsey.

"I'm pleased to know that when it came to making a choice, you opted to be a British subject and not an American citizen," Prince Edward said in a friendly manner to Ernest, and then, to Wallis, "In which part of America were you born, Mrs. Simpson? I know parts of your country very well."

His eyes were the bluest she had ever seen, his hair an even paler blond than she remembered it being when she had seen him from a distance in San Diego. Then, it had been silkily smooth. Now it was slightly and very attractively wind-rumpled. He was no taller than she was and as far removed in looks from every previous man she had ever been attracted to as it was possible to be.

It didn't matter.

She was dazzled by him. Utterly, totally, completely bewitched—and she knew she would have been even if he hadn't been heir to a kingdom and an empire.

She flashed him the wide smile that came so naturally it never occurred to her it might not be quite the done thing to do.

"I'm from Maryland, sir. The most northern southern state in America."

As Edward was accustomed to only stiffly correct behavior and monosyllabic replies to any question he might ask, his eyes crinkled at the corners with amusement. "It isn't a state I am familiar with, Mrs. Simpson, though maybe I will be one day."

With a smile tugging at his lips, he turned his attention toward the patiently waiting Benny.

Thelma, not knowing quite how she felt about the way Wallis had so swiftly and unself-consciously made an impact, stepped forward and introduced her to Prince George.

Wallis executed a perfect second curtsey. Prince Edward's youngest brother was much more like John Jasper, Win, Felipe, and Ernest in physical type, being tall and dark-haired. He didn't, though, send her head reeling and her senses spinning. Nada had told her that George was the black sheep of the Windsor family. "He's like me, dahlink," she had said in her heavy Russian accent, "in that he likes his own sex as much as he likes the opposite sex. He also prefers cocaine to cocktails. David is trying to help him break the habit."

As Wallis wondered how long she would have to be on social terms with the Prince of Wales before being invited to call him David, Thelma introduced the tall, military-looking man to her.

"Brigadier General Trotter, groom-in-waiting to the Prince of Wales."

"Please call me 'G,' Mrs. Simpson," he said, shaking her hand. "Everyone does."

Fresh tea was brought in. Small talk began. Benny, aware that Ernest and Wallis would be unfamiliar with many of the names being bandied about, deftly brought into the conversation people they knew well.

"The Milford Havens had a riotous country house weekend a fortnight ago," he said, his manner easy and relaxed. "We played charades and Mrs. Simpson stumped us all as Pocahontas. It turns out Pocahontas is a distant ancestress of hers. The literary allusion, of course, is from William Makepeace Thackeray's poem about her."

From the expressions on their faces, it was obvious that neither Prince Edward nor Prince George was overly familiar with Mr. Thackeray, but both of them were interested in Wallis's exotic ancestry.

"Just what is it your Native American ancestress is famous for, Mrs. Simpson?" Edward asked, leaning forward, his hands clasped between his knees, as if not wanting to miss a word of her answer.

Wallis took in a deep breath and, trying to keep her voice steady, said, "In the very early sixteen hundreds, sir, when Virginia was first being colonized, an Englishman, Captain John Smith, was captured by Native Americans and taken before Chief Powhatan. This mighty Indian chief ordered that Captain Smith be killed. At the last moment, just as the ax was about to fall and end Captain Smith's life, Chief Powhatan's thirteen-year-old daughter, Princess Pocahontas, threw herself on the captain's neck, risking her own life in an effort to save his."

"Good God!"

Everyone present could see that Prince Edward was absolutely spellbound.

Thelma, aware that Wallis was effortlessly—and very unexpectedly—stealing her thunder, was furious and taking pains not to show it.

Ernest was puffed with pride.

Benny was vastly amused.

Prince George and Averill were as spellbound as Edward.

"And then what happened?" Edward demanded, his blue eyes holding hers.

Despite her nerves, Wallis once again shot him a grin. "Her father spared Captain Smith's life. A few years later, when she was eighteen, Pocahontas saved the lives of many in Jamestown by warning the settlers of an Indian attack."

"And then?" Edward said again, not wanting the story to come to an end.

"And then she became a Christian, married a Jamestown settler, John Rolfe, and came to England where she was presented to King James I and his consort, Queen Anne."

"So the story had a happy ending?" Prince George asked.

"No." Wallis shook her head. "Pocahontas wasn't accustomed to English cold and English fog. She became very ill and shortly after boarding a ship that would take her back to her beloved homeland and while the ship was still sailing down the Thames River toward the open sea, she died."

Edward gave a heavy sigh. "That's a wonderful story, Mrs. Simpson—and you told it so very well."

Thelma's polite, tight smile became even tighter.

Ernest's pride soared into the stratosphere.

Benny's amusement deepened.

Before anything more could be said, they heard the front door opening and Prince George rose to his feet.

"That will be the friends I am expecting who are taking me on elsewhere for dinner. Good-bye, Benny; hopefully I'll be seeing you again before too very long. Good-bye, Mr. Simpson, Mrs. Simpson." He shook hands with them. "It's been a pleasure meeting you."

When it came to Thelma, he kissed her good-bye on the cheek. Despite such intimacy, Thelma dipped him a curtsey. Realizing that she should also have curtseyed, Wallis hastily curtseyed for the third time.

Later, as she and Ernest dressed for dinner in the suite of rooms that had been prepared for them, Ernest said, "You were marvelous, darling. Not a hint of nerves, though I know you must have been feeling them." He fastened a stiff collar onto his dress shirt. "Wasn't the Prince of Wales wonderful? So natural and he put one so much at ease. I've come to the conclusion that you Americans lost something that is very good and quite irreplaceable when you decided to dispense with the British monarchy."

When they went down to dinner it was to discover that the "handful" of people Consuelo had spoken of was instead a large group of at least thirty, none of whom they knew. They were seated a good distance away from Thelma and Prince Edward, and even after dinner was over they were still not in a position for him to speak to them, as Thelma deftly sorted everyone into different groups, some to play poker and some to play bridge.

The poker players went off with the prince and Thelma to a connecting drawing room, and Wallis, designated by Thelma to be a bridge player, had no choice but to resign herself to an evening spent at a card table in the company of people in whom she had little interest.

The next day was the kind of day she had feared it would be. The prince and "G," together with Benny and a great many other of Thelma's guests, went off in the direction of the stables, dressed for a day spent on horseback.

"The prince will be with the Quorn hunt," a female guest who also hadn't chosen to spend the day in such a manner said when she met Wallis strolling in Burrough Court's large and formal grounds. "He has a terrible seat on a horse. One of the worst I've ever seen, but he's absolutely fearless. He's always in the front, always taking fences other riders deem to be too risky. I've heard the king wants him to give up fox hunting and steeplechasing, thinking them sports too dangerous for a man who is heir to the throne. If he doesn't give them up, he'll end up by breaking his neck. Bound to."

The woman continued on her way back to the house, and Wallis continued with her walk. She hadn't wanted company. She wanted solitude in which to think about Prince Edward.

As a schoolgirl at Arundell, when she had first begun collecting news cuttings and photographs of him, she couldn't have even imagined meeting him in the way she had the previous evening. Even when, married to Ernest and living in London and being introduced to people like George and Nada, she had quite feasibly been able to hope of one day being introduced to Edward, she had never imagined that if she were, she would awaken his interest in the way she knew she had awakened it the previous evening.

She sat down on a stone seat, looking out over a sea of rosebushes rimed with frost. He had been the theme running through her life from childhood until now. The culmination of all those years of thinking and daydreaming about him had been yesterday evening when, for a few brief precious moments as she had told him the story of Pocahontas and Captain John Smith, it had been as if they were the only two people in the room—two people deeply enthralled by each other.

The sensation was one she wanted to experience again, but

she could see no way of doing so. One weekend house party at which he was also present was not enough to bring her into his rarefied world.

The only way to do that was by nurturing her tentative friendship with Thelma.

She looked down at her watch. If she was to be bright and sparkling that evening, she needed to get rid of the last of her cold, and the most sensible way of doing so was to spend the rest of the day in bed.

She rose to her feet, premonition telling her that the coming evening was going to be very little different from the previous one, with Thelma keeping Edward very much to herself. It was something she could do absolutely nothing about.

With her hands deep in the pockets of her tweed cape she walked back to the house, wishing that she could see into the future, wishing she knew what it held.

Chapter Twenty-Nine

As Wallis expected, there was never another occasion when she could engage Prince Edward in conversation during their stay. Royal etiquette was such that she couldn't engage him in conversation first. "There won't ever be another weekend like it, Wallis," Ernest had said to her on the train as they returned to London, "but wasn't it splendid? The chaps at my club will be goggle-eyed when I tell them where we spent the weekend and whose company we were in."

Wallis wasn't interested in name-dropping. She was only interested in meeting Prince Edward again.

"You haven't the remotest chance of doing so for months and months," Pamela said to her the next time they lunched at the Ritz. "He's en route to South America at the present moment in order to bolster British prestige, which, thanks to cutrate German and Japanese competition, has apparently fallen alarmingly and is affecting the economy badly. It will all be a terrible bore for him. He hates grand banquets that last for hours and hours, and on a trip like this he'll be enduring one every night of the week."

Wallis toyed with the salad on her plate. On the two evenings at Burrough, when she had been seated at the same table with him—though at the opposite end of it—she had been able to watch every flicker of expression that had passed over his face. Mostly he had been animated, treating those seated on either side and opposite him to his engaging quizzical smile, quite often laughing at things that were said.

The laughter never reached his eyes, though. There was always a wistful expression in them, as if he were battling a deep melancholy he could never quite overcome. She had noticed it when seated opposite him before the roaring fire in Burrough Court's principal drawing room.

"Do you," she said to Pamela, "think the prince is truly happy? He's the most famous man in the world. Millions of women idolize him. He has vast wealth and prestige and isn't at risk of ever losing it. He has everything any man could ever ask for, yet having been in his company I'm convinced he carries a terrible burden of sadness."

Pamela took a sip of her wine and then held Wallis's eyes over the rim of her glass. "That is extremely perceptive of you, Wally."

She took another sip of wine, put her wineglass down, and said, "He hates the constraints he lives under. Way back in the days of the Great War, when he was writing to me from Flanders and Italy, he said how he hated never being able to live as other people lived—able to make his own choices. Then, of course, it was because he wanted to be in the thick of the fighting, and as heir to the throne he was kept as far from the front as the generals, who were terrified of having to take responsibility if he was killed, could manage. He must have been the only man during the entire course of the war struggling to be where the action was most dangerous."

She picked up her fork. "Nowadays it's the barrier that exists between him and other people that he hates. No matter how close people in his circle are to him, the barrier of royalty always prevents real intimacy. I doubt if it's something he's ever known, even with Freda and Thelma. People simply don't treat him with the informality he craves. They are too intimidated by his title and the fact that one day he will be not only king of the United Kingdom and the Dominions of the British Commonwealth, but emperor of India as well. It's enough to intimidate anyone."

Wallis stopped toying with her salad and speared a mushroom. She, too, had been intimidated at the thought of meeting him, but the intimidation had evaporated when she had been in his presence, telling him the story her Grandmother Warfield had so often told her when she'd been a child.

Then, there had been real rapport between them. If she told Pamela of it, she knew Pamela would tease her and tell her she had been imagining it.

She knew differently, though. Prince Edward had been as attracted to her as, initially, John Jasper, Win, Felipe, and Ernest had been. After this conversation with Pamela, she knew why. It had been because when talking to him, she hadn't been overawed by him. Her natural vitality and friendliness had penetrated the barrier that usually surrounded him. To her great astonishment she realized the Prince of Wales had been as happily at ease in her company as she had been in his.

With Edward in South America, Thelma responded warmly to Wallis's attempts to become better friends with her. Tarquin invited her to a party at which Ernest and Wallis were also present, and Wallis was wryly amused at how gaily Thelma flirted with her host.

At a weekend house party given by the Milford Havens at Lynden Manor, Thelma was a fellow guest, as were Pamela and

John Jasper. Thelma treated her as if her *froideur* at Wallis steal-ing her limelight at Burrough had never happened.

"Don't be so surprised, Wally," Pamela said to her. "Thelma is an empty-headed little fluff. I don't believe she's ever had a se-rious thought in her life, and she's not the type to hold a minor grievance. She doesn't seem to be missing Edward much. She and Tarquin dined out together three times last week."

At the beginning of the summer, when Edward's return to England was imminent, Thelma declared her intention of holding a welcome-home party for him.

"Prince George says the king has scheduled a visit to a north-ern provincial town for David the very day after he returns, which I think is absolutely beastly of him," Thelma said at one of Wallis's cocktail parties, her indignation deep. "It means by the time David returns for my party for him he's going to be absolutely shattered, poor darling."

"Have you permission to call Prince Edward David?" Wallis asked Pamela a little later when Thelma was happily prattling away to Nada. "I know you often do when talking about him, but I've never thought to ask you if you did during the time the two of you were close."

"That, sweet Wally, is a very sore point." Pamela's cat green eyes glittered with hurt pride. "Considering how long I've known him—since childhood—the answer is no, and it's some-thing I'm probably never going to forgive him for."

"Do you think Thelma does so?"

"In private, or when other people present are also royal—people such as George and Nada—then yes, she does."

Wallis, seeing that one of her guests had nearly finished his Virginian Sherry Cobbler, began making him another before it was asked for.

"So no one is ever asked to call him David—not unless he is

very much in love with them?" she asked, pouring a measure of Amontillado into a small cocktail shaker.

"That's just about it." Pamela remembered the way the Houghton family called him David but decided not to mention it. A private secret was no fun once it was shared. "I assume you've been invited to Thelma's welcome-home party?" she said, changing the subject.

Wallis poured a dash of Grand Marnier into the cocktail shaker. "Yes." She added a slice of orange and two tablespoons of sugar. "I'm looking forward to it."

It was the understatement of the year. She wasn't merely looking forward to it, she was counting off the days and hours to it.

Faced with the choice of what to wear, when the evening arrived she decided on a backless silver lamé evening dress she had bought in Paris in which she knew she looked devastating. Her glossy dark hair was arranged in the style she hadn't changed since her debutante days. Parted in the middle, it was combed back in deep waves over her ears to be coiled in an elegant figure-of-eight chignon at the nape of her neck.

Her jewelry was a problem, as, because she had few good pieces, she had so little choice. In the end she decided on her Grandmother Warfield's choker of pearls—the same pearls she had worn the evening at the del Coronado when she had come so close to being introduced to Prince Edward and Lord Louis Mountbatten.

As a finishing touch she sprayed herself with her favorite perfume, Mitsouko, and then, taut with tension, joined Ernest in order to walk downstairs and outside to where their chauffeur was waiting for them.

"There's going to be a crush of people there," Ernest warned as the car neared the Furnesses' town house on Grosvenor Square, "and I doubt if Prince Edward will even recognize us."

It wasn't a doubt Wallis shared. When the prince saw her, he would remember her. Ernest was right, though, in that it was a very crowded party. The entire house was blanketed in flowers, and as they walked into the drawing room, Wallis was grateful for the weekend house parties she and Ernest had spent at Lynden Manor. It meant she was already acquainted with many of Thelma's guests. Pamela and John Jasper were there, of course, as well as George and Nada and other people, such as Tarquin and Cecil and Sibyl, all of whom she counted as being not just acquaintances, but real friends.

Despite the number of guests, the party was informal. "Thelma knows the Prince of Wales well enough to know it's what he prefers," Tarquin said as they each lifted a glass of champagne from the tray a footman was proffering. "He won't be in the room long before the dancing starts."

When Thelma and the prince entered the room, Wallis's first reaction was that he looked far more than the "exhausted" Thelma had predicted; he looked shattered. There were pouches beneath his eyes that hadn't been there at Burrough Court, and though he was smiling as readily as always, Wallis thought she detected signs of strain around his mouth.

He and Thelma began making their way through the crowded room, greeting people as they did so. When they reached Wallis and Ernest, the prince stopped. "Mr. and Mrs. Simpson," he said with a warm smile. "How nice to see you again. I remember our meeting at Melton."

Flushed with pleasure at being not only recognized but called by name, Ernest bowed. Wallis dipped into a by-now-confident curtsey.

The prince, with Thelma at his side like a limpet, moved on.

Tarquin was right in that there was soon dancing, but it seemed to Wallis that Edward wasn't throwing his heart and soul into it—and he didn't ask her to dance.

"But then, apart from Thelma, he isn't dancing with any-one," John Jasper said, sensing her disappointment. "Will I do as a substitute? I can't do the Black Bottom, but I can do a fairly competent foxtrot."

They foxtrotted and whenever Wallis caught sight of Ed-ward, she was struck by how very preoccupied he looked.

Later in the evening the reason became clear to her.

"I'm just back from some dreadful provincial northern town," he said to George Milford Haven.

Dancing was still going on, but he'd given up on it and was sitting on a sofa, Thelma at his side. George was in a comfort-able chair nearby, nursing a brandy, and Wallis, always a strate-gist, was seated on a nearby sofa with Nada.

"I thought it was too utterly horrid that you had to travel to some boring town in the north on your first day home from Argentina," Thelma said cooingly, laughter in her voice. He didn't respond to her. Instead he said, still talking to George, "Those poor devils up there have absolutely no work, George. I've spent the whole day talking to men who have no shirts be-neath their jackets, worn-out boots—that's if they have boots—and no hope."

"Oh dear." Thelma's voice was still laughter-filled. "A jacket without a shirt must be very scratchy."

Her gaiety fell on deaf ears.

"Something must be done to help them, George." Fiercely Edward slammed a clenched hand into his fist. "Something *must* be done!"

The music changed to a quickstep. "Brilliant!" Thelma sprang to her feet. "I just *love* quicksteps. They're so racy!"

Edward remained where he was, his finely featured face deep in grave thought.

It was a moment that could have been embarrassingly sticky, but George rose swiftly to his feet, took hold of Thelma's hand,

and, telling her that he simply *adored* quicksteps, headed her speedily in the direction of the adjoining room and its small dance floor and orchestra.

Nada, reading Wallis's thoughts, said languorously, "When you are a cousin of the Prince of Wales, you can ignore usual etiquette, lovely Wallis."

For Wallis the little scene was a revelation. Pamela had said she doubted if Edward had ever experienced true intimacy with anyone, even with Freda or Thelma. Wallis now knew for a certainty that where Thelma was concerned, Edward had certainly never experienced it, for Thelma had not been remotely attuned to his mood. Even worse, she had been totally uninterested in the kind of difficult official tasks he had to undertake as Prince of Wales.

He looked up from his now-clasped hands and said apologetically, "I'm sorry, Mrs. Simpson. I'm being a bore."

"No, sir. You're not."

She held his eyes in the way she had done at Burrough Court.

"Was the town you visited a mining town, sir?"

Even as she asked the question she knew she was seriously breaking the rules of royal etiquette. It was up to the prince to lead in any conversation. Pamela had been quite explicit about it when she had given her last-minute pointers before her visit to Melton. "If the prince holds you in conversation, Wally, never introduce a new subject into it and never, *never*, discuss politics or anything of a controversial nature."

That it was totally unheard of for anyone to question him went so much without saying that Pamela hadn't even reminded her of it.

"It was a steel town, Mrs. Simpson." He paused, unclasped his hands, and fiddled nervously with his bow tie. "May I call you Wallis? Mrs. Simpson sounds so formal when we're beginning to be such good friends."

Wallis caught her breath, not at the honor, but at the realization that he was shy.

"Yes, sir," she said, beginning to see him in an entirely new light. "I'd be honored if you would call me Wallis."

All around them was laughter and chatter and from the adjoining room the strains of a Jerome Kern quickstep.

They were oblivious to it.

"It's this damned economic depression," he said, his brow furrowed, his voice passionate. "It's crippling the working classes. You've no idea of the misery I see when I travel north, or into South Wales. Men who can't feed their families. Children going hungry. I spoke to a man today and asked him what his trade was. He said he was a foreman riveter. I asked him how long it was since he had worked and he said it had been five years. Five years! He wanted hope from me, Wallis, and what hope could I give him? Was I supposed to tell him that the government was doing all that it could and that he simply had to be patient? What possible solace would that have been to a poor blighter who, through no fault of his own, has been on the dole for five years?"

Wallis hesitated and then said, "The fact that you were there, sir, would have been a comfort to him. It would have shown him that you care, that the monarchy hasn't forgotten about him and the thousands of others like him."

The expression in his eyes changed. He was now looking at her like a drowning man seeing a life raft.

"Do you think so, Wallis? Do you really think so?"

"I'm sure of it, sir, and I know that you'll do everything in your power to help men like the one you have just spoken of."

"Royal power in British politics is limited to the power of

suggestion, but I'm certainly going to do something, Wallis. By God I am!"

The foxtrot had come to an end. The small orchestra was now playing a tango. Edward's ability to tango with great panache was legendary, and Thelma came back into the room at a tripping little run, George in her wake.

"It's a tango, sir," she said to Edward, her dark eyes shining. "And as you are just back from Argentina, I just know you will be aching to dance it."

Wallis had never seen a man who looked less like wanting to tango. Nevertheless, he rose to his feet. "Anything to please," he said with a tired smile. "Excuse me, Wallis."

Thelma was too busy chattering away about how the tango was in her Latin-American blood to notice Edward's use of Wallis's first name.

George noticed it, though. As Edward escorted Thelma toward the adjoining room and the dance floor, he raised an eyebrow queryingly at her.

Wallis ignored it. Her newfound relationship with the Prince of Wales was her affair and no one else's. Without a word of explanation she rose to her feet and strolled off in search of the buffet table.

She was still in the supper room, eating grapes that had been stuffed with cream cheese, when from the drawing room she heard Edward bidding everyone good night.

"I've had a long day," she heard him saying, "and am still recovering from my long return journey from South America. It's been a splendid party. Good night, everyone."

From the supper room's open doorway Wallis saw Thelma accompany him out into the hall in order to say a personal good night to him at the door.

She ate another grape, wondering how it was that Thelma had been so blindly unable to pick up on Edward's mood and his need to talk about his day and of how defeated and crushed it had made him feel.

She remembered the change in his mood at the end of his conversation with her. Of his fervor and determination. The change in him was one she had achieved and, if she were given the chance, it was something she knew she would always be able to achieve.

"So there you are," Ernest said, breaking in on her thoughts. "I wondered where you'd got to. The orchestra is now playing a waltz. I can manage that even if I can't manage a tango."

As they waltzed, Wallis's thoughts were still full of her extraordinary conversation with Prince Edward. His compassion for the unemployed had been real and touchingly deep. She wondered whom else he spoke to in such an agonized and confiding way and suspected it was no one.

Thelma danced past them with Tarquin.

Ernest removed his hand from hers in order to glance down at his watch. "It's after midnight, darling. Unlike most people here I have an office I need to go to in the morning. Let's call it a day, shall we?"

Wallis nodded. Now that the prince had gone she had no further need to stay.

They said their good-byes and retrieved their coats. Thelma, the party now being in full swing, didn't trouble to accompany them to the door.

When it was opened for them, only the butler saw the royal Daimler still parked outside and the Prince of Wales leaning against it, smoking a cigarette.

"I wondered," the prince said, as they walked down the steps to the pavement, "if I might offer you both a lift home?"

A shell-shocked Ernest opened his mouth to stammer that it wouldn't be necessary, that they had their own car and chauffeur waiting for them.

Wallis, anticipating what he was about to say, said swiftly, "That would be most kind of you, sir. We would much appreciate it."

The royal chauffeur opened the near door of the Daimler. The prince stepped inside. Wallis and Ernest followed.

"G" Trotter was in the front passenger seat and greeted them as though their being given a lift home by the Prince of Wales were quite in the normal run of things.

"Whereabouts do you live, Mr. Simpson?" Edward asked.

"Bryanston Court, on George Street, sir. Not far from Marble Arch." Ernest's voice sounded as if hands were squeezing his windpipe.

Edward repeated the address to his chauffeur and then said, "I've just found myself a marvelous new home. It's called Fort Belvedere and it's an eighteenth-century house owned by the Crown on land near to the castle at Windsor. When I told the king I would like to move into it, he called it a queer old place, but I already love it. It's been neglected for years and I'm going to have a wonderful time fixing it up. When I've done so I would like it very much if you would both visit me there and tell me what you think of it."

Wallis thought Ernest was going to pass out with pride and pleasure.

"Does it have gardens, sir?" Wallis asked. "If the house has been neglected for a long time, I imagine the gardens will have been neglected as well."

He shot her the smile that over the last two decades and his many tours abroad had charmed millions.

"It has a wonderful garden, Mrs. Simpson. The land descends in a gentle slope toward Virginia Water, where as a child I paddled in a rowboat with my brothers. It is, though, as you have suspected, desperately overgrown. The first thing

I shall need when I move in, is a billhook in order to clear the undergrowth."

The short journey was nearly over.

The Daimler slid to a halt outside their block of flats in George Street.

When the chauffeur opened the rear doors for them and they stepped out of the car, Edward stepped out onto the pavement with them.

"Good-bye," he said to Ernest, shaking him by the hand. "And don't forget that when you visit the fort, billhooks and scythes will be an absolute necessity."

"No, sir." Ernest sounded as if he were in desperate need of a restorative drink of brandy. "Thank you for the lift, sir. It's been a great honor."

"Good-bye, Mrs. Simpson." Edward shook her hand, and Wallis dipped into a curtsey. "It's been a pleasure meeting you."

"The pleasure has been all mine, sir."

He turned away from them, toward the Daimler.

The fairy-tale evening was at an end.

On unsteady legs Ernest mounted the steps leading to Bryanston Court, and Wallis followed him.

As Ernest disappeared into the building she paused on the top step and then, in order to see the Daimler drive away, turned around.

The Daimler was still there and the prince was still standing beside it.

She knew, just as she had known when she had left the party, that he was standing beside it because he was waiting for her.

Slowly she began to walk back down the short flight of steps toward him.

"No one," he said thickly as she reached him, "has ever made me feel as if they truly know me in the way you have done this evening, Wallis. No one before has ever shown any interest in my job of work as a Prince of Wales."

The street was silent of traffic. The night very still. The moon and the stars very bright.

Wallis was aware of a sensation she had felt only once before. The sensation when, in faraway China in a small, dark, incense-filled room, Madame Xiuxiu had placed scrawny, birdlike hands on her head.

The singsong words said then came back to her now.

"You are a woman of great destiny. The man who will love you will love you with every atom of his being. Kissed by the sun, he will be the ruler of kingdoms and you will be his shadow queen. The love you will share will echo down the centuries."

She had dismissed the prediction as being nothing but fanciful imaginings.

The description of a man who would one day be the ruler of kingdoms had clearly never applied to either Felipe or Ernest.

It did, though, apply to Edward, Prince of Wales.

As she looked into his eyes, saw the need there and the hope, she knew there had been nothing fanciful about Madame Xiuxiu's prediction. The old Chinese woman had seen into her future, and it was a future beyond all her imaginings.

"Will you talk with me again, Wallis?" There was urgency in his voice and in his eyes. In the moonlight his hair was the color of pale wheat. "Will you dine with me tomorrow night?"

Knowing that tomorrow night was only going to be the first in a lifetime of such nights, her lips curved in a deep, radiant smile.

"Yes, sir," she said. "Of course I will."

AUTHOR'S NOTE

Wallis's many biographers have all had to face up to the mystery of her sexuality and have done so in many different ways. Some have perpetuated the myth of the "China Dossier," a dossier drawn up allegedly at King George V's request and in which Wallis is said to have accompanied her husband, Win Spencer, to Chinese "singsong houses" where, virtually a prostitute, she learned sexual arts that later bewitched and enslaved Prince Edward. (At the time of the abdication, no slur about Wallis was too salacious.) Other, very different speculations, have been made: that she was not really a woman at all, but a man, or that she was a hermaphrodite. She certainly had masculine characteristics in that she was angular and flat-chested with unusually large hands and a very strong jawline.

The Shadow Queen is a novel and, though it is based on the factual elements of Wallis's life, the fact is mixed with fiction. (Pamela, John Jasper, and the Houghtons are all fictional characters.) The freedom that comes with being a novelist and not a biographer has enabled me to come to my own theory about Wallis's sexuality, and I based it on things Wallis is quoted as having said, and on the surmises of some of her many biographers.

Greg King, in his excellent biography *The Duchess of Windsor: The Uncommon Life of Wallis Simpson*, quotes Wallis as having said in 1936 to Jack Aird, Prince Edward's equerry—and prior to her marriage to Edward—"I have had two husbands and I never went to bed with either of them." Donald Spoto, in his 1995 book *Dynasty*, cites Wallis as having told Herman Rogers, who gave her away on her marriage to Edward, that she had "never had sexual intercourse with either of her first two husbands nor had she ever allowed anyone else to touch her below what she called her personal Mason-Dixon line." Greg King also cites Wallis's lawyer in her later years, Maître Suzanne Blum, as saying, "Wallis remained a virgin until her death." Wallis's mother is quoted in several biographies as having said that Wallis could never have children. I coupled these intriguing quotes with the mystery of why Wallis's first husband, Earl Winfield Spencer, should have changed in attitude toward her after their marriage, becoming violently abusive and accusing her of "not being a real woman." In the most recent biography of Wallis, *That Woman*, Anne Sebba writes that Wallis may have been born with a disorder of sex development (DSD) or intersexuality, a term that embraces a wide range of conditions and would have explained much about Wallis's distinctively masculine appearance and the hints Wallis herself gave about her intimate relations with Win Spencer and Ernest Simpson.

The conclusion is my own, a theory not based on fact, for there are no facts to base it on. If it were true, though, it would answer a lot of the speculation that has been made about her.

The Shadow Queen ends in 1931. In January 1934 Thelma sailed to the United States in order to be supportive to her sister, who was engaged in a custody battle for her daughter. By the time she returned, Wallis had become the great love of Prince Edward's life. In January 1936 he succeeded his father as king of the United Kingdom and all her Dominions beyond the Seas and as emperor of India. His one desire was to marry Wallis and, at his coronation, to have her crowned as his queen consort. The prospect of a twice-divorced woman becoming queen was one the British government and church violently opposed. Faced with the choice of remaining king or of marrying the woman he loved, Edward saw no choice at all. On December 10, 1936, Edward abdicated from the greatest throne in the world. Thereafter he and Wallis were known as the Duke and Duchess of Windsor and made their home in France. To the end of Edward's life, his love for Wallis never faltered. He died in 1972 and is buried in the royal burial ground at Frogmore, Berkshire. Wallis, who died in 1986, lies next to him.

Historical Main Characters

Royalty

King George V
Queen Mary
Prince Edward (David)
Prince Albert (Bertie—Prince Edward's brother)
Prince George (Georgie—Prince Edward's brother)
George Mountbatten, second marquess of Milford Haven
    (Prince Edward's second cousin)
Nada (Nadejda) Mountbatten, marchioness of Milford
    Haven

Others

Felipe Espil (first secretary at the Argentinean embassy,
    Washington, D.C.)
Lady Thelma Furness
Bessie Merryman
Corinne Mustin
Lieutenant Commander Henry Croskey Mustin
John Freeman Rasin
Ernest Aldrich Simpson
Lieutenant Earl Winfield Spencer
Freda Dudley Ward
Wallis Warfield
Alice Montague Warfield Rasin Allen

ACKNOWLEDGMENTS

Thanks are due to my editor, Christine Kopprasch, who has been enormously helpful and supportive; Tina Pohlman, my publisher; and Amy Schneider, my copy editor. My agent, Sheila Crowley at Curtis Brown, has been constantly encouraging, and I am deeply grateful for her pep talks and friendship.

The Shadow Queen

READER'S GUIDE

1. Very early in the novel, a young Wallis hides beneath the table as her Uncle Sol violently confronts her mother about the nature of their relationship. Though Wallis is too young at this point to understand the substance of their conversation, what impact does this event have on her as both a child and an adult?

2. Uncle Sol offers Wallis a chance, as his adopted daughter, to live as "one of the richest heiresses in Baltimore," on the condition that she has no future contact with her mother. Is it fair to ask a child of Wallis's age to make that choice? What would you do in this situation?

3. Before Pamela departs for Europe, she and Wallis form a blood pact, stating that they would be friends forever. Considering Pamela's betrayal of Wallis in the following years, do you feel Pamela was sincere about her end of the pact? How might she and Wallis differ in their notions of fairness, friendship, and even morality?

4. After receiving word of John Jasper's delayed return from

Europe, Wallis can "hardly believe the battering that fate was giving her." How else does fate—in the forms of history, chance, and the actions of others—affect Wallis?

5. Wallis lies to her friend Corinne about her desires to become engaged while in Pensacola, and we are told that "every girl her age was looking to get engaged, because there was no other future for a girl but for marriage." Does this statement prove true? How does the time period Wallis was born into influence her actions? How would Wallis have conducted herself in the modern age, where the pressure for women to marry is far less significant?

6. In the course of an argument with her husband, Henry, Corinne quotes the Monroe Doctrine—an act considered a "surprise so startling as to be almost unbelievable." Why is this startling to the other guests? What does this say about what is expected—and suspected—of women in Wallis's time period?

7. Following Uncle Sol's refusal to pay for her lavish wedding, Wallis vows that "the day would come when her Uncle Sol would eat his heart out to be publically recognized as being her relation—and when it did, she wouldn't even give a nod in his direction." Does Wallis ever make good on this promise? Is it fair for her to feel this way about her Uncle Sol, who, despite his flaws, did much to keep Wallis on her path to a royal destiny?

8. After being beaten by Win, Wallis feels that "violence had become a standard part of their life together" and that she had no alternative but to put up with and accept it. Following the revelry and high hopes of the European Armistice, Wallis is "determined yet again to soldier on with her difficult marriage," stating that "quite simply, it seemed to her she had no other choice." Why does Wallis see no immedi-

ate alternative to this lifestyle with Win? How does her past influence this mind-set? What are the factors—society, family, and her past—restricting her from seeing other options?

9. Relishing her early success with the Prince of Wales, Pamela wishes she could tell Wallis of her new affair, stating that despite their falling out, "there was, quite simply, no one else quite like [Wallis]." Who else could say this same thing about Wallis? What is it that gives her that unique, memorable quality?

10. As a child, a teenager, and an adult, Wallis has defied her family's wishes many times. Despite this, she obeys Uncle Sol's orders to not pursue a divorce from Win. Why does she act so differently in this instance? Why is she unable to break free from her uncle's wishes?

11. Wallis spends much of the novel dreading an encounter with Pamela after their falling out. However, their reunification happens unexpectedly, and without drama. In what ways is their reunification actually fortuitous for Wallis?

12. Following the end of her relationship with Felipe, Wallis feels that "it was her physical disability that had ruined their marriage, just as, eventually, it had ruined her relationship with Felipe." Is this a fair statement for Wallis to believe about herself? In what other ways does Wallis potentially misappraise herself and those around her?

13. Throughout the novel, Wallis is forced by necessity to move around from home to home, living in a wide variety of locations. Where do you feel she is the most happy?

14. Toward the end of the book, Pamela notes that the Prince "hates the constraints he lives under . . . hated never being able to live as other people lived." Does this mirror Wallis's own experiences throughout the novel? How so?

ABOUT THE AUTHOR

REBECCA DEAN is British and lives in the pretty harbor town of Whitstable in Kent. She is married and has five adult children, two of whom are married to Americans. Her eldest daughter lives in Chicago, and her youngest daughter lives in Nashville. She is a former chairman of the Romantic Novelists' Association, and in 2011 her novel *The Golden Prince* was short-listed for both the RNA's Romantic Novel of the Year Award and the Best Historical Novel of the Year Award. Her passions are recent royal history—she is currently writing a sequel to *The Shadow Queen*—family life, and her two small dogs, Pip and Bruno.